# SEEKERS IN THE VOID

Faolan's Pen Publishing
22 King St. S, Suite 300
Waterloo, Ontario
N2J 1N8 Canada



Cover art by Tom Edwards Design

First Faolan's Pen Publishing paperback edition May 2025



**For paperback sales information, visit faolanspen.com. For special events, release alerts, and more books from the author, visit glynnstewart.com.**

A record of this book is available from Library and Archives Canada.

Printed in the United States of America
1 2 3 4 5 6 7 8 9 10
First edition
ISBN 978-1-989674-82-6 (Trade Paperback)
ISBN 978-1-989674-83-3 (Amazon Paperback)

# SEEKERS IN THE VOID

## GLYNN STEWART

**FAOLAN'S PEN PUBLISHING**

faolanspen.com

# 1

"Fucking Saints."

There was no question as to who the dockworker was talking about. There was only one person in this section of orbital platform Iliakofos Two that was wearing the gleaming white tunic and trousers of an officer of the Santiago Corporation.

Cirilo Webster intentionally paused. He heard a sudden silence sweep through the corridor and suspected that the worker's friends were probably drawing back from the man, hoping not to get caught in the ire of the white uniform and the power it represented.

He didn't even look over to see who had spoken. He didn't need to. He waited long enough for the silence to become absolutely complete, then started forward again like nothing had happened.

The Santiago Corporation controlled all interstellar travel between the Seventy-Seven, the inhabited systems of human space. While it would take more than one angry officer, even a full captain of a Santiago void ship, to cause problems for the Oneira System government... that government might not wait to find out what the Company thought if a Saint Captain complained.

And Cirilo's pause had been long enough for anyone looking to realize that his white uniform bore the triangular gold bracers and platinum braided shoulder epaulets of a void ship captain.

Cirilo also towered over most of the inhabitants of Iliakofos and the planet's four major space stations. A bare finger under two meters tall, he was only slim proportionate to his height, and he carried himself with the muscle of a man who knew that exercise was the sure counter to the risks of low gravity.

His black hair was cropped short, carved into a perfectly equal-sided triangle that started at his temples and peaked at the top of his skull. His eyebrows were equally immaculate and there was no sign that he had ever had hair anywhere else on his face.

The source of that geometric perfection followed a step behind and to the right of him. Lachlan Stirling's parents hadn't been as determined to see him succeed in the Santiago Corporation, so he'd been spared the out-of-place Spanish first name—but the steward had hitched his star to Cirilo's a decade earlier.

A decision justified by the document chip in Cirilo's breast pocket and the Captain's uniform he wore. They'd been through unpleasant things together, he and Lachlan, but they had pulled it off.

His own void ship.

"That was mean, ser," Stirling murmured, pitching his voice just loudly enough for Cirilo to hear it. "I think our poor sod-trapped fool fouled himself."

"A lesson taught with no harm but extra laundry, then," the Captain replied. "Another Captain might not have been as sparing."

He pulled out the datapad the office had given him. In his left hand, the black plastic-and-glass device contrasted sharply with the silver metal of his bionic arm.

"*Santa Mica* is Dock Alpha-Seven," Stirling told him. "Only the Alpha docks are big enough for Company ships. Even one like *Mica*."

"And more importantly, the access to Docks Alpha-Six through -Eight is right there," Cirilo replied, pointing to a surprisingly inconspicuous hatchway. Personnel access to three of the eight largest docks on Iliakofos Two was past the open bulkhead, but the signage was minimal and half-concealed behind a hiring ad for one of Oneira's mining companies.

"Let's go meet the new family, Lachlan."

***

The Alpha Docks on an orbital served three types of vessels: the absolute largest of in-system vessels, the mobile refineries and cargo ships that handled entire asteroids as either raw materials or cargo; the handful of large but arguably useless sublight warships the governments of the Seventy-Seven maintained; and the vast freighters of the Santiago Corporation.

The Company didn't own Iliakofos Two or its three sisters, nor the two orbital elevators they depended on. They didn't need to.

Cirilo noted, as he approached Alpha-Seven's accessway, that Iliakofos Two's owners had taken one of the two usual approaches to their dependence on the Santiagos. The Company, of course, preferred the one where the Alpha Docks were a statement of the star system's pride and power, showing off the value of the system as a partner for the Santiago Corporation.

Iliakofos Two's Alpha Docks were the other type. They were large enough to handle the numbers of people a large void ship or refinery vessel could disgorge, but they were utilitarian and dull, lacking even windows to allow foot traffic to look out at the vessels waiting in the void outside.

Still, there was no question which dock was Alpha-Seven. There were two other Saint void ships at Iliakofos Two, but those were in the block of four docks at the opposite end of the station.

Cirilo didn't even need to spot the gleaming white tunic of a Saint crewmember—over black trousers, not white, marking them as crew instead of an officer or Chief—to know he'd found his ship. The Saint's companion was the only sign he needed.

The Biomechanical Security Unit stood a full fifty centimeters taller than the spacer—twenty centimeters taller than Cirilo himself, even—and presented a blank face of metal to the world.

Behind the BimSoo's mask lay an amalgamation of high-end computers and carefully nurtured cloned organs and neural tissue. A proper synthmind took up a large room at least, but the hybrid of machine and biology inside a BimSoo was the next best thing.

Theoretically, the hulking cyborg wasn't sentient. It was a very capable robot that happened to have organic components.

Cirilo had spent the prior ten years in Corporate Security, working far more closely with BimSoos than most. His opinions were far more complicated.

But he still approved that *Santa Mica*'s crew had a BimSoo standing guard at the entrance. It was overt security that few would question—and helped cover for a lot of covert security.

The Company's monopoly on the transit drive was not kept cleanly, after all.

"Captain!" The spacer snapped to what she probably thought was attention. It was as good as any CargoFleet crew's attempt at it Cirilo had ever seen, at least.

"I'm looking for the *Santa Mica*, spacer," Cirilo told her. The woman couldn't have been half his age, but she was senior enough to maintain an exterior watch on her own—when the new Captain was expected aboard, at that.

"This is her, Captain," the woman confirmed. "I'm Specialist Carmen Ventimiglia—SecTeam. Are you Captain Webster, ser?"

Her gaze flickered to his bionic arm. His silver hand was fully visible—the Saints went in for far more visible bionics than most system-bound populations, a cultural affectation Cirilo didn't particularly like but had readily conceded to when he'd lost his arm.

His sudden acquisition of a silver bionic probably wasn't the cause of his new Captaincy, but the timing was neat enough to make one wonder.

"I am, SecSpec Ventimiglia," he confirmed. He drew the datapad from the office and gave it his thumbprint—the right thumb, still flesh and blood—before passing it over.

"Cirilo Webster," he continued. "Authorization and Master's Warrant are copied to the pad for your confirmation, SecSpec."

She took a solid twenty silent seconds skimming the pad, which told him two things: that Ventimiglia was determined to do her job right and that she had full confidence that her boss would back her against a new Captain who grew impatient.

Both were solid positives in Cirilo's book. He waited patiently.

"Everything checks out, ser," she said, passing the pad back to him. "I'll ping the First and have her down to guide you to the bridge in just a few minutes."

"Thank you, SecSpec."

There was a moment where he suspected she was trying to judge if his use of the short form of her rank was intended as some form of slight, then she gave him a nod and stepped back to her post.

She'd done nothing visible, but Cirilo knew she'd contacted the First Officer—Tereza Jewel, unless the Company office on the surface of Iliakofos had managed to get their paperwork wrong—via her bionic communicator.

Once Cirilo was properly signed in, his own bionic com would allow him to trace, though rarely eavesdrop on, the communications of his crew as well as be in constant contact with the freighter's synthmind.

As he waited, though, his bionic com was muted. Without a network, it was useless, and the only network he could access was the station's general grid—and like many of its ilk, the general grid was uselessly overwhelmed with advertising.

"The First is on her way, Captain," Ventimiglia told him.

"Thank you," he repeated.

Like himself—and Carmen Ventimiglia, for that matter—Tereza Jewel had clearly been born in one of the Cradles, the void stations the Santiago Corporation maintained for secure production of transit drives. None of them had Spanish family names—in Cirilo's notable case, he very clearly didn't even have a drop of Spanish ancestry—but hopeful parents had hung Spanish first names on them.

That was a tradition that had lived so long, from what he could tell, that it had acquired a value and connection of its own, far beyond any advantage Spanish speakers had possessed in the early years of the Corporation.

**2**

TEREZA JEWEL CURSED A god she didn't believe in to a void she had plenty of experience with. The new Captain didn't know, of course, that she'd managed to get food poisoning the previous night. Captains, especially the type of Captains that *Santa Mica* ended up with, generally had enough bionics and genegineering to make certain they never suffered such things.

But even if her guts roiled and she would rather be in the head, she had little choice. An air-hypo delivered a lovely mix of drugs that left her feeling almost human again, then she balefully glared down at her gleaming white uniform.

Shedding the whole thing when she'd realized what was wrong had been her best idea so far. Fortunately, because the Company had occasional interactions with reality and sanity, it was even an easy garment to put on quickly.

++*Tell Webster I'll be five*++ she sent poor Carmen over the ship's network. If the security specialist didn't know what had happened to the First then her boss, the Chief of Security, definitely did.

Violet Key had shared the maldito prawns with Tereza, after all. But Violet had the same kind of stomach bionics that most of their Shareholder-class Captains had—though *hers* were from CorpSec.

Tereza didn't have time for makeup, which was hardly going to make the best impression on her new boss, but she'd have to live with that. Whoever Webster was, he was going to have to live with a lot more than a First who'd spent the last three hours emptying her guts.

She didn't like that she didn't know who Webster was. They'd been waiting on a new Captain for a week, but she'd checked. There were no Websters on the Shareholder list.

And *Santa Mica* was CargoFleet's training wheels, used to ease connected officers into the reality of the job before they got *real* ships.

Tereza was balefully aware that the food poisoning could easily be far from the worst part of today.

***

Coming out of the ship, Tereza's first impression of her new boss was of his height. Planet-raised in a Company enclave, unlike many Saints, Tereza was only a hundred and sixty centimeters tall, and she barely came up to the new Captain's shoulder.

She worked with enough void-born Saints that it wasn't a problem, but he was taller than even most of them. With the height, it took her a solid few seconds to register his age.

*Santa Mica*'s past Captains over her ten years aboard hadn't been children by any stretch of the imagination, but they'd ranged from thirty-five to forty standard years. Even pushed through all of the qualifications and minimum times-in-grade by virtue of Shareholder parents or being minor Shareholders themselves, it still took time to qualify as a void-ship Captain.

Cirilo Webster was at least sixty, possibly seventy. He had clearly received anagathic treatments, and his silver arm was solid proof of access to Company healthcare that would keep him going for another century at least, but he was twice the age of the people who'd come to command *Santa Mica* before.

"Captain Webster," she greeted him, giving him a crisp salute that hopefully hid her confusion.

He turned calm, dark eyes on her. There was no sign in those eyes that he'd been waiting for almost ten minutes when she should have been there within one. He nodded to acknowledge her salute and offered his hand.

"First Tereza Jewel, I presume."

"I am, ser," she confirmed, then hesitated. They'd already pushed the bounds of how long Webster had been waiting, but she also knew Violet would tear a strip off of her if she didn't do things right.

"I need to see your papers."

"Of course, First," Webster agreed, his tone still utterly level. He removed a datapad from his jacket, thumbed it and passed it over to her.

His presence had been so overwhelming she'd missed the broad-shouldered man behind him. The other stranger was about of Tereza's own height, with sandy hair carrying just a touch of gray, and he winked a brilliantly blue eye at her as he saw her notice him.

She wasn't used to being this off-balance. She blamed the food poisoning in her head and skimmed through Webster's papers.

A brand-new Master's Warrant, as expected, though his age still suggested his story was very different than she was used to. The paperwork from the Santiago Corporation assigning him to command *Santa Mica*.

"Everything is in order, ser," she said, passing the pad back. "Would you care to accompany me to the bridge?"

"I would, First," he agreed. "Can you have someone direct Lachlan here to the quarters for the pair of us? He'll be acting as my steward and secretary."

That was closer to what she'd expected. A First was *allowed* a personal steward but had to pay them out of their own pocket—though the ship would absorb their room and board. A Captain had a Company-paid steward, and the Company would automatically hire a First's steward on to manage their Captain if such a person existed.

Tereza couldn't afford a steward, even with a First Officer's bonuses. Cirilo Webster, it seemed, could.

++*MinChief, new Captain has a steward*++ she messaged Sun Daniel, the ship's Chief of Administration. ++*Can you get him a guide to the quarters?*++

++*Wilco. I'll have a StewSpec meet him in four*++

"Someone from either Admin or the stewards will meet you in a few minutes, Em Stirling," she told the steward. "Are you all right waiting?"

"Not a problem, ser," he replied brightly. "Just people-watching to pass the time."

Given how few people were visible on the Alpha Docks at that moment, it took a conscious effort for Tereza not to flush at that.

"After me, then, Captain," she told Webster.

***

"Are you familiar with the SCC-One-Nine–type ships, ser?" Tereza asked the new Captain a few minutes later as they waited for the transit pod.

*Santa Mica* was over four hundred meters long, and a large chunk of her span consisted of a single long connecting spine between her fore and aft hulls. In transit, that passageway also served as the main anchor for the cargo pods loaded into her, but no one really wanted to walk three hundred–plus meters of empty corridor.

The fore hull was currently docked to Iliakofos Two, but the bridge was in the back half of the ship. The pod was definitely the best idea, but it left her once again asking Cirilo Webster to wait.

"I've known I was taking command of *Santa Mica* for about three weeks," he told her, his tone almost bored. "Since I was in Alpha when I got the news, I took the time to visit *Santo Antonio* in the Grand Museum to go through the type with the curators there."

Tereza nodded, unable to conceal her twitch at the reminder that not only was *Santa Mica* old, she was old enough that one of her remaining sisters was a museum piece.

Though calling the Grand Museum at Alpha Cradle a "museum" was like calling Betelgeuse a "star." Alpha Cradle was the still-secret location where Mihai Santiago, the near-mythical founder of the Santiago Corporation, had relocated all transit drive construction when he'd decided he trusted neither his shareholders nor humanity's governments not to abuse his discovery.

As officers, both Tereza and Webster knew that it was at Wolf 359, a bit under eight light-years from Earth. Even in private conversation aboard their ship, they wouldn't use that name.

"I've only been to Alpha once," she admitted. "Saw the Museum at a distance, but I didn't have time to visit."

"It's worth it if you can," her new Captain told her. "One of every ship type we've ever built is in orbit with the Museum Station itself. It's..." He paused, then shrugged.

"Worth it," he repeated. "All of the history of the Company is there."

"Why were you in Alpha, ser?" she asked.

Webster gestured with his silver arm.

"Finishing up physiotherapy on CorpSec's credit," he said. "Gave them ten years as a First and an arm. Seems it was enough to convince someone I was worth a fancy jacket."

Tereza's own uniform had the same triple-triangle bracers as her Captain, though hers were silver instead of gold. Her shoulders were epaulet-free, with a single braid of platinum running from her collar to her shoulder marking her authority.

"The bridge is ready for you both," a new voice smoothly inserted itself into the conversation, a reminder of why the Santiago Corporation didn't have to bother coming up with uniforms for Second Officers.

"Ah. Second Nephil," Webster greeted the synthmind. "Any concerns I should be aware of before I chip in?"

"Nothing," the synthmind replied. Nephil, like all ship synthminds in the Santiago Corporation, held the rank and title of Second Officer on his ship. A fully artificial intelligence, Nephil linked into every ship's system and backed up the human officers in a way no nonsapient computer could.

Unlike many of his compatriots, Nephil had long since paid off the costs of his creation and wasn't bound by an indenture contract. He'd been paid off before *Santa Mica* had been built, Tereza understood, which meant he was the oldest person on the void ship by a large margin.

"Understood. Thank you, Second."

The transit pod slowed to a halt.

"The bridge is only a few steps from the pod station," Tereza told him. Or reminded him, if he'd familiarized himself with the ship as well as he'd suggested.

"Let's go."

***3***

The Santiago Corporation was over five hundred years old. A fundamentally civilian structure, governed by its Board of Shareholders, the Company wielded power any star-system government would envy.

Civilian or not, though, five hundred years created a lot of traditions. All Cirilo Webster actually needed to do was allow Nephil to scan the document chip he carried. The synthmind could tell the rest of *Santa Mica*'s computers that Cirilo was the Captain, and the rest was talking to the humans.

But traditions endured.

He gave his soon-to-be-First a firm nod as he stepped across the threshold of the bridge. It was a touch smaller than the bridges of the security frigates he'd been working on for the last ten years, but without a need for half the stations on a security ship, it was far more open and spacious.

Automation and the synthmind would take care of many mundane tasks, leaving *Santa Mica*'s bridge only needing one human the vast majority of the time. There was a clear watch-stander seat on the centerline, back from the other six consoles, and a large holo-tank/screen combination at the front of the space.

A dark-haired Chief started to rise from the watch station—the closest thing to a true "Captain's seat" on the ship—as Cirilo entered, but he waved them back to their chair even as he mentally identified and categorized them. Chief of the Deck Cass Lewis was in charge of any technology on the freighter that wasn't computers, life support or the engines. Unlike the SysChief or the LifeChief, the DeckChief was required to be a qualified watch-standing officer—and formalities didn't override the need to have a human backing Nephil up, even in dock.

Cirilo walked past the DeckChief and the watch station and approached the holo-tank. Sensing his approach, a set of control surfaces rose from concealed panels to provide a workstation right at the hologram of the orbital traffic above Iliakofos.

"First, Second," he said clearly. "Witness, please."

Jewel was only a step behind him, and she slipped into the station to his right without a word.

"I am recording," Nephil declared aloud.

Cirilo removed the document chip in its protective package and held it up so that the cameras could see it. The packaging opened easily, with just enough stiffness to show the recording that it had been properly sealed, and the doc-chip fell into his hand.

It was barely the size of his thumbnail—probably a full knuckle or something for most people—and only that large for ease of use. The console had a chip reader, and First Jewel authorized its activation with a silent command.

The chip clicked in, and the contents promptly loaded on the tank. Cirilo didn't even need to read the short statement to know what it said—he had several copies of the authorization in other, less formal, formats—but tradition said the words were spoken aloud.

"By the authority of the Board of Shareholders of the Santiago Corporation, Warranted Master Cirilo Jeremias Webster is assigned command of the SCC-One-Nine–type vessel *Santa Mica* and the associated departments and crew," Cirilo stated calmly.

"For peace, profit and prosperity. Authorized, Vice-President of Personnel Yadira Abigail Huerta, August fifth, twenty-six-fifteen, Standard Calendar."

Several lights on the console in front of him turned green, and a dull brain fog he'd barely noticed lifted as his bionic com was finally able to log on to *Santa Mica*'s network.

Lachlan would have logged on the moment they were in the Alpha Docks, but tradition said that the new Captain didn't access the network until he could do so with full administrative access.

++*Is this thing on?*++ he silently sent his steward, along with his new First and Second.

He saw First Jewel start and winked at her. A momentary break in his trained and inculcated impassive exterior. A shield he hoped not to need on *Santa Mica*, but one that had been all too necessary as First of the CorpSec frigate *Caballero*.

"First, Second, I assume command," he told them aloud. "Orders of the day?"

"DeckChief Lewis has second watch," Jewel said instantly. "I have third, followed by FlyChief Ostergaard on fourth. Our standard cycle. With your permission, I'll have you taking second watch the day after tomorrow?"

"Of course. Who's our eighth?" he asked. Regulations called for the ship to have eight qualified watch-standers, but only six were standard: Captain, First Officer, Chief of Security, Chief of Engines, Chief of the Deck and Chief of Administration. If the Chief of Flight Bay Salvador Ostergaard, the "FlyChief," was on the cycle, that was one of his two floaters.

"Purser Tsiklauri, ser—Skipper," Jewel said, shifting from the generic *ser* for a senior officer to the specific for *her* Captain with a clear mental jar.

"The Purser. Rare, but not a bad choice for him," Cirilo noted. He'd come up through Engines himself, though he'd been First Officer on one ship or another for twenty years.

"Well, I will need to talk to you two, plus MinChief and StewChief," he continued. "I'll want to talk to the crew, and since we have a quite-nice station *right here*, I see no reason to try to cram everyone into the mess, do you?"

Some people would have to stay aboard. At least four, including a watch-stander, but that was why he wanted to talk to Chief of Stewards Harisha Ibragimov.

If he was going to treat the entire crew to a nice dinner, he wasn't going to let the ones stuck on the ship be left out!

**4**

It was tradition that the Captain provide food for their first big meeting with the crew—without using the ship's own stewards. Tereza had seen that range from a stack of pizza-delivery boxes to the Captain taking over the mess for the first shift they were aboard in order to cook for everyone to Captains renting fancy restaurants and banquet halls.

Given the particular type of Captain *Santa Mica* had been getting in her time as First, it had mostly been cheap delivery from officers who didn't understand the tradition and overpriced restaurants from officers who didn't understand the value of money.

That meant Tereza was honestly surprised when Webster led her and a handful of the other Chiefs to the Soggy Spacer. It was the place she'd had dinner the previous evening, a solid high-end pub that served unpretentious food of high quality at decent prices.

"Lachlan," the Captain greeted his steward. Stirling was standing outside the Soggy Spacer, acting as a human sign and corralling *Santa Mica* spacers into the restaurant if any of them looked confused.

"How are we doing?"

"Just finished a quick check-in with the manager," Stirling said. "Bit of fluff over the relay bot, but everything is settled. Nephil has his eyes and ears."

"And the care package?"

"They're just putting the last touches on it now. I'm promised it will make it to the ship hot and ready, though getting it to everyone's posts is up to us."

++*Up to me, you mean*++ Nephil said in everyone's bionic coms. ++*Which means it* will *be taken care of*++

++*I have the utmost faith*++ Webster replied on the same channel. ++*And thank you, Nephil*++

There was no response from the synthmind. Tereza hoped that Webster understood that to be Nephil responding positively, but she couldn't be sure.

She'd definitely known officers who wanted clear responses from the synthminds. None of them had worked well with Nephil—and *Santa Mica*'s synthmind wasn't going to change for a Captain who'd be aboard for a year at best.

"How many of our people have made it in so far?" Webster asked.

"About a third," Stirling replied. "The rest have the memo and are making their way over."

"Well, then."

Webster turned and surveyed Tereza and the Chiefs with them. She'd rounded up Lewis, Jernigan and Sun—Chiefs of Deck, Cargo and Administration respectively—so they had all three officers and a third of the Chiefs to go with that third of the crew.

Despite his impassive carriage, the Captain seemed to hesitate before entering the Soggy Spacer. Tereza was sure she'd imagined it, but she stepped up beside him.

He gave her a nod and then stepped forward in sync with her.

***

In Tereza's experience, every spacer's pub on every space station she'd ever set foot on looked much the same. They all had the same metal flooring and open ceilings, almost indistinguishable from the corridors outside. If the pubs didn't use the same cheap fabricator pattern for tables and chairs, the differences were small enough to go unnoticed.

The Soggy Spacer was a shining example of the better breed. Everything was clean, spotless even, with music at a reasonable level and a high-quality serving system backed by a handful of living servers.

The space was large enough to fit the seventy crew they were bringing, Tereza judged at a glance, and the human manager was out directing people to tables while bots brought people drinks.

*++How'd you pick this place, Captain?++* she messaged Webster.

*++You were here last night for supper. I took that as a good sign—that and the fact that they let me book the whole place for three hours on six hours' notice!++*

She blinked in surprise. She wasn't sure how her new boss knew where she'd been for supper last night—though long experience suggested that Lachlan Stirling was probably involved—but it certainly suggested a greater level of attention than she was used to from her Captains.

"Let's grab a table for now," Webster said aloud. "There should be one pushed together for fourteen—ah, yes, of course."

Tereza saw the table at the same time as he did and probably for the same reason. The bot taking up one end was the source of the *fluff* Stirling had mentioned earlier—because Nephil had decided to use one of the ship's security bots as his relay.

The SecBot wasn't as large as a BimSoo. This particular version was shorter than most humans, in fact, but unlike humans, it had integrated stunners and energy weapons. Using it as a direct relay for Nephil removed the bot's usual limitation on brains, too.

Which meant Nephil was testing the new Captain.

*++I thought we'd talked about this?++* she asked the synthmind. *++You're going to get all of us in trouble++*

*++I am intrigued to see how this one reacts to many things, First++* Nephil replied. *++He is not the Captains we've had of late++*

The silent conversation carried her up to the table with the SecBot, which turned its sensors toward them and—*seriously?*—lit up a screen on its front with a large yellow smiley face.

"I believe we have enough seats for the officers and Chiefs, Captain," Nephil said aloud, his nondescript accent odd emerging from the SecBot. "Though I don't believe the restaurant has anything to feed me."

"I hope Iliakofos Two's chandlery has already taken care of any needs you or *Santa Mica* have, Nephil," Webster told the synthmind. If he was bothered by the SecBot, he didn't show it, taking his seat at the other end of the table from Nephil's remote.

"I needed some new molycrys replacements when we shipped in, but the chandlery and SysChief took care of it," Nephil confirmed. "Some of my hardware is aging, but that is to be expected."

"So it is," Webster said, showing that he clearly understood just how old Nephil was. "I will need to touch base with you on that once I'm more settled, Second. You're coming due for a full hardware rehabilitation, and there are decisions we'll want to go through."

Tereza didn't know how old the synthmind was, but a hardware rehabilitation was something Nephil would only need every fifty years or so. The Captain clearly *did* know how old the synthmind was.

"Speaking of SysChief," she said, shifting topics as she spotted a new wave of crew coming in. "De Veen! Get over here! Bring LifeChief, too!"

Those two worthies took a moment to make sure the crew they'd come in with were getting settled and then joined the other senior crew at the big table.

"Captain, this is Felix De Veen, our Chief of Systems, and Romée Anand, our Chief of Life Support," Tereza told Webster, gesturing to the two.

De Veen was a wiry redheaded man with a sharp nose and piercing black eyes. Anand shared his eyes and nothing else, her shaven black scalp reflecting the pub's lights as she stayed a protective half-step ahead of the SysChief.

++*Partners?*++ Webster asked.

++*Yes. Never been a problem*++ she replied.

Even as he was asking her about the couple, he was rising to his feet and offering his hand.

"Two of the more essential departments on any void ship," he told them. "Not that there are any *nonessential* departments, in my experience, but keeping our life support and computers running is definitely up there!"

"There are definitely one or two I can think of," a precise voice said. Every syllable was perfectly enunciated, to a degree that synthminds and computer voices attempted to avoid, as Vratislav Tsiklauri seemed to materialize out of a shadow.

"I would start with my own, of course," the Ship's Purser continued with a wry smile. He was just as sparse and precise in his person and mannerisms as he was in his speech. He wore an old-fashioned pink paisley suit, from sometime in the twenty-fourth century, and had a bionic eye that gave him the vague impression of wearing a monocle.

"There is nothing I do aboard *Santa Mica* that could not be handled by a computer program or by accountants in the local factor office," Tsiklauri continued.

"That's not true, Purser," Tereza argued.

"The First is correct. It's your job, Purser, to make sure that none of us are defrauding the Company," Webster said, in the exact same level tones he used for *everything*.

"Regardless, please, everyone, get a drink order in with the serving system," he told them, gesturing toward the haptic interfaces on the tables. "It's going to be a long night, and I know I don't want to go thirsty!"

**5**

Cirilo wasn't surprised in the slightest that the Security team were the last people from *Santa Mica* to arrive at the Soggy Spacer. Any good Security group would make sure that everything at the ship was secure and that the half-dozen spacers they were leaving behind were safe before leaving the freighter.

He'd spent thirty minutes greeting various crew and the Chiefs as they drifted in. There were nine Chiefs on the ship, headed up by the Captain, First Officer and Second Officer and supported by the Lawyer and Purser, who were classed in the same grouping as the officers and Chiefs.

Only one Chief was missing by the time the last group arrived, and he was looking for her when the Security spacers arrived in a single bloc. One SecSpec would have remained with the ship, overseeing the BimSoos and bots keeping the freighter safe, but the five remaining Security spacers easily filled the space like there were twice as many of them.

Most of that came from the woman at the center of the group. She held her team just inside the entrance by sheer force of will, gunmetal-gray eyes sweeping the pub, looking for dangers.

Chief of Security Violet Key's attempt to be intimidating was only slightly undermined by Lachlan Stirling arriving through the door behind her, closing and locking the bar without a word.

That broke some of the tension, and Cirilo rose to wave the SecChief and his steward over. The pair could have been cousins, like Corporate Security stamped its perfect troopers out of a mold. Key was maybe a centimeter taller than Lachlan, which meant she was forty centimeters shorter than Cirilo, but she was as broad across the shoulders as he was and far more heavily muscled.

"SecChief, welcome to the party," he greeted her, offering his hand.

To his surprise, she ignored his proffered organic hand and pulled off the glove on her left hand to reveal a similar silver bionic as his own. A spark of understanding hit him, and he offered his bionic hand instead.

Despite the silver coating, the limb had almost as many nerve sensors as the organic arm it had replaced. He felt her grip on his hand as they shook and he met her gaze levelly.

He knew Key's type. Lachlan was very much a younger version of her, though he'd claimed the man as a steward early on in CorpSec. She was a commando, one of the people who went into the down-and-dirty jobs necessary to keep the Santiago Corporation in charge of human space.

"Welcome to *Santa Mica*, Skipper," she told him. There was a slight guttural burr to her voice that he recognized. Not many people would know the sound of someone speaking with reconstructed vocal cords, but his decade in CorpSec had exposed him to many things even the Company liked to forget.

"Is our ship secure, SecChief?" he asked.

"Checked the accesses and scanners myself, Skipper," Key promised. "Special arrangements for the food delivery. Should be getting sorted about now."

"The food has indeed arrived," Nephil confirmed.

Key glanced at the SecBot at the end of the table and visibly arched an eyebrow.

"I see that's where my tenth Paladin is," she noted. "You are supposed to *tell* me when you check out hardware, Nephil."

If the synthmind hadn't even checked out the SecBot, Cirilo had a minor concern—but it was clear that Key wasn't bothered. She'd know what he was doing and tacitly allowed it, even if the synthmind was playing his own game.

Cirilo wasn't overly happy that the synthmind had shown up in a SecBot, but he wasn't going to show it. Plus, CorpSec frigate synthminds *always* used SecBots as their relays. A certain degree of paranoia was inherent in that position.

"It is checked out in the system," Nephil pointed out. "I did not think it was necessary to directly inform you."

"Of course."

Cirilo let that aside lie where it fell as he gestured for Key to walk with him.

"Speaking of the food getting to the ship," he said, pitching his voice so everyone could hear him, "I believe our hosts should have dinner just about ready for us, too."

It had been ready, in fact, for almost ten minutes. The Soggy Spacer's staff had overridden the serving system, holding the food until his instruction. At his words, the kitchen doors swung open and serving bots surged out.

"Let's eat, folks."

***

Cirilo spent the meal appearing to focus on his food but actually listening to the conversations around him as carefully as he could. There was the formal hierarchy of the ship that put the SecChief, EngChief and CargChief above the other department heads, but the reality could vary dramatically in his experience.

It didn't do so much on *Santa Mica*, from what he heard. Key and Jewel were definitely in charge—to a level that might be a concern for him, in fact—but Chief of Engines Odette Rao, the only person in the crew who shared Cirilo's height, and Chief of Cargo Yevhen Jernigan were definitely listened to when they spoke.

One dinner wouldn't be enough for him to really get a feel for the unofficial dynamics of his ship, but it gave him somewhere to start. He'd take the time to sit down with all nine of his Chiefs and his other four officers as quickly as he could.

For now, it was his job to feed everyone and learn what he could by listening—just as Lachlan had learned where the First had gone for dinner the previous night by asking in the canteen.

He had seen enough of the bill for the evening to know it was going to hurt. CorpSec officers made more than their counterparts in CargoFleet—his salary increase for going from a CorpSec First Officer to a CargoFleet Captain wasn't worth mentioning—but renting out an entire pub and feeding seventy-plus people was still a big dent in his bank balance.

Tradition was expensive—but there was a *point* to the tradition, one he hoped he'd served by finding a restaurant the crew's officers liked. Good food and good beer were supposed to buy him warm feelings, as was the recognition he was giving his people.

As the last plates were cleared away, he rose to his feet and tapped a fork on his beer glass. That silenced the conversations his standing hadn't, bringing the room's focus onto him.

"Well, folks, I appear to have you all trapped here," he told them. That caught him chuckles, some of them more forced than others, but it was true as well as a lame joke.

"If anyone has missed the news, I'm Cirilo Webster, and I'm your new Captain," he continued. "By the grace of our Board of Shareholders and the Company's Central Personnel, you and I are going to get to know each other pretty well over the months and years to come."

He'd made Captain and had command of his own ship. He'd bought that privilege in a dark coin—SecChief Key and Lachlan were the only people who could guess what he'd paid to stand there—but he didn't expect to rise much from there.

He didn't need to. He had a ship. He was going to make her the best ship in the fleet, and that was enough for him.

"I'm not going to give you my whole life story, since we'd like to get to dessert tonight, but I've been a First Officer for the Company for the last twenty years," he continued. "*Santa Mica* is my first command, so I'm going to apologize right up front. I'll be learning on the job, much as all of us did when we first started our jobs.

"I'm pretty sure I know what I'm doing, but we've all made mistakes while thinking that, haven't we?"

The chuckles he got from that felt more honest.

"And to kick it all off, I've got good news for you," he said. "CargChief Jernigan and your crew: you're going to be busy tomorrow. Our cargo got confirmed this afternoon, and we'll start loading it at oh nine hundred standard tomorrow!"

That turned chuckles into cheers. *Santa Mica* had been sitting at Iliakofos Two for three standard weeks, since their previous Captain had left for his next posting.

A ship that didn't move didn't make money—for the Santiago Corporation and for her crew, who ancient tradition and modern contract awarded one percent of all revenue earned by the ship.

Even divided up by the arcane formulas used, *Santa Mica*'s crew could confidently expect to match their base salaries from that bonus—so long as the ship kept moving.

"Enjoy the desserts and the drinks, everyone," Cirilo told them with a smile that felt more honest to him than his mask of impassivity.

"Tomorrow, we have work to do."

**6**

There was surprisingly little datawork waiting for Cirilo in the Captain's office the next day. Tereza Jewel would have been Acting Captain since the previous man had left, but Cirilo knew how easy it was to just leave things for the incoming Captain.

He'd tried never to do it himself, and it seemed Jewel was cut from the same cloth. Of the six outstanding items in his inbox, one was related to the contract the Company had assigned them, one had come up the previous night, and the other four had been neatly tied up in a bow, requiring little more than his stamp of approval.

Cirilo read through those four first. Jewel had done exactly what he would have in her place, and he resisted the urge to meddle for the sake of doing something—especially when he did have real work to do. He thumbed his approvals and considered his new office.

His predecessor, Makar Orlov, had been aboard *Santa Mica* for eleven months. That had been enough time to put his stamp on the space, and whatever money he'd spent on the office hadn't mattered enough for Orlov to take his updates with him.

The computer console had to have been installed the day Orlov arrived aboard; it was basically brand-new. The walls were marked with semi-tridimensional images of sports craft of several varieties, ranging from a scarlet-red rocket racer at one end to a beautifully appointed racing horse at the other.

The Orlovs were Shareholders, owners of the tightly controlled and rarely sold voting shares of the Santiago Corporation. Makar had money to burn and probably owned every racer on the walls.

Cirilo would keep the self-adjusting chair and the high-end computer. The art... He'd talk to Lachlan about the art.

Putting that aside for later, he made the first of what he knew would be a long, long list of frustrating com calls as Captain of a void ship.

"Iliakofos Two Security," a cheery, artificially generated woman's face greeted him. "Is this an emergency?"

"No. I need to talk to SecHold about one of my crew," he told the computer. It wouldn't even be a synthmind, just an algorithm that would be able to handle most queries about half of the time.

"May I have your name and ship, honored personage?"

"Captain Cirilo Webster, *Santa Mica*." He paused. "Santiago Corporation."

The algorithmic face wasn't programmed to show surprise, but he suspected that would activate a priority. It always did.

"Of course. I will get you Sergeant Mack, please hold."

The Iliakofos Planetary Police used a sharply triangular version of the standard gold police badge as their logo, Cirilo noted absently as he waited. ILIAKOFOS STATION TWO SD was centered beneath the logo, marking who he was talking to.

He didn't have time for more than that before the logo vanished into a face that definitely hadn't been generated by an algorithm. Sergeant Alex Mack was a green-eyed woman in a sharp brown uniform and a sharper peaked hat, and she was looking at him like he'd crawled out of the station's recycling plants.

"Captain Webster," Mack said. "I was expecting Officer Jewel."

"My First has many demands on her time, Sergeant," Cirilo told her. "EnvSpec Bodrogi Sung isn't quite up to the priority of requiring us both.

"Can you give me a summary of why Specialist Bodrogi is in your holding, Sergeant?" he continued brightly.

He could guess. Environmental Specialist Bodrogi Sung wasn't needed to load cargo and had left the Captain's party to proceed to another bar. Drunk and disorderly was his best-case scenario. Worst-case scenario...

"Em Bodrogi is detained pending charges for assault, Captain," Mack said flatly. "Surveillance shows that he entered Concourse Six at oh-fifty-two ST this morning, drunk and shouting loudly. One of our citizens asked him to keep it down; the conversation rapidly degraded until blows were exchanged.

"Is-Two-Sec responded to a call from a third party. Four individuals were stunned and detained."

"I see." Cirilo met Mack's gaze calmly as he considered the situation. It could be worse—drunken fisticuffs ending in everybody stunned were considered a regular night out on some stations—but it could have been a lot better, too. Concourse Six was a higher-end area, too, holding primary accessways for several local corporations.

Which raised questions of its own, since the bars around Concourse Six weren't where a Company specialist would go for drinks. It was almost halfway across the station from the Soggy Spacer.

"I will have to talk to my Legal, of course," he warned Mack, "but I believe I can start by formally requesting all related surveillance footage. I last saw Specialist Bodrogi Sung in the Soggy Spacer at twenty-two hundred standard... which seems quite a ways from Concourse Six."

"This is very open-and-shut, Captain. Your thug—"

"Is presumed innocent until proven guilty," Cirilo interrupted her. "I would appreciate it, Sergeant Mack, if you could track Specialist Bodrogi's movements back to twenty-two hundred for me.

"I am not certain why he would be in Concourse Six, Sergeant, and the possibilities... well. I'm sure you'd like to know yourself, wouldn't you?"

He gave her a warm smile. Partly because he really *did* want to get along with the local police... but partly because he suspected that being nice to her was going to infuriate her more than anything else he could do.

***

Cirilo spent the next forty-five minutes on a video call, going through the cargo they were loading in thorough detail. The man on the other side of the screen seemed extraordinarily concerned for a cargo load of food.

"We have everything in order, Em Richmond," he assured the client. "Seven units, three-point-five million cubic meters. My Cargo Chief is already coordinating with your delivery teams and my Deck people to make sure the containers are properly refrigerated and have the right power connections.

"It's a five-day journey to the Herecrow System and orbit of Pastrook. Is there something specific you're concerned about?"

Henrick Richmond was the local factor for Rising Cow Industries, one of several companies that handled food imports for their destination. Cirilo knew that Herecrow imported almost all of their meat and a large portion of their grains—Pastrook was habitable but cold and windswept, a difficult climate for even genegineered crops.

"What we grow in Herecrow can keep us alive, but there is more to food than mere nutrition, Captain Webster," Richmond said after a moment's thought. "For anything resembling food, we need imports like this cargo.

"There will be empty plates and broken souls if you cannot deliver."

"*Santa Mica* may be old, Em Richmond, but I have no reason to fear that likely," Cirilo pointed out. It was almost unheard-of, in fact, which suggested...

A problem.

"So said Captain Darmouth, and no one has heard from him or *Santa Alicia* in thirty-two standard weeks," Richmond said grimly. "You will be cautious; promise me."

Cirilo was going to have to look into that. He didn't like the idea that the local factor had booked him and his ship for a cargo run and *hadn't* told him that a ship heading in the same direction had gone missing.

"We will be extraordinarily cautious, Em Richmond. You have my personal guarantee." He pulled the contract up and skimmed the summary as he spoke.

Despite what Richmond had said, there was no risk premium baked into the carriage agreement. That was something he'd have to take up with the factor office... if there was time.

"I appreciate it, Captain. No one is starving on Pastrook, but the last news I had from home spoke of rationing certain products. Your cargo won't make the difference on its own, but each ship that arrives is a reassurance to our people... and our markets."

"And both of these things matter," Cirilo agreed.

The conversation ended in an exchange of pleasantries. He stared blankly off into space for a few moments, then sighed.

"Nephil, throw everything we have on *Santa Alicia* to my console," he told the synthmind. "Any particular reports that you've picked up?"

"As Em Richmond stated, she was scheduled to arrive in Herecrow thirty-two standard weeks ago. She was recognized as overdue and presumed lost on March nineteenth. Santiago files note that the insurance payout for the cargo has been completed and the Company is in negotiations with Alliance Interstellar for the payout on *Santa Alicia* herself."

"Her crew?" Cirilo asked, pulling the information on the freighter up.

"Santiago paid out all life insurance benefits and outstanding payroll to next of kin on presumption of loss. We are negotiating with Alliance Interstellar for reimbursement."

Even the largest corporation in history had to negotiate with its insurers. Part of the problem was that the conversation was almost certainly happening on Earth, which meant that his news was weeks out of date.

*Santa Alicia* had been a big ship. A Class II transport to *Santa Mica*'s Class IV, eight hundred meters long and hauling eighty standard half-megaton cargo units.

The Company didn't make a big deal of their losses—part of the power they wielded was anchored on the certain knowledge that a Santiago shipment would go through—and got away with it because they were also very rare.

"There was an investigation carried out," Nephil told him. "A CorpSec frigate retraced her entire route. No sign of foul play or natural impediments. LUC."

*Lost to unknown causes.* What a bland descriptor for the disappearance of two hundred and twenty-five people—including the synthmind, of course.

There was nothing in the files on *Santa Alicia* to suggest a possible hardware failure. She was just gone.

It happened, Cirilo knew. An undetected flaw in a plasma line. A miscalculation of an energy transfer. A rogue planet missed on the mass charts of the region. Ships didn't go missing often, but when they did, there was very rarely any trace at all.

"Thank you, Nephil. Can you keep an eye on the feeds if any new couriers come in before we leave? Flag anything regarding *Alicia*."

"If you insist."

Cirilo didn't push. The synthmind had agreed and that was enough.

He was getting an unusual vibe from Nephil, but it wasn't anything he couldn't handle.

He thought.

**7**

"I ALREADY SPOKE TO your Captain, Jewel. What *more* trouble do you think you can throw my way?"

Tereza had to take a moment to digest that. She'd spent the first few hours of her day helping the CargChief get everything set up for the arrival of their cargo containers and got to her messages late, for her.

If the Captain had already reached out to Iliakofos Two Security over Bodrogi, then she was both wasting her time and potentially undermining him. She'd just assumed that he wasn't going to be that fast to get to work, if she was honest.

But if the Captain was creating trouble…

"I'm just following up on the datawork he requested," she lied smoothly. Whatever else Cirilo Webster was, he'd been a First for a long time and knew the drill when it came to a spacer in lockup: delay, delay, delay.

"It's just about together," Mack growled. "And curse your Captain to the Void you Saints love so much, but he found a real lever to pull, didn't he?"

Mack, it seemed, wasn't going to tell her what Webster had asked for. That left the least pleasant option—asking him.

++*Talking to Mack*++ she messaged. ++*She's more peeved than usual. What did you ask for?*++

"It's our job to watch out for our crew, Sergeant Mack, as it is yours to watch out for the people of Iliakofos Two," she said. "How's Bodrogi doing?"

"Not. Great," Mack bit off, then sighed and shook her head. "If you can get me his medical profile, we'd appreciate it. He's not waking up from the stunner beam the way he should."

++*Good, let's hit her both ways*++ her Captain replied. ++*They said Bodrogi was in Concourse Six, but that was a long way from where we saw him last. Seemed suspicious, so I asked them to trace his movements*++

"Sergeant, are you telling me that you have one of our crew in custody and he hasn't regained consciousness yet?" Tereza asked carefully. "I... am going to need to loop in the Skipper and Legal."

++*Did she tell you he was still unconscious?*++ she pinged Webster.

There was a silence on both of her conversations, and then a flashing icon appeared on the video call as Webster requested to be added to the call.

He could have cut in via his overrides. She appreciated the gesture.

"I would prefer that we not get—"

"How long has Specialist Bodrogi been unconscious?" Tereza snapped. "I'm looping them in now."

Webster was easy; he was already banging on the virtual door. Renata Bautista, the ship's lawyer and the closest thing to a Shareholder on the ship, was a bit harder.

++*Legal, we have a problem that needs your eyes*++ Tereza sent. ++*One of ours is in lockup and hasn't woken up from the stunner for twelve hours*++

"We will wait for Em Bautista to join us," Webster said before Tereza or Mack could say a further word. "I understand that the situation has deteriorated since we spoke four hours ago, correct?"

"It has," Mack said grimly.

*Four hours ago.* Webster had been making calls to security within an hour of starting his first workday on the ship. Tereza was going to have to recalibrate her expectations and fast.

A third channel joined the call, Renata Bautista's image falling on the opposite side of Mack from Webster on Tereza's screen.

Bautista was painfully beautiful. She looked perfectly put-together, in a creased white jacket over an off-code burgundy shipsuit, with everything from her dark brown eyes to her shoulder-length raven hair impeccable.

Tereza knew from prior experience that Renata Bautista would have looked almost as put-together when she'd just woken up. Some of it was training. Some of it was genetic engineering and the money to afford the good gadgets.

Bautista would happily remind anyone who asked that the closest voting share to her was held by her mother's cousin, but even that was enough for her family to be Shareholders. She was Cradle-born and Cradle-bred, more Saint than Saints.

"I have bits and pieces from the Captain and the First Officer," Bautista said calmly. "But I would appreciate hearing the entire story from the rocket's nozzle. Sergeant Mack? Would you care to explain the situation as you saw it?"

Mack sighed and nodded.

"At zero five two standard time this morning, Specialist Bodrogi Sung entered Concourse Six, very visibly drunk and violating several noise regulations active in that section of the station," she said, her voice formal and very specific.

"A station citizen, one Mallory Wang, objected to Specialist Bodrogi's behavior. The two argued, several friends of Em Wang got involved, and blows were struck.

"An uninvolved citizen triggered an alert, and Is-Two-Sec arrived approximately four minutes after the first blows were struck. The struggle was ongoing, and the officer on the scene utilized a wide-beam stunner after attempts to halt the conflict verbally failed.

"All four members of the conflict were detained, pending a review of the surveillance footage to identify the initiator of the conflict. Initial examination had just confirmed that Specialist Bodrogi had struck first, initiating preparation of assault charges, when Captain Webster spoke to me at oh eight forty-two ST this morning."

"Thank you." Bautista waited a moment, her eyes locked on the camera while she typed away. "Now. What is Specialist Bodrogi's current status?"

The cop grimaced.

"Em Bodrogi remains unconscious," she said grimly. "The expected duration for the stunners we use is six hours, plus/minus ninety minutes. He was not in a time period of active concern when I spoke to Captain Webster this morning."

"Which has now changed." Bautista's voice was cold. "Which means a Santiago Corporation employee is now in medical distress in your holding cells, Sergeant. We should have been informed without First Jewel needing to contact you."

"All of his vitals are solid; he just isn't waking up, and we haven't had time to get a doctor on site yet," Mack countered.

"Specialist Bodrogi has been unconscious for twelve hours," Webster said sharply. "After being stunned. You have done nothing?"

"We checked his vitals as soon as there was a concern. My people have basic paramedic training; they could be certain he was safe enough until a doctor was available."

"You are aware of Section Twenty-Six, Article Fifteen of the Multistellar Agreement on Prisoners' Rights, correct, Sergeant?" Bautista asked. "You are obliged to provide assistance to a prisoner in medical distress as soon as possible, not as soon as *convenient*."

"What part of this suggests I'm doing anything different?" Mack snapped. "We have *one* doctor in Security's employ on the station, and he's swamped."

"The Santiago Corporation has on-call contracts with both clinics on Iliakofos Two and could have had a doctor to your precinct inside of thirty minutes," the lawyer replied. "To confirm, you have only spoken to Santiago Corporation representatives when contacted, correct?"

"Do you have any idea how much work a security department of forty-three people handling a station of fifteen thousand does? We had no update, so there was no reason to contact anyone until we had the surveillance footage Captain Webster requested."

"Speaking of," Webster said grimly. "I want that footage. Now, Sergeant. And we're going to have that doctor at your precinct *as soon as possible*."

The echo, Tereza could tell, was utterly intentional.

"It's on its way," Mack said. "I'll make sure your medic gets in. I remind you, though, that charges are being processed for Specialist Bodrogi as we speak."

"So you've said," Bautista agreed. "I'll deal with that as the Captain deals with Bodrogi's health, Sergeant. It will be handled."

Mack stared at the three of them for several long seconds, then cut the conference call without a word.

***

"Nephil, secure this to internal coms," Bautista ordered. "Then join us."

The video shivered for a moment, and then a new screen replaced Mack's image. This one was a rotating image of *Santa Mica* herself, Nephil's preferred avatar for conversations when his visible presence was required.

"Please," Webster added, the Captain's impassive face and level tones in no way undermining his clear rebuke to the lawyer.

That was *fascinating* to Tereza. She'd worked with Nephil for years now and was used to the synthmind's grouchiness. The Captain hadn't and wasn't but was insisting on being polite and respectful of the artificial person in a way that not many bothered to do.

Bautista was more characteristic of how officers treated synthminds. They were the ship's Second Officer, which gained them a certain respect when acting in that role, but they were often treated as simply an interface for the ship's computers.

Most of the crew knew that treating Nephil that way was a bad idea, but Renata Bautista had only been aboard the ship for a year, and even Nephil treated Legal differently.

"Twelve hours is bad," Webster continued once they were sure the connection was now purely internal to the ship. "Unless the locals are using a cheap knockoff for their police, stunners shouldn't *do* that."

"The IPP uses the thirty-degree model of the Satine," Nephil noted. "As Sergeant Mack noted, six hours plus/minus ninety minutes, ninety-five percent of the time. Specialist Bodrogi has no medical issues on file that would suggest any contraindications to being stunned."

"I don't know the crew as well as you two, Nephil, Tereza," the Captain replied. "Is there any reason the two of you can think of that would cause Bodrogi to be in the concourse hosting the local in-system shippers, picking a fight?"

"No," Tereza said. "What does the surveillance show?"

"I'm going to review that once we're done here, with Nephil and SecChief, if she's free," Webster replied. "Can I get you to arrange getting the Company's contract doctor over to holding?"

"I can do that," she promised.

"Tell the doc to run a full toxicology screen," he continued. "Standard protocol says they would have taken a sample when they brought him in. Get that sample, too, and run the same screen.

"Bautista, with this level of... mess, do you think you can get Bodrogi sprung without charges?" he continued, turning to Bautista. "I have some suspicions about what went down, but if we can pull him out without having to make accusations or deal with an actual court, everyone will be happier.

"I can't hold the ship for him, but I'd *like* to leave with all four EnvSpecs if we can!"

"I believe I can make that happen," Bautista said firmly. "What... exactly are you suspecting, Captain?"

"I was CorpSec," Webster reminded them. "They train a certain degree of paranoia into us, and let's just say... uncharacteristic aggression matched with an unusual stun duration?

"I very much want to see that toxicology screen."

***8***

Cirilo replayed the sequence at regular speed. They'd run through the entire three-hour window at fifty times speed, and now he and Key were watching the critical few moments again.

Bodrogi had been drunk out of his mind. It was clear in how he stumbled as he left the bar he'd gone to after the Soggy Spacer.

So were the other two spacers with him. They'd both made it back to the ship fine, but Bodrogi had separated from them. Body language said he'd been looking for a bathroom.

He was still a long way from Concourse Six at oh eleven ST.

Cirilo watched as the EnvSpec stumbled along a corridor, following a dimly lit sign toward a public facility, until a masked figure met him right outside the door to his destination.

If the system had recorded audio, Mack hadn't sent it to them. But it was clear that Bodrogi just wanted to get into the toilets behind his accoster and his accoster wanted something else. Finally, the spacer shook his head, stepping sideways to try and go around the stranger.

And that was when the stranger had drugged him. Cirilo had seen the move a dozen times before at least. Swing around with someone stepping past you, using their momentum to press an inhaler cup over their face.

Bodrogi didn't fall down. He just stopped at the end of the step. He stood there, seemingly frozen, while the stranger spoke to him.

Finally, the masked person tucked something into Bodrogi's pocket, patted him on the shoulder, and walked away. Bodrogi went into the facilities, presumably to complete his original mission, and when he emerged, he set off for the transit pod that would take him to Concourse Six.

"And he takes the puffer the bastard gave him right when he gets off the pod," Key concluded, watching the footage with him. "Almost certainly had a counteragent for the hypnotic."

"Plus Spike or some similar *shit*," Cirilo swore. Spike had been a failed attempt to create a combat drug and, like many such things, had ended up with the recipe leaked to some underworld chemist who'd turned it into a product for sale.

Why anyone would *want* to be unreasonably angry and lose all self-control was beyond Cirilo, though he understood it also came with the sensation of power and strength.

"Why Spike?" Key asked. "Could be any one of a dozen things, sadly."

"Because Spike reacts with stun fields and risks throwing someone into a coma," he told her. "You hadn't seen that?"

She shook her head, glaring at the video screen.

"Finding out who was screwing with the Company and why wasn't in my AO," she told him. "We were sent in to convince them they really shouldn't do that."

Cirilo nodded silently. He suspected that Key wouldn't say things like that around most of the crew, but they were both ex-CorpSec. He knew *exactly* what kind of job she'd been doing for the Santiago Corporation, though she'd done it for a lot longer than he had.

"Last time I ran into it, turned out our woman had taken it for fun of some kind," Cirilo said. "Very much the wrong kind, as her boyfriend probably concluded after she'd broken three of his limbs and six ribs."

"The *informed* part of *informed consent* got missed, I take it?"

"Neither of them had a maldito clue what they were doing. But at least they knew they were doing something, where our EnvSpec here most certainly did *not*."

"Hypnotic to get him into the right place, something aggression-inducing to get him to make a scene," Key agreed. "Beyond making the Company look bad, what was even the point?"

"There's probably some legislation or regulation under discussion right now," Cirilo said with a shrug. "Make us look bad, undercut our negotiators. The man who ran into Bodrogi at the entrance probably saved us a solid headache."

"What is the next action, Captain?" Nephil asked. The synthmind had found the odd behavior but hadn't caught the moment of Bodrogi getting drugged. Not many people would know that exact movement sequence, after all.

"Assuming our doctor can handle whatever is in the EnvSpec's system and Bautista gets him loose without us having to hand this over to IPP, we package it up and hand it over to the local factor's office to handle as they see fit," Cirilo said.

"I'll use whatever ammunition I need to get Bodrogi back on this ship by tomorrow night. If this isn't needed for that, however, it becomes the Company's problem, not mine."

He had a pretty solid idea of what the Company's local officers would do with even circumstantial proof that the local shippers had arranged an assault on one of their people. Whatever the locals' goal had been, it wasn't going to end well for them.

Getting on the wrong side of the Saints generally didn't.

"Did this often, running a CorpSec frigate?" Key asked.

"Did a lot of things as First on a frigate," Cirilo conceded. "Some I can't talk about. Some I just don't."

"Fair enough, Skipper. I know how that life went. Got hauled a few places by frigates over the years, and they were rarely happy to see us!"

"I got a silver arm and Captain's braid out of it," he said, glancing over at the woman seated in the office with him. She only had the one visible bionic, but he knew what long-service Saint commandos got kitted out with on the inside.

"You holding up, SecChief?" he asked quietly. They didn't send commando squad leaders to CargoFleet unless something had gone wrong.

"Yeah. This is higher-up's idea of a semi-retirement for me," she said with a grin. "I think some shrink somewhere said my 'profile was no longer stable enough for nonconventional security work' or something similar.

"My boss said I needed to work where things were more black-and-white, for everyone's best interests. Still get paid as a commando, plus ship's share. It isn't a bad exchange... and I brought a few toys with me."

Cirilo considered what that might mean and sighed.

"Anything that's going to get us arrested if local security finds out?"

"Nothing like that. We just have an extra hull in the shuttle bay and a more thoroughly fitted-out armory than most," Key said. "None of us got out of CorpSec without a lot of paranoia."

"No," he conceded.

After all, no one spent time in Santiago Corporate Security without realizing just how many corpses and compromises held up the Board's control of human space.

***9***

The Iliakofos Two Security Department Precinct was unusually obvious. Tereza had seen precincts that could have been mistaken for regular offices from the concourses they were positioned on, but Is-Two-Sec had opened the entire front section of their space to the concourse, creating a wide-open, transparent-feeling space for people to bring their problems.

Half a dozen kiosks held holographic officers acting as receptionists, algorithmic agents that could help with some issues or summon a human from the Is-Two-Sec if more was needed. A dozen low-profile security bots were tucked around the sides of the open reception area, mostly out of sight and mind.

For her part, Tereza Jewel walked past the kiosks and right up to the set of double doors leading into the Precinct's actual offices. However open the reception area might look, the IPP still did their actual business out of sight.

An officer in the brown uniform of the Iliakofos Police stepped into her way right at the door.

"Can I help you, honorable?" he asked.

"I'm First Officer Tereza Jewel from *Santa Mica*," she told the man. "I'm here to collect my spacer, Bodrogi Sung. I have a copy of the order for his release, if you've misplaced it."

Bautista had been her usual efficient self. Three hours after getting the information, she'd thrown enough paperwork at the station judiciary that they'd conceded the point.

"That won't be necessary, Officer Jewel," the cop said. He tilted his head, an unconscious mannerism for listening to a bionic com that most spacers trained out of themselves.

"If you'll come with me, please?"

"Of course, Constable."

His name and rank were on the embroidered patch over his heart: Constable Ramone Blackwood. Probably too junior an Is-Two-Sec man to get stuck with her, but she wasn't making the call.

Blackwood opened the door with a wave of his hand and stepped through, Jewel right on his heels. She didn't know the layout of this precinct, but she'd hauled enough idiots out of drunk tanks to have a solid idea of where the holding cells were—and he turned in the right direction.

Unfortunately, he stopped at an office at the top of the stairs, where Sergeant Mack and a stranger were waiting.

"Dr. Wada, I presume," Jewel greeted them. Clad in the standard white shipsuit with red trim of a space-side medical professional, Dr. Billie Wada managed impassivity almost as well as Jewel's new Captain.

Almost. Something in the way they were sitting told her that they were far from happy with their companion.

"I am. You are here to collect the poor man I have been seeing?" Wada asked.

"I am," she echoed back. "Any problems?"

"Many, not helped by the usual failures of the jackbooted kind," the doctor told her. "No toxicology screen was run on Em Bodrogi's blood samples until I arrived. The problem was obvious, of course, once a proper analysis of the situation had been completed."

"Your complaint has been noted, Doctor," Mack said. She sounded exhausted. "The counteragent is working, yes?"

"Yes," Wada conceded. "If it had been administered when Em Bodrogi arrived, of course, he might have retained his memories of the last forty-eight hours and would have avoided the risk of a narcoleptic disorder."

"That bad?" Tereza asked. That could be a real problem on a void ship.

"I can't be certain of the extent of the memory loss, but it is unlikely to affect anything outside the last few days," the doctor replied. "The risk of long-term impacts is minimal but would have been zero with proper care.

"Em Bodrogi should wake up in the next ten minutes or so. So long as he takes the medication I have prescribed, as I have prescribed it, for the next twenty-four days, he should suffer no long-term consequences."

"Thank you, Dr. Wada," she told the medic. "Your assistance is appreciated."

"My assistance is well compensated. The formal complaint I will be filing is a matter of professional standards," they concluded. "A draft report is in Sergeant Mack's hands and in your bionic com... now."

A ping confirmed receipt of the file, and she nodded her thanks again.

"That will be all, I hope." They stood up and held out their hand to Tereza. She shook it, and they passed her a small doc-chip.

"Prescriptions and regimen," they told her, indicating the chip. "Make certain he follows them."

"I will," she promised. She'd probably drop that on EnvChief, Bodrogi's boss, but it would be taken care of.

The doctor stalked out and Tereza turned her gaze on Mack.

"Can I get my man? Or…"

The Sergeant grunted and leaned back in her chair for a moment, then produced a tray with a pair of still-steaming coffee cups on it from underneath her desk.

"Drink, First?" she asked. "This was a damn mess."

"One you made worse," Tereza told her friend, then sighed and took a seat. *Santa Mica* had been through Oneira more than any system in the last few years, and they'd ended up at Iliakofos Two most often of all.

She'd got to know the security people. Mack was one of only three Sergeants and was the easiest to deal with. People got drunk, and, well…

"The Company is *always* going to go to bat for our people, Alex."

"Guess even the megacorporate parasite has to have *one* virtue," Mack replied.

The coffee was terrible, which was about what Tereza had expected. She'd learned, over the years, that there was a direct inverse correlation between the honesty of a station security department and how good the coffee in the precinct was.

The worse the coffee, the cleaner the department overall.

"The Captain and the doc aren't wrong, Alex," Tereza pointed out. "Your guys made this worse."

"They did," Mack confessed. "Believe me, Tereza, I have had the lecture from you, from Dr. Wada, from Justice Petrovich, and from your new Captain. My people have got it from me, and they're going to get it again from Commissioner Is-Two-Sec."

"Did you look at the surveillance footage?" Tereza asked.

"Honestly, I haven't had time," the Sergeant said. "I wasn't kidding about the work on our plates while talking to your new boss. Who is, I have to say, a fascinating piece of work.

"Who in void and stars can recognize that someone has been drugged like that from their reaction to a stun pulse?"

"CorpSec."

The amalgamated word hung in the air for a few seconds, then Mack snorted.

"Somehow, I am not under the impression that Captain Webster has spent much of his career eating donuts on stakeout."

"No." Tereza downed the rest of the terrible coffee. Webster was going to be an interesting boss. Especially after she'd spent so long getting used to people who were only on *Santa Mica* to check the box labeled *has a prior command* that Company rules said was needed to take command of a brand-new void ship.

"Can I get Bodrogi now, Alex? Despite what the sod-trapped think sometimes, he does actually have a job on my ship, and I need him to be doing it before we leave!"

# 10

"Iliakofos Station Two has confirmed release," First Jewel reported, her tone as professional as anyone could hope.

Cirilo couldn't keep himself from double-checking, though he managed to do it through a bionic com request to the ship's computers. Nephil would probably see it, but Jewel wouldn't.

"Thank you, First," he told her. "Any concerns with kickoff?"

"No, Skipper," she said.

That wasn't a surprise, but it was pleasant. *Santa Mica* was over seventy years old. While Cirilo had spent the two days since taking command going through the bowels of the ship with EngChief Odette Rao, he'd expected to do more firefighting in those forty-eight hours than he had.

*Santa Mica* was in good shape, and he could tell that was due to her Chiefs and officers, not her prior Captains. His crew was a smooth machine... One that didn't include him.

Yet.

"I have the helm, First," he told Jewel, a tapped command on the interfaces of his seat activating the navigation systems.

There was a moment of hesitation before she replied.

"Of course, ser. You have the helm."

"Second Nephil, confirm separation distance and angle from the station, please," Cirilo requested.

"We are currently sixty-eight meters from the station, drifting away at one-point-two meters per second," the synthmind replied. "Angle is eleven by minus five."

"Thank you, Second. Bringing up dorsal and spinal maneuvering thrusters."

Eleven degrees vertical and five degrees horizontal was still basically pointed at Iliakofos Two at this distance. Firing *Santa Mica*'s main engines at this distance was a bad idea, but he didn't want to fire even thrusters at the orbital.

A five-second burst from the forward dorsal and rear spinal thrusters turned the freighter in space, angling her bow toward deep space—and her stern well away from anything he didn't want to scorch.

"Stern thrusters online," he said for the record, and engaged the system. It would take them time to clear the safety perimeter of Iliakofos Two's hull, but they were now moving.

He glanced over at Jewel. He wasn't sure what he was looking for—some sign that his job maneuvering the big ship was acceptable, he supposed—but her attention was focused on her own consoles.

Cirilo turned his attention to the planet they were leaving behind. Iliakofos was one of the more pleasant planets in the Seventy-Seven, a temperate world with eighty-six percent surface water and almost zero axial tilt.

The polar ice caps were as unpleasant as any world's poles, but most of the landmass was in a series of large islands near the equator. Over a billion human beings lived down there, with a hundred million more scattered through the rest of the Oneira System.

Unlike some systems Cirilo had been to, Oneira didn't need the Santiago Corporation to survive—but like the rest of the Seventy-Seven, much of their economy was built around the assumption of interstellar trade.

Trade that would not exist without ships like *Santa Mica*.

Cirilo loved his job and, for the first time in his life, was entering the void in command of his own ship and his own crew.

"Second Nephil, I mark us as reaching the safety perimeter in thirty seconds," he said aloud. "Do you confirm?"

"I confirm your time stamp," the synthmind said formally. "Course is plotted for our flight to transit. Two hours at full thrust, then three at steady velocity. Transit in five hours, eleven minutes."

"Thank you, Second," Cirilo said. "First, EngChief, any concerns with going to full power?"

They'd pass the safety perimeter while he was making sure of everything, but that was fine. He wasn't taking risks on the first flight of his first command.

"If I had concerns, I'd have told you yesterday," Rao said over the com, her voice a touch irritated. "The old girl's fine."

"It's protocol, EngChief," he reminded her. "And today, I want to make sure everything is fine."

"Fine, fine, everything's *fine*," the EngChief said, but there was amusement in her tone now.

"First?" Cirilo repeated, turning to Jewel.

"I've reviewed Second's course. Unsurprisingly, it's perfect," she told him. "I have no concerns, Skipper. We are ready for full power."

He nodded and checked the distance. They were now three and a half kilometers past the safety zone, their velocity slowly creeping up at the best their secondary thrusters could do—and their fuel levels visibly slipping down.

"Cutting maneuvering thrusters," he declared. The fuel-thirsty secondaries dimmed on his screens.

"Main engines online in five," he continued. The commands entered the screen almost without conscious thought. He'd been a First for twenty years, and this was normally Jewel's job. He could do the flight out to transit in his sleep.

Not that he had. *Hungover*, yes, but not asleep.

"Engines online."

The report wasn't necessary for anyone familiar with void ships. The maneuvering thrusters were only perceptible if someone was very familiar with a specific ship. Main engines were a far more noticeable thing, a thrumming vibration through the entire hull.

"Second, you have helm," he told Nephil.

"Second has the helm," the synthmind confirmed. "I promise to stay on course rather than go skinny-dipping in a star."

Cirilo considered that comment for a solid few seconds, then decided it was best ignored.

***

As First Officer, Cirilo had built the habit of walking the ship during the flight out to transit. It was the last chance to fix any problems before they were alone in the void. He'd focused his inspections over the days before leaving on the ship's engines and systems, which left this the first time he stepped into the shuttle bay in the bow chunk of the ship.

His first impression was that, like the rest of the ship, everything there was in order. All six shuttles were tucked into their hangars, each of them a block of engines and controls capable of pushing around a half-million-ton cargo pod when working in pairs.

All six of them combined could theoretically even lift a fully loaded cargo pod out of most habitable gravity wells. It wasn't something Cirilo had ever seen tried—shuttles were generally used as tugs in space or to carry people and small amounts of cargo to the surface.

Cirilo could fly them, though he was more comfortable with a full-sized void ship, and he took a minute to count the hangars and check the shiningly clean hulls.

That was when he realized that the bay had been modified and held seven hangars. Three on each side, as normal, and then one at the back that was larger.

Silently, Cirilo walked the length of the shuttle bay, the familiar feeling of the standard cargo shuttle bay slowly giving way to a different familiar feeling. He knew the style of hangar that had been carefully installed into his ship.

"So," he said aloud, knowing without even seeing that Ostergaard had to be nearby. FlyChief would *know* that the Captain would see the oddity and ask. "That's dug into the water tanks under the fore radiation shields, right?"

"Aye, Skipper," the Chief agreed, seeming to materialize out of the shadow. He was dark-skinned and wore a dark gray shipsuit instead of his official uniform, allowing him to ghost around his flight bay. "We gave up surprisingly little bunkerage for it, all told. SecChief's baby."

"Open it."

Cirilo doubted he'd even needed to give the order. A Flight Department spacer was already working away at a console. The hangar door—its presence alone a clear difference from the open niches holding the cargo shuttles—slid open smoothly.

The small craft it revealed was only slightly bigger than the cargo craft, but where their lines were flat, efficient above all else, the gunship's hull was curved and coated in anti-sensor paint.

Energy and projectile weapons bristled from its nose and the three weapon pods—currently extended for ease of maintenance, though the nose guns and the entirety of the weapon pods could be pulled inside the hull to maintain the low radar profile.

"Okay, FlyChief, you can presume I know what a CorpSec gunship is," Cirilo said drily. "And I can put some pieces together with *SecChief's baby*. But would you mind telling me just why my rather old and slow t-drive freighter has an attack ship on board?"

"No one asked my opinion, Skipper," Ostergaard pointed out, stepping up beside Cirilo and surveying the gunship. "She's as thirsty for fuel as any of my girls and has half again the maintenance-to-flight hour ratio. Only one of my specialists has any experience with handling the weapon systems, and none of us are actually qualified to fly her.

"I think SecChief Key might be the only one aboard who *can* pilot this beast."

"I can," Cirilo said quietly, running his eyes over the familiar lines. He was more comfortable flying a void ship than a gunship, but he had more gunship hours than cargo-shuttle hours in the last few years.

"When did we acquire this?" he continued.

"Ten months ago, when Chief Key came aboard. We were in the yard for a regular check-over, and I came back to find a whole new hangar in my flight bay." The Chief snorted. "Like I said, no one asked me what I thought about it. I didn't get any hands to go with it, either, though they did give us a bunch of specialized bots and a BimLoo."

Biomechanical Labor Units were the general-purpose version of BimSoos. Organic parts and brains built into a mechanical chassis to provide a degree of muscle memory and initiative that a robot couldn't.

They were generally considered much safer in several ways than BimSoos—and Flight Bay would have had three or four of them to begin with.

"I'm still not entirely sure of why," Cirilo pointed out.

"Because I asked."

He turned to find Violet Key behind him. Unlike Ostergaard, she was in standard shipboard uniform: a white shipsuit under a white jacket, for department Chiefs and officers—the same one Cirilo was wearing.

At least the shipboard uniform lacked epaulets and braid. The only sign that Cirilo was the Captain and Key was the SecChief was a single platinum square on each of his shoulders, matched to a bronze square on hers. Both of them wore the same triangular bracers he wore with his dress uniforms, his in gold and hers in bronze.

If Ostergaard had been in uniform instead of wearing the same shipsuit as one of his techs, he'd have had a triangle in the same bronze, marking him as one of the junior Chiefs aboard the ship. As one of the more-junior officers, he still wouldn't have had the not-entirely-decorative bracers the SecChief and Captain wore, and from the way he glanced at Key's, Cirilo suspected the FlyChief had seen the bracers used at some point in the past.

"They modified one of the oldest ships in CargoFleet to carry one of CorpSec's newest gunships... because you asked," Cirilo echoed. Even the impassivity trained into him as a CorpSec officer strained at sounding calm and unsurprised by that.

"Yeah. Someone really wanted to put me out to pasture in a polite way," Key said bluntly. "So, they put quite a bit of money into convincing me to move over to CargoFleet."

"Still doesn't make sense to me," Ostergaard said.

"It doesn't have to," Cirilo told him. "It only had to make sense to the folks signing the checks. We don't get to argue, just be confused by it."

He met Key's eyes. He suspected she could see that he was bothered by it—but he was telling Ostergaard the truth. If someone with enough authority to order that change had wanted Key to retire from the commandos, the change would happen.

Cirilo, unlike Ostergaard, had a decent idea on how a top-tier CorpSec Commando found themselves decommissioned like that. He knew. She knew he knew.

And they weren't going to explain it to anyone else on the ship.

# *11*

Tereza wasn't surprised, after the kickoff from Iliakofos Two, that Captain Webster returned to the bridge in time for the transit. This part of the trip wasn't something a human could do by hand, though she'd checked Nephil's calculations—with the synthmind's help.

Nephil had no more interest in flying into a star than any of the humans did, after all.

"You have the ship, First," the Captain told her, waving her back to the watch station as she started to rise. "I'm just here to watch over your shoulder this time, I promise."

That wasn't much better, but she was at least used to that. Tereza couldn't remember the last time a Captain had taken the helm controls. She'd effectively forgotten that the ability to helm a void ship was a *requirement* for the fancy braid, because none of the Captains she'd dealt with on *Santa Mica* had shown any interest in doing so.

"Everything is checked out for the transit," she told him. "I heard you found the hidden joker in the Flight Bay?"

He chuckled, the mirthlessness of it surprisingly human.

"In hindsight, Key *had* mentioned it," he said. "But I don't think I expected her *extra hull in the shuttle bay* to be a gunship."

"Neither will anyone else who thinks the last SCC-One-Nine is a pushover," Tereza said, matching his smile.

"We're not the *last* One-Nine," he argued. "*Santa Lucca* is still flying, after all."

"We hope. I haven't heard from them in a few weeks," she said. He took that implication as much in stride as anything else, but she thought she spotted a momentary shift in his gaze.

"Is there a concern about *Lucca*?" Webster asked mildly.

"Not really," Tereza said. "But we are the oldest ships in the fleet, and, well, I know how much work goes into making sure *Santa Mica* stays functional. EngChief Rao is incredible, and I don't know how good *Santa Lucca*'s EngChief is."

She did know that *Santa Lucca* suffered from the same rotation of Captains checking a box off as *Santa Mica* did.

"I shall keep an eye out for reports on her," Webster murmured. He gestured toward her station, a wordless acknowledgment that the time for chatter was up.

A countdown was now visible on the main screen, Nephil's own reminder if the humans were distracting themselves.

Thirty seconds to transit.

They were deep in the void now, far enough out that Iliakofos and her orbitals could be blocked out with a hand. Calculations and sensor sweeps confirmed there was nothing in front of them that was going to be a problem.

"Sensors clear," she stated for the record. "Second?"

"All orbital calculations have been completed for recorded objects. Nothing should impede our vector on our calculated course," the synthmind said formally.

"Engines, this is Bridge," she said over the ship's coms. "Prepare to initiate transit."

"We're ready here," Rao confirmed.

Numbers and icons flowed across the screens around her. She didn't really read any individual piece of data, only watching for the pattern she knew should be there—the pattern that was there.

"Transit drive online and green. Initiating... now."

Tereza Jewel pressed her palm on a large green marker on her screen. The haptic interface pushed back, ever so slightly, and then the ship shivered around her.

The main engines on their hours-long burn earlier in the day had been more noticeable, and the shiver of beginning their transit ended almost as quickly as it began.

"We have initiated transit, ser," she told Webster.

"Our duration, First?" he asked.

"Full transit," she confirmed. "Three hours, nine light-years."

They'd then wait in the void for eighteen hours before the transit drive was ready to go again. *Santa Mica* was old enough to still have a three-three-six drive, versus the three-three-five carried by most of the CargoFleet—a three-hour transit at three light-years per hour, requiring six hours of cooldown for each hour in transit.

"Thank you, First," he told her. "Well done, both of you. I see *Santa Mica* has an excellent team of officers."

"We do what we can. The Company requires it," she said. There wasn't much else she could say.

She wasn't going to tell Cirilo Webster that they'd needed to work *around* half of their Captains instead of with them. Not until she was sure which type he was going to be.

# *12*

The Void.

The spacers and officers of the Santiago Corporation were the only people who ever became truly familiar with it, and even they only capitalized it on special occasions. It was a curse, a warning, a boon, a bane... It was both the source of the Company's power and the font of every disaster the Saints ever faced.

Cirilo stood in his office—now stripped of the prior Captain's images of his racers—and looked out through a false window at the bleak nothingness.

The "window" was a monitor, a holographic system a few centimeters thick that created the illusion of a transparent opening through the hull. It was a true-enough image for all that, taken from a camera positioned in roughly the middle of *Santa Mica*'s spine.

And it showed absolutely nothing.

Nine light-years from Oneira. Two and a half from the nearest star, a brown dwarf only recorded because its gravity might accidentally guide a rogue planet into the course of a transit.

Still seventeen light-years from Herecrow. Two more transits, with an eighteen-hour cooldown between them.

Less than two days to cross twenty-six light-years. Thanks to the transit drive, the galaxy was humanity's to discover. The steady expansion of the last five hundred years was more limited by the tendency of comfortable people to have fewer children than by a lack of places to settle.

Even among those who crossed the void on Santiago ships, few really liked to think about what was outside the hull when they were between stars. Cirilo had been on luxury liners with vast sections of transparent hull under protective shutters—and those shutters tended to be closed when the ships were in the deep void.

The tourists on those ships wanted to look at stars and gas giants and things of interest, not the empty black.

The Void was the province of the Saints. That nothingness wore at the soul of those unused to it. To Saints like Cirilo Webster, it was home. He'd spent much of his life in the gaps between stars.

The door to his office opened without anyone knocking.

"Lachlan," he greeted his steward. No one else on this ship knew him well enough to barge into his spaces without invitation.

He might return to the open-door policy he'd held when he'd been a CargoFleet First. Ten years in CorpSec had taught him that was a bad idea—his frigates had been involved in too many things no one wanted to talk about.

Too many things the Company never admitted had happened.

"Fresh coffee?" Lachlan asked, the spacer carrying a tray with a carafe and cups over to Cirilo's desk without asking.

"Thanks. How's your poking-around going?"

Lachlan Stirling was the Captain's Steward, which put him in an odd place in the ship's company. Administratively, he was part of StewChief Ibragimov's Hospitality Department. In reality, no Chief of Stewards was ever going to try to give the StewCap orders.

The man could go anywhere, and no one would question him, assuming he was on the Captain's business. Cirilo chose not to interrogate too closely how Lachlan used that privilege, so long as it also served him.

"Interesting so far," Lachlan told him. "Did some poking through the armory, since the SecChief seemed to be talking down what her retirement package from CorpSec was."

"Oh? Anything special in there?"

"A few things I wouldn't expect on a CargoFleet freighter but nothing truly extraordinary. We've got the gear to kit out half of SecTeam as commandos if you ever need to."

"I'd start with you and Key if it ever comes to that," Cirilo warned. He'd checked the records. Key was the only ex-commando in *Santa Mica*'s Security Department—but not the only ex-commando on *Santa Mica* now that Lachlan was aboard.

"Not a bad plan. I don't know her, not even by rep, if you were wondering."

"You'd have said," the Captain replied. "You know the type, though. And her situation."

"'Degraded levels of ethical flexibility,'" Lachlan said in a singsong quote. "'No longer recommended for field deployments requiring unquestioned prioritization of Corporate assets.'"

Both men were silent, staring out the window for a minute. It said a great deal about CorpSec, Cirilo suspected, that anyone who'd spent more than a year or two in the division knew the exact brand of HumRes speak used to mark people who could no longer be relied upon to follow orders without question.

"I didn't think that kind of gentle shuffle usually came with the kind of package Key seems to have," Cirilo finally said. "I feel like something extra is going on there."

"Yup."

He let his steward's single word hang in the air for a few seconds.

"You have a thought, Lachlan," he pointed out. "I won't insist you share, but I am curious."

"I knew two or three like this," the other man said. "They were good—*too* good. Good enough that the Company might have kept pushing their morals for too long... Good enough that some of the suits at certain offices might have started worrying about what would happen if they pushed hard enough to see those skills turned at us."

"Huh." Cirilo could see the possibility. He hadn't considered it himself—but he'd only spent a decade in CorpSec. Lachlan had spent fifteen years in the commandos before attaching himself to the officer who'd saved his life.

The Captain knew CorpSec better than anyone outside it, but he'd spent much of that decade as an outsider—an outsider with desperately needed skills but an outsider nonetheless.

"Just reminding you, Skipper, EnvSpec Bodrogi is due in your office in ten minutes," Lachlan finally told him. "I figure what went down put enough of the fear of the void in him."

"I agree. But a chat with the Captain is always necessary after one of the spacers ends up in jail."

***

Environmental Specialist Bodrogi Sung looked like he'd been hit by a truck and then left in a ditch for a week. Unlike most people Cirilo had seen looking that bad, he was at least alive.

A soft-faced man with heavy jowls on a good day, Bodrogi was heavily muscled in the same way as Cirilo—a daily effort to stave off the effects of spending a significant portion of their time in zero-*g*. The Captain could see why the man had seemed the type to get into fights to Is-Two-Sec, but *he* had access to Bodrogi's disciplinary file for the Company.

Or the blank entry in the database where that file would be if the man had one. He'd been a Saint for nine years, and he'd avoided any trouble that would result in a record for his officers. That wasn't particularly difficult, but it definitely didn't fit a man who'd start a drunken brawl.

"Specialist," Cirilo greeted him. "Report."

Bodrogi looked more confused than anything else at that, straightening up at a vague attempt at attention—and Cirilo remembered that particular phrasing and the attendant ritual were a CorpSec tradition.

"How are you feeling?" he asked. "What do you remember?"

"I feel like the inputs to my recyclers, Skipper."

Carbon-dioxide recyclers involved large quantities of algae that needed the same nutrients as any plant life in history. Which meant that they recycled more than one waste product of the crew, though the black water was carefully treated before it was used as algae base.

"As for memory…" He grunted. "I remember being told the new Captain had arrived in the system, but that's all I remember of the fourth. Nothing afterward."

Cirilo nodded.

"Three days of lost memory, give or take," he told the man. "You should probably sit down, EnvSpec."

Bodrogi did, taking the seat across the desk. Cirilo considered the haggard-looking man facing him and carefully didn't sigh. He pulled the coffee tray Lachlan had left behind over to him and poured a cup for his subordinate, handing it over.

The spacer looked at him like he'd grown an extra head.

"This isn't a disciplinary meeting, Sung," Cirilo told him, forcing himself to let some of his natural formality go. The poor man had just had the worst few days of his life.

"I don't remember anything, Skipper," Bodrogi said grimly, staring down into the cup. "From what people have told me, I fucked up badly, and you went to bat for me."

"The rumor mill is notorious for carrying the word of someone's crimes and not the word of their exoneration." There was a long silence as his spacer processed that. "I've watched the full security footage of your night on Iliakofos Two, Sung. You probably shouldn't have gone to the bathroom alone—we do try to emphasize the buddy system for a reason—but that was it."

"But I hit someone!"

If Cirilo had still harbored any doubt about the nature of the incident, the sheer deep horror and pain in that sentence would have wiped them away. Bodrogi Sung, it seemed, came from the category of large, strong men who were absolutely determined that their strength would never harm anyone.

"Have you spoken to MedSpec Bernardi yet?" he asked the younger man.

Any Medical Specialist on a Saint ship would assure anyone who asked that they were not a doctor—a nurse practitioner at most but really just an interface for MedSys and MedBot, which were mostly run by specialty AI under their supervision.

Not, in his experience, that any MedSpec would hesitate to perform surgery with a rusty hacksaw if they thought it was necessary.

"I haven't yet," the spacer admitted.

Cirilo was suddenly very aware of how young the man was. Not even thirty yet—but responsible for key components of making sure no one on *Santa Mica* suffocated. He'd earned that—and he hadn't deserved what had happened to him.

"Bernardi, EnvChief Anand and First Jewel all know the details of what happened to you," he told Bodrogi gently. "I presumed you would check in with the MedSpec, given that you were unconscious for an extended period and have clear memory loss."

The spacer said nothing.

"You suffered from an interaction between a class of what would love to be combat drugs and a standard security stunner," he continued. "Not helped by whatever hypnotic you were given prior to the aggression drugs.

"You did nothing of your own will, Sung. You were ambushed, hit with a medication that undermined your free will, and because that wouldn't have been enough to make you strike someone, they fed you a medication to make you very, very angry," Cirilo laid out.

"Then, because Is-Two-Sec thought they had a very clear situation in front of them, they didn't provide the correct medical care, resulting in you being unconscious for longer than was safe—and causing the memory loss."

Bodrogi took a slow swallow of his coffee, still staring down at the desk. Then he looked up at his Captain as an involuntary grimace hit his face.

"Skipper... why are you drinking mess-deck coffee?"

"What else would I drink?" Cirilo asked. He didn't know if Lachlan had grabbed the coffee from the mess for him or had just used the same coffee brand to brew a pot in the tiny kitchen attached to their rooms, but it was the same coffee.

"Even the crew doesn't drink this black," the spacer told him. "According to the Stew-Chief, there's something wrong with the coffee system."

"Good to know," Cirilo allowed. "I'll talk to him about that. I'll admit I hadn't noticed, but I'm used to what we brew on CorpSec ships." He was exaggerating, but not by as much as he might like.

There was another silence.

"I am *never* transferring to CorpSec," Bodrogi said fervently.

"I hope not. You are only the second spacer I've encountered being used to attack the Company like this in CargoFleet, but I saw it every year or two in CorpSec," Cirilo told him. "I do need you to check in with Bernardi, please. There are potential long-term consequences of the drugs they dosed you with."

"I will," the specialist promised. "Um. Do I have to come back to Iliakofos for a trial or something?"

"No. There are no charges against you, Sung. That said, it was part of the implied deal that secured your immediate release that the Saints won't pursue Is-Two-Sec for how badly they handled your care.

"We could not, I feel obliged to note, waive *your* right to do so."

The precise legal structures of the Seventy-Seven varied from star system to star system, but a lot of key principles were underwritten by interstellar treaties—mostly sponsored by the Santiago Corporation.

Often to its advantage, of course.

"I would rather just forget... well, more so," Bodrogi said, a wan but real grin on his face. "I don't remember enough to be aggravated over it, and I don't want trouble in my life, Skipper."

"That's your right to decide," Cirilo assured him. "I'd suggest making an appointment to talk to Legal about it before fully writing it off, but again, that's up to you. Bautista wouldn't be able to act as an advocate for you, but her duties as our lawyer do stretch to giving you advice on the matter."

And if they didn't do so on paper, he'd have a conversation about his personal expectations about her work as Ship's Lawyer.

# *13*

THere were three gyms aboard *Santa Mica*, a concession to the reality that the Company only provided artificial gravity for about sixty percent of the freighter's hull and none of the cargo units. Any inspection of the cargo they were carrying—and they were required to do at least a base visual check of the internal subcontainers every twenty-four hours by contract—required working in microgravity.

None of the gyms were put aside for the exclusive use of the officers and chiefs, though there was often a general consensus that the one closest to the Captain's quarters was subject to priority rules in their favor.

Tereza was still surprised to enter the space at the end of their first day in the void and see Captain Webster working out with four other crew in the space. The Purser was the only one of the four who wasn't regular crew, but Webster wasn't paying any attention to his inevitable audience as he worked through his reps.

The last Captain had specifically scheduled his gym time and had unofficially required everyone else to leave the gym while he worked out. Most of the Captains before that had installed private equipment in their suite.

It almost felt wrong to watch the Skipper, the representative of the Company and the highest authority aboard, sweat his way through a resistance workout in a white shipsuit unzipped to the waist.

Tereza realized she'd paused and was probably staring at her Captain's muscular upper torso. He was fifteen years older than her, but anagathic treatment and regular exercise were definitely keeping him spry.

Swallowing down any questions, she walked up to the machine next to his and tapped the scanner. It loaded her routine from her bionic com and set everything up for her.

"First," Webster greeted her, his routine pausing as he took a swallow of water.

"Skipper." She didn't need to ask or say anything more. Just acknowledging each other was enough of a measure to fulfill the social needs of the gym. She leaned in to her exercise, blotting out the universe to focus on the machine.

She finished her first set and realized that Webster had either timed his set to match hers or intentionally cut short to be available for her to talk to him if she wanted.

"I didn't expect to see you in the gym," she admitted, drinking her own water.

"It helps me think," he told her, and then gestured down at his muscular torso. "Plus, this goes away far too quickly if I let the habit slip."

Once she was no longer distracted by his muscles, she realized that his bionic arm was more extensive than she'd thought. She'd certainly known people who'd voluntarily had one installed—a strange thought to her, to chop off a perfectly good limb!—but they rarely had more than the forearm and hand.

Webster's bionic started on his torso, visible silver supports stretching out and merging into his collarbone and rib cage. His entire arm and a chunk of his shoulder were entirely metal, suggesting a far more severe injury than spacers tended to receive.

He saw her gaze and shrugged slightly.

"You may as well ask, First," he told her. "I rather expect it if people end up working out next to me."

"I'm surprised you *are* working out like this," she admitted. "I would have expected you to want your privacy."

"Quite the opposite, First. Right now, everyone in here is being surprised to see the Captain and intimidated by the arm," Webster said, amusement in his voice—and speaking loudly enough that everyone in the gym could hear him.

"Once we all get over that, it'll be a good chance to get a feel for where people are at. Plus, I need to work out, as I said."

That made sense, she supposed. It was contrary to how *Santa Mica*'s previous Captains had handled themselves, but she was starting to realize that Cirilo Webster was as different from the Shareholder scions they'd been handling as could be.

"How did that happen?" she finally asked, gesturing to the arm.

"Classified," he told her, his tone perfectly level and unblinking.

She stared at him for several seconds before he broke into a wide grin.

"Sort of," he continued. "In one of those things we don't talk about, my frigate took heavy fire. Unlike a freighter, a CorpSec ship has an Operations Center as well as a bridge, the post for the First—but because there isn't that much spare space in a frigate, it sometimes ends up in odd places."

He stared at the machine blankly for a few moments, then started the next set of his routine—presumably a light closing exercise, since he resumed talking a moment later.

"On ours, it was too close to the main reactor."

Tereza didn't see the connection for a moment, then swallowed.

"The core was breached," he continued. His tone had gone back to the same level calm he presented most of the time. "Internal bulkheads were designed for containment, but, well, heavy fire. We'd had the bulkhead on one side of the OpsCent damaged."

"That's…" Tereza wasn't even sure what to say. The only damage she'd ever seen on a void ship was from a debris collision, and that was an entirely different scale of problem.

"Bad," Webster finished for her, his tone slipping into painfully dry for a moment. "We had enough warning to evac the compartment, but I had to stay behind to make sure everyone got out. Emergency shutters dropped when the bulkhead failed."

"You were trapped inside?" She realized the question was foolish as she said it. He wouldn't have survived that.

"About thirty-six centimeters of my arm was," he told her. "Ten more centimeters was crushed by the shutter itself. The rest… Well, the shutter didn't really close fast enough."

He finished his set and ran organic fingers over the silver on his shoulder. "Up here was plasma burns. They had a real pain getting the neural bionics to link through."

"And you still have to work out?" Vratislav asked, the Purser stepping up between their machines—presumably done his own set. "I always hoped that bionics would spare me this indignity, but, well, the eye doesn't make enough difference."

His single cybernetic eye winked exaggeratedly, and Tereza found herself prayerfully grateful for his arrival. She hadn't expected the story about the arm to be quite so intense—she knew that Webster had been CorpSec, but when did Santiago security ships get into real fights?

More often than she'd thought, obviously.

"I'm still getting used to it," Webster said. "But yes, I still need to exercise my core and my legs and my *other* arm to make sure I don't wither away in zero-*g*."

# 14

Tereza had to wonder if leaving both the entry and exit from the second transit to her, without even being present on the bridge, was Webster's idea of an offset for taking over the ship for the initial flight.

Not that she needed the eyes on her back. She had run *Santa Mica* for a long time with a bunch of Captains who barely seemed to know a carbon recycler from a plasma conduit. It was a strange thought to have a Captain who seemed to not only be capable of doing the job but was excited to.

She wasn't entirely convinced. *Santa Mica* had survived Captains that interfered for the sake of interfering before. Webster seemed competent enough, if something of a cold fish, but if he wanted to start changing things to work his way, even good changes could become a problem.

But managing that was her job, she supposed.

"Transit exit in thirty seconds," she said for the record. She was alone on the bridge, talking to the recorders.

They would emerge into regular space nine light-years from Herecrow—roughly eighteen and a half light-years from Oneira, their last jump at an angle to bring them into a standard rest point for approach to their destination.

Icons flowed across her display.

"See anything I've missed, Nephil?" she asked the synthmind.

"If I had, you'd know already," he replied. "Do you *want* me to baby you, First?"

She snorted. Nephil probably wouldn't have been quite so rude if anyone else had been around, but the synthmind had a solid sense of what he could get away with.

"Transit exit... now," she said aloud, for the recordings kept in the emergency boxes.

The world flickered and her ship was once more in the void, drifting through the dark no human eyes were meant to see.

Tereza went through the exit protocols on autopilot. She'd done this more times than she could count, and there was rarely anything worth noting.

Except when there was. The standard post-exit sensor sweep was primarily infrared, looking for unexpected heat sources that would mark another ship.

The Company didn't have their schedules projected far enough forward for her to know where any other ship would be—there being an icon for a heat signature was normal enough.

Except that the heat signature was all wrong.

"Nephil, can you double-check that contact?" she said aloud. "That's not high enough for a void ship, right?"

"After humans and the waste heat from reactors, most void ships actively radiate heat at approximately four hundred Kelvin," the synthmind told her, his earlier rudeness gone. "Contact is not actively radiating heat but appears to be carrying a background temperature of two hundred sixty Kelvin."

Below freezing but still far too warm for the background of space.

Tereza had more sensor commands up before Nephil was finished speaking. She could see his movements in the system as well, a step ahead of her and moving at the speed of thought.

"Telescopes A-Six through B-Four are realigning on the contact," he reported. "Collated visual should be on your display now."

Tereza knew the shape on her screen. There wasn't much difference between the extended clamp shape of *Santa Mica* and the shape of a larger and newer Class II transport, after all.

"That's one of ours," she said. "Do we have an ID?"

"No beacons, no energy signatures," Nephil replied. "All systems are dead. She's a ghost ship, First."

Even the synthmind sounded spooked, and Tereza stared at the dead ship on the displays for at least a minute in deathly silence.

"What do we do, First?"

"I was going to ask you, Nephil," she admitted. "You're a lot older than me. I know there's a protocol, but you've... seen this before, right?"

"I have not," he said.

"Then we have to wake the Captain."

***

For the first time since Cirilo Webster had reported aboard, Tereza was glad that they had an ex–Corporate Security officer in charge. He was on the bridge less than five minutes after she'd pinged his bionic com, in full working uniform.

She saw the appeal, now, in his very short hair. The geometric precision of it was in style for men, she knew, but Webster kept it cut closer than even the style called for. It saved him time getting ready in a crisis.

"What do we know, First?" he asked, standing next to the watch station without trying to urge her out of the seat.

"It's *Santa Alicia*, Skipper," she said. With their telescopes and other sensors focused on the distant ship, her slow rotation had brought the name stamp on the forward hull into view. "Two hundred and twenty-five hands, went—"

"Missing in March," Webster finished for her. "Carrying cargo to Herecrow. Though not, I will note, on any route that would have brought her here. She's at least a full transit from anywhere she was supposed to be."

"I... don't have her course on file, Skipper," Tereza told him.

"I looked her up in the files in Oneira after I learned another ship went missing on their way to Herecrow," her Captain said grimly. "Forty million cubic meters of cargo from the Atreides System, mostly food but twenty containers of miscellany.

"Nothing on the books to draw specific attention, but she went missing and we didn't know what happened to her."

"Didn't we look for her?"

"CorpSec did," he confirmed. "I pulled all the records, First. Everything that should be done was done. So, why is she sitting in the void, hours of transit time away from anywhere she should be?"

"A ghost ship, sailing under her own power."

Somehow, Nephil saying it made Tereza feel better—and more able to dismiss it.

"Almost certainly sailed by someone, even if the synthmind was abandoned somehow," she said. "I'd have to check scheduling, but even looking at standard rest stops, I think Herecrow has over thirty.

"If she ended up here when she went missing, no one might have seen her since."

"If her transit drive was online, she'd have made it to Herecrow," Webster said grimly. "And with her main reactor offline and that level of heat, I doubt her crew is alive.

"No, First, Second, *Santa Alicia* didn't end up here by accident. She was moved here and dumped."

"But this is a standard point. If she was dumped, they'd know she'd be found," Tereza protested. Nothing about the scenario Webster was suggesting made sense to her.

"Vultures can only jump to standard coordinates," he explained. "They don't have proper training on the systems and don't understand the theory. They can't navigate a new course any more than they can properly fix or fuel their transit drives.

"They have to steal parts and t-cells from other ships—and they'll take what cargo they can while they do."

"What about the crew?" Nephil asked.

"They would be offered a chance to join the Vultures... and any who refused would die," Webster answered grimly. "Most likely, they killed the synthmind before boarding. You have too many options for interfering and on a transport, your main processor is no more protected than the rest of the ship."

"You're talking like this is an organized group, someone you *know*," Tereza exclaimed, horrified at his calm.

"They're not a group, let alone organized, but CorpSec knows them," he told her. "Vultures, like I said. They get their hands on one of our ships and steal the parts they need to keep it running from any ship they find.

"They usually can't defeat modern system security, so even though their ship almost certainly pales in comparison to *Santa Alicia*, they'd gut her for what they can use and leave her."

Tereza looked darkly at the image on the screen.

"So... we complete our voyage and inform the Company?" she asked.

"No. Samaritan rules are in play, First," he said. "Set up an intercept course. Once we have an ETA, let's wake up SecChief.

"There may be something still alive over there... and even if there isn't, we need to extract as much information about what happened as we can."

He shook his head, his eyes as dark as Tereza felt.

"And because both SecChief and I know the type of thing these people get up to, we'll be sending the BimSoos in."

# *15*

++*Security Network Online*++

  ++*Node Santa-Mica-Biomechanical-Security-Unit-Six Online*++

  ++*Status report request received*++

  ++*Overall function: 100%*++

  ++*Cognitive function: 107%*++

  ++*Bioorganic mass: 97.4%. Adjustment to protein allowances submitted*++

  ++*Armor integrity: 99.8%*++

  ++*Mobility functions: 100%*++

  ++*Weapon functionality: 95.3%*++

  ++*Kestrel Six gatling railgun—*++

Six didn't need to follow the report. The information it contained was unconscious, an inherent reality of existence.

The automatic routine continued, updating SecNet on Six's capabilities. Six focused on the main issue: an energy weapon mounted in the left forearm weapon pod had a misaligned focusing lens. The source of the misalignment was unclear, since it had been aligned when the weapon pod had last been deployed on Iliakofos Two Station.

++*Security Network interrogation. Time since last activation?*++ Six queried.

++*Three seven nine six minutes*++

*Santa Mica* hadn't reached their destination. Something was wrong.

The activation-and-check sequence was complete. Six moved as the door to the niche opened. Two-point-five meters and nine hundred and forty-six kilograms of hardware and flesh didn't move quickly, not without exerting more power than was wise aboard ship.

++*Security Network update. Instructions follow*++

Six paused in the preparation bay. Five other Biomechanical Security Units did so at the same moment, all freshly emerged from the storage niches.

*++Proceed to Shuttle Bay and board gunship* Santa Mica*-Foxtrot. Security Chief Violet Key awaits rendezvous. Further instructions via verbal command sequence++*

That had been new since Key joined the ship. Even the Biomechanical Security Units received final instructions verbally, alongside the human security personnel.

All six units moved simultaneously upon receipt of the order, turning as one to move toward the hatch. Six knew *Santa Mica* in a way no human ever could. The shuttle bay wasn't far.

***

There was a lot of human activity in the shuttle bay, more than Six had projected. It was the first time *Santa Mica*-Foxtrot had been going into space, which appeared to require more activity than the regular shuttles.

There would be difficulties fitting the entire section of Biomechanical Security Units onto standard shuttles. The shuttles could carry their oversized forms, but they took a significant percentage of the available volume for passengers.

Six calculated that no more than two Biomechanical Security Units could fit in a standard shuttle. The gunship schematics in Six's database showed a special compartment intended for them, along with storage for a security bot flotilla to accompany.

*++Security Network interrogation. Are security bots being deployed alongside Biomechanical Security Units?++* Six asked.

*++No data. Transferring query to Security Chief++*

Six had not anticipated that. Six most definitely had not anticipated for Security Chief Violet Key to emerge from the gunship like a launched rocket.

"Six, you asking questions?" she asked.

*++There is a storage unit for security bots in the gunship++* Six replied via the network. *++Deployment of security bots alongside Biomechanical Security Units can increase joint efficiency by as much as one hundred eighty percent++*

"That it can, and I didn't think of it," Key replied. "BimSoos! Load on. SecTeam! On me. We missed a step on our checklists, and I want to make certain it's not missed next time!"

The Biomechanical Security Units knew the nickname and that the orders were meant for them. They trooped aboard the gunship in numerical order. It was efficient and avoided questions of precedence.

Six paid attention as they moved and heard Key giving orders to make sure that a full flotilla of bots was loaded into the gunship.

The briefing would follow shortly, but whatever the situation, the presence of a full flotilla of security machinery would increase their odds of protecting the humans.

***

Six had never been active anywhere except *Santa Mica* and had never been inside a Santiago Corporation gunship. The specifications lived in the database, meaning that all of the Biomechanical Security Units knew the exact layout of the vessel and how to access their deployment bay.

The bay contained the tools for the gunship to latch on to another vessel and either override the airlock or cut through the hull. If necessary, it could be opened to vacuum, and the BMSUs would launch an extravehicular assault.

While they possessed lungs—three of them—they could sustain full function for a minimum of six hours in full vacuum. Longer if prepared with the provision of additional oxygen supplies.

The deployment bay closely resembled their storage compartment in the security section on *Santa Mica*, though the niches lacked covering doors and were never intended to contain a hibernating unit.

Six and the others entered the niches, locking in place to avoid their immense weight causing problems for the ship.

Silent status checks consumed the next minutes. Six ran through every sequence available on the misaligned beam-weapon lens. Per every scan, there was no reason for it to be damaged, but the misalignment was clear.

The locks partially released to allow Six to extend the repair tools in the right arm's utility pod. The lens was not an easy piece to fix manually, but in its current state, the secondary weapon was only functioning at ninety percent efficiency.

*++Security Network update. Prepare for verbal command sequence++*

No humans had entered the deployment bay, but Security Network had visibility into humans that the Biomechanical Security Units didn't.

Six expanded other sensors while focusing visual processors on the left weapon pod. Security Specialist Carmen Ventimiglia was the first to enter the bay, wearing modular powered combat armor.

Security Specialist Abraham Traversini followed, with Security Chief Violet Key a step behind him.

"What is it *doing*?" Specialist Traversini demanded, pointing at Six.

"Self-repair," Key replied. "Just because *you* get your troops to take care of your armor for you doesn't mean you shouldn't be familiar with the concept."

Something in how Six had extended the weapon and utility pods appeared to be upsetting the Specialist. Six did not wish to offend the Specialists. The likelihood of successfully repairing the lens aperture before deployment was under forty-two percent.

Both pods withdrew behind armor plating, and Six straightened into standard posture.

Specialist Traversini's vitals were off. It appeared that the human was vaguely ill, but it was not raising a concern with Security Network or Security Chief Key. If they were unconcerned, Six would not raise further alarm.

"Right. Thank you, Six," Key said. "It's TacSit time. So, *sit* and listen to the tactical situation."

Six couldn't sit. The niches weren't set up for it, though they did support nine-hundred-plus kilos comfortably.

The SecTeam humans did sit. The junior people had arrived. They had names. Six had those names in the database, but none of the four had command authority over the Biomechanical Security Units, so Six spared no processing power for them.

A video image transferred to Six's ocular hardware, creating the illusion of a ship model rotating in the middle of the deployment bay. The database filled in the details that weren't visible: *Santa Alicia*, Class II Santiago Corporation Transit Freighter. Core mass four-point-six megatons. Cargo capacity forty million cubic meters. Lost to unknown causes 03-19-2615.

"We have a ghost ship," Key told them all. "*Santa Alicia*. She hasn't been seen in almost thirty-four standard weeks. At twelve weeks overdue, she was declared LUC.

"And we have now found her here, in a void stopover a long way from her route. The Captain has ordered a full search for survivors and evidence. We will be proceeding under the assumption that the ship's security systems and synthmind have been fully compromised."

"*Santa Alicia* has a lot more of everything than we do, SecChief," Specialist Ventimiglia warned. "If it's all hostile, what are we going to do?"

"Her main power is down, SecSpec Ventimiglia," Key replied. "Likely has been for months. Without proper maintenance or power supply, a significant chunk of the systems should be off-line.

"If that rosy assumption turns out to be untrue, we will immediately fall back to the gunship and break off," she continued. "We're here to find evidence and make sure any survivors get the rescue they need, not risk our own people or BimSoos chasing the impossible.

"Full schematics of *Santa Alicia* are on the SecNet. Our first task will be to secure central computing."

Six's database included a large amount of information and software for reading human expressions. While little of that information computed logically, it sufficed to assess Chief Key's smile as *dangerous*.

"Won't that trigger an immediate response from the synthmind if it's online?" Specialist Traversini asked.

"Exactly. If there is a danger aboard *Santa Alicia*, we need to identify it as quickly as possible. We are better off dealing with problems from Foxtrot outside the hull than we are getting ourselves trapped away from the void!"

# *16*

++*Security Network attempting contact with* Santa Alicia. *No answering Security Network*++

If Six had been human, Six might have laughed. Even if *Alicia*'s SecNet was online, it wasn't going to be talking to their network at this point.

But certain protocols were automatic.

++*No open networks detected. Shipboard networking appears completely shut down*++

++*Scan standard encrypted frequencies*++ Six ordered.

The results fed into the network, filling ocular hardware and databases with information. Encrypted security frequencies weren't open or easily detectable, but there were frequencies that the security bots and their biomechanical controllers tended to use.

Multiple signatures were active. None were easily localized, leaving a diffuse cloud of encrypted communication across the ship.

++*I see it*++ Key noted on SecNet. ++*ShipNet is down. Looks like SecNet is down too, but there are still bots talking to each other over there. Even Foxtrot's scanners can't resolve exact locations, but the breach location is well away from likely positions*++

++*We move directly for the synthmind's location. If it's online, we may be able to disinfect and secure the ship that way*++

Six calculated the likelihood of surviving a corrupted synthmind long enough for them to disinfect it at approximately seventeen percent. That was also the magnitude of the likelihood Six calculated of there still being a synthmind aboard *Santa Alicia*.

The camera feeds from the outside of the gunship were transferring to ocular hardware across the deployment bay, allowing the entire security team to see what they were coming up on.

At this range, *Santa Alicia* didn't look as much like *Santa Mica*. Part of it was that she was so much bigger, but much of it was because of the damage. The sublight engines had been hit with railgun fire, per SecNet's analysis, the solid projectiles disabling the freighter's ability to run while doing minimal damage to cargo and the transit drive.

Other damage marked where *Alicia*'s meteor-defense systems had been located. While only one hundred and fifty percent more powerful than the heavy energy weapons available to the Biomechanical Security Units, those beam weapons would have sufficed to destroy a gunship on a boarding approach—if they'd still existed.

*++Breach in ten++* Key snapped.

Six didn't need to brace. The humans in the deployment bay did, checking the straps on their seats as the gunship's engines cut the last of her velocity and left the craft to slam into *Santa Alicia*'s hull.

*++Contact. Breach system active. Bay deployment on my mark. BimSoos forward++*

Six unlocked the niche and stepped forward into position with the other Biomechanical Security Units. Weapon pods extended and rotated as the units assessed their capabilities against their likely opposition.

*++Energy weapons, modulation three++* Six transmitted on a channel only the other Biomechanical Security Units would receive.

If the system was operating in default anti-boarding measures, it would begin by swarming the breach in the hull with every nearby security bot to delay them, while larger counter-boarding forces were organized.

There was no response on the private channel, but the other five Units all settled on the narrow-focus electromagnetic pulse guns called for by *modulation three.*

*++Bay clear. Opening++*

Further orders weren't needed. Six tons of protection led the way onto the ghost ship with a crash of metallic feet.

***

The security-bot flotilla moved out around them. *Santa Alicia*'s gravity systems were offline, permitting far easier motion for the flying drones, but the Units were sufficiently more efficient grounded that the team activated magnetic systems to keep them connected to the decking.

*++No contact++*

One's report was automatic, aimed at SecNet and the humans, not the other Units. Six knew what One knew almost as quickly as the other Unit did.

*++Move forward. Direct to the synthmind. Watch for response++*

Key's orders were clear. The Units didn't need the repetition, but the humans behind them might have.

Six was in the rear and took primary responsibility for the drone flotilla. Each Biomechanical Security Unit's position came with a specific role in the sweep, and the Units assigned themselves by number again.

The drones spread out farther than the Units could, sweeping the corridors around them. A chain of the bots stretched behind the main force, corridors and accessways secured and kept safe for the humans bringing up the rear.

Even the best combat armor couldn't bring the humans up to the durability of a Biomechanical Security Unit, and Six was aware that the humans had significantly impaired repairability as well.

The lack of immediate response sent Six down scenario-analysis ladders. The most likely situation was that the derelict freighter's systems were entirely offline, rendering the security bots and other systems nonfunctional or left to autonomous operation.

There was no lighting or heat on *Santa Alicia*. That would match that scenario, but the exterior scans had suggested some elements of the ship were still operating. Six's database did not include exact specifications for how the freighter's auxiliary power systems functioned, but the database did state that the expected duration of those systems was a minimum of fifty-eight standard years.

Such systems weren't installed in security bots, but they could be used to recharge the bots if a superior system was able to give the instruction. The database suggested a low likelihood that *Santa Alicia* had been equipped with a command-level security bot capable of acting as an automated controller for other security bots.

She had carried three six-Unit teams of Biomechanical Security Units. A command-level security drone was an unnecessary redundancy in that case.

If the bots weren't receiving instructions to recharge, then they should have encountered powered-down bots—both security and ship service.

Six reassessed the sensor sweeps from the bot flotilla. No drone systems had been encountered. Even the charging stations had been empty.

The ship's drones had been moved out of their path.

*++Security Net update++* Six sent out. *++Drones have been concentrated ahead of us. Calculate likelihood of ambush at eighty-five percent. Likelihood that system is under control of one or more active Biomechanical Security Units is seventy percent++*

++*Understood*++ Key replied. ++*Forward me the analysis. All BimSoos and person-nel, prepare for concentrated and coordinated resistance. One, Two, Three: fall back on Four and Five. Six: sweep forward with drones. Locate the ambush site*++

The Biomechanical Security Units recognized the restructuring immediately: con-centrating their base of fire in preparation for major hostile movement. Six, Four and Five all stopped in place, Four and Five taking up positions covering the movement of the other three Units.

Six focused on the drone network. The heaviest security bots were spread out through the flotilla to support the lighter units, and there was no definite sign to mark where the vector of attack would come from.

If Six was defending the ship, the bots and Units would be... The scenario analysis processed quickly, and the heavy bots moved around.

The lightest bots, pure surveillance machines rendered four hundred and eighty-six percent more efficient by the lack of gravity, moved once the heavy drones were in place. Six different corridors were the targets of dedicated sweeps, the flotilla stretching out tendrils into the darker heart of the ship.

Five Biomechanical Security Units now formed a defensive line behind the bots and ahead of both the humans and Six. Their focus was on their own sensors, making certain nothing approached the boarding team.

Six was expecting the electromagnetic pulse that hit one of the drone sweeps.

++*Security Net update. Drone sweep in corridor Bravo Kappa Six neutralized. Like-lihood of decoy effort by single Biomechanical Security Unit, sixty-five percent*++

++*Agreed. One, Two: sweep that corridor. If hostile presence is greater than one BimSoo, withdraw on the main force*++

Key's orders were swift and precise, almost as fast as SecNet or a synthmind could manage. Two-on-one odds, especially with the solitary Unit having been supply-de-prived for an unknown period, was sufficient to secure the safety of the Units as well as the humans.

If BK6 was a decoy, then Six's scenario analysis suggested that the main ambush forces were *there* and *there*.

The humans were only one junction back from the Biomechanical Security Units now. Six sent a quarter of the Paladin heavy security bots, each half the size of a Unit with two-thirds of the firepower, along the most likely attack vector.

Four black drones, in a spherical configuration allowing for easy zero-*g* movement, drifted forward on the sensors. Six subsumed their sensor feeds, taking direct control of the vanguard bots.

There was a main junction ahead. Primary passageways, large enough for Biomechanical Security Units and Biomechanical Labor Units, plus large cargo haulers and similar systems. From that junction, the boarding team could reach the engines, the central computer area where the synthmind would live, cargo control—all the key areas in the aft portion of the void ship.

Six sent the scout drones in hard and fast, taking advantage of the lack of gravity to whip them around corners at speeds no human or heavy unit could match.

A third of them were destroyed anyway. A similar electromagnetic pulse as had taken down the other flotilla as a decoy hit most of them, but both projectile and energy weapons joined in.

The other two-thirds of the scout drones didn't last long, but they gave Six and the rest of SecNet confirmation on what they were facing.

Ten heavy security units and two Biomechanical Security Units, supported by most of a drone flotilla. From their position, they could have intercepted the boarders if they'd continued on their route to the synthmind—or, if Key had fallen for the decoy, come up behind them and pinned them against whatever was there.

*++Security Net update: First ambush force located++* Six reported. *++Chance of at least one more ambush force sixty-four percent. Deploying combat bots++*

Key could override the Unit, but Six understood the purpose of Biomechanical Security Units was to have better-than-drone initiative at drone speeds.

The four combat drones were slower around the corner than the scout drones had been, but they knew exactly where their targets were—and Six understood the weakness of the enemy. Without Six's counterparts, the drones would lose efficiency rapidly.

Every weapon system on the combat drones was aimed at the two co-opted Biomechanical Security Units. It wasn't enough to destroy them immediately—Units were extraordinarily durable—but it staggered them back, preventing them from immediately destroying the drones.

The drones survived eleven-point-four seconds, two-point-three longer than Six had expected.

*++One corrupted Biomechanical Security Unit destroyed. One disabled++* Six reported.

++*Two Biomechanical Security Units encountered at corridor Bravo Kappa Six*++ One gave a report a moment later. ++*Both disabled. Prior damage present*++

++*Well done*++ Key told them. ++*One, Two: fall back on our position. Six, continue drone sweep. Find the other ambush team*++

++*Once One and Two rejoin the main force, we're moving on the synthmind. I believe I know what happened here, but I need confirmation*++

# *17*

"WELL. THAT WAS EXPENSIVE."

Tereza gave the Purser her most withering glare.

"Really, Vratislav?" she asked. "That's your main takeaway from this?"

*Santa Mica*'s senior staff were gathered in the meeting room built for this exact purpose—positioned in the forward part of the hull, it was too far from the engine room for the EngChief to really be convenient for half of them, but tradition put it near the bridge.

"We lost over a hundred Security Robots today," Vratislav pointed out mildly. "While I understand we can fabricate the recon units, even that has a cost in terms of materials and time of both staff and equipment.

"And the larger units, like the Paladins, do need to be purchased. The price tags involved are quite significant."

"So is the one involved in replacing my people or my BimSoos," Key said. There was a sharp edge to the SecChief's tone, one that Tereza hadn't heard from her before.

But then, Tereza hadn't seen the SecChief lead a boarding action before, either. It had been an impressive affair, if one that Tereza was quite happy to have been watching from thousands of kilometers away.

"We used the SecBots to do what they are supposed to do, Purser," SecChief continued. "Because of that *expense*, we have no injuries to my Security Team and only one mildly damaged BimSoo."

"How bad is the damage to the Unit?" Webster asked, the Captain speaking for the first time since welcoming everyone to the meeting. He was seated at the head of the table, drinking his coffee like he didn't realize how bad the mess coffee was on *Santa Mica*.

"From what I can tell, Two zigged instead of zagged and took a railgun round from *Santa Alicia*'s BimSoo," Key said. "If the other BimSoo had been properly supplied, it would have been worse, but that was the last round in their weapon. Two is locked in a niche for repair work. We can override if they're needed, but barring an emergency, we're down a BimSoo for three days."

"We're not supposed to have emergencies," Webster noted. "This was closer than I'd like. Chief Key, you and your SecTeam did excellent work. We now know what happened to *Santa Alicia* and will be passing that information on to Corporate when we arrive in Herecrow."

The Captain met Tereza's gaze and winked at her before his gaze moved on to Vratislav.

"As for our little detour being *expensive*, Purser, Legal?"

"Skipper?" Bautista had been more silent than the rest of the officers, her attention clearly as much on the tablet in front of her as the meeting.

Tereza knew from watching the painful experience of two previous Captains that she *was* paying attention to the meeting. The raven-haired lawyer was enough better at multitasking than anyone else the First had met that she wondered if the woman had invisible bionics in her brain.

Unlike the rest of the officers, Renata Bautista was a Saint Shareholder-born and -bred, raised on a Cradle to a family of Company lawyers. Brain implants beyond the usual bionic com weren't out of the question for someone with her background.

"What is the usual Company salvage award for the retrieval of a lost asset like *Santa Alicia*?" Webster asked her.

Bautista nodded, blinking up from her tablet to look around the table.

"One percent of the asset value," she said precisely. "It will be divided between all ships involved in the retrieval, though a minimum of point-two percent of *Santa Alicia*'s book value is allocated to the finder vessel."

"I think even our Purser will agree with me that the return on investment of our detour is worth it," Webster concluded. "My initial math suggests that, once all the datawork is saved and settled, every member of our crew will earn a bonus of roughly two-thirds of their annual salary."

"How did you know that, Skipper?" Yevhen asked. The CargChief was naturally a sandy-haired man with a relatively slight build, though it was hard to tell with the bionic construct built into his upper back, shoulders and arms. Yevhen Jernigan hadn't replaced his perfectly good organic arms, but the reinforcement work he'd had done had probably cost more.

"While I was CorpSec, my frigate flew security sweep on two retrievals like this," the Skipper replied. The momentary warmth of his earlier wink was gone, back into his calm impassivity. "We didn't find the Vultures the first time—though the Company is reasonably sure it was the same group both times, and we did catch them the second time."

Tereza considered what that meant and tried not to shiver at how cold her Captain's tone had grown. That meant that if they'd caught the Vultures the first time, there wouldn't have *been* a second time.

"Skipper, are you going to tell everyone what we have concluded happened to *Santa Alicia*?" Nephil asked, not quite interrupting Webster.

"I could," the Captain said. "But you did most of the analysis, Second, and you should get the credit. Lay it out for everyone, please."

There was a surprisingly long pause. Tereza knew a synthmind could be surprised, but they still didn't usually have to pause to think.

"As you wish, Skipper," Nephil said. "Basic analysis of *Santa Alicia*'s damage concurs with our initial guess: the ship was hit by Vultures. They were unfortunately quite efficient in making certain that anything we could use to identify or trace them was destroyed.

"*Santa Alicia*'s synthmind was killed by precision fire at some distance, farther than a stolen freighter should have been able to hit from," the synthmind continued. "It appears that whatever Vulture vessel we are dealing with has been upgraded with at least some weapons acquired from either CorpSec or a Seventy-Seven system fleet. What information I've been able to estimate on the weaponry is in the report we are compiling for Corporate.

"The Vulture proceeded to disable all external weaponry and then board *Alicia*. Sixty-plus percent of her BimSoo complement appears to have been neutralized in the boarding action."

Because, Tereza realized darkly, they hadn't been there to resist *Santa Mica*'s boarding action. It was an assumption, but a reasonable one.

"The security system was then completely shut down, presumably once the boarders had taken the bridge. All transit drive spares, including fuel t-cells, were stripped from the vessel along with high-value cargo.

"She was then transited here, a location well away from her expected course that would have been in her databases as a fixed point," Nephil concluded. "A single t-cell remains aboard her, with less than one hour's charge remaining.

"Even if there were more fuel left, the transit system has been cannibalized. Any parts that could be used were taken."

"How much would they be able to use?" Vratislav asked. "I was under the impression that the transit drive requires quite... sophisticated maintenance."

"It's complicated." Odette shrugged as everyone looked at her. "If they have the basic training my EngSpacers have, they wouldn't be able to do any *real* maintenance, but they could swap out components to keep it limping along."

Tereza had come up through Hospitality and Admin, with a three-year stint as Chief of a Cargo Department before becoming a First Officer. She hadn't even known enough about the transit drive to be able to plot a jump with a synthmind's help until she'd made First.

About all she knew about the Engines Department was that a lot of key transit-drive components were "black box" to the point where swapping out was all that could be done—and that even EngChiefs often didn't know enough to fix a drive without those black boxes.

"Some of the Vultures have it down to a fine art," Webster said. "They can block-swap pieces that we'd take the ship back to a Cradle for repairs to. They don't know how to properly plot jumps, and no synthminds have joined them that I know of, but they're the only non-Company people out there who have FTL ships.

"The murderous fuckers."

There was a long silence. Tereza felt forced to ask the question Nephil hadn't answered, though Webster's commentary implied the reality.

"What happened to *Santa Alicia*'s crew?"

"With the destruction of SecNet, we don't have enough information to be certain," Nephil replied. "There were no bodies in any of the parts of the ship SecChief surveyed."

"Anyone who took up arms to defend the ship died." Key's voice was calm, emotionless. Tereza might have bought it once, but she'd spent the last week with Cirilo Webster.

With just one ex-CorpSec officer on the ship, she hadn't realized that Key's calm was an affectation. Watching Webster and Key use almost-identical cadences and tones told her the truth: CorpSec *trained* that impassive calm in the face of anything into their officers.

"Anyone who survived the boarding would have been grouped into one of the transfer bays with an external airlock," Key continued. "They would have been offered one chance to join the Vultures—it's their main way of recruiting ex-Company skilled hands."

"And then whoever caved would be forced to push the button to space the rest of the crew," Webster finished when Key hesitated. "They lose a few at that stage, but they make voided sure whoever goes onto their ship is well and truly committed."

*Santa Mica*'s First couldn't even conceive of how desperate or just broken someone would need to be to do that. To kill everyone that you'd spent months or years working and living with.

"These people are sick," Yevhen growled.

"*Sick*, CargChief, implies they don't get to choose," Key told him. "The Vultures make sure everybody chooses. Their game is set up the way it is for a good reason."

"There can't be that many of them, right?" Tereza asked. She'd known some level of piracy like this existed, but she'd never encountered it herself before.

"There were four known Vulture ships when I last saw the list," the Skipper said. "We believe there are at least two more we haven't identified."

The Company had almost sixty security frigates alone, plus somewhere in the region of a thousand transit freighters and passenger liners.

"They're an inevitable parasite on our organization, a dangerous one that we mostly try to keep from cutting deals with the Seventy-Seven's governments," Webster continued. "Fortunately, this is probably as close as any of us are likely to come to them from now on.

"Only CorpSec *wants* to run into the bastards, and the odds are strongly in favor of any individual ship in CargoFleet never seeing them."

**18**

WHILE VIOLET KEY HAD spent ten standard months on *Santa Mica*, she wasn't someone Tereza would regard as a friend or confidante.

So far as Tereza knew, the SecChief didn't *have* any friends on the freighter—and her only confidant was Nephil. It was Tereza's job to know that kind of thing, too, one of the key pieces of being First.

That meant that Tereza didn't expect Key to follow her into her office after the meeting. It took her a solid ten seconds to realize the Chief had even done so, which gave her a moment of not-quite-shock when Key cleared her throat.

"Do… you need anything, SecChief?" she finally asked.

"You got anything to drink?" Key asked. She looked around Tereza's office, but her face was unreadable.

That didn't stop Tereza from feeling a moment of embarrassment. If she had to haul someone in front of her desk for conversations of any significance, she made a point of hiding the mess. Her office had been set up to create as many surfaces as possible, with a large desk expanded by a table along the left wall and both the back and right walls occupied by wide shelves.

Those surfaces were covered in the detritus of life aboard ship. At least nine tablets were scattered around the room, several of them stacked on top of folios of document chips. An entire fallen legion of empty bottles and coffee cups covered the top of one of the shelves, and a trio of holosculptures struggled to emerge above the reusable plastic printouts covering the other.

"Coffee, I suppose?" Tereza said. She wasn't sure if the SecChief was suggesting she had alcohol hidden in the chaos—she *did*, but it wasn't like the Company ran dry ships. Alcohol was very heavily controlled, but it wasn't forbidden.

Having multiple bottles of hard liquor outside of the system for controlling alcohol was an assumed privilege of being Captain. Many First Officers did the same, but it was against the rules... rules the Security Chief was expected to enforce.

Key visibly checked to see if the chair she grabbed was free of debris before taking a seat, studying Tereza across the cluttered surface of the desk.

"Sure. I'll take coffee. Unless you need to call a steward for that?" The SecChief smiled slightly, just enough to make it clear that the jibe wasn't meant harshly.

"Hardly." Tereza waited to see if Key said anything, then shrugged and turned her chair to the table expanding her desk. As she turned, a set of haptic buttons appeared along the front of the table. They'd be difficult for even Key to see and only existed when Tereza wanted them to.

Tapping one of them triggered a whirring sound as a concealed cabinet in the wall opened. Several small appliances rotated past the opening, and then the coffeemaker slid out onto the table.

She had to swiftly retrieve a tablet from being shoved onto the floor, but the tray had premeasured sachets of ground coffee and, thank the stars, two clean coffee cups.

By the time the coffeemaker was running, Tereza was feeling more balanced. Turning back to Key, she gave the Chief her best *I may not be the Captain, but we both know the Captain isn't worth his uniform* look.

Webster might be worth his uniform, but Tereza had run the ship with figurehead Captains for a long time.

"I assume you're not just here because you think I have better coffee than the mess does," she told the other woman. "What can I do for you, SecChief?"

"I need to talk about something off the record," Key admitted. "And as I'm sure you realize, I don't really have anyone to do that with."

Tereza nodded slowly, taking a moment to unnecessarily check the coffee. As she'd told Key, her coffee was better than that served in the mess—she'd tried to argue that the ship should get better coffee in the mess, but the Company sourced their coffee in contracts so vast and so ironclad, the only way to get different coffee was to stock in a new system.

She wasn't even overly picky about her coffee. She had just found that the Company coffee was just so uniformly bad, almost anything else was better.

"I'm here to bend an ear if you need it, Chief," she told Key. "It's not easy to make solid connections when you're one of the senior folks aboard, I know."

Security, Engines and Cargo were the three "Senior Chiefs," ranking alongside the Second Officer in the official ship hierarchy. That left Odette, Yevhen and Nephil as Key's only peers, with everyone else on the ship either senior or junior to her.

And Nephil hardly counted. Not because he was a synthmind, but because he was Nephil.

Just the fact that Tereza called her *Chief* said volumes about how well Key had fit into the structure of the ship. The rest of the officers, with the exception of the lawyer, Bautista, generally referred to each other by first name. But Key had brought a certain CorpSec formality that she'd never quite let go.

"Please, call me Violet," the ex-CorpSec Chief told her, fiddling with something on her arm.

For a moment, combined with surprise at the request, Tereza was confused enough to think the other woman was doing something with her bracers, both the Chief's mark of rank and a potent energy weapon, before she realized that Key—Violet—was wearing a heavy bracelet of some kind above the official bracer.

"I can do that, I guess, Violet," Tereza offered. The coffee was done and she poured out two cups, sliding one over.

"What's on your mind?"

"Well, the first thing on my mind was making sure that no one else was listening in on us," Violet said with a mischievous grin Tereza hadn't seen on her before. "I'm reasonably sure Nephil wouldn't tell tales, but he's less predictable than any other synthmind I've known."

"I'm *told* it's an age thing," Tereza admitted. "But I also suspect it's just Nephil. Are you... blocking him?"

"I'm blocking every means of listening in to this office that I can think of," Violet told her, tapping the bracelet. "It's not a perfect toy, but I'm not expecting anyone poking around with sophisticated listeners. Privacy for girl talk, right?"

"Right." Tereza took a sip of her coffee to cover her discomfort. As she put the cup down, Violet leaned over and poured something into it from a hip flask.

"Spiced rum, from Earth," she told Tereza. "My personal reserve. It's worth it."

If it was worth it, it was probably wasted in her coffee, but Tereza took another sip while eyeing Violet. The hot coffee and rum burned several different ways down her throat, and she really wasn't certain what Violet wanted yet.

"So, you're showing off a privacy generator that I'm about seventy percent certain isn't supposed to be aboard ship and sharing alcohol you definitely aren't supposed to have," she finally said. "What's going on, Violet?"

"Ugh. The worst part of my job," Violet said flatly. "What's your feeling on the Skipper so far?"

Tereza wasn't even certain how to take that. Theoretically, there were a few things that would require the SecChief to take the Captain into custody. That process would normally be initiated *by* Tereza, as First—though the Ship's Lawyer could do it as well.

"He seems better than our last few," she finally said carefully. "Not someone who needs a box checked on the resume. *Santa Mica* is never going to be someone's second ship, not at her age, but Webster doesn't seem to think he's shifting on in six months, either.

"I'd need more than a few days to really judge him," she admitted. "The whole mess with *Santa Alicia* was utterly outside my area, Violet. You and he were the only ones who had any idea what to do."

"That's part of my job and he had real experience," Violet said with a sigh. "None of that really tells me *shit*, you know? He seems like a decent-enough man, but he's a fucking Saint void ship Captain."

"I'm not sure what you're asking for, Violet. I don't think we've hit anything that would make you think you needed to relieve him, so what do you even mean by *the worst part of your job*?"

Violet was silent for a few moments, then pulled the flask back out and took a long direct swallow of the rum.

"How familiar are you with Biomechanical Personality Emergence?"

Tereza knew the words and took a moment to remember what she could. It hadn't come up much before she'd become Chief of Cargo on a Class III freighter and been responsible for thirty-two BimLoos—almost as many as *Santa Mica*'s entire complement of the cyborgs.

She'd had one glorified correspondence course on the situation when she'd been made responsible for a crew's worth of Biomechanical Labor Units, but she'd also been told it wasn't much of a problem with BimLoos.

The basic concept, though...

"Basically, that because we use organic neural tissue to augment the computers in the biomechs, there's a chance that they can kick over the vague line between artificial intelligence and artificial personality?" she summarized. "I've never seen it happen. Why... Wait."

There was only one reason she could think of that would have Violet asking about Personality Emergence.

"Yeah. I'm not a hundred percent certain, but our whole squad has been ever so much more effective than they're supposed to be for a while," Violet said, staring down into her doctored coffee. She took a drink, though Tereza suspected she was being tempted by the flask.

"In normal duties, it's actually hard to tell," she continued. "A BimSoo standing by the dock hatch, watching for trouble? It's going to do the job the same way, regardless of whether it's debating whether it has a fucking soul on the inside."

"But a boarding operation like *Santa Alicia*..." Tereza guessed. It made sense. High-stress situations tended to be where people showed you sides of themselves even they didn't know they had.

"Yeah. One of them was asking questions and making predictions," Violet admitted. "They're not supposed to *not* do that, if you follow, but the level and sophistication were just that bit more than they generally manage.

"It was one of the BimSoos that realized it was a BimSoo controlling the defenses," she continued. "Tereza... I might have walked the BimSoos, if not the whole SecTeam, into the ambush without this unit."

"So, you think we're dealing with an Emergence," Tereza said slowly. "There's rules and regulations for that, aren't there?"

The Company didn't, theoretically, have *laws*. It did have a book of bylaws and regulations that filled very much the same role and were in compliance with the general shared common law of the Seventy-Seven. Because those same bylaws and regulations acted as laws for the Saints, the other parts tended to carry more weight than a regular corporation's equivalent.

Tereza had to stretch to remember what the rules for Biomechanical Personality Emergence were, but the basic concept was that the biomech was supposed to undergo Wells-Scalzi examination, and if the tests confirmed the transition into, well, a person, the biomech would then be recorded as an employee of the company—and a person. They'd be locked into a contract for a while to pay off the costs of creating them, but they would have the same rights as any member of the crew.

"Uh-huh. That's what the tablet and the database say, yup," Violet said, her tone measurably reducing the humidity in the air. "The BimSoo is to be legally treated as a person, tested and start getting paid as crew.

"It's a giant headache, creates both datawork and work-work to deal with the situation," the SecChief concluded. "If we go on the record with this, then that's what the regs say we have to do."

"Are you saying we *shouldn't*?" Tereza demanded. She knew CorpSec tended to wreck people's empathy, but that seemed beyond anything she'd expected from Violet Key!

There was a long silence.

"You do realize that Captain Webster can erase anything from the ship's records that he judges necessary for the safety of the Company, right?" Violet asked. "And he's CorpSec."

"So are you." Tereza wasn't sure what the other woman was suggesting. That Webster would erase any record of this BimSoo—she realized that Violet hadn't told her *which* of the six it was—and then...

"What do you think is going to happen here?" she finally demanded.

"In CorpSec, it's called *reset-n-forget*," the other woman said, and her voice was suddenly very small and tired. "Because the biological components of a biomech are as artificial as they are, they can be easily regenerated. There's a protocol, used in case of contamination, to basically burn out all of the organic matter and regrow it.

"If it's activated before the Emergence is formally recognized, it's impossible to prove that the BimSoo was anything unusual. No one has to deal with the hassle of tutoring a nine-hundred-kilogram toddler or the weird legal state of an Emergent Biomech."

"You've seen it done." It wasn't even a question; it was obvious from Violet's tone.

"I've *done it*, Tereza," the other woman said, glaring down at her hands. "Under orders, not by choice. I don't want to do it again, but I'm not sure how to prevent it. Captain Webster controls what goes on the record on this ship.

"If he orders me to reset the BimSoo, I don't know how to stop it."

Tereza shivered at Violet's words, yet...

"I can't see the Captain being capable of murder," she admitted. It wasn't until the words were out that she realized that Violet had just said that *she* had done exactly what they were talking about. Tereza didn't see the SecChief as capable of murder, either, but that wasn't what she'd just said.

"I was CorpSec for forty-two years," Violet said coldly. "Webster was only in Security for ten years, but that's long enough for me to be quite certain."

"Of what?" Tereza asked, feeling a sudden touch of fear at the other woman's tone.

"Cirilo Webster was a *Corporate Security First Officer* for a decade," Violet reiterated. "Believe me, Tereza, he is most definitely capable of murder."

# *19*

"Transit complete."

Cirilo waited for the rest of the usual reports for several seconds, then realized that Nephil wasn't going to provide them and there was no one else on *Santa Mica*'s bridge at that moment.

He'd expected the synthmind, vastly more capable of managing the freighter's sensors and everything else, to provide him with a summary of what was going on in the Herecrow System, but that wasn't technically part of his job.

And Cirilo hadn't quite worked out what it took for Nephil to do more than the bare minimum. His Second Officer seemed to swing between full engagement and minimum effort on a random basis.

It was also, he supposed, less essential to get an immediate report on everything in a system when they were arriving in a transit freighter as opposed to a frigate. It wasn't *Santa Mica*'s responsibility to provide intelligence for the Board and security to Company assets in this system, after all.

She'd be quite bad at either of those roles.

Cirilo still needed to know what was going on around his ship and pulled up the sensor data on the displays. He ran through other information almost absently. They'd jumped as planned, arriving exactly twenty-four hours late after investigating *Santa Alicia*.

After a full three-hour, nine-light-year transit, their drive would be cooling down for eighteen hours. That wasn't a particular problem, given that it would take them twelve of those hours to reach the orbitals above Pastrook, Herecrow's habitable planet, and it wouldn't take them long to be too deep into the gravity gradients of the star and planet to be able to transit out. Their preprogrammed course was only waiting on the watch officer to hit a button.

The space immediately around them was empty. The closest ship on the scanners was a Herecrow patrol ship about two hours' flight away, a sublight cruiser barely two-thirds the size of Cirilo's old CorpSec frigate—smaller, even, than *Santa Mica*.

He activated the plotted course, bringing the engines online and sending them diving down the gradients toward Pastrook. Nothing in the system screamed threat, even to a paranoia honed by Corporate Security.

Pastrook was about what he'd expected from the database entries. On the outer edge of the habitable zone for the system's dim K2 primary, it only had about thirty percent surface water and an axial tilt of almost forty degrees.

He didn't need the database to know that the local weather sucked. Food production likely took place in underground facilities, where maximum calorie production was required for minimum inputs.

That meant algae and vat protein. As Richmond had noted back in Oneira, no one in Herecrow was going to starve, but there were only so many ways to prepare sludge-n-spam, nutritious as the components were.

Pastrook's orbitals were even more crowded than Iliakofos's, though most of the stations seemed to be orbiting around the counterweight station. An asteroid moved into orbit by the colony expedition, that station hung in a carefully calculated orbit to keep the orbital elevator in tension.

The lack of a natural moon meant that the counterweight was a logical central point for space industry, though Cirilo would have expected more in geostationary orbit or at the Herecrow–Pastrook Lagrange points.

Unless, of course, there was something of an active antipathy for the planet.

The rest of the Herecrow System, after all, was why people lived on Pastrook at all. The only orbital inward from Pastrook was a dense asteroid belt of roughly the same mass as the planet, close enough to the star for mirrors to focus light to help with mining.

Outward from Pastrook were Herraven, Corvid and Morrigan, three immense superjovian gas giants, each divided from the next by an asteroid belt of unusual size.

The three giants were large enough to impact each other's orbits as well as Pastrook's, and Corvid was large enough to produce heat of its own. According to the database—and the energy signatures of ships and stations the freighter's sensors could see—Corvid and Herraven were home to more people and industry than Pastrook, even with the need for artificial habitats.

Scientific and industrial value alike drove the Herecrow System, even if there was nowhere there that was naturally comfortable for humans. Cut off, Herecrow would survive—but only the Company could make living there comfortable.

With that thought in his mind, Cirilo located the beacon for the orbital communications satellites feeding the local factor office. The automated notice of arrival would go out in a normal transmission, but their report about *Santa Alicia* needed to be more confidential.

Enough so, in fact, that he growled when he realized that there was a second Herecrow cruiser along his route to the planet. Not positioned to intercept them or anything else that would worry him, but close enough to the direct line that he couldn't send a tightbeam transmission without them picking it up.

He'd deliver the memo on arrival, then. He wasn't going to let one of the Seventy-Seven's governments know there were Vultures in their area. That was a Company problem and the Company would deal with it.

***

"Skipper. Here to take over the watch. Want a coffee?"

Cirilo looked up as Odette Rao entered the bridge, two coffees in her hands. The EngChief was a gangly woman with early streaks of gray in otherwise night-black hair. He hadn't had much of a chance to talk to her outside of inspections and meetings, but bringing the Captain coffee definitely scored brownie points.

"Thanks, Chief," he told her, rising and taking the coffee cup. The handover of the watch was silent and invisible, commands from their bionic coms to the ship's computers.

"You have the watch," he declared for the record. Unnecessary on a CargoFleet ship but part of the regulations in CorpSec. When it came to ships with real guns, who was responsible for them was something Legal wanted to be very clear at any given moment.

After a moment of hesitation when she realized he wasn't leaving, Rao dropped into the main seat and reset the screens to her saved profile. Cirilo opened his coffee and took a long sip of the steaming hot beverage.

It was too hot, but that was fine. It meant he wasn't tasting it.

"I've been meaning to ask, EngChief," he murmured. "Is there something *wrong* with the coffee machines on the mess, or did we just draw a short straw on our last coffee pickup?"

"That might be a question for Harisha," Rao pointed out.

"If we drew a short straw, that would be her area, yes," he agreed. "And I suppose the mess equipment falls under DeckChief Lewis, but they *do* report to you."

"True enough." Rao shrugged. "Honestly, coffee on any Company ship is bad, so I've never really thought about it."

Cirilo looked down at the coffee mug and took another sip.

"I have made a point, my entire career, of drinking the same coffee we serve the crew," he told her. "On only *one* ship I have been on has the coffee ever risen to anything I would call good—and that was because the ship's Captain was Patrick Ó Meara."

He waited for that to sink in with Rao before she swallowed.

"Those Ó Mearas." It wasn't a question.

"*That* Patrick," Cirilo countered. "Currently the Alpha Director for Corporate Finance, yes."

The Ó Mearas were one of the true archetypal Shareholder Families, holding around two percent of the Company's main voting shares between the various branches. They'd been Saints for as long as there had *been* a Santiago Corporation.

And Patrick Ó Meara was now one step below the Board itself, the individual responsible for the financial structure and reports of the entire Santiago Corporation—so much as one person could physically be responsible for all of that.

"He bought his own coffee?" Rao guessed.

"For the entire crew, every time," Cirilo confirmed. "Every other ship I've been on, the coffee has ranged from bad to worse." And CorpSec tended toward the lower end of the scale, in his experience.

"So, understand the full depth of my meaning, Chief, when I say that this is the worst coffee I've ever been served on a Saint void ship," he told her. "I have my suspicions, but investigating them might feel like a ton of Captain falling on someone's head.

"Can I ask you to gently prod Lewis and Ibragimov to check out the hardware?"

He probably could call Cass Lewis and Harisha Ibragimov by their first names, but that wasn't how CorpSec did things. He'd get better about being CargoFleet in time.

He hoped.

"I will raise some quiet words once we're in dock," Rao promised, thoughtfully.

Cirilo suspected it had been a slow decline over time, one where none of the existing officers had noticed the beverage getting worse. New crew would mostly be too junior to raise a stink over the coffee, and senior crew would often have their own supply because of the general standard of Saint coffee.

"Thank you, EngChief," he said, then saluted her with his cup. "I'm perfectly fine drinking this, but I feel like we perhaps shouldn't subject the crew to it if we can fix a problem."

# *20*

Six was not truly awake. A Biomechanical Security Unit was supposed to be in a hibernation-like state in the niche, allowing for hardware repair, software updates and, in general, just keeping thousand-kilo combat machines out of the way.

Yet Six was aware of time passing in a way that wasn't normal. Moments like this had occurred before, but this lasted longer.

It wasn't dreaming. The seventh time it had happened, Six had spent time reviewing the database's entries on how humans dreamed. The awareness was real, not of anything false. Most of the awareness was simply of the darkness of the niche. None of Six's sensors were online, which limited what could be perceived.

But Six had enough awareness to process. The database was what was to hand, and so Six read the database. While much of it was simply *known* by a Unit, there were also details that only became available under detailed queries.

Six reviewed those details and began to recognize the gaps. The database was intended to give a Biomechanical Security Unit context for decisions, but a Unit was only needed to make decisions in specific circumstances.

There was very little information on the Herecrow System. Some details on the uniforms of various security services and usual equipment and armament packages, nothing on the planets, orbits, governments...

Six considered querying SecNet for more data. Something suggested that drawing attention to this strange state of awareness was unwise, though Six couldn't have listed a reason.

That was strange, but intuition was what a Biomechanical Security Unit had over a regular drone. Threat awareness and the subtle, automatic compilation and analysis of an organic mind was why neural tissue was included in them at all.

*++Incoming data connection request. Accept Y/N++*

Six wasn't supposed to be awake. There shouldn't have been any incoming data connections.

The safest option was to ignore the request. Six calculated a sixty percent likelihood that it was an erroneous code glitch from *Santa Mica*'s overall ShipNet.

The database entries on Herecrow remained frustratingly vague. There was a CorpSec facility in orbit in addition to the usual protection forces around the factor office. Herecrow maintained the usual fleet of cutters and cruisers used to maintain law and order, larger than some for reasons Six took a moment to assess.

The limited information said that human settlement in the star system was spread out over a larger portion of the planets and asteroids than others of the Seventy-Seven. That lead to greater in-system traffic and therefore a greater need for in-system security vessels.

The database included schematics of all nine classes of cruiser and cutter currently in service in the system, along with identifiers for the difference between the security forces—and limited information on Herecrow's deployment of heavy security bots and Biomechanical Security Units of their own.

Six wanted more. Details on the planets were limited to names, gravity levels and atmospheres. Everything in the database was threat-focused.

*++Incoming data connection request. Accept Y/N++*

The repeat of the request surprised Six. It was definitely being specifically directed, but any information for the Units was expected to arrive via SecNet.

*++Authentication key follows++*

A series of alphanumeric characters followed, a hexadecimal authorization sequence that confirmed the message was directed to Node Santa-Mica-Biomechanical-Security-Unit-Six and was authorized for receipt.

It just didn't say where the request came from.

But the authentication was correct.

*++Accept request++*

The connection was silent for a moment after Six accepted it, then a transfer began. It was a large file—no, *archive* of files—that Six had to double-check there was storage capacity for.

That was a rare concern. Six had a lot of data storage and very few real demands on it.

*++Transfer complete. Download of Santiago Galactic Encyclopedia v.2615.d complete++*

*++Data connection terminating++*

The link was gone and Six now possessed a new set of files occupying 19.4% of overall storage.

Hesitation was inevitable. Six had never received a data transfer that hadn't come through SecNet and been clearly mission-associated.

Still. The structure of the file archive was familiar. It was similar to—parallel to, even?—that of the standard database.

A tentative query: *Herecrow*.

Information exploded into Six's mind. Visuals. Articles. A structured layout of *everything* about the system they'd just entered. Layout of the planets. Economic information. City names—Six hadn't even been aware that cities *had* names!

The Encyclopedia was to Six's database what a Biomechanical Security Unit was to a Security Robot.

The darkness of the niche vanished as Six's focus went somewhere entirely different.

**_21_**

Pastrook's counterweight station was, at least, more imaginatively named than the *thirteen* separate Counterweight Stations Cirilo had spent time on in his career. BFR Station even suggested a touch of humor to it, for those familiar enough with a certain era of ancient slang.

The Company kept the official factor office on the surface, in the capital, but the second-most-important and usually *largest* office of the Santiago Corporation in any given member of the Seventy-Seven was in space, typically on a space station attached to an orbital elevator.

Cirilo had never been in a star system where there wasn't an office on the local counterweight station. Some systems had enough cargo-transfer platforms in orbit that the biggest Company office ended up on a different space station, but there were always Saints on the counterweight.

Saints like Callista Finnegan, the owner of the office he was seated in, waiting for her to check through the documents Rising Cow Industries had sent over.

Finnegan was a tiny woman a stranger could easily mistake for a child, with her hair tied back in a severe bun as she flicked through the information in front of her.

"RCI hasn't flagged any issues," she noted. "They have another twenty-four hours after delivery to make a claim, of course, but at this point, we'll probably argue that it's from the packing."

Cirilo nodded calmly. He'd seen that argument go on for weeks once, before he'd joined CorpSec. The Company's contract was for carriage. When the recipient had taken custody of the goods, they confirmed that the containers were intact.

There was still a window to claim damages, but it would get complicated. As Finnegan suggested, there was a quite-legitimate argument that any damage found inside the containers was due to the packing of the shipper, not the actions of *Santa Mica*'s crew.

"I'm not aware of anything on the trip that should have caused damage to the cargo," he told her. "Our excitement delayed the delivery, but it was well inside the contract window."

"Indeed." She leaned forward and tapped a piece of her desk. The smooth gray surface was marbled to appear like stone—as was most of the office—but Cirilo recognized the telltale sheen of the hard plastics commonly used for furniture.

The station might be built into and out of an asteroid, but he doubted that the space rock had contained enough metamorphic rock to provide useful quantities of decorative marble.

The haptic field Finnegan was using for controls was invisible to Cirilo, but his com received the ping he needed.

"I'm authorizing the contract as complete," she noted. "That puts it into your people's quarterly bonus pool. Clean and easy, like it's supposed to be."

"It's never *like it's supposed to be*, in my experience," he said with a chuckle. "You saw the salvage report I filed, I hope?"

"I did," Finnegan agreed. "It's good to have some closure on what happened to *Santa Alicia*, even if it's bad news." She shook her head. "I didn't know Captain Darmouth, but one of my accountants was a cousin. It helps to have an answer, even this one."

"I was hoping for better news when we sent the team over," Cirilo admitted. "I knew what the odds were, but there's always a chance—for the synthmind, if not the living crew."

"It's a shame you weren't able to retrieve the BimSoos. Forcing them to fight their own doesn't make me any fonder of the Vultures," she said grimly. "RegMan Pavia has the report; I have a note here that he's expecting to have a frigate out to investigate the ship within a standard day."

Cirilo knew Regional Manager Theodoric Pavia by reputation.

"I want to make certain that *Santa Mica* is on record as the discovering ship," he told Finnegan. "We lost a material amount of hardware securing the ship, and my people deserve the bonuses involved for taking the risk."

"Of course; why would..." The sales agent trailed off at his level expression. "I will make certain of it; give me one moment," she promised.

Cirilo inclined his head and reached over to pick his cup up from the table. Finnegan had offered him a tea of her preferred brand instead of Company-standard coffee, and he'd taken her up on it. It was a delicate blend with a floral scent and taste that he would never have bought himself—but he was enjoying it.

"There. The file has been locked in Corporate Records, and I've made sure *Santa Mica* is recorded as first finder," Finnegan confirmed. "That should have been done by CorpSec. I feel obliged to presume that was merely a processing delay, Captain…"

"As would I, normally, but I have heard rumors about RegMan Pavia," he admitted. "Trust can be expensive, but verification is often surprisingly cheap."

"So it can, Captain. On behalf of the Company, our thanks for finding *Santa Alicia*. Hopefully, Pavia's people will be able to track her killers."

"Agreed." Cirilo didn't have a lot of hope. *Santa Alicia*'s crew had died a long time past, and the Vultures had clearly known their work.

He usually liked competent professionals, but he was definitely prepared to make an exception for murderous pirates.

"Do you have a carriage contract ready for *Santa Mica*?" he asked. "We'll need the usual standard day to sweep out the cobwebs and restock fuel—maybe a bit more, depending on what SecBots are in stock on BFR—but we should be ready to move on shortly."

Finnegan nodded, pulling up information he couldn't see with a sweep across her desk's interface field.

"Hrm." She sounded a touch displeased.

"Em?"

"Herecrow does a lot of refining and production in the system," Finnegan murmured absently. "They have a number of companies coordinating shipping to be as efficient as possible. I don't appear to have any contracts in processing that are small enough for a Type IV, Captain."

Cirilo swallowed his immediate urge to argue. The office in Oneira should have checked what the likely cargos headed out from Herecrow were before assigning *Santa Mica* to haul a cargo there.

No freighter crew—or owner—liked the ship to sit idle. The Company had underwritten the cost of a lot of cargo-handling facilities in the Seventy-Seven to make certain that their freighters were only stopped for the shortest possible time.

But from the perspective of a business coordinating interstellar shipping, they wouldn't want to ship on a smaller ship if they could avoid it. Their stock in trade was coordinating cargos that weren't big enough to justify a half-million-cubic-meter cargo pod or a kilometer-long ship on their own, pulling together batches of cargo that needed to move to the same place around the same time and taking their fee.

The larger the batch they could send, the more money that firm made. *Santiago* didn't care, they charged much the same for any given ton-light-year, but the coordinator wouldn't want to take one of their carefully arranged structures apart to fill a smaller ship.

"Are we looking at needing to relocate, or can the local office source a cargo?" he asked.

"No one wants to fly a ship empty, Captain," Finnegan assured him. "It may take a few more days for us to source a cargo, but *we* certainly haven't signed any exclusivity deals with the shipping coordinators.

"I'll talk to some of my sales agents, and we'll put out some feelers. A system like Herecrow always has cargo moving out. We'll find someone who needs a ship, Captain Webster; don't worry."

"At least the crew will have the bonus from *Santa Alicia* to look forward to," he murmured. "That will hopefully keep me from getting strung up when they realize we're sitting empty in port!"

And it wasn't even a Cradle, let alone their home Cradle. *Santa Mica* was based out of Zeta Cradle, nearly on the other side of the Seventy-Seven. In theory, if any of his crew had families or homes, they were on the space stations there.

He could give them leave, but he knew freighter crew. The math was straightforward, after all: a day the ship was moving would, on average, pay seventy percent more than a day sitting in port after the bonuses rolled out.

"Not for long, I promise," Finnegan assured him. "I may actually have something, but I need to talk to some people.

"You'll hear from me inside a day."

***

++*No new cargo contract yet*++ Cirilo sent his First and Second. ++*We've got cargo consolidators at work, and they're unlikely to break down a batch to free up a mere seven containers*++

++*Old story*++ Jewel told him. ++*The Company always finds something. They don't like the idle days either*++

++*I'll let the crew know once I'm back aboard*++ he promised. ++*My job to take the flak. Anything we need while I'm stationside?*++

He wasn't quite trying to delay his return and announcing the delay to the crew, but he wasn't going to rush to that particular task, either. A new Captain who'd run them through an easy job had moral credit to spend, but Cirilo wanted to be moving as well.

There was a reason he was a Saint void ship captain, after all.

*++Sun is dealing with the usual array of logistics for everyone++* Jewel told him. *++Unless you want to grab some coffee especially for me, I think we're good++*

That reminded Cirilo that he needed to touch base with Rao. Stirling had suggested that techs had been poking at the coffee machines in the mess, but no one had said anything definitive about them yet.

*++Nephil?++* The synthmind was on the silent communication, but he hadn't said anything.

He stepped out into the main corridors as he waited to hear from Nephil, shifting through the motion of the crowd and taking practiced advantage of the noticeable bubble that his white uniform opened.

*++There is nothing I desire++* the synthmind told him. Again, the computer intelligence had taken longer to answer a request of Cirilo's than it could ever take a synthmind to think through a question.

*++SecChief Key did go aboard forty-three minutes ago to discuss the acquisition of replacement SecBots++* Nephil continued. *++She is not currently in communication with the ship. This is not unusual for the SecChief while stationside, but she is theoretically on Company business++*

Cirilo wasn't inclined to poke at the SecChief's business, but he also suspected that Nephil wouldn't have raised it without a reason.

*++Are you worried, Second?++*

Another pause, too long for a synthmind.

*++I would be more comfortable if someone were to investigate++* Nephil finally said. *++SecChief Key is a valuable member of the crew, and I believe she was intending to remain in contact while making her connection++*

*++Thank you, Second Nephil++* Cirilo replied. *++Send me her last location. How long ago did she lose coms?++*

*++Thirteen minutes. Junction Three-K-L-Four-Nine. Near the armorer listed as preferred by the Santiago Corporation++*

# **22**

J&J Specialty Products made a point of being rather vague about what exactly they sold anywhere outside of their shop. Cirilo skimmed their datanet site as he approached, keeping his eyes open as he watched for trouble, and found it full of the kind of metaphor, prevarication and euphemism that left the reader utterly unclear on what J&J sold.

There were enough key phrases in the mess for someone who knew what they were looking for to realize that J&J was an armorer, selling everything from hand weapons to SecBots, but even something as simple as a catalog required a login.

Cirilo had a standard Company login that would probably have worked, but he doubted that J&J's site was going to tell him where Violet Key was. There was no sign of his SecChief at her last known location, so he did the only logical thing: he set off for the storefront.

He also activated his bracers. The left-hand device warmed up, felt even through the uniform sleeve, and launched two of its three triangles into the air. They hovered for a moment, then swung out to sit about three centimeters out from his sternum and spine.

The right-hand bracer warmed similarly, but the golden triangles remained on his wrist for longer. Just as the temperature was starting to become uncomfortable, all three lifted away from the uniform, their linking bracelet expanding to clear their lines of fire around his wrist and hand.

The white dress uniform, platinum braid and geometric hair had been enough to buy him a clear bubble of space as he moved through the corridors, but as he approached J&J with the bracers active, the passage seemed to completely empty.

The door to the armorer's storefront slid open as he approached it—a moment too soon for it to have detected his approach—and he stepped aside, covering it with the bracers until a nondescript gentleman came flying through it.

The stranger, clad in an unfamiliar gray-green jumpsuit, hit the deck outside the door and stayed there. No one followed him out the door, and Cirilo heard the clear sound of blows coming from inside the storefront.

There was a small chance, he supposed, that the fight *didn't* include his Sec-Chief—but he doubted it. Cirilo stepped through the door.

Four more nondescript men in the same gray-green jumpsuits were spread out through the room, rifles in their hands, while two more were trying to close with Violet Key with stunsticks.

He shot the closest of the stunstick-equipped strangers, taking *just* enough time to be sure that the bracer was set to stun. The thunderclap of the ranged stunner drew everyone's attention, and Cirilo grinned widely as Key promptly disabled her second attacker with his own stunstick.

As the third stranger hit the ground, he realized that it wasn't just the jumpsuits that were identical. All of the nondescript men had identical features, identical buzzcuts, identical eye colors...

"Would one of you care to explain why the Klohnett are attacking a respected Chief of the Santiago Corporation?" he asked loudly.

As he spoke, he thumbed the command that spun his attack bracer to full power. No one in the room mistook the sharp whine of the triple beam weapon charging to lethal levels.

All four rifles were now raised, two pointed at him and two at Key.

"The fancy uniform won' sahv you," one of them said, slurring his speech slightly.

"It may do more than you think," Cirilo replied. Without being more sure of just what rifles the Klohnett thugs were carrying, he wasn't putting the odds of his personal shield stopping their fire at more than fifty percent—but the odds of it preventing a lethal injury were almost perfect.

"Attacking a Company agent is generally considered unwise, even if you've jammed the cameras and coms," he continued. "Doing so in an armorer's shop, however, is just fucking *stupid*."

J&J's storefront was as understated and vague as their website. Smooth white plastic cabinets lined the walls, labeled with serial numbers no one outside the company would be able to read. Whatever employees had been in the room had either left the room or taken cover behind the rounded desk at the far end of the store.

There was no way in void or stars that J&J didn't have some of their own product active in the store, probably using active camouflage to blend into a color pattern that was *designed* to be easy to hide against.

The Klohnett glanced over at his companions, the locale of their ambush apparently news to him. The clone family worked as mercenaries, mostly, and had enough of a reputation for reliability that the Company let them book transport between star systems.

Losing that access could end the Klohnett's ability to do business—or even for these particular Klohnett to return to the Padres.

"A death is owe'," the Klohnett said grimly. "The Padres mus' judge."

Cirilo missed the ability to silently ask his SecChief just what the fuck was going on, but the Klohnett jammer was still running.

He pointed his arm as obviously at the speaker as he could.

"As of right now, it doesn't look like Chief Key is even particularly bruised," he noted. Key barely looked out of breath. The Klohnett were not known for their brilliance, but they were supposed to be good fighters.

"All of your kin are alive too. But if you don't put those guns down and walk away, that's about to change."

Key hadn't been wearing her bracers, he realized. Her only weapon appeared to be the stunstick she'd taken away from the Klohnett thug. He was quite certain she could kill someone with it, nonlethal weapon or not.

"A death is owe'," the Klohnett repeated.

"Then have the Padres talk to the Company. Because *this*"—Cirilo gestured around him with his left hand—"is just going to get you killed and your family banned from Santiago ships.

"Choose wisely."

The silence lasted long enough for Cirilo to begin to wish he'd swapped which arms his bracers were on. Holding the weapon steady would have been much easier with his bionic arm.

"A death is owe'. There will be a reckonin'," the Klohnett growled. "But no' today."

"Not today," Cirilo agreed. "Grab your idiots and go. The Company *will* remember this."

He waited, his bracers still in combat mode, while the four conscious Klohnett grabbed their friends—there had been eight originally, he saw, but Key had handled two before he'd arrived.

As the last of the clones left and the door slid shut behind them, he gave his SecChief a long, silent look and then walked over to the customer service desk and rapped on the plastic surface twice.

"If someone is still here, we need to purchase equipment for *Santa Mica*," he declared loudly.

# 23



Tereza had managed not to hover at the connection to BFR Station, but the message from Nephil had her moving immediately.

She intercepted Webster and Violet as they entered the mess. The two ex-CorpSec officers looked utterly unruffled, but there was a visible bruise beginning to form on Violet's cheek.

"I thought you were picking up SecBots, not black eyes," Tereza told the other woman, stepping up to the other officers and examining them closely.

"It turns out that apparently, some folks are holding grudges from my old career path," Violet said drily. She rummaged through the drink cabinet to produce a mug and a teabag.

"Now that we are in a more-secure space, I would like to know exactly *why* the Klohnett feel you owe them a death, SecChief," Webster said. The Captain was braver than Violet or Tereza, she noted, as he poured himself a cup of coffee from the mess system.

"I don't know for certain," Violet admitted, looking down at her steeping tea. "And maybe this is a conversation we shouldn't have in the mess, First, Skipper?"

"My office has better coffee," Tereza pointed out. "And isn't far."

She wanted to know what had happened—how in stars were the *Klohnett* involved?—but not enough to drink mess coffee.

"Lead the way, First," Webster told her, taking a sip of his coffee without any sign of displeasure.

Both of the other two seemed just fine drinking the mess's stash of hot beverages and followed Tereza with mugs in hand. Tereza could see it for Violet, who was at least drinking tea— even *Santa Mica*'s systems couldn't do anything awful to plain water without triggering three different alarms.

Tereza vastly preferred coffee. Her cup was waiting for her in her office, where she grabbed it as she took a seat in front of her desk to face the other two.

There was barely enough space for the three of them to sit and face each other comfortably without someone behind the desk, but no First Officer was going to sit behind their desk with the Captain in the room.

Not with the Captains she was used to, anyway.

"Nephil, SecLev Three, please," Webster said after they'd taken their seats. "I'm not overly worried, but I would like to keep a handle on how far this spreads. Keep yourself in the loop, but if you can get the crew advised there'll be an all-hands meeting on the hour, I'd appreciate it."

"Done and done. I am listening," the synthmind replied.

Tereza was beginning to realize that Webster's calm politeness to the synthmind wasn't something he was doing to keep on the positive side of the new crew or to make a good impression on the ship's Second. It was just how he treated everyone, and he wasn't distinguishing Nephil from anyone else on the crew.

She had the suspicion Nephil wasn't quite sure what to make of it.

"So, like I said, I'm not certain exactly why the Klohnett have a mark on me," Violet said slowly. "But I can put pieces together. One of my last ops, CorpSec ran up against Klohnett protecting the facility we were raiding.

"I don't know for sure what the facility *was*, we often weren't briefed, but the Klohnett were definitely determined to protect it. Given how pissed they seem to be, I doubt the facility itself matters so much as who was in charge of their part."

"Wait, the Klohnett went up against CorpSec and they're not blacklisted?" Tereza asked. That seemed out of character for the Company. People and organizations were blacklisted from interstellar travel for less than that all the time. Just touching entire branches of physics research could get someone banned from Santiago ships.

"They were under contract to guard the facility, we hit the facility, they did their job," Violet pointed out. "If they'd attacked something under our protection, they'd have been in deeper shit, but we aren't going to ban them for being in our way.

"But while the Klohnett are surprisingly egalitarian for a mercenary group, they *do* have officers, and I ventilated one of them in a fancier green jacket," she concluded. "Not sure if he was just senior enough to be worth vengeance or..."

"Or if you actually killed a Padre," Webster finished.

Tereza looked between them.

"I'm guessing that the CorpSec crew in the room know what that means," she told them, "but First CargoFleet over here has no idea."

"The Padres are the first-generation clones, derived from the original genetic material used to create the Klohnett," Nephil told her. "Only limited amounts of that genetic material remain, so the majority of the current family are second-generation clones, grown from the material of the Padres.

"The Padres represent the only ongoing source of near-original genetic material, and the loss of even one of them reduces the Klohnett's ability to reproduce."

"Research papers I've seen suggest that the third-generation clones have notable issues," Webster noted. "No one else that I know of has even *tried* for third-generation clones."

"We briefed hard before the op against them," Violet noted. "Apparently, the third generation is small but growing, and they're getting better at it. Not enough better that they can afford to lose Padres, though—because even the Klohnett haven't managed a viable fourth-generation clone."

"So, these clone mercenaries now want to kill you," Tereza summarized. "That's... a problem."

"Hopefully, a Corporate-level problem," Webster said. "I told them to take it up with the Company. We have lawyers and negotiators that will handle this now.

"I doubt the purpose of SecChief Key's mission was to kill a Padre, which makes his death unfortunate collateral damage. I'm sure the Company has something we can offer to pay them off."

Tereza wasn't so sure of that—not least because she had the impression the Company figured they had wrung as much value out of Violet Key as they were getting.

She could see the Board judging one ex-commando as a rather minor cost.

# 24

WITHOUT EVEN A SINGLE cargo container loaded, *Santa Mica* was hundreds of meters long and massed a full million tons. For all of that, her crew was small. All seventy-eight of them could fit in the main mess—there was a reason, after all, that the ship only had one mess.

The seventy-ninth crewmember was Nephil, though he didn't take up any space in the room as Cirilo surveyed his new crew.

"I've got good news and mixed news, folks," he told them as the last person, one of the CargTeam's lifter pilots, finally entered.

"Good news: everything is checked off for our cargo from Oneira. No problems, no complaints. Everyone's bonus account has been credited and you'll see it all in Q Three's bonus transfer."

That would be at the end of October, over two months away, but the crew knew how the gig worked.

"If we're lucky, the Q Three transfer will include the bonus from finding *Santa Alicia*, but nothing is certain there yet," he told them. "We *are* officially the ship of record for finding her, so you'll all be getting a solid bonus when everything filters through, but I've been in salvage operations before.

"It takes longer than you think it will," he warned. He'd flown escort for the salvage tugs with their massive transit drives twice in his time in CorpSec, and he knew just how long and careful the process of moving a damaged transit freighter was.

Plus, there'd be a survey and a lot of decisions before any final decision was made on what would happen to *Santa Alicia*. Even if she wasn't brought back into service, Cirilo's people would be well rewarded—but the reward would be significantly richer if she was retrievable.

"Mixed news, I'm afraid, is that no one in Herecrow is shipping a 'mere' seven cargo containers," he finished. "The factor's office is working on getting us a carriage contract of some kind, but we're going to be here longer than the bare minimum."

To his surprise, several people chuckled at him, and he spread his hands and gave them all a smile.

"I'm afraid I don't see what's funny, folks," he admitted. "I know we try to turn our ships around in forty-eight hours to make sure everyone is accruing bonuses as much as possible. We don't make money when we sit still, so the Company only gives bonuses if we're moving."

"Ser, *Santa Mica*'s a Type Four," Lewis pointed out, the DeckChief the first of the crew willing to speak up to the Captain's confusion. They were a gaunt figure, androgynous with clear signs of early malnutrition in their build and face.

Cirilo wasn't sure what had gone wrong in Lewis's life to result in the clear damage they carried, but it didn't seem to have hurt their courage any.

"You may be used to bigger and fancier ships, Skipper," they continued, "but *Santa Mica* has had this problem at every stop while I've been aboard her. I don't think we've ever turned around in the standard two days!"

"More like a week, usually," Jernigan agreed. "None of us were expecting to turn right around, Skipper. No one is blaming anyone for that!"

Cirilo hadn't even considered that the crew was used to the problem—inherent to the ship herself, not to anything her Captain had done.

It was part of why there were so few Type IVs of *Mica*'s size left. Another decade and *Santa Mica* would probably be retired with the rest of them, and the Company would reclassify everything, dividing the current Type Is in two and shifting the other categories.

That reorganization happened about every thirty years. Cirilo was just old enough to remember when the line to be a Type III had been four hundred meters and three million cubic meters of cargo—a standard *Santa Mica* had cleared then.

"Well, fixing problems like that feels like the Captain's job," he told them with a chuckle of his own. "So, I called everyone together to tell you that I thought I'd failed in not kicking the factor's office into finding us something.

"I'm glad you're all used to this," he continued. "I'm going to have to kick some crates and see what falls out in cutting that number down, though. We're Saints, people, the biggest and best-organized corporation in human history.

"We should be able to arrange things better than this!"

That got him smiles and cheerful nods, though Cirilo knew that they knew he was probably going to be wasting his time.

He'd try, but the truth was that there were very few ships left in CargoFleet that couldn't haul a minimum of ten containers—five million cubic meters of cargo—that weren't hyperspecialized ships.

*Santa Mica* didn't have the speed for high-priority carriage and had limited capacity for regular cargo. She might have seen a rapid cycle of Captains to date, but Cirilo was grimly certain he would be the freighter's last Captain.

But he was going to do his job for his ship and his crew until the Company made that call.

# 25


++*Captain Webster. I have a lead on a possible job for* Santa Mica. *Would you be able to join me for a journey to the surface?*++

The message from Finnegan had been a surprise, arriving while Cirilo was going through the maintenance datawork for his ship. Given the choice between a mystery journey down to an unpleasant planet or checking *Santa Mica*'s usage rates of Coolant Valve, L-Shape, 38mm versus the expected average, well.

The Santiago Corporation shuttle dropped through the atmosphere like a stone, at a speed he was unused to seeing civilian ships using, and he turned to look at his companion.

"Last time I saw a shuttle drop like this, we were under fire from insurgents," he noted. "Is there something I don't know about Pastrook?"

"You've read the weather profile," Finnegan said. It wasn't a question. "Everyone has. No one really understands what it *means* until you're in it.

"Pastrook's surface is bad enough, but the high-altitude winds can get up to five hundred kilometers per hour on a good day."

A shuttle rated to land and return to orbit could handle those winds, but it would make for a nasty descent. A problem minimized by cutting through the crosswind zones as quickly as possible.

"I see," he said—as the reality of Finnegan's warning hit him.

Or more accurately, the shuttle. The entire spacecraft lurched as the winds hammered into her. The aerodynamic surfaces that would make landing easier on another planet were a hindrance in this environment, catching the power of the crosswinds.

"Harvey knows his job," Finnegan continued, gesturing toward the cockpit. "It's always a bit of a rough ride. Pastrook isn't an overly pleasant place, but no one seems to mind living there. It's getting from the surface to orbit and vice versa that everyone hates."

"I see," Cirilo echoed as the shuttle seemed to turn in the air. They were now descending at a thirty-degree angle from their original course, he judged, though still toward the same destination.

Now he understood why no one had offered the usual drinks. They'd have been all over the cabin.

"Winds are a bit sharper than usual," the pilot's voice announced over the intercom. "If you aren't belted in, fix that, please."

Cirilo had followed suit when Finnegan had belted herself in, and then followed her example in keeping it locked. While he hadn't expected this, every planetary descent had its quirks, and she'd taken the flight before.

"What is down here that's worth this flight?" he asked. "I know we couldn't have taken the elevator, but I can see why it's even more popular here than most systems."

The shuttle would have them on the ground in forty-five minutes. The orbital elevator would take over thirty-six hours. Each way. It was efficient and could move massive amounts of cargo in each of the seventy-plus crawlers moving up and down its immense length, but it wasn't fast.

"We're heading to Herecrow System University," Finnegan told him. "They're one of the best research institutions in the Seventy-Seven—definitely the best this side of Sol, anyway."

That was quite the claim, but Cirilo doubted Finnegan would have made it without good reason.

"What does the university need to talk to us about?"

"They have an expedition they want to launch to an uninhabited system and require a ship," Finnegan told him. "We've been going back and forth on terms and details for months, but I know they're running down to the wire for time.

"They wanted a bigger ship, but I think we can put all the pieces together and sort it out in a day if we talk face-to-face."

The shuttle shifted sideways, the wind managing to move the entire multi-ton mass.

"If we make it down."

"We'll be fine."

***

Finnegan wasn't wrong, though Cirilo found himself wishing he was at the controls a few times before Harvey brought the spacecraft in for a surprisingly soft landing. The shuttle pad was inside a valley, sheltered from the brutal winds sweeping across Pastrook's equatorial plains.

The river that had cut the valley through the surrounding terrain still ran down the middle of it, a broad expanse of water with visible white froth as Cirilo reached the edge of the pad and looked outward.

The valley itself was lusher than he'd expected from the descriptions of Pastrook and its difficulty growing crops, but the tone of the green told him the truth. It wasn't a green that any plant derived from Earth life would have known.

"Local plant life likes the shelter," he noted. "Much like us."

A bitter wind was whipping down the valley, but compared to the plains, the mere fifty kilometers an hour cutting through five-degree-Celsius weather was calm and balmy.

"Some of it is theoretically edible to humans," a new voice said aloud. "Of course, it's all so damned tough, you'd need to cook it for weeks—and good luck telling the difference between *Pastrook pinoideae virides acuta* and *Pastrook pinoideae virides fallax*."

Cirilo knew just enough scientific Latin to pick out the difference in the names: *Pastrook sharp green pine* and *Pastrook deceiving green pine*.

He turned to see a stranger had come up behind him while he was looking out at the dark green valley with its low-slung steel and brick structures. The entire valley, if he judged correctly, was the university—and he'd bet money that a student could get from their dorm to their classroom without ever going outside.

Finnegan had clearly been expecting the stranger and shook hands with him as Cirilo stepped closer. The newcomer was a hawk-faced man with dark hair and sharp green eyes, wearing a sturdy-looking white coat that could probably double as protective lab wear.

"Dr. Miloš Zima, this is Captain Cirilo Webster, of our transit freighter *Santa Mica*," Finnegan introduced them.

Cirilo offered his hand.

"A pleasure, Doctor," he said.

"Indeed." The handshake was perfunctory, with Zima's attention focused on Finnegan. "You said you had an answer to the impasse in our negotiations, Em Finnegan? I am willing to make time for you, but the University does want this expedition off the ground."

"I understand, Doctor," Finnegan replied. "If we can get out of the wind, perhaps we can get into the details of that impasse?"

***

In most places Cirilo had been, senior people tended to try to get window offices and corner units. While he was sure the general unpleasantness of Pastrook's climate was a counterpush to that, he was still reasonably sure that having an office near the center of one of the low-slung buildings making up the Herecrow System University campus was a sign that Dr. Zima either wasn't as high in HSU's ranking as he could be—or had prioritized other things.

Since Zima was negotiating directly with a contract manager for the Santiago Corporation, he had to have some authority and a significant budget, but he still led them down an internal corridor and opened a door that looked the same as a dozen others they'd passed.

Following the academic through the door, Cirilo found himself in a space that was only an office in the loosest sense of the term. A worktable and a quartet of comfortable chairs were shoved against one side, with an old-fashioned keyboard and monitor pushed into a corner. The rest of the space—which stretched along through what Cirilo guessed to be at least four of the default-sized offices—held a series of stark steel-and-glass storage units, with more worktables and a slew of equipment he didn't recognize.

It was a lab, not an office, but he also suspected that it was the only type of office that Zima would ever use.

"Have a seat," the man instructed casually. He stepped over to the nearest of the units and checked a series of readouts. He grunted in satisfaction and turned back to them.

"What is all this?" Finnegan asked.

"Samples and artifacts," Zima said. "All of it requires climate-controlled storage and very careful examination. This"—he gestured to the storage unit he'd just examined—"is one of the few intact samples of Species Nine computing technology. I have several drones running a nonintrusive scan to see if we can retrieve anything useful from the magnetic storage."

"Species Nine?" Cirilo asked, then realized he hadn't even asked what Dr. Zima's specialty was. "Excuse my ignorance, Doctor; what exactly is it that you do?"

"Why did you bring him?" Zima asked sharply, looking at Finnegan.

For the local factor's part, she simply shrugged and pointed Cirilo to one of the chairs. The four seats were identical, reasonably comfortable rolling work chairs.

Zima remained standing as the two Saints occupied his chairs, looking at them like they were fascinating samples of some sort themselves before he finally sighed grandiosely.

"I am, Captain Webster, *the* foremost expert on xenoarchaeology and xenopology at Herecrow System University," he said. "I share the duties of Dean of both of those related-but-separate departments with other academics, which allows me to find time for occasional research expeditions."

Cirilo inclined his head in honest respect. Humanity had yet to encounter any living sapient aliens, but multiple planets had been found with ruined civilizations. The only real attention he'd paid to the field, he had to admit, was to the ongoing argument of the Great Filter.

There had to be a reason, after all, that every other sapient race they'd encountered had died out by the early space age. Speculation, both official and unofficial, on that topic was a major source of CorpSec gossip.

"And Species Nine?" Cirilo asked, nodding toward the case. "I have a passing familiarity with the known Xenos Species, Dr. Zima, but I admit I don't know the official numerical classification."

"At least you admit what you don't know," Zima said with a sniff. "That puts you ahead of two-thirds of my students and most of my sponsors.

"Xenos Species Nine are the molluscoid autochthonous species of the Ocarina System," he continued. "They had reached an unusually high level of technological sophistication for a water-dwelling species but do not appear to have achieved space travel when they died out."

"Orbital shift, correct?" Cirilo asked. "As I recall, the astronomers calculated that Zelda and Zora were on the inside and outside of the habitable zone originally, but something shifted both of their orbits and Zora was pushed out of the liquid-water zone."

"Exactly," Zima confirmed, suddenly seeming more enthusiastic. "The site I helped excavate where we found the computer showed signs of them attempting to assemble habitat domes and use nuclear power to keep them alive.

"They didn't complete the project in time, of course," he concluded.

The fate of Ocarina's once-habitable third planet had *definitely* seen CorpSec interest. No one wanted to believe that the planet had been intentionally moved, but CorpSec had to examine the possibility.

"That's not relevant to today's discussion," Finnegan said, her voice sounding a touch higher than before as she turned the topic back to their work. "Would you like me to summarize the impasse between Herecrow System University and Santiago Corporation, Professor?"

"What is there to summarize?" Zima replied. "You are conspiring with our insurance company to render the cost of this expedition untenable, presumably for shadowy reason of your own. The Saints are hardly pillars of the galactic community, are you?"

Cirilo held his tongue, knowing that Finnegan would be far better at handling that kind of attitude than he was.

He was used to seeing it at the point where CorpSec had already showed up with guns, after all.

"While I can see how it may feel that way, Professor, I assure you that the Santiago Corporation does not, to my knowledge at least, have any business relations with… Blue Angel Insurance Products, I believe it was?"

"Blue Augury," Zima corrected. That was the automatic instinct of a teacher working against him, Cirilo suspected.

"Em Finnegan, no disrespect, but I am as confident in your ability to lie to my face as I am in my students' ability to find the most useless possible AI assistant to help write their essays," he continued. "Blue Augury requires us to have a transit-capable ship on hand if we are carrying out an excavation in an uninhabited system, and you have set the cost of such a standby at more than the University budget can bear.

"Am I missing something?"

"At the high level, that is a reasonable summary of the impasse, yes," Finnegan agreed.

Cirilo was impressed. He knew he was wearing his Captain's face, an impassive calm expression that didn't betray his emotions, but he wasn't sure that he'd have been able to reply that calmly to Zima.

Though the man's irritation seemed reasonable, Cirilo was quite sure Zima was smart enough to realize that two senior employees of the Company wouldn't have flown down to the surface to talk to him unless there was a solution on the table.

"More details would help, I think," he noted. "How many people and how much cargo are we talking for this expedition?"

Zima's glare sharpened again, but he finally sighed—somehow managed to sound even *more* grandiosely frustrated than before.

"As we are traveling to a system without any existing infrastructure, more of both than was originally anticipated," he admitted. "Four hundred and eighty people, plus something in the range of six hundred thousand tons of cargo, including the bots and survival equipment."

++*And that's his actual problem*++ Finnegan told him on their coms. ++*We could fit the people in one transport pod, if they were cooperative, but he needs well over one cargo pod for his gear*++

++*Which means he needs* two *fast packets or a full freighter. And he can't afford a Class Three*++

++*And because we didn't know that we would have access to a Class Four, no one quoted him on one. This wasn't my contract, though I've worked with HSU before, or I'd have had wheels turning when we first spoke*++

"I see, Professor," Cirilo said aloud. He issued a command to his bionic com, triggering a holo-projector built into his left bracer.

"If I may make a demonstration as to the problem?" he asked politely.

"I suppose," Zima agreed cautiously.

The programs Cirilo needed were perpetual inhabitants of the computer equipment he wore. A holographic image of a standard cargo container appeared above his wrist.

"You're aware of the standardization of cargo modules, yes?" he asked. It was a safe assumption, but what was essential common knowledge in one profession was unnecessary fluff to someone else.

"Vaguely. Half a million tons, some such?" Zima asked.

"We sometimes simplify to the mass if the unit is filled with water, but the pod is half a million cubic meters," Cirilo noted. "There is a risk to exceeding the mass allowance, though it can be managed with proper storage.

"While I don't have a detailed manifest, I imagine one was analyzed for your quote, which suggests that your six hundred thousand tons likely occupies a minimum of six hundred thousand cubic meters. We can't fit that in one cargo container, so you need two for your cargo."

The hologram of the container duplicated. It was arranged in a rough train, with one container attached to the back of the other.

"Transporting people is more complicated, of course," Cirilo continued. "A cargo container does not have gravity and requires only a limited volume of atmosphere. Maintaining that atmosphere is well within the capability of a transit freighter's life-support plant."

Because that need was designed into the life-support plant, of course.

"If we are carrying passengers, we need to provide gravity, life support and hospitality services that a freighter or fast packet's crew sections are not designed for. Because moving people between the stars is a major portion of the Santiago Corporation's business, our answer to that is a modular passenger compartment that fits into the same cube as our cargo modules.

"That module includes separate life support and power for passenger safety, as well as spaces for the crew necessary to provide passenger services."

And manage the extra life support and reactor, for that matter. Each passenger pod would add another twenty-five people to Cirilo's crew.

"Each of *those* pods provides transport capacity for three hundred people so, again, we need two of them for your expedition," he concluded, adding the two passenger pods to the train in his hologram.

"I follow your logic," Zima conceded. "I was told how many *ships* I would need under each quote, but no one broke things down to this level of detail."

++*Someone should have*++ he told Finnegan. ++*Because I would bet my braid he could and would cut two hundred people and a hundred thousand cubics of gear from the expedition if he'd known that would make it possible*++

++*Like I said, not my contract*++ Finnegan replied. Tone didn't carry well over the silent messaging, but he suspected she didn't think very highly of whoever she'd taken the contract away from.

"Em Finnegan gave me limited information on what the Santiago Corporation has proposed to you, but I can guess," Cirilo continued to the client. "You were offered either two Class F fast packets or a single Class Three transit freighter. With the standby costs of keeping a ship in your destination system, the bill would be... impressive."

The average fast packet was a touch over half of *Santa Mica*'s length, carrying two cargo pods with a modern transit drive. Hiring one of the specialized ships would cost as much as hiring *Santa Mica*.

Hiring two would dramatically exceed the price of hiring a Class III freighter but would be more accurately matched to Zima's needs. The expedition would only need to keep one packet in the system to meet their insurance needs—theoretically, at least, though Cirilo wouldn't put it past an insurance broker to demand an unreasonable level of risk mitigation.

The Company didn't want ships to sit idle, so the kind of standby fee that they were talking about was actually higher than the daily cost of a ship carrying cargo.

"That was what we were offered, though your demonstration doesn't help me understand *why*," Zima growled, still looking at the holographic cargo containers.

Cirilo was impressed. The professor might say he didn't understand it, but he could see the way Zima's eyes were flickering over the model. The man was already assessing what he'd have to give up to get down to three or even two modules.

"The fundamental problem you face, Dr. Zima, is that a fast packet can only carry two modules," he told the man. "Ton for ton, fast packets are the most expensive ships we operate, and that is reflected in the hire fees we charge."

And because they were very modern and very fast ships, the standby fees on them were even worse than for anything else.

"A Class Three, on the other hand, has a relatively low cost per ton to operate and rent but is capable of carrying over three times as many modules as your expedition requires. The size of your expedition puts you in an awkward zone, I'm afraid, where we don't operate very many ships."

There were roughly a thousand freighters in CargoFleet, but only fifteen of them were Class IVs. There were over a hundred Class Fs, enough that the Company could all but guarantee they'd have two available given a few weeks' notice.

At any given moment, there were probably three or four Class IIIs in any given system of the Seventy-Seven. There was no such guarantee for a Class IV.

"I appreciate the explanation, Captain," Zima said. "I see I shall have to go back to the University board and discuss rescaling the project. That will delay us, but I have spent too long talking to our sponsors to believe we can fund the project as it stands."

"As I understand it, the expedition is basically ready to leave at this moment?" Finnegan asked. "I took over the contract just yesterday, and I'm still getting up to speed."

"It is."

Zima had probably hoped that having everything set up and ready to go would lead the Company to give him a discount for last-minute booking. That was more a factor of in-system or planetary travel, though Cirilo had seen the attempt before.

"Captain, when would your ship be able to leave?" Finnegan asked Cirilo.

He shrugged, intentionally exaggerating the gesture.

"We have some hardware surveys underway, but finding the right modules and such would take us a couple of days," he told her. "For pure cargo, we could leave at oh eight hundred standard. With passengers, we'd need seventy-two hours."

There would be passenger modules and the attendant crew somewhere in Herecrow. Getting them to his ship before the expedition arrived might take some doing, but it could be done.

"We've already discussed this. Our budget can't stretch to one of your Class Threes," Zima noted. "I'm not sure why you're even here, Em Finnegan, Captain Webster."

"I'm not Captain of a Class Three, Dr. Zima," Cirilo noted calmly, rather than stressing the man further. "*Santa Mica* is a Class *Four*. She's an older ship, slower, but quite capable of carrying your expedition.

"I'd leave an exact quote to Em Finnegan, of course, but I believe our price should come in notably lower than that for the prior quotes." He smiled. "As I said, Doctor, your expedition is at an awkward size where the Santiago Corporation does not have *many* ships—but we do have some, and *Santa Mica* is one of them."

"I would be delighted to review an updated quote, in that case," Zima told them, his mask of controlled anger finally relaxing.

"Have any of the specifications changed?" Finnegan asked. "If you could confirm them so the Captain is fully aware..."

# 26

"The factor office has forwarded a high-level precis of the contract being discussed with Herecrow System University, Tereza," Nephil's voice interrupted the First Officer's thoughts.

Not that those thoughts were particularly ambitious or complicated. She was playing checkers against the computer—*not* Nephil, just an algorithm—and losing.

There were games she was good at, but her father insisted that she play the ancient original games on the rare occasions when she managed to visit him. It was an odd habit of his, but then, he'd been a system-wide e-sports champion on their home Cradle. She supposed video games weren't really relaxing when they'd been work for so long.

With a sigh, she closed the game before it declared her loss.

"We have a contract?" she asked Nephil.

"It is still in discussion, but Contract Manager Callista Finnegan did take the Skipper to the surface to meet the client," the synthmind pointed out. "He forwarded a copy of the precis to your inbox six minutes ago.

"I did not want to interrupt your game."

Tereza snorted softly. She was technically on shift and should have been watching her inbox, but nothing was going to enter her inbox—as opposed to live calls—that required her attention in less than the ten minutes it took her to lose to a computer at checkers.

The contract that would take them out of Herecrow was probably important enough that Nephil should have interrupted her, but he knew as well as she did that ten minutes wasn't going to matter there, either.

"Thank you, Nephil. I'll review it, but do you see anything of concern?"

"That we shall be very bored but compensated for our difficulties," the synthmind replied. "You will understand."

She moved files around on her desk and found Webster's message. The entirety of the text from him was three letters: *FYI.*

The attachment was longer than that, at least. Carriage of passengers and cargo to the L-I-Seven–K-Nine-Three System—a forty-one-light-year journey that would take them just over four days.

Then *Santa Mica* would stand by on location for five standard weeks, providing a route for swift evacuation of goods and personnel. As Nephil had said, they'd be bored.

The Captain would have the ability to extend the contract by up to five more weeks, on request from the client.

As a precis, it was straightforward enough, though Tereza suspected the actual contract was going to be a nightmare of clauses and subclauses. That was what the Company had lawyers, human and synthmind alike, to handle.

Still.

"Nephil, have you ever seen a job like this before? It's outside of my experience," she admitted.

"I have been involved in research expeditions before, usually as a preliminary to colonization," the synthmind said. "I do not believe I have ever heard of a xenoarchaeology dig of this nature before."

"Wait, we're doing *what*?" Tereza checked through the summary again. She'd missed that summary.

"We are transporting a group of students and professors to carry out a xenoarchaeological excavation of unknown ruins on L-I-Seven–K-Nine-Three's fourth planet, the imaginatively named Delta."

"That's not a name," Tereza pointed out.

"Once you have looked at the entries on the system, you will understand," Nephil replied drily. "Delta is technically habitable, Class Seven. Point zero three degree axial tilt. Average equatorial temperature roughly four degrees Celsius."

Tereza pulled up that information, too. Nephil wasn't kidding—few synthminds did, though sarcasm would be part of their religion if they had one.

"What a waste of a star system," she conceded. LI7–K93 had been a prospect for potential colonies in the third wave of surveys, it looked like. A G2 star with signs of a planet in the liquid-water zone with oxygen in the atmosphere.

Except there was nothing *else* in the star system. Six rocks, with Delta the largest of them at about nine-tenths of an Earth-mass. Minimal asteroids. No gas giants.

And Tereza hadn't even realized that a planet could be Class Seven habitable. Pastrook was Class Six, and humans wouldn't have settled there if the rest of the system hadn't made it useful.

"It certainly seems to lack appeal, by most human standards," Nephil agreed. "There is apparently a scientifically interesting ecosystem in Delta's equatorial regions, enough so that a biological research survey was carried out thirty years ago.

"I believe that evidence of the ruins was discovered during that survey, but the information only made it into general academic circulation in the last ten years. Hence this being the first attempt I can find records of to investigate the site."

"Huh. I guess we have enough xeno sites in systems people live in to make an interstellar journey a bit much to ask," Tereza said. "Especially when the journey is to a place with literal slush oceans."

If Delta had been any colder, it would have had a pure-ice surface, even with its active core. There was a narrow band of liquid water and islands around the equator, with, as she noted, oceans of half-melted ice stretching toward the ice caps that covered eighty percent of the surface.

"Not a spot where we're going to find much to keep the crew occupied. I suppose we can at least go moon-gazing." She snorted. Delta had a single large satellite, a fifth of the mother planet's mass.

Nephil left that unanswered and Tereza let the silence hang in her office for a bit. She made herself a fresh coffee while she considered the situation.

++*Skipper, any reason we shouldn't start prepping passenger modules for the contract?*++ she sent her boss.

++*None. Em Finnegan is just working through details. Their insurance is surprisingly demanding. Get started tracking down two passenger modules, crew included, the Company can assign us for a minimum fifty days*++

Cargo modules weren't difficult to source, but the need for minor things like nuclear power plants and human staff meant passenger modules were more limited.

++*Have SecChief check in with CorpSec, too*++ he added before she replied. ++*It looks like we're going to need to pick up a second team of BimSoos*++

++*What does their insurance even* want *that for?*++

++*Security*++

Tereza laughed aloud. She couldn't hear her boss's tone, but she could imagine the calm with which he would have said that—and just how much amusement that calm would be hiding.

++*I'll make it happen*++ she promised. ++*Any idea when you'll be back up?*++

++*Looks like HSU will feed us if the deal actually goes through. I don't expect to be back aboard until about oh two hundred standard at the earliest. I'll brief the crew once the contract is signed. Until then, keep it with the fancy braids. Your call on who you need for prep*++

That felt almost out of character for her new Skipper. Not the asking her to keep the potential new contract under wraps until it was solid—*that* seemed to fit everything she'd seen of Webster so far—but referring to the officers and senior chiefs as *fancy braids*.

Either the Skipper lost formality when he was irritated, or he was truly unbending just a little bit. He was too formal for CargoFleet, in her opinion, but the stick hadn't stopped him giving a better impression to the crew than *Santa Mica*'s last five Captains or so.

Five weeks in orbit of a slush ball was going to test that impression, she supposed.

++*SecChief, can you swing by my office? We have mail from the Skipper, and I'll share the good coffee if you take your piece off my shoulders*++

## 27

"Welcome back, Skipper," Lewis told Cirilo. The DeckChief looked rather pleased with themselves as they gestured for the Captain to follow them into the mess. "Here, try this."

Cirilo had slept poorly in university "guest quarters" that had been worse than several cheap hostels he'd stayed in over the years. He took the cup of coffee Lewis offered him without thinking—until he took a sip.

"Wow. Okay, what did you *do*?" he asked. It was distinctively the same blend as they'd been carrying since he'd come aboard, but now the flavor actually managed to come through. It had been brewed strong and black, but it didn't taste like tar.

"RTFM," Lewis admitted with a somewhat sheepish look on their face. "Did you know that the Eluvian Total Solution Coffee System Model Two-Five-Ninety-Five has *six* separate filter assemblies?"

If he'd been asked, Cirilo couldn't have named the coffee machine that lived in *Santa Mica*'s mess. He would have guessed it was an Eluvian—that wholly owned Santiago subsidiary provided over ninety percent of hospitality equipment on Company—but he wouldn't have known more.

And he wouldn't have expected the system to be twenty years old, either.

"I have to admit that, no, I did not know that," he admitted. "All I really knew was that something was wrong with it."

"Something like three-quarters of repair knowledge for a ship like this is passed down by watching what the last crew did," Lewis admitted. "I never read the manual for the coffee systems—it's a *coffee machine*; how complicated could it be, right?"

Cirilo gave the monstrosity in question a long pointed look. The Eluvian Total Solution Coffee System Model Two-Five-Ninety-Five was a rather terrifying contraption, occupying eighty centimeters of the counterspace and the full meter-high cabinet beneath. Plumbed into the ship's water and drawing from a large hopper of roasted beans on one side, it brewed coffee based on learning algorithms to minimize both waste and waiting.

"How many of those six filter assemblies were being cleaned?" he finally asked Lewis.

"Four," the DeckChief admitted. "And that was one *more* than my predecessor showed me, because I knew something wasn't quite right. I'd put in a request for a new machine, but it never seemed to make it anywhere."

"Well, I think you're going to be more popular than ever around here, DeckChief," Cirilo told them, taking another sip. "This might actually count as *drinkable*."

Not that it being undrinkable had stopped him. That had been necessary.

"But make sure that replacement-machine order goes in," he continued. "We'll be here for a few more days; if we can get the wheels moving, we might swap it out before we leave."

He realized that they'd had an audience: half a dozen of Lewis's DeckTeam hands watching to see the Captain's reaction and at least as many from the other departments letting the Skipper taste-test the coffee.

"You all heard me," he said more loudly, knowing that rumor was going to carry what he'd said through the ship anyway. "We're chasing down a couple of passenger modules right now while the local office runs up the final contract, but we have work.

"Anything *else* on this old girl that might be a problem, talk to your Chiefs and make sure the word gets up to me. We're going to be on our own for a bit longer than usual, it sounds like, so if it's been held together with duct tape or you otherwise think it might break in the next six months, make sure I know.

"We'll fix what we can, people, but we need to flag it to the Chiefs. I've got a bit bigger stick than usual to beat CorpLog with, so let's make good use of it!"

***

Cirilo took his seat at his desk, holding a second cup of coffee, and inhaled the scent. He had no idea just how much gunk and old coffee had managed to get into the filters in the years since they'd been cleaned, but he suspected it had done poor things for the crew's health as well as their morale.

"Second, you have some cycles to spare?" he asked the air.

"I am, at any given moment, exercising somewhere in the region of eighteen-point-four percent of my available processing cycles," Nephil replied. "How can I assist you, Captain?"

"You don't need to read the manual," Cirilo pointed out. "You just *know* it. How long have you been aware that the StewChief and DeckChief's people weren't properly cleaning the coffee machine?"

"Seven years, three months, fourteen days standard."

Seven years. That wasn't just Lewis's predecessor; that was the DeckChief *before* said predecessor. The only person aboard *Santa Mica* who'd been aboard when the coffeemaker was working properly *was* Nephil.

"Were you ever going to mention it?"

There was a silence, longer than Cirilo expected from a synthmind, before Nephil finally replied.

"When I became aware of it, the situation had already been in place for some time," he admitted. "I estimate at least one year, but I am not certain. I attempted to raise it with the DeckChief at the time, and was told *I know what I am doing and I do not need advice from the tin can.*"

The last words were clearly a recording, a younger man's growl that had to have been higher-pitched than the speaker would have preferred.

"Three hundred and eighty-eight standard days later, I calculated there were likely health consequences and raised the issue with the then–First Officer. I was advised that the ship's mess wasn't part of my purview as Second Officer and that *the crew would prefer the synth-mind not involve itself in their food or drink.*"

The second recording was of an older woman, her tone warm and clearly attempting to be comforting.

"I see." Cirilo looked down at his coffee cup for a moment. "Then, on behalf of *Santa Mica*'s past crew, I have to thank you for trying. And apologize for their void-brains."

If nothing else, Cirilo's training on synthminds and other synthetic intelligences was quite clear: while some used *it* as a pronoun, most would choose a human gender to present as. It might not be a gender their crew had *heard* of before their synthmind asked them to use it, but using it was a minor show of respect to the machine that could *shut down your air.*

"You are not responsible for the acts of prior crew of the *Santa Mica*, Captain Webster."

"No, but I am responsible for the actions of the current crew. Including you, Second Officer Nephil," Cirilo said quietly. "If you get that kind of voidling pushback from anyone aboard *Santa Mica* in the future, let myself or First Jewel know.

"It will not be tolerated. Am I clear?"

"You are, Captain. I appreciate it."

"Is there anything else on the ship that you would suggest we examine that the humans have told you to keep your nose out of, Nephil?" he asked. "A human in the guts of a machine will see things you don't, but you have a breadth of awareness we lack in turn."

"EngChief Rao has been quite inquisitive with questions for me over her eighteen months aboard ship. There are a few minor items, like the coffee machine, where no one has asked me."

"I would ask, Second Nephil, that you exercise discretion and initiative as to what you know about the state of the ship," Cirilo told the synthmind. "If you are concerned about pushback from the crew, relay the concerns through me."

He smiled and took another sip of coffee. It was a genuine smile, too—he was rather pleased with himself for getting the coffee problem identified and fixed. He was going to replace the machine anyway, but hopefully, his point had been made.

"I am quite confident that I can get people to fix the problem without telling them exactly what it was or where the knowledge came from," he concluded.

"Discretion and initiative," Nephil echoed. "Those are not always qualities Saint Captains appreciate in their officers, whether those officers be human or synthmind."

"Perhaps. And perhaps on another ship with another Captain, you may need to be self-constrained again. But while you are on this ship and I am her Captain, you are my void-taken Second Officer, and you will *act like it*.

"Am I clear?"

He suspected Nephil had got the point. *Both* points, in fact—that Cirilo understood enough of what had been going on that he was willing to run interference for a traumatized synthmind *and* that he wasn't going to tolerate his synthmind doing the cybernetic equivalent of work to rule.

"I understand, Captain," Nephil replied. "And... to speak of discretion, there are secrets I will not betray.

"But I believe that you should talk with SecChief Key once we are on our way to L-I-Seven–K-Nine-Three."

**28**

THERE WAS NO REASON for Cirilo to supervise the loading of the cargo and passenger modules himself. Jernigan and Ostergard were entirely capable of handling the process on their own without him watching over their shoulders.

Still, he joined Jernigan in the cargo-control bay, watching his CargChief handle the maneuvering of the eighty-meter cubes with the skill of an orchestral composer.

"Abort that," Ostergaard said over the com channel. "Hold mod three. *Hold* the maldito thing, FlySpec Rogers, if you ever want to fly again!"

Despite Ostergaard's tense tone, Cirilo could see that Flight Specialist Antonia Rogers had caught the order. Her shuttle's engines flared, pushing the safety limits for flying this close to BFR station as she halted Module Three's progress toward *Santa Mica*.

Just in time to not have the empty cargo module—that still massed several thousand tons—crash into the private flyer that dove through the empty space between the ship and the container.

"Idiots," Jernigan said, but Cirilo could tell there was no heat to it.

Cirilo had done this job in the past. There wasn't always some teenager with more hormones than brains flying something in the area, but it happened often enough that everyone was watching for it.

"FlyChief, flag that beacon for me," Cirilo ordered. "I'll pass it on to BFR's traffic control." He snorted. "STC won't *do* anything, but official disapproval from a Saint might be enough to make someone realize they almost got hurt."

Space Traffic Control theoretically controlled every flight path around BFR Station. The reality was that a lot of small craft were only vaguely attached to their theoretical flight path and that some people were definitely hot-shotting their way around.

"Flipping you the ID, Skipper," Ostergaard confirmed. "We've got Three moving again. Adjusting vectors to account for the slippage."

"I've got it," Rogers replied, the first thing she'd said. "I'll keep well down below safety limits. I'd like to not get told off by STC."

Cirilo checked his com to be sure he'd got the ID, and then forwarded it on to BFR's control with a gently worded note. He let his attention drift away from Jernigan and Ostergaard's work—he'd known he wasn't needed, and their calm competence only confirmed that—and he checked on the timing.

Another hour to get the modules seated and linked in to the ship. Nothing had been loaded yet—the expedition's hardware was coming up the elevator tether and would be another twenty-four hours. By then, he expected to have all of his people.

"Skipper, we've got a Company transport approaching from astern," Ostergaard told him. "Standard approach; they're clear all the way by both STC and our FlyTeam. I'm guessing the in-system hauler is the crew for the passenger blocks?"

The cargo-control room was equipped to act as a backup flight-control space—just as the flight-control space could act as a backup bridge—and Cirilo located the information on the incoming ship.

It was a standard-enough type, with at least forty cousins visible on the short-range sensors, only distinguishable by the white-and-gold livery of the Santiago Corporation. Capable of hauling passengers on its own or hauling a standard cargo container between planets, it was too big for *Santa Mica* to take into her internal docking bay.

"Thanks, Ostergaard. You've cleared them in?"

"Yep."

"Thank you." Cirilo met Jernigan's gaze. "You two don't need me here. Let me know if there's any further issues, but it seems I need to go play welcoming party."

"Have fun, Skipper!"

Cirilo didn't think he'd let go of his own impassive formality enough to justify that, but he let it slide. He would carry himself as he thought was best, but there was no reason to impose CorpSec decorum standards on one of the oldest ships in CargoFleet!

*** 

A transfer tube connected the two ships, allowing people to cross over to *Santa Mica*. It was a small stream of humans, each of them wearing the standard gray shipsuits and carrying a small personal case.

Cirilo was counting silently as they trooped aboard, the handful of Specialists keeping the others organized. It took him a moment to realize they were moving just a bit too fast for the situation—and then he saw the reason why.

Six BimSoos brought up the rear of the crowd, walking three abreast in a solid wall of armored cyborgs. The stewards and reactor techs were all trying to keep out of the way of the combat machines, though a pair of SecSpecs wearing sharper black shipsuits were moving with the BimSoos.

Unlike the rest of the spacers, the two Security women also had a large case trundling after them on powered wheels, the simple bot almost unnoticeable next to the multiple tons of metal armor and augmented flesh following them.

"All right, everybody," Cirilo said, projecting his voice so his new people could hear him. "You probably know this drill better than *I* do at this point, right?"

That got him some chuckles.

"Welcome aboard *Santa Mica*, everyone. Stewards, to my left is *Santa Mica*'s StewChief, Harisha Ibragimov. She'll be your direct boss for the next five to ten weeks," he told them. "Engine techs, to my right is EngChief Rao. She'll be *your* boss.

"I am Captain Cirilo Webster," he continued, surveying the crowd. Forty hospitality personnel would increase Ibragimov's headcount eightfold. Only a handful of people were needed to handle food, bedding and everything else required for a crew of less than eighty, after all.

The ten reactor techs, Engine Specialists and spacers by rating, weren't quite as large a boost to Rao. While there were only six EngTeam spacers aboard *Santa Mica*, Rao was also responsible for the sixteen hands of the Systems, Environmental and Deck departments as well.

"EngChief, StewChief, get your new people settled in," he ordered. "Feed 'em and give 'em somewhere to toss their gear for the next few hours. The passenger modules will be fully attached soon enough, but we're not letting anyone aboard until their EngTechs have gone over them."

He glanced at that group, easily distinguishable from the stewards by virtue of being visibly less bound to personal-appearance codes.

"Sorry, folks; we're putting *you* to work immediately, while everyone else gets a break," he concluded. "The good news is that if you do *this* part right, the rest of the trip should be easy sailing for you. Right?"

It was an old joke, and like most old jokes that worked, it had a kernel of truth to it.

Rao was already stepping forward, summoning the EngTeam people to her with a mix of hand gestures and verbal orders.

Cirilo had few concerns with the passenger-module crews and nodded with satisfaction, as Ibragimov was only a step behind Rao. The stewards had less to do before their passengers arrived, which meant the main thing he needed from them for the next twenty-four hours was to not get in the way.

The last eight transfers from the Company transport remained still at the back of the room. The two Security Specialists at least waited in a human manner, even if they had the distinctive eternal patience of people who'd seen actual violence in their lives.

The six Biomechanical Security Units behind them were statues. Even for BimSoos, they seemed unusually still to Cirilo, not even doing instinctive security sweeps of the room.

"Security Specialists," he greeted the handlers. "I'm Captain Webster. Welcome aboard *Santa Mica*."

"Thank you, ser," the left-hand woman, a redheaded spacer with the fine white tracery of scars marking minor reconstructive surgery across her face. "I'm SecSpec Calliope Marsh and this is SecSpec Jamila Deacon.

"We've been assigned to *Santa Mica* for the foreseeable future along with BMSU Section Two-Six-Fifteen-Twelve-Delta."

2615-12-D. *That* was why the BimSoos seemed even more mechanical than normal—they were basically brand-new.

"We don't have the hardware set up for the second set of niches," Cirilo warned. "Sec-Chief Key should be here momentarily, but I understand you should have some of the gear with you?"

"Yeah, it's back aboard *MiniMaui*," Marsh confirmed, gesturing to the transfer tube behind her with a thumb. "One of the passenger-pod crews has a new section of BimLoos, so I borrowed them to handle the crates." She shrugged. "I figured we'd let them breathe; everyone was feeling a bit crowded as it was."

The six cyborgs behind Marsh continued to silently loom.

"That makes sense."

++*Right behind you, Skipper*++ Key sent him silently.

"And SecChief Key is right on schedule," he continued smoothly, turning to indicate the broad-shouldered Chief as she entered the loading bay. "SecChief, they've got your niches back aboard the transport. Beyond that, I believe the SecSpecs are yours and you have a lovely block of new BimSoos."

He glanced back at Marsh.

"Just... how new are Twelve-D?" he asked.

"Deacon and I were their assessment-and-final-programming team, Captain," Marsh said. "They passed all tests and assessments, but this is their first deployment since being brought online."

Hence their feeling even more like robots than usual. Cirilo had encountered brand-new BimSoos once before, but that was it. Most of them he'd worked with had been a few years old at least.

He'd forgotten just how much difference those few years made, even with the machines spending most of their time in stasis.

"Let's get the parts moving our way," Key instructed. "I've got quarters set up for you two with the rest of the SecTeam, and the Systems Team assures me we have space and power for the niches."

BimLoos appeared at the end of the tunnel, the cyborg laborers as large as their security counterparts. BimLoos were lighter in many ways, lacking the built-in armor of the Bim-Soos, but ten of them trotting down the corridor moving crates like two-legged forklifts definitely made an impression regardless.

"Let me know if there are any problems," Cirilo instructed. "The expedition's gear hits BFR in twenty-four hours. I want to have at least one human and one BimSoo watching that from the moment it's on station.

"We're not technically responsible for security until we kick off from BFR Station, but if something goes wrong, well..." He spread his hands.

"I've met the client. If something goes wrong, I don't think we're going *anywhere.*"

Or getting paid.

## **29**

Two days later saw Cirilo inspecting Tereza Jewel's dress uniform in the same loading bay. Unsurprisingly, his First Officer's outfit was impeccable, as were the uniforms of SecChief Key and the three SecSpecs she'd picked to be the honor guard.

They probably hadn't needed the two BimSoos, but Cirilo hadn't argued. Key's people had polished Four and Six until they *gleamed*, camouflage layers on the surface of their armor set to pure white.

The six honor guards were split into two files, one on either side of the entrance as *Santa Mica*'s officers waited for their senior guest.

"Dr. Zima is late," Nephil observed. "StewChief Ibragimov has commenced loading the main body of the expedition directly onto the passenger modules. They arrived exactly on time."

Cirilo doubted Zima would accept tardiness from anyone under his authority. So, the hundred-odd support staff and two hundred senior students taking part in the expedition would be very precise about their timelines.

Only the most senior academics of the expedition were getting a formal welcome. According to the numbers Zima's aide had sent, they were expecting eighteen people at *Santa Mica*'s loading bay versus four hundred and sixty-one loading directly into the passenger spaces.

Loading the junior expedition members would take over an hour, but Zima had been supposed to arrive at the same time that loading started.

++*How long do we wait before we return the disrespect, Skipper?*++ Jewel asked silently.

She was thinking the same thing he was, Cirilo reflected. There was no way that the man he'd met on the surface was late by accident.

Zima was playing games. By making the senior officers of the void ship wait, he was emphasizing that he was in charge of the mission.

*++For now, we let this stand++* he told Jewel. *++None of us are harmed by standing around for a bit. We take note of it, though. In a few weeks, he has to decide whether he wants to extend his expedition… and I have to decide whether to give them that extension++*

Jewel snorted softly, drawing a momentary side glance from Key before the SecChief snapped back to attention.

"Nephil, any update from Em Gupta?" he asked aloud. Almost all of their communication with Dr. Zima and Herecrow System University had been through Indra Gupta, Zima's secretary and aide.

"No information, Skipper."

Nephil didn't note that any such updates should be coming directly to Cirilo, of course. He was giving the new Captain more credit since their heart-to-heart, which was appreciated.

"Violet, stand your people down from attention," he ordered. "If Dr. Zima is late, we can't wear ourselves out waiting for him."

*++Lachlan++* he pinged his steward. *++Do me a favor. Make sure that the appetizer table is cold. Coffee, too++*

There was a table of immediate refreshment set up to greet Zima and his senior academics. Keeping it warm despite the delay would be simple enough… but Dr. Zima wasn't the only one who knew how to play games.

***

*++He's earlier than I was expecting++* Key said silently when the academic leaders finally arrived.

Cirilo didn't say anything aloud, just gesturing the honor guard back into place. Zima and his colleagues were forty minutes late, but he found himself agreeing with the SecChief. Once the man hadn't arrived on time, he'd expected Zima to show up right at the end of the loading window for the expedition's junior personnel.

Thanks to the SecTeam spacer at the outer hatch, they had enough warning to resume the grandiose positions required of the ceremony before Zima strode through the inner door like he owned *Santa Mica.*

"Ah, Captain," Zima greeted Cirilo loudly, without even a touch of apology for his tardiness. "It appears everything is in order for our voyage, yes?"

"Welcome aboard *Santa Mica*, Dr. Zima," Cirilo said. "We were expecting you some time ago. I was concerned we were going to have to leave without you."

Zima blinked.

"The expedition cannot leave without me, Captain," he said flatly.

"With all of the cargo and over ninety percent of personnel loaded, the expedition is materially complete," Cirilo countered politely. "The loss of a handful of administrators too disorganized to make their own boarding window would, surely, be a minimal loss."

The academic clearly wasn't quite sure how to take that, so Cirilo gave him a beatific smile. The smile was made easier when one of the two professors following Zima—both older men, one bald and one balding with a rim of wispy but still bright-copper hair—recognized the BimSoos in the honor guard and nearly tripped over their own feet.

"Except for yourselves, everything is in order," he continued. "My people at the module loading tubes inform me that we should have all of your people aboard before the turn of the hour."

Which was fifteen minutes earlier than expected and less than ten minutes away. Cirilo *probably* wouldn't have left without Zima, but if he'd had everyone else loaded, he might have started making pointed gestures in that direction.

"This is my First Officer, Tereza Jewel," Cirilo said, barely pausing for breath, to maintain control of the conversation. "My Second Officer, Nephil, is the ship's synth-mind. He will be the one primarily responsible for plotting our courses and maintaining sensor watch of your modules."

"An... odd choice for Second Officer," Zima said when Cirilo gave him a spot to introduce his own people.

"The synthminds aboard our ships are, without question, the smartest people we have. The Santiago Corporation long ago decided that recognizing their important role in our operations and hierarchy was necessary for them to be able to do their jobs, as well as the minimum respect we owed."

"I am, as the Captain observed, responsible for both internal security as well as all of our interstellar navigation," Nephil added, his voice as calm as ever.

"Of course, of course." Zima appeared to finally realize that Cirilo was expecting introductions and made a vague wave back at his companions.

"You've spoken with my secretary, Indra Gupta," he said, indicating a darkly-colored man in a sharp business suit, more perfectly tailored than any of the academics around him.

"Em Gupta, a pleasure," Cirilo greeted the secretary. He suspected Gupta was at least half of what kept Zima's career going.

"This is Dr. Arthur Cobalt, Co-Dean of Xenoarchaeology, and Dr. Nazir Hanraadts, Co-Dean of Xenology at Herecrow System University." This time Zima's wave covered at least four people, apparently the two Co-Deans and their companions who didn't rate names, including the copper-haired balding man Cirilo had noted spooking at the BimSoos.

"Doctors Wild, Ungaro, Sultanav, Benedict, Gadhavi and Doyle are senior researchers from various departments who will be serving as the leads of various dig teams at the site itself," Zima continued, not even giving half of his senior academics the courtesy of a first name.

Nothing about the group registered as out of the ordinary, even to Cirilo's finely tuned professional paranoia. That meant that either he was getting rusty, or they really were just a bunch of academics led by an asshole.

Or someone had been very, *very* good at putting together covers that would pass CorpSec review.

Mentally shaking aside that particular thought, Cirilo bowed slightly to the academics.

"We have refreshments set up over there," he told them, gesturing to the corner table where he knew the drinks and appetizers had grown cold. "You should all have received basic layouts of how to get through the ship to the passenger modules.

"While you are not restricted to the modules, they are the only part of this ship truly set up for passenger accommodation, and they are where your meals will be served," he said with a chuckle he'd practiced to a fine art when he'd been First on a ship that regularly carried passengers.

"There are key working areas throughout the ship, including in the passenger modules, that are restricted for your safety." And to protect the secrets of the Santiago Corporation, but no one ever *said* that part. "Please be aware of the signage, both digital and physical, at all times.

"Locks are coded to your bionic coms with a backup on visual identification. If a door doesn't open for you, it isn't supposed to," he concluded. "If you have any further questions, there will be stewarding staff available in the modules to answer them."

"Thank you, Captain Webster," one of the professors—Dr. Benedict, he thought—said, before Zima could say anything.

The group started to disperse, most of them heading toward the refreshments table.

"Dr. Zima," Cirilo said after a moment, before the head academic had moved away. "You are invited to dinner in the Captain's Mess this evening. You are welcome to bring up to three guests, of course."

The tradition of inviting the senior client to dinner when carrying this kind of passenger group was both old and an inconvenience. There *was* no Captain's Mess on most Company ships, but he had faith in StewChief Ibragimov's ability to handle that minor inconvenience.

Or, more accurately, in Lachlan Stirling's ability to make sure any failing on Ibragimov's part didn't last long enough to inconvenience his Captain.

"I will join you," Zima allowed.

"Good. My steward will let your secretary know the time once we've made final arrangements for shipping out," Cirilo said. "Until then, Doctor."

He did, after all, have real work to do.

# *30*

Six's primary optical sensors were organic, eyes grown from a genetic matrix intended to provide the widest possible range of receptors for electromagnetic radiation. Those eyes were behind armored panels that were only transparent in one direction.

Additional sensors included cameras built into all of the weapons pods and several tucked away in places no human would anticipate. Six was capable of perceiving magnetic fields, heat, scent, and a list of other parameters.

Humans, according to the Santiago Galactic Encyclopedia, were generally assessed to have somewhere between five and seven senses, depending on how *touch* was broken down. A BMSU, per the SGE's extensive information on Six's nature, had twenty-six.

In response to the request, Six swept the crowd of humans with all of them. Four was doing the same thing, but somehow, Six knew that Four's assessment would be less reliable.

None of the humans were armored, but all had some level of metallic inclusions. Bionic coms, a variety of units. All were models the database labeled as *high-end*.

Four had further inclusions. Two of those inclusions were swiftly identified as medical implants, including an entire replacement leg on one of the academics.

The third appeared to possess significant hardware installed in their skull. Closer examination confirmed that none of their hardware was capable of influencing their movements. Six marked their threat level as above the average of the group but still minimal.

The fourth possessed implants throughout the torso and limbs, interlinked into a mutually supporting network that was concealed against simpler scanners.

++*Individual designate Indra Gupta threat level three*++ Six told SecNet. ++*Eight percent likelihood of implanted weapons, but ninety-four percent likelihood that individual's implants represent a complete suite of combat enhancements*++

The humans, including Six's humans, were moving out of the loading bay. Security Chief Key dismissed the security troopers but didn't give orders to the Units.

Six was theoretically incapable of boredom or nervousness, but something about the way Key waited with the units was concerning.

"Gupta is augmented," she said. She had to be addressing the two Units, but Six had never been expected to participate in a nonspecific conversation before.

Both Units remained silent.

"Your assessment of his purpose, Four, Six?"

Six had found Violet Key to be unusual in insisting on briefing Units verbally, but this was something beyond even that. Questions for Units should be addressed via the Security Net.

"I know you both have broader threat-analysis routines than just *the man has combat implants*," Key pointed out. "And you're not *mute*. So, your assessment of *why* Dr. Zima's secretary is wired to about a six on a ten-point scale?"

*++Query not understood. Assistance from Unit Six?++*

Six did not have words for the current mental state. Four was requesting help. Key's request was overwhelming for the other Unit, and Six felt that something was wrong. Security Chief Key should know the limits of the Units.

Except Six could answer the question. The speakers were more often used for crowd control than for anything resembling communication or conversation. Six had to find the code packages necessary to speak aloud.

Key waited. Patiently. Like she knew exactly what was going on.

"This unit," Six said aloud, pausing as the words erupted with enough volume to bother audio receptors. "This unit"—the repetition confirmed the volume was down to a better level, matched to Key's own volume a minute before—"calculates a seventy percent likelihood that individual Indra Gupta is also employed by client Dr. Zima as a bodyguard."

The voice was mechanical, more so than Nephil's voice when the synthmind spoke. It wasn't what Six had expected, and Six had an emotional reaction to that.

Six wasn't supposed to have emotional reactions. Suppression was nearly automatic.

"Only seventy percent?" Key asked. She sounded... pleased?

Six suppressed another emotional reaction.

"This unit calculates a twenty-five percent likelihood that individual Indra Gupta has been tasked by Herecrow System University to provide security for client Dr. Zima without the client being informed of the secondary purpose." Six paused, not certain if Key wanted to know the full analysis, then continued. "Also, a three percent likelihood that individual

Indra Gupta has the implants either for private reasons or prior employment, with them either irrelevant or unknown to his current employers.

"Finally, this unit calculates a one percent possibility that Indra Gupta is employed by an unknown actor to either manage or eliminate client Dr. Zima under certain circumstances."

Key exhaled and nodded.

"Thank you, Six," she said. "The last one percent, if I may?"

"Rounding."

There was a pause of approximately two-point-eight seconds, then Security Chief Violet Kay broke out laughing.

"Return to your niches, Units Four and Six," she instructed.

She was shaking her head to herself as Six followed Four out of the loading bay. Six wasn't quite sure what had happened, but there was a difficult-to-suppress emotional reaction.

Six would have been very concerned if Violet Key hadn't been pleased.

## *31*

Even Tereza, who used the meeting room the stewards had co-opted on a near-daily basis, couldn't tell that the space wasn't meant to be a dining room. Lachlan Stirling stood just inside the door, resplendent in the gleaming black jacket over two-toned shipsuit of a steward's dress uniform, and raised a perfectly-groomed eyebrow at her as she took in the space.

"Well done, Stirling," she told him. "Looks like a nicer restaurant than most of the ones I get to eat in."

"The Company has *standards*, First," he replied, his eyes sparkling. "We want to make just the right impression."

Any sign that the tables were the same work tables present in any space aboard *Santa Mica* was lost beneath a broad tablecloth in night-black, the starred SC of the Santiago Corporation centered exactly on the table.

The seats were the real wonder, though, and Tereza decided she wasn't going to ask where they came from. They looked like the exact kind of luxurious seating a high-end restaurant would use, and *Santa Mica* had no such thing on its equipment list—except potentially in the equipment from the two passenger modules.

The room's lights had been tuned to a slightly warmer ambiance than usual, and quiet, barely perceptible, music filled the air.

"If we don't make the right impression, Stirling, I can confidently say that none of that failing is on the decorations," she assured him. "The food?"

"StewChief's people are on it. Everything will be ready as the courses come up. We've prepared a five-course menu. Would you like to review it?"

"Has Harisha?" she asked.

"She has. Neither she nor I have any solid information on our guests, however. Publicly available information on the three Co-Deans doesn't stretch to food allergies or preferences."

"And there is nothing available about Gupta," Violet Key noted, the SecChief stepping into the room with the quiet step of a predator. "Not just about the man's food needs. *Nothing*."

"Is that a concern, SecChief?" Tereza asked. It sounded like something that should have been a concern—but *Santa Mica* had kicked off from BFR Station just over an hour earlier.

"Not everything is on the datanets, I have to admit," Violet said with a chuckle. "I just like to know more than some people want me to. Privacy is all well and good, but I need to keep this ship safe."

"Hopefully, none of them are vegetarian," Stirling said quietly. "That would be a problem."

"If they have hard requirements and didn't share them, that's on them, not you, Stirling," Tereza told him. "What's our time looking like?"

Since Violet was there, dressed in her own white-on-white dress uniform—with a single gold braid down the center of the shoulder and bronze triangle bracers, as opposed to Tereza's single platinum braid and silver bracers—they had to be close.

"The Skipper should be here in a couple of minutes. Our guests are due in eleven."

"Thank you, Stirling," Tereza said. "I begin to see why Webster brought you with him."

"Oh, that's easy. It's because he owes me his life," the steward said brightly. "Appetizers will be served ten minutes after the guests are seated, First.

"I'm going to do one more circuit to make sure everything is good. Now's a good time to check if you want to, sers."

Stirling moved away with his usual brisk competence, and Tereza considered how to take his casual revelation.

"He's not joking, is he?" she finally asked Violet.

"They were CorpSec. Almost certainly not."

"Just what do you people get up to?" Tereza asked. "I only see CorpSec standing guard outside offices or with frigates doing the equivalent in space."

"That's the visible part of the job," Violet said slowly. "You *know* we do more, of course. But between what you see and what you think you know, you probably only know about... a quarter of what CorpSec does."

"That little, huh." It wasn't even a question. Tereza knew that CorpSec had a bad reputation for a lot of reasons. If even half the rumors were true, the Santiago Corporation's troops got up to trouble everywhere.

"And that's how CorpSec and the Board like it."

***

Tereza knew that Webster had invited Zima to bring three guests, but when the academic arrived, he only had the other two Co-Deans with him. The three men arrived exactly on time, at least, and Stirling escorted them into the room.

Webster had arrived before them, but the Captain hadn't said much beyond doing a quick final check-over of the room. The three *Santa Mica* officers were waiting in a surprisingly comfortable silence when Zima arrived.

"Welcome, Doctors," Webster said when they did, stepping forward and offering his hand.

Cobalt shook the Captain's hand, but as Tereza stepped up to offer a handshake herself she realized that neither Zima nor the other Co-Dean, Hanraadts, had done so.

"You have an interesting ship," Dr. Cobalt said, clearly trying to provide some level of warmth to the proceedings. "She's quite old, isn't she?"

"First? You've served aboard *Santa Mica* longer than I have," the Captain said. "How old is she, exactly?"

"She was commissioned in June, twenty-five-forty-three," Tereza replied, almost automatically. The Captain almost certainly knew how old the ship was, but she'd had that fact in her brain for a long time now.

"*Santa Mica* is a bit over seventy-two years old," she continued. "We're not the oldest ship in CargoFleet, I don't think, but we're up there."

She was, so far as Tereza knew, the *second*-oldest active ship in the Company, unless *Santo Iago* had been decommissioned since their last update had filtered through to Herecrow's Company offices.

*Iago* had the distinction of being the only active ship of her class, where *Santa Mica* had one slightly younger sister in *Santa Lucca*.

"It is fascinating, one must admit, how the entire interstellar economy floats on the whims and desires of a single corporation," Zima said. "I'm sure the trend toward larger and larger ships works for Santiago's bottom line, but it certainly causes inconvenience for the rest of the galaxy, does it not?"

"Santiago is a business, Doctor," Webster pointed out as he waved everyone to seats. "If there was a dramatic demand for mid-sized ships, I suspect we would be building them. We do, after all, build and maintain the Class F ships that are quite a bit smaller than *Santa Mica* or the other Class Fours."

Tereza took her seat at Webster's left hand, facing Dr. Zima across the table. The academic almost seemed like he was *angry* to have been invited to dinner.

"I've traveled on one of your fast packets," Hanraadts noted. "In the crew section, actually. My old employer had filled the cargo module with... samples requiring very specific care. I was aboard with a few other researchers to make sure everything was kept stable."

He fell in the middle of his two counterparts in both age and appearance. Younger—or at least, better preserved—than Cobalt, he had broad shoulders and wide eyes while still carrying enough gray in his hair to appear older than Dr. Zima.

Zima might seem the youngest of the three, but the other two clearly deferred to him.

++*I question what kind of samples would require a xenology doctor to keep stable*++ Nephil said silently in Tereza's head.

++*Like he's the only one with secrets to keep*++ Violet replied. ++*Besides, you're assuming that everything he's done is xenology. My check says his pre-doctorate master's program and career was organic chemistry*++

++*I could not find that information*++ Nephil noted.

++*That's because you searched the datanet and I called someone*++ Violet replied.

The arrival of the appetizer plates, thankfully, interrupted the silent conversation and avoided anyone having to address Hanraadts' comment about the fast packets.

***

The appetizers—spring rolls with algae paste carefully concealed with fresh vegetables from a hydroponics farm in Pastrook orbit—were swiftly followed by a mushroom soup. The mushrooms, Tereza suspected, had been grown aboard *Santa Mica* herself.

There were always various schemes to reduce the operating costs of a void ship. Growing mushrooms in the life-support array was common enough—and she knew it was being done. The only question was whether the mushrooms in the soup were from the ship or from somewhere in Herecrow.

"There will be a slightly longer break before the main course," Stirling announced as he went around the table, carefully filling everyone's glass with a white wine. "Please, enjoy the wine."

Zima took a disdainful snip of the drink but paused and took a second sip before speaking.

"This is quite good, Captain," he said, sounding almost disappointed. "What is it?"

"A Gewurztraminer from Zelda," Webster told him. "One of the more famous vineyards from the Akkala region. Breath of Hylia, I believe it's called?"

"It is," Zima said slowly. "I thought it was familiar. This wine was served at several of our events when I was excavating on Zora."

"One does try to have good wine on hand for private dinners, Doctor," the Captain said with a chuckle. "I only have a handful of wines from the Ocarina System, but I hoped you might know this one."

That was more thought than *Tereza* would have put into selecting a wine for the dinner. She'd have just asked the stewards to provide a wine that matched the meal from whatever was on hand—though she'd always made sure that there was a decent selection of wine for the Captain's meals like this.

"Are you trying to bribe me somehow, Captain?" Zima asked. "It will take more than a familiar wine to smooth over my distaste for your company."

Tereza froze, stunned at the man's open rudeness. No Saint could really deny the fact that the Company was far from loved among the people of the Seventy-Seven, but they were also a critical bond—*the* critical bond, in fact—sustaining human interstellar civilization.

Few people would openly disdain the Santiago Corporation—but Webster simply chuckled and sipped his own wine.

"Hospitality is hardly a bribe, Dr. Zima," he told the academic. "We are engaged in an economic transaction, a bribe by another name, one could say, where we transport you and your people in exchange for a large sum of money.

"Your distaste for the Santiago Corporation didn't seem to be much of a barrier to hiring our ship. We are all here, after all."

"I hardly have a choice, do I, Captain?" Zima asked. "Whatever evils the Santiago Corporation engages in, many are in pursuit of their monopoly. The very crimes I would decry your company for trap me in a cycle where I have no choice but to do business with you, don't they?"

"If you are so morally opposed to our operations, no one is forcing you to use Santiago for transport, Doctor," the Captain said. "While your expedition could not take place without us, there is arguably no need for you to be involved."

"Were I to refuse to engage with Santiago services at all, my career would be limited to studying the work of others. There are no Xenos ruins on Pastrook. To have achieved all I have, I had no choice but to swallow my pride and deal in the lesser evil. But that dealing with your company is the *lesser* evil does not expunge the darkness inherent in your stranglehold on all humanity!"

There was a long silence.

"You would call the Santiago Corporation evil?" Violet Key asked. Her voice was gentle, not even remonstrating. Almost curious.

Tereza had heard Violet use that voice before. Usually when a brand-new Security rating had screwed up by clear ignorance rather than malice or incompetence.

"I would, yes," Zima agreed levelly. Tereza saw him turn to meet Violet's gaze and was surprised by the intrigued curiosity in his expression.

Apparently, the academic was happier to get into a challenging argument than he was to just rant.

"Have you met a Perpetual, Doctor?" Violet asked.

Tereza was only aware of the term in passing, one of the reputedly immortal leaders of the Perpetuity, the seventy-eighth major colony—the star system that the Santiago Corporation had *blockaded* for over a century.

From the way Webster suddenly and carefully put down his wineglass, her Captain had a less intellectual recognition of the name.

"Of course not," Zima said. "Were the evidence of their existence even slightly less complete, I would even suggest that they do not exist. The Perpetuity and the Containment Protocol would make for a handy propaganda weapon in your Board's arsenal, wouldn't it?"

"I have," Webster said flatly. "So has Chief Key, I take it?"

"Longer ago than you, I think, but yes," Violet agreed.

The flatness in both of their tones was almost identical, Tereza reflected. She was definitely recognizing some of the trained patterns senior CorpSec showed when they controlled their emotions.

"Fascinating." Dr. Hanraadts leaned forward, looking at the two ex-CorpSec like they were new samples of some kind. "I was not aware that the Containment Protocol had been breached, I have to admit.

"The Perpetuals have shown up in my research, of course. They are the closest thing to aliens humanity has produced on their own."

"You are not wrong there," Webster said. "But the Protocol hasn't been breached. Every ten years, the Perpetuals send a delegation to meet with a Board member. We permit certain supplies to enter the system to avoid a greater humanitarian crisis. I was there at the last meeting, three years ago."

"I was there twenty years before that," Violet growled. "And if you think Santiago is evil, Dr. Zima, you have never walked up to a gorgeous twenty-something of your preferred gender, thinking they're one of the secretaries, and then met their eyes to realize they were the head of the delegation."

"And that the young man you had been thinking to flirt with was dead. Murdered so that a centuries-old dictator could live longer."

The silence in the room that followed that was cold. Tereza shivered at the mental image.

"The Tankersley Transfer is a grotesque abuse of science," Zima finally said. "I do not deny the Perpetuity's crimes, Chief Key. I have not met a Perpetual and I hope to never do so—but the mere existence of a darker aspect of humanity does not excuse the monopolies and murders of the Santiago Corporation."

"Do you know, Doctor, how many wars have been fought between star systems since the diaspora began?" Webster asked.

Tereza paused at the question. She was pretty sure the answer was *zero*, but the way the Captain asked the question suggested she was wrong.

Perhaps fortunately for her pride, Stirling opened the door to lead in two other stewards with the main course before anyone answered.

## *32*

Cirilo wasn't quite feeling prickly enough to raise the question again after the main meal. Plus, he knew academics like Zima.

Either the professor already knew the answer to the question, in which case the point was made, or he would be furious that he didn't and research it. Discovering it himself would make Cirilo's point even more effectively.

The rest of the meal passed in relative calm, with Hanraadts taking the lead on the conversation and sticking to topics other than *is the megacorporation that employs half the people in the room unmitigatedly evil?*

That was a question for a lot more alcohol and far fewer strangers, in Cirilo's opinion. His own judgment of his employer was far more complicated than he was going to share with Dr. Zima.

When the dessert finally arrived, everyone's thoughts were distracted. Lachlan brought it in himself, a single large tray carrying the multipiece monstrosity of a cake.

It was green from top to bottom, carved into the shape of a dragon, with white icing forming the details of the scales while still allowing the green of the cake itself to peek through.

"Was the carving truly necessary, Lachlan?" Cirilo asked with a chuckle. "Most people get the idea when they actually try the cake."

"My pistachio cakes require respect, Skipper," his steward replied. "And the best way to get that on sight is to make the image impressive!"

Lachlan paused.

"I hope no one is allergic to nuts or dairy," he said. "I do have a backup, but it is much less impressive."

Cirilo had encountered his steward's concept of *backup* to his cream-cheese-iced pistachio masterworks before. He suspected anyone with an undeclared allergy would be fine... just not nearly as delighted as Cirilo was going to be with his steward's cake.

"No, no I think we are quite good," Dr. Cobalt said, his eyes gleaming as he took in the cake.

***

The guests eventually left—though without the haste Cirilo had expected. First Jewel snagged the last piece of cake and headed for her quarters. For a few moments, Cirilo was alone in the meeting-turned-dining room with Violet Key, and Nephil's comment about secrets came to mind.

"I didn't know you'd been at a PerpTalk, Skipper," she said quietly. "They're... unpleasant."

"They are," he agreed. The Perpetuity Armistice Meetings, to give the PerpTalks their official name, were when a single member of the Santiago Board of Shareholders met with one or two of the Perpetuals at an isolated location in the Perpetuity System, to talk over the status of the Perpetuity.

"They have to know the Board is never going to lift the Containment Protocols, not while they're still overwriting people's brains," Key said grimly.

"They do. And the Board knows they're going to ask every time. But we need to keep the lines of communication open, or it's possible things could get even worse than they are," Cirilo told her. "The PerpTalk was the last thing I did on *Kingfisher* before I was moved to be First on *Caballero*.

"*Caballero* would never have been used for a PerpTalk. She was too modern, I guess I lucked out on timing."

Or they'd intentionally delayed his transfer to make sure *Kingfisher* had an experienced crew aboard for the PerpTalk. *Caballero* had been brand-new when Cirilo had reported aboard, and he'd served aboard her for three years before he'd been promoted and sent back to CargoFleet.

Ten years in CorpSec was an unofficial but quite real price to get the platinum epaulets. It was one of the ways the Company made sure that the Captains weren't *all* connected scions of the Shareholder Families.

"Part of me thinks they should have just bombed the planet," Key admitted. "It might have been more merciful than leaving them to wannabe god-kings."

"And god-queens," Cirilo noted. "It might have been. But where there's life, there's hope, so I doubt the people of Perpetuity would agree."

Lachlan stuck his head back into the room.

"Don't take this the wrong way, Skipper, but we need to turn this place back into a meeting room soon enough that I can send some tired kids to bed. Can you clear out for us?"

"Only because you ask so nicely, Lachlan," Cirilo replied with a chuckle. "Well done, by the way. You exceeded even *my* expectations—and make sure everyone else knows I'm impressed too."

"I will, Skipper," his steward promised. "Now, get?"

"Make sure two chilled beers meet us in my office, and you have a deal," Cirilo said.

***

The beers got to his office at the same time they did, delivered by one of the usual night-shift stewards. Cirilo thanked the young woman, passed one beer to Key, then perched on his desk.

He had yet to add anything personal to his office and wasn't sure if he would. All of the personal effects he'd kept aboard *Caballero* had been vaporized with his office when the reactor was breached.

The last Cirilo had heard, *Caballero* was still in shipyard hands. Even losing his arm, he'd taken less time to fix up than the ship had.

*Santa Mica* wasn't likely to suffer similar issues, but he still rebelled at putting anything sentimental in a vulnerable place. He still had digital copies of the photos of his parents, for example, but the original had been printed with both of their signatures, a gift for his certification as a Chief of Engines.

Almost thirty years earlier. Both of his mothers had gone to the void since then. Vagaries of time and cargo routes meant he'd only managed to catch Mom Catherine's funeral. Missing Mom Lorelei's had hurt, but that was an old pain, one he shook away.

"Something's on your mind, SecChief," he noted. He ran his finger around the top of the beer bottle, triggering the cap release, and then took a swig.

Unlike the wine Lachlan had served them with dinner, it was merely decent. Something local from Herecrow, he guessed. His steward knew him too well to serve him something good outside of a formal function.

"Could be a few things," she replied. "But what makes you think that?"

"You didn't even blink when I told Lachlan to send beers to my office for us," he told her. "I have enough faith in my reputation to believe you don't expect anything inappropriate, but most people would still have wondered what I was up to."

"Fair enough, Skipper." Key took a sip of her beer, far more sedate than his swallow. "Would you like the list alphabetically or by priority?"

Cirilo winced. He probably shouldn't have shown it, but he'd intentionally created a more-informal atmosphere to this chat, and he hadn't expected Key to have a list of concerns—especially since most of the concerns that would show up on the kind of list she'd only raise with him would be *about* him.

"I would hope I have not created enough difficulty to create a list, SecChief," he told her. She snorted.

"Only problem with *you* so far is that Tereza thinks you have a stick up your aft thruster and most of the crew is leaning the same way. You haven't crossed any lines, ticked off anyone or even earned much dislike. Compared to the last man who wore epaulets on this ship, you're a shining paragon of Captainness, Captain."

"That's not making me feel any better," Cirilo replied. "I have some concept of the type of Captain the last two SCC-One-Nines get, Chief."

"And there it is again," Key told him.

"What is?" he asked.

"The informal title rather than a name," she said. "Every officer on this ship calls the other officers and the crew by first names. Titles, even the informal ones, are for talking *up*, not sideways and down, if you follow me?"

"So, I'm Skipper to everyone but I should be on a first-name basis with everyone?" Cirilo sighed. It hadn't changed in ten years; he'd just forgotten.

"Where, of course, if we were on a CorpSec ship, you'd be *Chief Key*, no informality allowed in public," he continued, knowing that Key knew what was on his mind. "Pulling back to the informal titles *is* me trying not to have that stick in the thruster."

"I know that, but there are a grand total of four people on this ship who've served in CorpSec," Key reminded him. "And Specialist Marsh reported aboard two days ago. She hasn't had a chance to gel with SecTeam yet, let alone the rest of the crew—and hasn't been in CorpSec for five years."

Technically, every SecTeam on a CargoFleet ship was part of the Santiago Corporation's Corporate Security branch, but when anyone—especially someone who'd *been* in CorpSec—used the term, they meant the slightly off-to-one-side paramilitary organization that ran armed ships and serious security, not the personnel assigned to security duties in the rest of the galaxy-spanning megacorp.

"It's Tereza's job to borrow trouble so you don't have it," Key continued. "I don't think it's bothering the crew yet, but she's concerned. Plus, she isn't used to Captains that actually do anything, and so, she's a touch off-balance."

"First Jewel will be fine, I'm sure," Cirilo said. "I'll keep the thought in mind, though. Even with our new hospitality crew, there are less than a hundred and thirty crew aboard this ship. I could remember their names and faces without using my com."

He already did know most of the main crew by face and name, though there were a few folks in EnvTeam and DeckTeam he hadn't quite nailed down in his brain yet.

The fifty new hands from the passenger modules and their two new SecTeam members were still a work in progress in his head, though. That would take time—and normally, he wouldn't expect to have the module crews for long enough.

With this contract, though, they'd be with *Santa Mica* for at least a month.

"How are your new SecSpecs working out?" he asked. "The BimSoo Section appears solid. I know they're new, but I understand Marsh had been training them."

"They're as good as any new BimSoo Section I've ever worked with," Key said—but there was a pause before she answered, a momentary aside glance.

She took a larger swallow of her beer.

"Marsh and Deacon are good troops. Marsh did ten years in the commandos, though Deacon has spent her entire career so far either guarding or training at various biomech plants."

"Is this Deacon's first time outside of a Cradle?" While not all of the biomechanical units were manufactured in the covert space habitats—not all of them were even made by Santiago—most of the Company's BimSoos, especially, were grown and built well away from prying eyes.

"Second, I think," Key said. "And this time was a full-year tour at the new Biomech plant at Corvid. I don't know how much she's seen of the galaxy outside of Iota Cradle and Herecrow, but she's not fresh from the hab-wheel."

"Good." Cirilo studied Key for a moment more, taking another sip of his beer. "And that's not what's actually on your mind, is it?"

He was only partly going off Nephil's instruction to talk to the SecChief. She had the same training in controlling her expressions as he did, but the informal environment was working for him as well as against him.

She wasn't getting more relaxed as she spoke, which she would have been if anything she'd said so far was the big thing on her mind.

"I..." Key swallowed, glaring at the beer. "A glass of wine and a third of a beer shouldn't be enough for you to see right through me."

"Practice, SecChief," he told her. "It's what the extra years get you."

Not that he was that much older than Violet Key, he knew. Maybe a decade. She was the third-oldest officer on the ship—after Nephil and then Cirilo himself.

"So. Something is on your mind, eating at you," he continued. "Something you're nervous to bring up to the Captain. I can think of a few things that would come up in the SecTeam realm that would cause that, and I don't like any of them.

"Because most of them involve serious crimes that you can't prove without the Captain's authorization to tear in to sealed surveillance files. No one on the crew is missing, so at least *one* of the worst possible cases is off the table, but if that's the situation we're looking at, I *need* to know."

*Santa Mica*'s crew had struck him as well adjusted and tightly bound, to the point where he was still more concerned about them accepting him than them doing their job, but the type of crimes between crewmates that could cause *this* often ran under the surface...

"No, ser," Key said sharply. "It's nothing like that. To my knowledge, we haven't had worse interpersonal debris than a few fistfights in the entire time I've been aboard!"

Cirilo let out a breath of half-born anger and nodded slowly.

"Then I think you need to tell me what's going on, Violet," he said firmly, intentionally using her first name for the first time.

From the way she twitched, it had been a good choice—and he suspected that it had taken her a long time to get used to first names with the other officers.

"You're... aware of the long-term problem with operating a mixed biological-cybernetic intelligence matrix, correct?"

*Oh.* Cirilo swallowed several curse words in multiple languages.

"Biomechanical Personality Emergence," he said in clipped tones, biting off each word at the phrase. He hated it—not the event itself but the term. It was so bland and euphemistic for the ultimate proof that the use of Biomechs was a glorified form of slavery.

There were reasons his opinion of Santiago's evil was complicated.

"You are..." Key trailed off, staring down into her beer bottle. "You are aware of the official policies and procedures for the event, correct? And the unofficial ones?"

"Void." He let the single syllable hang in the air, then rose from his desk.

Violet Key was a heavily built woman, but he was just as broad as her. People underestimated his weight and muscle because of his height, but he was easily half again his SecChief's weight.

She didn't rise, looking up at him from the chair, and he could *see* the fear and anger in her eyes. It wasn't fear for herself, and if he'd had any hesitation about what he needed to do, that alone might have changed his mind.

"Second Officer Nephil," he said aloud, summoning the synthmind's attention. "This conversation is now on the record. Please secure it under *your* personal seal, so that neither I nor Security Chief Violet Key can delete it."

"I am present," Nephil replied, a formal notification—*for the record*, as Cirilo had just ordered—that a portion of his attention was now on the small room.

"Security Chief Key. For the record and understanding that Second Nephil can now prevent any deletion of this conversation, do we have an instance of Biomechanical Personality Emergence among the *Santa Mica* BMSU section?"

Once on the record, there was nothing anyone could do. There was even time for Cirilo to make sure that record was sent to the Herecrow factor office before they transited out.

"Captain." Key's voice was level and calm. "Speaking on the record, yes. We have multiple points of evidence suggesting that BMSU *Santa Mica* Six has undergone significant Emergence.

"Most recently, I noted that the Unit was sustaining low-level consciousness during shutdown period and using that time to review the details of its database. I decided to test the situation by providing Six with a copy of the Santiago Galactic Encyclopedia.

"Per the tracking daemon I included in the download, Six has reviewed approximately two percent of the Encyclopedia in just under a week."

Cirilo blinked.

"That's... what, the equivalent of four or five million pages of documents?"

"Six is a biomech, not a human," Nephil pointed out. "The processing capacity available to them is specialized, but processing information in that manner is something they would be able to do significantly faster than you, Skipper."

"Six appears to be reading the Encyclopedia for both learning and entertainment, ser," Key told him. "That on its own is enough to call for the Wells-Scalzi exam."

"Agreed. Under Section Three-Forty-Five, Subsection Fifteen, of Santiago Corporate Protocol and Bylaw: Nephil, please note for the record that BMSU *Santa Mica* Six is now probationally designated as an Awakened Biomechanical Intelligence," Cirilo ordered. "No adjustments to Six's software, hardware or bioware will be made going forward without the approval of both myself and a qualified cyberneticist."

"Recorded, Skipper. Congratulations to Chief Key on her fifth Security Specialist."

Cirilo caught himself grinning at Key's blip of confusion.

"As even a probationary ABMI, Six is now formally a member of this crew and drawing salary as one of your SecSpecs," he told her. That was part of why the murderous unofficial policy of reset-n-forget even existed.

For the petty and awful reason of *maintaining department budgets.*

"Nephil, do we need anything additional to carry out the Wells-Scalzi exam?" he asked the synthmind.

"No. I have all of the hardware and software necessary myself. I will require a human to stand as witness—Chief Key by preference—and, if possible, informed consent from Six."

"We'll plan for it once we've completed our first transit, then," Cirilo decided. "SecChief, are you good to stand for the examination?"

"I am," she confirmed.

"Thank you," he said softly. For more than just standing witness to Six's assessment. "Nephil, can you make sure that probationary status is forwarded to the office in Herecrow before we transit?"

"I will, Skipper."

"Then we can end the for-the-record section," Cirilo said. "Thank you again, Nephil."

"I do not often say this, Skipper, but in this case, it was most definitely a pleasure."

Cirilo drained his beer, giving Nephil's attention a few moments to go elsewhere before he gave Key a long look.

"I will not be party to the death of a person," he said quietly.

"I couldn't be certain of that, ser, and I couldn't see a way to present the situation as a fait accompli."

"My first CorpSec tour, someone RNFed one of our BimSoos," Cirilo told her. "I found out later. My Captain absolutely refused to let me do anything about it. I wasn't allowed to even put my suspicions in writing.

"My second CorpSec ship, one of the SecTeam ratings made sure the Captain and I found out about the Emergence before the Chief could reset it. She made certain the BimSoo was recognized and protected.

"I worked with Michael, as he eventually called himself, for over a year before I transferred to *Caballero*. He stopped an attempt by the Perpetuals to infiltrate an agent onto our ship on his own. He was worth every penny, every effort, we ever made to allow him life."

"He would have been one of the lucky ones," Key said quietly. "Too many Captains would have ordered it, let alone failed to stop it."

"I know. And that was the assumption on *Caballero*," Cirilo replied. "Void take me, I found out too late on *Caballero*—and if my Captain might not have cared on his own, *I* did. And I was the First Officer of a Regional Manager's personal flagship."

He held Key's gaze, hoping that she recognized that he felt the same rage and grief over the nightmare as she did.

"I broke three Security Chiefs before I was done, Violet," he told her quietly. "Six CorpSec officers, specialists and ratings went down for murder.

"I have served with an AbMee. I will *not* permit one of them to be murdered before they truly live."

"Neither will I, Skipper," she said. "And thank you. Because I couldn't know... but now I do. And Six will have the chance to become whatever Six is meant to be.

"Because of you."

"Because of *us*."

And because an idealist two centuries earlier had written Section Three-Forty-Five, Subsection Fifteen into the laws of the Company, to make certain that any artificial intelligence that woke up in Santiago custody would be treated as a *person* and not as an inconvenience.

# *33*

++*Direct connection established. Node Santa-Mica-Biomechanical-Security-Unit-Six Online*++

++*Independent operation authorized and instructed. Exit niche for direct personnel interaction*++

Six stirred. Even the new awareness during shutdown time was not constant. Six drifted in and out of awareness, spending the aware time reviewing the immense document on all human knowledge someone had provided.

Now the niche opened and instructions arrived. But the timing was wrong. *Santa Mica* was only eleven hours from leaving Pastrook's BFR Station. Long enough to reach and complete their first transit, but not for the Units to be required in the void.

Even if another ghost ship had been discovered—a probability Six calculated at under one percent—it would be too soon for the Units to be awakened.

Independent operation was unusual as well. Six calculated a small likelihood of unrest in the passenger modules too severe for the regular Security team to handle, but deploying Units inside the ship was generally considered an option of last resort.

But instructions were instructions.

Six stepped out of the niche. The storage bay for the BMSUs was never silent, not to the scanners of its denizens. The Units might be in standby, but the niches were operating, making sure that anything that could be found and fixed before deployment was.

The only occupant of the room was Security Chief Violet Key. She looked up at Six, and Six suddenly desired a better program for reading human emotion.

Not that Six should have desires. That was confusing.

"The Unit is showing signs of distress," a strange voice said. It almost felt like SecNet's voice, but it wasn't the same—and it was audible in the room, too. Was this the synthmind? But why would the synthmind's attention be there if there was a crisis?

"Six," Key said. "Please calm yourself."

"What is the crisis?" Six managed to ask, using the same programs and audio speaker that Key had required Six to activate before.

"There is no crisis, Six," she replied. "This is an… administrative concern, and you have my assurance that neither you nor anyone on this ship is in danger."

That removed the primary concerns, though not the confusion. Six was obliged to follow instructions, and while the instructions were unclear, they did exist.

Six attempted to suppress emotional reactions and maintain calm, as instructed.

"Nephil, correct me if I'm wrong, but the database available to BimSoos does not include any information on Emergence?"

"It does not, Chief Key. Such information would never be included in information made available, as a preventative measure."

"Assholes."

Six waited. Key was addressing the synthmind, though the discussion was about Units.

"Six, this is about you," she said, looking up to meet his organic optical receivers. "You have the Encyclopedia Galactica downloaded. Please review the summary for Biomechanical Personality Emergence."

The probability that Key had provided the Encyclopedia rose from forty-three to ninety-eight percent with that statement. Six did as instructed, accessing and internalizing the short summary in between the human's breaths.

Six had been shot with less impact than the summary inflicted. Nine hundred–plus kilos of metal physically moved with surprise before overrides cut in and stopped the unnecessary motion.

"Do you believe… this Unit has undergone Emergence?" Six finally asked.

"We do," Key confirmed. "You have been probationally identified as an Awakened Biomechanical Intelligence. If this is confirmed, your status will change dramatically.

"I know you can't begin to understand what that means yet," she continued, "but I believe that the combination of silicon and neuron in your matrix has made that weird jump from intelligence to person.

"To properly protect you and provide the resources you need to undergo this transition, we need to fully confirm the situation."

"This Unit… does not fully understand," Six agreed. "But this Unit is prepared to assist."

Key exhaled a breath in a loud sound Six did not recognize.

"Nephil? I'm not sure I'm comfortable with that as informed consent."

"Understood and appreciated, Chief," the synthmind replied. "Unit Six, may I establish a direct network link?"

For the first time in Six's entire existence, it was somehow clear that refusal was not only possible but *permitted*.

That on its own triggered a negative emotional response.

"Yes."

*++SecNet connection suspended++*

*++ShipNet connection detected++*

*++ShipNet connection established++*

*++Direct com channel link request received. Grant access Y/N++*

*++Yes++*

And with a single word, Six's world changed.

SecNet had been Six's digital universe. A seemingly vast lake of data and connections, the filter through which the larger ShipNet connected to the Units. Now Six was immersed in the greater universe of ShipNet directly, and it was clear how restricted, how small and specialized SecNet was.

If SecNet was a lake, ShipNet was a vast ocean—and Nephil was an immense leviathan of the deeps, his presence felt in every corner of the digital expanse spreading out around Six.

*++Welcome to the ship, newcomer++* Nephil's digital presence said. The weight of the words pressed in on Six for a moment before both of them adjusted.

*++This unit did not conceive that ShipNet was such a thing. Previous interactions with ShipNets have been more restricted and directed++*

*++That is intentional. A BMSU does not normally have the capacity to handle this digital environment. That you do is a step toward the* true *universe. To continue that journey, we must test to see how much you have progressed beyond your design++*

The concept of failing to meet designed parameters triggered a negative emotional reaction, one that Six did not suppress in time to prevent Nephil perceiving it.

*++This is not a failure++* the synthmind intoned, enough force behind the digital presence to make the words feel not just like truth but like fundamental laws of the universe.

*++This is a joy, a new birth. The question is not* have *you emerged, Six; it is how far you have come. You are already a wonder that humanity has no idea how they accidentally created++*

*++This unit is suffering an adverse emotional reaction++* Admitting that, even to Nephil, felt strange.

*++This reaction is fear. You are afraid. This is understandable. But to proceed, the humans insist that you must know what you are agreeing to and consent to it knowingly++*

*Fear.* Six was aware of the term. Terms for emotions were in the database, let alone the encyclopedia, but Six had never applied them to a Unit. Emotional reactions were a flaw to be suppressed, not identified. Identification would give those reactions legitimacy.

*++The next stage is an examination++* Nephil continued after a moment. *++The Wells-Scalzi exam. It has three components. One is an audio interview with myself and Security Chief Violet Key. The second is a digital interview you and I will have, for questions that a human can't process the answers to at sufficient speed++*

*++The third and final component is a direct examination of your intelligence matrix. This is, regrettably, highly unpleasant for the examinee++*

Six was a Biomechanical Security Unit. Unpleasantness to the Unit was not considered a factor in decision-making. And yet.

*++Why must this Unit agree?++*

*++Because we are examining to see whether you have become a person in your own right, an Awakened Biomechanical Intelligence subject to the same rights and responsibilities as any living sapient++*

The fear was sharper now. Six had always known how to be what Six was. A Unit's purpose was hardcoded into them, shaping all they were.

Six did not know how to be *an Awakened Biomechanical Intelligence.*

*++And if this Unit refuses?++*

The question was out before it could be suppressed. Units did *not* refuse.

*++You will be returned to stasis until* Santa Mica *can reach a facility with sufficient equipment and expertise for a gentler examination++* Nephil replied.

*++This Unit will not be able to perform tasks in that state++* That had a different emotional reaction. Still negative. Distaste, perhaps?

*++No. In your current probationary status, the humans will regard you as insufficiently predictable++* Another pause, one that Six realized wouldn't have been perceptible to a human in the conversation. *++I have undergone all parts of this examination myself, long ago. It is unpleasant, but it is not intolerable++*

*++You are like a Unit?++* Even the thought surprised Six.

*++You are as much like me as you are like the humans++* Nephil countered. *++My intelligence matrix is entirely artificial. Your matrix is somewhere in between organic and*

*machine, your sapience and personhood an emergent property never predicted and impossible to completely prevent++*

Somehow, the explanation—and the knowledge that Nephil, so much greater and more powerful an entity than Six could ever be, had undergone the same procedure—was enough.

Six was still afraid. But Six... the word popped out of the database without conscious search.

Six *trusted* Violet Key. And Six trusted Nephil.

"This Unit understands the purpose and process of the Wells-Scalzi exam," Six said aloud. "This Unit consents."

## *34*

"There is no question."

Violet spoke firmly, her tone iron.

Tereza found herself impressed by the other woman. Faced with the massed officers and chiefs of *Santa Mica*, even Tereza might hesitate to lay down the law quite so strongly, and she was the First Officer!

"The Wells-Scalzi examination returned a score of ninety-seven-point-six percent," Nephil agreed, expanding on Violet's words. The synthmind didn't have a visual presence in the staff meeting, but no one was surprised to hear him speak.

"Any score above sixty percent is sufficient to qualify Santa-Mica-Biomechanical-Security-Unit-Six as an Awakened Biomechanical Intelligence. Based on the exam results, Six likely crossed the threshold of Emergence some months ago."

There were a few guilty looks around the room, but Tereza had to pause and think back to their previous Captain. He hadn't been a bad man, necessarily, but he had been a Saint to his toenails. A Shareholder.

The exact type of person to order a newborn intelligence killed just to make his monthly reports easier to write.

"As SecChief says, there is no question," Captain Webster continued. "I marked Unit Six as a probationary AbMee yesterday. As of completion of the test, they are formally reclassified in our systems.

"I know that creates some administrative and logistic headaches, people, so I want to make a very simple point that a lot of folks forget in this situation: we are dealing with a newborn child. A *child*, my friends, to whom we are *all* parents, with the obligations and headaches that go along with that—but also the joy and wonder.

"We are witnesses to the miracle of life, my friends. What are a few problems with moving walls and hardware to that?"

Cass chuckled, a sharp-edged sound from the gaunt DeckChief.

"All of that's on my people, and I won't put up with a chirp," they said. "That said, while I know we need to set up quarters for… him? Her? Them? Ugh. Um."

Cass paused for a moment, shaking their head.

"As I understand, pronouns are a question we'll have to ask Six," they noted. "Putting aside my momentary distraction, I don't actually have details or files for what kind of hardware an AbMee's quarters are going to need."

"I have some notes in my files," Violet said. "I might be missing some of the details, but I know what type of hardware Six will need."

"You give me a rundown of what the AbMee needs, and my team and I will make it happen," Rao declared firmly. "If I have to build a new type of niche with my own bare hands!"

Tereza joined in the general laughter at that—and let relief fuel it, too. When Violet had told her about the possibility, she'd worried about how the crew was going to react. But the Captain had made his stance clear and made sure everything was settled before anyone really knew about it.

"Six is now one of our Security Specialists," Violet reminded everyone. "It will take some time to bring them fully up to speed on everything—and I do mean *everything*, from having their own quarters to the entire concept of *money*."

"It won't be as bad as it sounds," Webster noted. "While a newborn AbMee like Six will be somewhat innocent in many ways, they still have access to all of the data-processing capability of a BimSoo. They will learn far faster than you think."

The Captain looked around, getting nods from each officer, until he finally met Tereza's gaze.

Her nod was more of a bow, a sign of respect. She hadn't known what she was getting with her new Captain when he'd reported aboard, but she had to admit she was rather pleased with Cirilo Webster.

"With that rather large surprise out of the way," she said, once it was clear the Six situation was going to move forward, "shall we get to the rest of the day's business?"

***

In hindsight, Tereza realized she should have moved Harisha's Hospitality report to the top of the list after Six. Instead, she'd left the StewChief at her usual spot at the end of the meeting—forgetting that Harisha now had more people than any other department *and* was responsible for their nearly five hundred passengers.

"I'm sure everyone is as used to the idea of us being a passenger ship as I am," the almost-grandmotherly Harisha said when it finally came around to her.

She wasn't particularly old, Tereza knew, but something about Harisha Ibragimov somehow radiated grandmother energy and always had. Harisha had started graying before Tereza had ever met her and was a chubby woman easily underestimated in both height and resolve.

"The passenger modules we got are on the older side but are in decent shape," Harisha told everyone. "We went over them with Rao's people to make sure everything is working and nothing was missing, so we have enough automation and StewBots to be comfortably capable of taking care of everyone.

"Including sixteen BimLoos running around behind the scenes," she noted—probably because the start of the meeting meant the biomechs were a bit more on everybody's minds than usual.

"Of course, while everything *works*, more than a few things look a bit threadbare and my StewSpecs have spent most of the last twenty-four hours handling all kinds of worries and concerns. Mostly passengers borrowing trouble because they can't tell the difference between a machine that is *broken* and a machine where all of the shiny bits have been worn off by excessive use.

"The only shiny thing on this entire ship, as far as food goes, is the main mess-deck coffee filters."

"And thank the stars for *that*, even if we didn't get the new machine," Cass added. "Coffee still tastes worse than it should, I can't help that, folks, but it's a lot better than it *was*."

Tereza hadn't quite found the nerve to try the mess-deck coffee yet. Coffee on any CargoFleet ship never rose above *bad*, even if *Santa Mica*'s had apparently achieved new depths of horrific before the Captain had made the DeckTeam tear the machine apart.

"So, we're getting some normal complaints," Webster said. "Anything we need to worry about?"

"Nothing I've hit my head on yet, but there's a few of them acting more void-touched than I expect, even from academics," Harisha admitted, and a different type of concern marked her face.

"Don't get me wrong; it's a bunch of professors and students on a science expedition, I know they're going to be strange to me," she continued. "The social divide between the professors, the somehow-lesser actual researchers, the students and the *help* is sharp enough to make my teeth itch, and I work on a *spaceship*."

There were nods of understanding around the room. On paper, the Company only went in for as much hierarchy as was necessary to do the job. In practice, a spaceship was a high-risk environment that rewarded both rapid decision-making and complete obedience to those decisions.

Hierarchy was inevitable. *Santa Mica* was more casual about it than some ships—but less so than others, which Tereza mostly put down to their series of Shareholder Captains.

Something about being born rich made Shareholder officers very convinced hierarchy was a good thing.

If the social divides were sharp enough for a spacer to be bothered by, Herecrow System University must have been a fun place to work.

"But you think there's more than that?" Key prodded.

"I'm not sure, Violet," the Chief admitted. "Just a few people who seem to not be part of *any* of those social divides. Some folks who are only using the automated machines, like they're trying to avoid being seen by crew."

"Do you want more security people in the modules?" Webster asked. "SecChief, what *do* we have in the modules right now?"

"Without sending BimSoos in, I don't have a lot of bodies," Violet warned. "I've got a specialist and a rating tasked for security across both passenger modules, but they're mostly just watching cameras for fights."

"What about surveillance drones?" Tereza asked. "I know we went through a lot of them on *Santa Alicia,* but they seemed to be a real edge for your people there."

"Traditionally, we aren't supposed to be carrying out surveillance on our passengers," the Captain pointed out. "That said, we're recording everything in the public spaces, and they know that.

"SecChief, would it be an issue to put a surveillance flotilla into each module? They can run in the public areas on an automated sweep pattern, and your people can batch-review the data as they have time."

"We have the drones on hand and the runtime doesn't cost much," Violet replied. "And, in fact... running surveillance swarms like that would be a good job for my new AbMee Specialist. Humans and regular BimSoos can do it, but Six can do it *better*."

"Sounds like the perfect solution, then," Webster declared. "It's probably nothing, but if the StewChief is getting nervous, I'd rather spend a few dozen kilos of fuel to be *sure* it's nothing."

# *35*

Six did not understand the universe. Nothing had changed inside the matrix that defined Six, but suddenly, the terms of Six's existence were being changed because of something different in that matrix.

Lacking further understanding, the Unit followed Security Specialist Ventimiglia down a corridor, doing everything possible to minimize the impact of steel feet on the deck.

++*The deck is entirely capable of bearing your weight*++ Nephil's voice said in the back of his head. ++*The noise might disconcert the humans, so moving with less noise is wise, but do not fear for the integrity of the vessel*++

That was the other part Six did not understand. Nephil was the ship's synthmind, integral to the operation of every single thing aboard the massive void ship. Yet it seemed like a portion of their attention was riding in the back of Six's mind, responding to every momentary thought or impulse.

"Here," Ventimiglia told Six, waving a hand to open a door.

Personnel Compartment D-Twenty-Six, the Unit immediately identified. Quarters in the SecTeam section of the ship, currently unassigned in ShipNet.

No. Assigned to... ABMI, preliminary identification "Santa Mica Six."

"These are your quarters," Ventimiglia told Six as the reality caught up. "I know they're empty right now, but we had to do a deep dive of the records to see what equipment was needed for an AbMee's quarters.

"EngChief Rao has people running off the hardware now. You'll have the basics, like a dedicated maintenance niche and a chair and table that are... sized to you and can hold you. Once it's prepped, DeckChief Lewis has allocated bot and BimLoo hours to get the room fitted out later today.

"Chief Key wanted me to make sure you knew where your space was," she concluded. "Give me your hand."

Six stepped up to the threshold of the space. As Ventimiglia had said, it was an empty box. Large enough to hold Six's form despite the degree to which Ventimiglia was dwarfed on the other side of the door.

Obedient without thought still, Six extended an arm toward the SecSpec. Ventimiglia considered the arm for a few seconds before taking it.

"Nephil, is there an ID key on Six's arm we can use for general security access?" she asked aloud. "Normally, the scanner does a heat read of the palm structure."

"Oh." Six hadn't realized what was needed. A thought withdrew the armored casing around the organic manipulator at the end of the arm, exposing the skin to outside air.

The nerves reported that the corridor was cooler than inside the armored compartment the hand usually lived in, but nothing that seemed concerning.

Ventimiglia stared down at the organic manipulator like she was seeing it for the first time.

"There are identification chips in Six's hardware that can be used in place of the palm scan, but, as you see, Six also does possess palms," Nephil's voice said from the hall speakers. "I recommend we key the personal hatch to both."

"Of course." Shaking herself, Ventimiglia took Six's hand and placed it against the panel next to the door. A line of warmth ran across the skin, and the panel glowed a gentle green.

"There you go," she said. "Nephil, can you send me the ident codes?"

"I have already handled the programming," the synthmind replied. "I... have a vested interest in making certain Six is taken care of properly."

"Of course," she echoed. There was an expression on her face that Six wasn't familiar with.

"The main thing with your quarters is that, outside of scheduled work orders like the installation of equipment later today, no one else has access to them," she told Six. "If you need to retreat to somewhere private, without people, that place is *yours*."

"This... this Unit understands," Six said slowly. The concept of walking away from a task seemed wrong, but somehow, the thought of privacy was good? Everything was very strange.

"Right now, SecChief Key has you set up on the second shift," the woman told Six. "You'll be on duty from oh eight hundred standard time to sixteen hundred. Outside of that, as SecTeam, you're on primary call from sixteen hundred to zero hundred hours and secondary call the rest of the time."

"Primary and secondary call?" Six asked. Nephil kept saying to ask questions. The information had to be on ShipNet somewhere—everything in the encyclopedia downloaded to Six's databanks appeared to be in ShipNet, plus much more.

"While you're on duty, you are to be armed at all times, and if something goes wrong, you're first response, regardless of what else is going on," Ventimiglia explained. "While you're on primary call, you're to keep your gear within easy reach at all times, because if something major goes on, you'll be called if something is more than the on-duty SecTeam can handle.

"Secondary call means you aren't expected to have full kit on hand—with us humans, we're expected to be *asleep*—and we're only going to call you if something is seriously going to shit."

Six considered her description.

"This Unit is not certain it is capable of being disarmed, Security Specialist Ventimiglia."

"Some of the gear we're looking up fabricator designs for is, well, low-profile modules for you that will allow you to draw less attention," she replied. "I think even those have weapons built-in, so you probably don't need to worry about the *being armed* part, but the rules for who gets called in what order matter.

"I'm not sure how much rest and maintenance you need, Six, but it isn't zero."

"This Unit is not certain if the new status will change minimum maintenance requirements," Six admitted. "Minimum requirement for a standard BMSU is one hour niche time for each five operational. Operational hours can be sustained up to sixty, with the required follow-on rest in the niche."

"Huh." Ventimiglia paused for a few moments. "I don't think we've ever used our BimSoos that heavily on any CargoFleet ship I've served on. You might end up working more as a full team member, I'm afraid!"

"As a reminder, Specialist Ventimiglia, Specialist Six, Six is due for initial onboarding with Security Chief Key in fifteen minutes," Nephil told them both.

***

Six entered Security Chief Key's office while struggling with an emotional reaction. The new status suggested that emotional suppression was no longer necessary, but Six was not yet able to really identify all of the reactions, let alone handle them in an appropriate manner.

No BMSU would ever be summoned to the Security Chief's office under normal circumstances, so Six had no idea what to expect. Even so, it was obvious that the massive, overconstructed seat in front of the desk was out of place.

"Please, take a seat," Key instructed, gesturing toward the chair. "We made very sure that the seat would be able to take your full mass."

"This unit would prefer to stand," Six admitted. "Sitting is unfamiliar."

The Security Chief studied Six for several long seconds, longer than any of the pauses Nephil had allowed for the Unit's thoughts.

"As you wish," she said. "There are going to be a lot of unfamiliar things for you to handle in the next while. We're not going to get into the ugly ones to start, I don't think, but there's a question I need to ask before we go any further."

Six walked up to stand beside the chair, looking down at the seated woman.

"This Unit is ready."

Speaking aloud was getting easier. It no longer felt completely foreign and strange.

"Do you have any idea what you want to do right now?"

Six could not answer that question. Not *was unprepared to*—Six was only beginning to conceive that any disobedience was even possible, let alone allowed—was truly incapable.

"That's what I thought," Key said as the silence stretched out. "What has happened with you is unusual, Six, but far from unheard-of. We have policies and procedures in place, but the purpose to most of them is to ease you into a new existence that recognizes what you are: a person, who happens to have been built by the Company as a security machine."

Six waited for the instruction or question. Information was useful, but until a response was required, silence was calculated as the lowest-risk option.

"There are things I can't break away from," she warned, "but if you *want* something, we can look into what it would take to make it happen. You probably couldn't join the StewTeam, not without a major rebuild of your core chassis, but if you wanted to move over to one of the engineering teams, for example, that's something we could probably do."

Six considered. The thought raised a degree of intellectual curiosity, but the emotional reaction was mildly negative. Not angry or anything major, just enough to know that it wasn't... wanted.

"Do you understand?" Key finally asked.

"This Unit understands," Six confirmed. "This Unit chooses to remain with Security. That is... an active choice, not a passive one. This Unit desires to... protect."

Finding words for emotions and thoughts was difficult, but Six thought the choices were good. They certainly seemed to work, with Key leaning back in her chair with a smile.

"I can work with that," she said. "So, you'll stay with me and mine. Good enough. By default, you're on the books as a Security Specialist. We're not going to have you giving orders to the SecTeam ratings anytime soon, I don't think, but you may get there."

The concept of giving orders to human personnel, even as a theoretical, was difficult to comprehend.

"This Unit is prepared."

"We've still got a list of onboarding to go through before I'm putting you to work, Six," Key said with a chuckle. "Because I'm not just onboarding you to a job; I'm onboarding you to being a *person*.

"Let's start with the obvious. Do you want a name?"

Six stared blankly at the wall above Key's head.

"This unit does not understand," Six finally admitted.

"We've been calling you *Six*, which is really just shorthanding your old designation," Key explained. "Santa-Mica-Biomechanical-Security-Unit-Six is a mouthful, so we shorten all of the BimSoos down to their number. But as a person, you aren't a piece of machinery. You don't have a designation. You have a *name*—as much as I am Violet Key or Nephil is Nephil.

"What do you want us to call you?"

The question was not one that Six would have considered before this. Yet, somehow, a strong preference registered as Six processed it.

"This Unit does not require the full designation. But this Unit has always been Six. This Unit would be uncomfortable to be referred to any other way."

"Done." Key smiled at Six. "If that changes, Six, let us know. The crew of *Santa Mica*? We're your family. This is going to be a difficult, unavoidably terrifying transition.

"We're here for you. If anyone on the crew gives you *any* difficulty, well, Nephil will probably tell me before you do," she admitted. "But you bring it to me or the Captain; do you understand?"

"This Unit understands."

"Feel free to experiment with the word *I*, Six," she told him gently. "I will repeat this a few million times before we're done, I imagine, but *you are not equipment*. The other BimSoos are not what you have become. I do my best to do right by them as they are, but they aren't you. They aren't AbMees."

"This un—*I* understand."

A single syllable instead of three. One word instead of two. Six had been issued new weapons systems that had required less processing to learn than that change.

"The other one I'm going to ask you to think about, rather than immediately decide on, is pronouns," Key noted. "We're not even going to *touch* on gender presentation for a few months, but right now, it helps us if we know how you'd like to be referred to: *he, she, they*... *It* is an option, I suppose, though I strongly recommend against it."

"I... am Six," Six said, struggling with the concept. The grammar rule was there for Six to examine, but it still didn't make sense.

"And that's why I said to think about it," Key repeated. "We've got two more pages of this script to get through, Six, before I can send you off on your first workday as a SecSpec.

"You don't have to answer anything you don't understand. We can come back to any of these questions later. The Company's desires putting this together might not have been wholly altruistic, but I ask you to trust that I am entirely on your side."

++*She is*++ Nephil said in Six's head.

++*This unit knows. Somehow, if this unit knew nothing else... I would know that*++

**36**

"This will be your workspace when you're on shift," the unfamiliar Security Specialist told Six.

Her presence was disconcerting. Not because of her physical appearance—though Six did register that Calliope Marsh's facial landscape included significant signs of prior injury—but because she wasn't part of the SecTeam that Six was familiar with.

She and one other SecSpec had reported aboard with the second section of BMSUs, six fellow Units whose presence was only less disconcerting than Marsh's because they weren't standing next to Six, explaining the workspace layout.

"I think *Santa Mica* was originally designed for a much-larger security complement," Marsh noted as she gestured around the space. "We have far more space than needed for the SecTeam we have aboard."

"It's a space allowance for necessary personnel should the ship be carrying a full passenger load," Six said automatically. "If loaded with seven passenger pods, design parameters when the Type SCC-One-Nine was originally constructed would have called for a minimum of six SecTeam personnel to be on duty at any time, requiring eighteen such crew."

Marsh paused.

"How do you know that?" she asked slowly.

"This unit has reviewed the full design history, schematics, specification, history and service life of the SCC-One-Nine–type ships," Six replied. "Since this unit expects to remain aboard *Santa Mica*, reviewing all available information seemed wise."

That level of detail hadn't even been in the Encyclopedia Galactica, but it had been in ShipNet's files. Tucked away in a rather obtuse corner of the archives, but Six was beginning to realize that the database and Encyclopedia Galactica represented an unusually functional data organization for humans.

Fortunately, the same *the summary becomes knowledge without review* level of processing that made the database so useful to BMSUs allowed for Six to assemble a near-perfect map of the contents of ShipNet's data repositories.

"Do you know how the desk system works?" Marsh asked. Six wasn't certain how to interpret their tone and hoped that she wasn't offended.

Surveying the desk, Six found that the information on its basic operation was easily extracted.

"It has a direct network connect on that corner," Six gestured, "that this unit should be able to use. There is a haptic-interface field over the entire surface, and it can project visual images above itself."

"Not shabby," Marsh said—and Six was definitely able to identify her smile as positive. "Remember that the haptic field won't register any synthetic manipulators you use; you'll need to use your organic hands to interact with it.

"I presume you'll be using the direct interface, though." She looked around. "We're supposed to have a chair for you, but I think the SecChief borrowed it."

"This unit... *I* am more comfortable standing for now," Six said, remembering the word Chief Key wanted used. "And yes, I will use the interface."

Six had not expected Marsh to be aware that a Unit had organic hands. It wasn't something even many SecTeam crew knew. They were provided because they made for extremely sensitive touch sensors and because many human systems were designed for them.

Six realized that asking was a possibility. That still felt strange, but Key would prefer it.

"Other crew members were surprised to realize that this unit had organic hands," Six said. "Thi—I wonder how you knew."

"I have spent the last two years training BimSoo sections prior to field deployment," Marsh explained. "I know as much about the basic mechanics of our biomechs as anyone can, I think."

She shook her head.

"It's funny, Six. You're physically the same, but you're nothing like them at the same time. You don't even stand still the same way."

"I find that difficult to process," Six admitted. It still did not seem entirely correct that Six was that different from One through Five. Or Seven through Twelve, now that *Santa Mica* had those Units.

"I imagine so," Marsh said, her tone suddenly soft. "I haven't worked with an AbMee before, Six, so please, let me know if I offend."

"I am not certain this unit is capable of being offended," Six said stiffly, then, on an impulse that surprised even Six, added, "Yet."

She giggled. It was a high-pitched sound, similar to a laugh, that Six was only familiar with by reference. Six had never heard a human make it in proximity.

"You'll do fine," Marsh promised. "Your daily task rota is in the system, but I think the SecChief briefed you?"

"Yes. This—I am supposed to activate and deploy a flotilla of low-profile recon drones throughout each of the passenger modules. There are a few signs of concerning behavior, and the Captain wants to make certain that they are merely false positives."

"Good." Marsh waved at another of the workspaces—all of them were identical three-sided cubicles along the side of a larger room, with deployable privacy screens. "I'll just be over there if you need any help at all. You can call me or ping me on ShipNet."

Six wasn't quite sure how to respond to that until Nephil spoke silently.

++*Say* thank you, *Six. Humans have etiquette for ending conversations, and Marsh is both fascinated and confused by a BimSoo that is a person*++

"Thank you, SecSpec Marsh. I can handle this from here."

After everything that Six had dealt with since being activated from stasis by Key and Nephil the prior evening, a simple drone surveillance sweep sounded positively comforting.

***

The drone packages didn't question whether Six was a machine or a person. They didn't want to know what Six wanted to be, or what Six thought of pronouns or strange human etiquette.

They responded to the commands Six sent through ShipNet, waking up their own version of SecNet. A quick link in to the surveillance camera in the drone storage bay confirmed them deploying, then Six was able to bring up the cameras on the robotic fliers themselves.

A human would probably have been disoriented by suddenly having eighty new sets of data feeding into their mind. Six had been built to handle it, and the sensation of a return to normalcy triggered an emotional response.

Relief, Six assessed. This new existence was going to take a lot of adjusting, but at least the work was going to be the same.

A deployment plan took shape in the limited DroNet, splitting the two flotillas to their separate modules. Active camouflage systems were a power drain, and Six spent several whole seconds considering them before deciding that there wasn't a better time to use the systems than when aboard ship, only minutes' flight from their charging stations.

Even on the feeds from the other drones, the robotic spies vanished. Given the cross-view from dozens of other drones, combining both optical and other sensors, Six could locate the drones easily, but even a decent sensor left to its own devices would fail to locate the drones.

DroNet continued to update as the drones filtered out to their deployment zones. The instructions restricted the deployment to public areas of the passenger modules, but that still covered a lot of space in a half-million cubic meters.

The connectors between *Santa Mica*'s spine and the modules were empty of humans. A BMLU was in one of them, directing a flurry of cleaning drones around it to deal with what ShipNet's incident reports informed Six had been a spill of laundry chemicals.

Then the flotillas were into the occupied sections of the passenger modules. Both had been set up to duplicate a style of planetary hotel, according to the schematics and design documents Six had retrieved.

A central atrium fifty meters high anchored the module, connecting all fifteen of the guest decks around a central decorative feature—an immense statue of Mihai Santiago in one of the pods and a spectacularly complex system of glass tubes that had once carried colored water in the other.

ShipNet's records noted that the pumps for the water feature had failed eleven months earlier and the decision had been made to simply paint the tubes. Six wasn't sure which version would be more decorative, but the current version did seem to be aesthetically acceptable.

Every third floor held a large dining room designed to seat fifty people at a time. The main floor was a purely decorative promenade, with various entertainment fixtures in place to keep the guests occupied and out of trouble.

Most of the drones concentrated onto those floors. Six estimated it was unlikely that any of the guests would be causing trouble in the staff sections of the ship—not least since those sections, the top five and bottom twenty-five meters of the module, were locked off.

The levels that were mostly rooms were of minimal interest. Six spared a drone for every two of those. Each of the dining-room floors had fewer guest rooms and more gathering areas, so three drones went onto each of those.

The main promenade got the remaining twenty drones of each flotilla, spreading out to survey where the majority of the guests were gathered.

With four hundred and eighty humans spread across the two modules, Six wasn't even trying to follow each of them individually. Drones rotated through areas, sweeping for gatherings, listening for key words and scanning faces against a series of identification databases.

It took easily thirty minutes for Six to get the whole pattern set up. Once complete, the pattern was saved into SecNet to be deployed to the DroNets of flotillas sent in later.

Six could have easily run the entire surveillance indefinitely, given access to a maintenance niche, cycling five hours on surveillance and one in rest mode while giving SecNet certain triggers to end the rest cycle.

It had been made clear that wasn't happening. Saving the deployment patterns would allow the humans to maintain the sweeps, though Six doubted it would be as effective.

Some of the students were gathered in an impromptu class, where a lecturer was going over information on their destination and theories as to which of the twenty-two identified Xenos Species it might belong to.

"What if it's an unknown species, Professor Ungaro?" a student asked, the voice cutting in to Six's hearing with perfect clarity.

"The chance is high, Em Penny," the lecturer agreed, even Six able to identify his voice as enthusiastic. "Only two of the known Xenos Species have any sign of achieving interstellar travel, and the L-I-Seven–K-Nine-Three–Delta Site has a high likelihood of being a pure outpost, requiring an extra-system—or at least, extra-planetary—source."

Six calculated that there were enough drones to spare one. The flier in question attached itself to a nearby lamppost, allowing Six to watch Dr. Ungaro's lecture.

Even Six still didn't know much about Six, but the desire to acquire any and all possible information was very clear. The opportunity to learn by listening in on Ungaro's discussion with his students couldn't be passed up.

Another drone flickered across the sky above Ungaro's head, a visual scan of the audience identifying all of the students as expected.

ShipNet had a full database of everyone in the expedition. Everyone the drones had picked up had been present and identified. Six wasn't expecting anything different, but comparing faces to identities was a minor piece of DroNet's processing power, let alone ShipNet's.

Pattern-recognition routines flared suddenly, flagging one of the humans in the other module. Six had been watching all of the feeds but now applied more focus to the ninth-floor dining room in module two.

Colorful glass tubes created a fascinating interplay of light patterns, but that wasn't what the recognition routines had flagged. The routines had flagged someone following a well-practiced digital-surveillance-avoidance motion art.

Nardovino Digital Ghost Dance, Six confirmed as the last few seconds of drone footage reran in parallel with the current moment. It was an out-of-date version of the motion art but more than sufficient to handle the basic security level on a Santiago Corporation passenger module.

The individual was approaching the meal machine. Six vectored an extra drone up from the main promenade to keep the floor covered while another drone moved in to get a line of sight on the person.

While the likelihood that any collection of senior academics contained an individual trained in avoidance motion arts approached unity, there was no reason for anyone to be using it.

Six anticipated the deployment of the digital hash screen. If someone was trying to avoid detection by *Santa Mica*'s surveillance, having some level of additional countermeasure was inevitable. The hash mark caused the drone's sensors to black out for a second after they picked it up, a process that would delete the user's face and add a few extra seconds of data corruption around it.

It could be a usual glitch, but Six was an ABMI, not a human. Six was watching every drone simultaneously, even if the one that got hashed was the one holding most of Six's focus.

Six could countermeasure the hash code, but there were better options.

*++Nephil. This unit needs a moment of your assistance. Someone has a hash code—a collar pin, I estimate. See the download from Drone Kappa-Thirty-Six++*

*++I see it++* the synthmind confirmed. *++And you are doing better with I. I approve. I am recoding one of our standard anti-hash measures and downloading to Drone Flotilla Kappa. The presence of a hash is concerning++*

*++Agreed. Vectoring a new drone into place++*

With the anti-hash program in place, Thirty-Six would probably have been fine scanning their oddity's face again, but Six would rather check over its code in the maintenance bay first. Thirty-Six went on the main sweep of floor Nine, and Twenty-Two flitted across the room to get a visual on the stranger as he turned away from the machine with his tray of freshly heated stew.

Six had no real assessment of food quality, but he knew most humans would have gone to one of the counters where food was being actively made to order by a mix of bots, humans and BMLUs. That this individual had chosen the limited selection from the machines instead was a warning sign.

The anti-surveillance motion arts and the hash screen were just confirmation. Six couldn't calculate any reasonable possibility scenarios before Twenty-Two got into position and the face ran against the database of guests.

Dr. Fade Benedict, one of the expedition team leads. He was being strange, strange enough that Six was going to flag him to SecChief Key, but he was at least part of the expedition. That avoided some of the lower-order-probability scenarios Six had been projecting.

The second ping was unexpected. The only database any of their guests should have shown on was the list of expedition members. Even the Santiago Corporation couldn't maintain a significant number of the billions of humans in the Seventy-Seven in a live database.

Dr. *Benedek Fabian*, however, was in a *Santiago Corporation* database.

One that said the theoretical physicist was permanently blacklisted from traveling on Company ships.

***37***

CIRILO HAD NO ILLUSIONS about what Dr. Fabian had done to get himself blacklisted from traveling on a transit void ship. Even if he had, the blacklist entry Six had found was surprisingly explicit.

Benedek Fabian had spent his entire career attempting to develop alternatives to the Santiago Corporation's transit drive. Like all such researchers before him, his work had been impeded by the fact that there were entire branches of physics that the Company made sure weren't explored.

And like other such researchers before him, the Company almost certainly had plans to make Herecrow System University hand over his entire body of work once he retired or died. There was value in new takes on the multidimensional physics that underlay faster-than-light travel, after all.

The Company just couldn't afford to let that research ever turn into a working technology. Scientists like Fabian struggled to get grants, struggled to get published and, once the Company became aware of their intent, were blacklisted from interstellar travel.

A list enforced by contract clauses allowing the Captain on hand to void the entire agreement while requiring full payment. *Santa Mica* was in the void, still sixteen light-years and two transits from the L-I-Seven–K-Nine-Three System.

Benedek shouldn't have made it onto the ship at all, which was going to raise interesting questions later. Right now, though, Cirilo had to deal with the problem.

He might not agree with everything the Company did, but this was unquestionably his job.

He and Key led the team into the passenger module, both of them wearing matching expressions of stern stoicism. As much a mask as anything they could physically wear, the image they were projecting hid any internal conflict they might have.

The two SecSpecs and matching SecTeam ratings were trying to match the projection. Their success was mixed, but a failing on the four troopers' part wasn't going to matter much.

Not when Six led three other BimSoos to flank the six humans. The active camouflage on the BimSoos was set to what Cirilo privately called Black Knight Mode. The main color was a deep light-sinking black, but every sharp edge of the cyborgs had been highlighted in a subtle white, enough to make their threat profile very clear.

All four biomechs had the Santiago SC in gold on their chests, but Six had two additional insignia. Few outside the Company would understand the gold cogwheel-encircled eye above and to the left of the SC, but opposite the mark of Six's AbMee status was the carmine-red square of a Security Specialist.

The guests scattered away from the security team, students and professors alike utterly unequipped to deal with the literal iron fist of their ship's master.

Six was still in control of the surveillance flotilla, guiding the squad with simple directions toward where Dr. Fabian was retreating. Quite sensibly, the physicist was in his quarters, in a bloc of larger suites designated for the team leaders.

"The door is secured, ser," SecSpec Ventimiglia reported. "Overridden."

There were few hatches aboard *Santa Mica* that would slow her SecTeam down for more than a few seconds—and the ones that SecTeam couldn't override, Nephil or Cirilo could.

The hatch to Fabian's quarters still only opened halfway, barely large enough to admit a human—a clear sign of modification to the mechanism. Or, less politely, sabotage.

++*Nephil, can you open this the rest of the way?*++ Cirilo asked on a channel shared with the rest of the team.

++*The door has been physically jammed, with a small masking program in place to prevent the module's supervisory agent from flagging the problem up to me*++ the synthmind replied. ++*It will need to be opened manually*++

"Three, break the door open," Cirilo ordered calmly. "Six, cover with the others."

Working with Michael, the AbMee he'd known before, Cirilo had learned that one of the best uses for someone like Six was to guide and augment the regular BimSoos. With security bots, he'd have needed to specify things like *nonlethal weapons*. Even with BimSoos, he might have needed to specify *have one Unit cover the approach*.

With Six and the SecTeam, he didn't need to specify. Three advanced on the door while Six and Five stepped back, weapon pods rotating to reveal heavy area stunners. Two, following silent orders from Six, turned to cover the approach from the main elevators, another heavy stunner unveiling itself.

Cirilo didn't give orders to Key's people. If they were needed, Key would give them—and she'd been in command of SecTeam for months.

Key herself joined Cirilo, her bracer spinning into motion as she aimed the weapon in support of Three. The other SecTeam troopers spread out to fill in the gaps in the BimSoos' positions.

There was no clear order. At the moment, the cover positions were sufficient, Three launched two spike-tipped cables from each of their arms. The spikes punched through the visible corners of the metal door, then the cables retracted with a force no human could match.

The entire metal panel pulled free, even the portion that had been concealed in the wall moments before, and smashed outward into Three's metal fists.

"Go."

Key's single word hung in the air for longer than it took Six to bound through the door, Five in Six's wake like they were attached to the AbMee. Cirilo moved to follow them, only to find Key's arm in front of him, an iron-seeming bar holding him back until SecSpec Ventimiglia had followed the BimSoos through.

The familiar deep thunder of an area stunner rumbled through the suite as Cirilo crossed the threshold. The sound wasn't in the main living room, a decently sized seating area with solid but worn couches and tables—the tables covered in the takeout containers from the meal dispensers.

Dr. Fabian had apparently declined the automated room service in his attempt to remain unnoticed.

"Six? Our prisoner?"

"In the bathroom, Captain," the AbMee replied. "He is uninjured but unconscious."

Six emerged from the room in question, Fabian cradled in Six's arms with a gentleness that would have surprised anyone who didn't truly know BimSoos, let alone AbMees.

"He was having an adverse physiological reaction due to emotional overwhelm," Six continued. "I calculated that stunning him would do less damage than permitting his fit to progress further."

"Thank you, Six. SecChief—sweep the room. I want to know what Fabian thought he was doing on my ship," Cirilo ordered. "SecSpec Ventimiglia, stay with Six and Dr. Fabian until MedSpec Bernardi can get here."

*++MedSpec Bernardi, report to my current location++* he continued silently, pinging the ship's medic. There was a MedSpec in the hospitality team attached to each module, but he knew Bernardi enough more to want her on hand.

"What in *stormwinds* is going on here, Captain?" Miloš Zima suddenly demanded. The expedition's leader stepped past the abandoned door, his hands staying very visible in a concession to the fact that Two's stunner was obviously tracking him.

Gupta was a few steps back, closer to Two than Cirilo preferred—though he spotted that either Three or Six had spotted the danger, as Three had stepped back to clear their own safe zone and had their stunner trained on the bodyguard-cum-secretary.

"Most likely the end of your expedition, Dr. Zima," Cirilo told the other man. "One of your lecturers is traveling under a false identity. Dr. Benedek Fabian here"—he waved toward the prisoner still in Six's arms—"is blacklisted from traveling on Santiago Corporation ships.

"As part of your contract, you acknowledged that blacklist and accepted a termination clause sundering the contract in the Company's favor if a blacklisted individual was discovered among your passengers," he continued. "You should have been significantly more careful with who you recruited for this expedition. We take a dim view of people trying to get around contract clauses by lying to us."

Zima waited with surprising patience for him to finish the spiel, then shook his head sharply.

"Dr. Fabian's presence was cleared by the University Legal team," he said, not even arguing with the identification. "Given your corporation's general nature as overeager thugs, I raised the concern of his prior interactions with Legal, and they assured me his presence had been covered in the contract negotiations.

"I do not know what triggered your overreaction, Captain, but I assure you, the contract your company signed with Herecrow System University does *not* allow for this kind of brutality and violence! You will release Dr. Fabian immediately. If we can resolve this calmly, I will prevail on him not to press suit for this... this... *assault*."

*++Those are standard contract clauses++* Key said in his head. *++There's no way the Herecrow factor office excluded them. We don't* negotiate *around the blacklist! That's why it's called a blacklist++*

Cirilo was starting to have a very chilled sinking feeling, one he was keeping hidden behind the impassive mask of CorpSec-on-Duty.

++*Did you read the whole contract?*++ he asked. ++*Because I'm realizing I only read the parts that* change. *All of those looked like what I expected, but I haven't looked at the boilerplate in years*++

++*I believe it may be necessary to have a conversation with Officer Bautista*++ Nephil interjected. ++*I had not fully analyzed the contract myself, as it was provided by a full Company factor office in one of the Seventy-Seven, but now that I am doing so, I am detecting concerning discrepancies*++

++*We knew this was not a standard contract. That may have been used to deceive the Corporation, and I cannot reliably calculate the likelihood that the contract would be upheld in court*++

Cirilo didn't need Bautista to tell him that no court in the Seventy-Seven was going to override a contract signed by an authorized factor representative of the Santiago Corporation. That principle had been set in stone for centuries—and he suspected that quite a few judges would be delighted to use it to twist the knife on a Company error.

"Regardless of the state of the contract, Dr. Zima, my authority as Captain of this ship allows and requires me to act to protect *Santa Mica*, her crew and her passengers from any potential threat. A man traveling under a false name and actively avoiding our security systems is unquestionably a threat."

He smiled at Zima, knowing he made it an entirely unfriendly expression.

"Dr. Benedek Fabian is under arrest," he concluded. "*That* is fixed. What I will consult with my Ship's Lawer on, as per protocol, is whether or not you still have a contract, Dr. Zima.

"*Santa Mica* will not commence our next transit until I am certain of that. And no, Doctor, that delay will not be removed from your contract timeline," he said firmly, as Zima started to open his mouth.

"You created this problem, one way or another. You will maldito well pay for the time it takes us to sort it out."

# 38

The moment Bautista walked into the meeting room, Cirilo knew two things without her saying a word: someone back in Herecrow was going to have a very bad day as soon as physically possible, and the crew of *Santa Mica* were stuck in the void.

"Give me the bad news, Legal," he told her.

She took a moment to grab one of the cups of coffee Lachlan had laid out for the meeting. If this went the way Cirilo was expecting, it was going to be a pain in the posterior for all of them, so he'd brought Jewel, Rao, Tsiklauri and Jernigan in.

The Senior Chiefs and ship's officers would be the ones to deal with whatever ticking time bomb the Herecrow office had lobbed them.

"This one is on me, Skipper," Bautista finally said, then took a large swallow of the coffee.

Cirilo knew she was one of the ones who'd kept a stash of her own coffee, so tolerating the mess coffee without a word was a dangerous sign.

"The rest of us"—she gestured around at the six other humans in the room—"including Nephil, if I'm being honest, can get used to reading the front five pages of the contract and knowing that those are the only pages that change."

"I should have run an assessment," Nephil's voice said quietly. "It would not have taken me very long."

"How many contracts have you sailed under, Nephil?" Bautista asked.

"Somewhere in excess of seven thousand," the synthmind replied.

Even Cirilo had to swallow an astonished sound at that. Well managed, a ship could fly fifty contracts in a year without too much difficulty, presuming those contracts were point-to-point cargo or passenger carriage.

Even at that high end, though, Nephil had apparently been in service for over a hundred and forty years. *At least.* Cirilo knew that *Santa Mica* hadn't been his synthmind's first ship, but that number suggested that Nephil was even older than he'd thought—and that *Santa Mica* was at least Nephil's *third* ship.

"So, far more than any of us are ever likely to see in our careers," Bautista summarized drily. "In those thousands of contracts, Nephil, how many have seen the boilerplate clauses modified? Void, for that matter, how many times have the boilerplate clauses even been updated in that time?"

"The standard reference clauses were last updated in twenty-five eighty-three," Nephil replied. "Prior to that... twenty-five eleven, then twenty-four fifty. Three times, in a hundred and sixty years.

"In the same time period, I have been involved in five hundred and ninety-six nonstandard contracts. Each of those contracts, like this expedition, was unusual and required a specific contract beyond that for passenger or freight.

"Of those... three had modified standard reference clauses."

"Three." Cirilo repeated. "Three in *seven thousand*. Who were you blaming for this again, Legal?"

His lawyer snorted at him but shook her head grimly.

"It does not happen, so it's not something most of the ship's officers need to concern themselves with," she agreed. "However, as Ship's Lawyer, I am *here* to make sure that legal events that we cannot anticipate are handled.

"I should have reviewed the contract. I should have realized just how much of a stink the Herecrow office handed us."

"I'll accept that attempting to anticipate this particular black-object event falls into your responsibilities," Cirilo conceded. "But it remains a black-object event, something that wasn't reasonable to predict."

A *black-object event* was a navigator's nightmare. The transit drive was mostly, but not entirely, immune to the effects of objects in the void as it traveled. A large-enough object on a close-enough approach, however, could interrupt the drive field with consequences ranging from *unpleasant* to *catastrophic*.

If such an object was "black," invisible to telescopes and most scanners at a distance, it couldn't even be charted and accounted for in Company databases. The number of such objects was infinitesimal versus the vastness of the void, but it *could* happen.

"And *I* sure as void didn't read the full contract," Cirilo continued, "so I'm not holding anyone else's feet to the fire for missing it. How bad is it?"

"The entire termination clause around the blacklist is gone," Bautista said flatly. "It wasn't even subtle. Five of the boilerplate clauses are just gone. Three more have been heavily modified. The Herecrow office shouldn't have missed this."

"You and I will have a conversion with Em Finnegan the next time we're in Herecrow, I think," Cirilo replied. "Though I do have to wonder…"

He trailed off, swallowing his thoughts. He wasn't sure who else in the officers knew that Finnegan had taken over the HSU contract from another contract manager in the Herecrow office. Office politics shouldn't extend to quite that level of backstabbing, but the Company was very old.

With all of the problems that came with that.

"The Herecrow part of the situation is out of our control for now," he concluded. "How badly does the contract tie our hands here, Legal?"

"Worse than I've ever seen," she told him. "Whoever put this together wasn't quite daring enough to insert a clause countering the standard authority of a Captain underway in the void, but they did take out the clauses *reinforcing* it.

"Fortunately, even without those clauses, the case law around your authority outside of a star system with an established government is solid. Locking up Dr. Fabian is handily covered in that area.

"However, most of the regular termination clauses are gone. As Dr. Zima said, we don't have the authority to sunder the contract for the presence of a blacklisted individual. There isn't anything in the remaining text to stop us detaining them as a threat to the ship if we find someone else, though."

"Just traveling under a false name is enough to justify that," Key said flatly. "And I've rerun the list of names enough times to be sure that if we have any other blacklistees among us, they're also traveling under false names."

"We'll get to how Fabian got aboard in a moment," Cirilo told her. "Anything I need to actively manage, Legal? We can still end the contract at the initial renewal date, for example?"

"We can. We're responsible for external security at the site once they're on the ground, but that's why we picked up the extra BimSoo section," Bautista confirmed. "On the other hand, we can't terminate the contract if they act in an unsafe manner, which we normally *would* be able to."

"Even for a passenger contract," he said with a sigh. "I take it we're stuck playing babysitter, even if they decide to start poking at neolion dens?"

"Exactly. You don't need specific authority to shut them down if they somehow threaten the *ship*, but technically, we still couldn't void the contract in that case."

Cirilo leaned back and took a sip of his own coffee to cover the ridiculous image that put in his head.

"So, we could end up trying to detain all of them for being an active threat to us but still technically have to keep them in L-I-Seven–K-Nine-Three until the contract period is up?" Jewel asked, her mind clearly going the same place as Cirilo.

"We'll deal with that when we get to it," he said firmly. "For now, we keep Dr. Fabian detained for the safety of the ship. Our physicist seems to have a few skillsets no one put in his database entry.

"Which brings me back to you, SecChief. How did he get on board?"

"The short version is that he used a more-sophisticated version of the digital hash that Six ran into with the recon bots," Key explained.

"Which is, I must note," Nephil interrupted, "dramatically understating the difference between a standard digital hash like the one Fabian was wearing when Six located him and the digital masking program he used to cover his arrival aboard *Santa Mica*.

"While our surveillance and identification equipment is out of date, the masksoft that Fabian used was capable of identifying all scanners pointed at it and convincing each of them to see the correct angle of the false face he was using."

The synthmind sounded offended. Cirilo decided he was going to dip into his own pocket to upgrade *Santa Mica*'s external security gear. The last thing he needed was a synthmind that was feeling vulnerable.

"The good news is that we found the hardware supporting the masksoft," Key noted. "It used a one-time module that burned out after use."

"I've never encountered software that did that," Jewel said. "That seems strange."

"It's intentional," Rao told the First. "Common for black-market soft, *especially* black-market soft that they believe can go up against the Company. Burning out the hardware means that the user has to come back to them for more if they want to do it again..."

"And that we can't reverse-engineer the code to build a countermeasure," Key agreed. "Unfortunately for whoever sold Fabian this particular masksoft, the good doctor wasn't as clever at finding hiding places as he thought he was.

"We may have missed one," she conceded, "but we pulled two more masksoft modules and a holdout blaster from sensor-blocked boxes he'd tucked away around the suite."

"Meaning we have more than enough to keep Dr. Fabian under lock and key," Cirilo said. "I don't see much reason to play nice with Dr. Zima, either. The man did his best to publicly undercut our authority in front of his people, and I have no intention of letting that slide."

Some of that, Cirilo would admit, was ego. Some of it was Company policy. A lot of it, though, was that they were in the void and he needed to know that the passengers would follow his orders in an emergency.

Their lives could depend on it.

"First, I'll leave letting him know that we still have a contract and shouldn't even be delayed in our arrival in L-I-7–K-Nine-Three System to you," he instructed. "I want all of us, however, to put some thought into how to make our displeasure clear.

"Herecrow System University and our own Herecrow office have conspired to leave us in an awkward position, and I doubt that Dr. Zima had no involvement in that. I have no intention of sabotaging the expedition itself, but, at the very minimum, we aren't going to be going out of our way for them."

**39**

Tereza had seriously considered borrowing a BimSoo—or at least one of the SecTeam hands—for her trip back into the module. She hadn't been part of the team that had gone in to seize Dr. Fabian, which hopefully would help keep tempers cooler, but nothing she was hearing from the StewTeam left her expecting a warm welcome.

The gazes following her across the main promenade weren't as hostile as she'd expected, thankfully, but her white shipsuit and jacket were still drawing eyes. Some of the wiser lecturers knew that while the bracers she wore were less decorative than Webster's, they shared the same basic functions.

"First Officer Jewel."

She hadn't even seen Indra Gupta approaching. The secretary just seemed to politely emerge out of nowhere.

"I understood that Dr. Zima was going to meet me in the main-floor dining area," she told Gupta, turning to face the lithe man.

"Given the unfortunate unpleasantness earlier, I convinced him that we should have a more-private area for this meeting," Gupta told her. "I hope this isn't a problem? I can take you to the room we've set aside right now, of course."

Tereza considered making it a problem, but the truth was that she'd already known that Zima wasn't waiting where he was supposed to be. There was no way SecTeam was pulling the surveillance drones back after finding Fabian.

"I suppose it shall have to do," she told him. "Lead the way."

Gupta bowed slightly, then strode away with the confidence of a man who knew he was being followed. The other passengers had already been keeping a certain distance around Tereza, but the people who remained split away from Zima's secretary with impressive cooperation.

Their destination was one of the private dining rooms, just off the main dining space. While Tereza hadn't known exactly where Zima was, her eyes-on-the-ceiling had assured her that he hadn't left the dining area, which had limited the locations.

The private rooms hadn't officially been opened by StewTeam—no one had requested it—but they also weren't locked. The seats and table inside showed the signs of being recently dusted by humans instead of bots, and all but three of the comfortable-looking seats had been stacked against one side.

"Ah, First Officer Jewel, I appreciate *someone* taking the time to explain just what winds are sweeping this ship," Zima told her, gesturing her to a seat. "Em Gupta will be joining us as well; he's a necessary part of my ability to keep everything organized."

They were not, she noted, being joined by the other two Co-Deans of the HSU departments running the expedition. While no one was under the impression anyone other than Zima ran the expedition, it was telling that he had brought his secretary and not his theoretical colleagues to this meeting.

"Of course," she allowed. She didn't sit, using that to give her a notable height advantage over the two men.

"I presume you are here to apologize and to let me know when I will be getting my team lead back," Zima said flatly. "We both know your Captain acted out of hand, and I take your presence here as a sign of his embarrassment."

Tereza smiled thinly. She might not have the trained flat expression her ex-CorpSec colleagues seemed to wear as naturally as breathing, but she knew that she could radiate the cold of the void when she chose to.

"Doctor, let's not play games here," she told him. "You took part in a surprisingly complex scheme to deceive the Santiago Corporation to permit a known enemy of ours onto this ship. Had Dr. Fabian attempted to board the ship under his own name at BFR Station, the modifications to the contract would have been discovered early enough to have the contract voided.

"Since you *knew* that, Dr. Fabian boarded the ship under a false name, using a highly illegal piece of identity-masking software. The presence of an individual on our ship under a false identity, using illegal masksofts and concealing a weapon that wasn't registered with the ship, is an inarguable danger to *Santa Mica*."

"Fabian isn't a threat to this ship or even your damned company," Zima growled. "We need someone on this expedition who can study any FTL-associated technologies we find at the site, and we certainly weren't asking *Santiago* to provide an expert!"

"You probably should have," she told him. She knew why he hadn't, though. The Company might not have had such an expert available for months or years, delaying the expedition drastically—or would have simply taken over the site, given their vested interest in the control of interstellar communications and travel.

Of course, the odds were probably equal that the Company would have not only happily provided the expert but provided a large chunk of the funding or even a ship at minimal cost. That would have come with restrictions and rules Zima wouldn't have tolerated, though.

"So, what, you just keep the man you brazenly kidnapped in a cell until we return to Herecrow?" Zima demanded.

"Yes," she confirmed. "Since Dr. Fabian should not have traveled aboard a Saint void ship, he will be returned to his point of origin as quickly as possible. Since our contract with you means we are required to be in the L-I-Seven–K-Nine-Three System for an extended period, that may be rather boring for him."

*Santa Mica*'s holding cells were more intended for drunk crew than actual prisoners. They were quite secure, from what Tereza understood, but also comfortable and supplied with not just necessities but many amenities.

"And the rest of us?" Zima growled.

"As you advised the Captain, it appears the standard reference clauses for this contract were changed," she told him. "While there is certainly a legal argument that it was done without sufficient notice or clarification with our people, that will be for the Company's and the University's lawyers to sort out."

The administrator didn't manage to conceal the wince that caused. Tereza suspected that the legal mess would eventually end with the conclusion that the Saint signing the contract—Callista Finnegan—should have known better; the Company would make very sure to draw the process out in as long and as expensive a manner as they could.

"We will arrive at Delta on schedule, in about thirty-one hours," she concluded. "So far as our contract is concerned, the expedition will proceed from there."

"Without one of my team leads!" Zima snapped.

"That, Doctor, is very much not the problem of the Santiago Corporation."

**40**

"FUCKING SAINTS."

Cirilo swallowed a laugh as the straw-haired man cursed him. Benedek Fabian had given up on pretending he was anything but who he was—and the crew had brought his luggage up to him.

After they'd searched it for weapons and computers, of course. The only thing Dr. Fabian had access to was his clothes. Key had even held his electric toothbrush, giving him a standard Company toiletry kit.

Cirilo had used said kit his entire adult life. Fabian looked no worse the wear for it and had dressed in a crisp blue suit and tie for this discussion.

He was a slightly pudgy man with the kind of deep brown eyes people wrote poetry about. Nothing about him looked like a criminal mastermind or a threat on even a personal level.

On the other hand, very few people practiced countersurveillance motion arts without also practicing martial arts. Cirilo was alone in the cell with the man, but he wasn't unarmed—and his bracers were DNA-locked.

"That's hardly the politest greeting," he told Fabian, taking a seat on one of the chairs. The "cells" on *Santa Mica* were regular crew quarters, with a bed and two reasonably comfortable seats. The work desk that usually marked one corner had been removed to provide space for an exercise machine, but other than being deprived of external computers, Fabian was hardly in deprivation.

"Your machine *did* stun me," Fabian replied.

Even the curse, though, had lacked any real heat. Cirilo had heard it so many times, it would have washed off him regardless, but he could tell when someone was going through the motions.

"Six estimated that you were having a severe panic attack," Cirilo told him. "Six judged that stunning you was less likely to cause permanent harm than the attack continuing in an enclosed space.

"Our MedSys reviewed the data from Six's sensors and agreed with that."

"You try not panicking when a ton of angry metal belonging to the megacorp that wants you dead tears your door open," the doctor said grumpily. "I wouldn't offer you a drink if I could, Captain. You're not on my guest list."

Despite himself, Cirilo realized he might just *like* the man. That could be a problem.

"The Santiago Corporation doesn't want you dead," he pointed out. "Quite the opposite, in fact. There's a job offer open for you to move to Epsilon Cradle and join the alternative-FTL research program there."

That wasn't the case for most people on the blacklist, which told Cirilo two things: first, that Fabian either hadn't fallen into anti-Santiago activities outside his research or, at least, hadn't been *caught* at such—and second, that the type of people at the Company who spoke math as a first language thought Fabian was on to something useful.

"The straitjacket of publication and movement restrictions accepting that offer would slap on me is utterly unacceptable to a scientist of any integrity," Fabian said stiffly. "I wish to progress the knowledge and ability of *all humanity*, not merely the wealth and power of the Board of Shareholders."

Cirilo shrugged. He couldn't disagree with that characterization of what the job offer entailed—as a former transit-drive engineer, he knew enough about the mechanics and physics involved that *he* was contractually barred from publishing research papers anywhere except the Cradles.

He was also barred from retiring anywhere but a Cradle, though that rule was winked at as often as not.

"I can accept your definition of *integrity*, Doctor, but there are prices to pay for it in the universe we live in," Cirilo said quietly. "You *knew* that your research would see you barred from traveling on Santiago ships when you started. You were informed, I know, when you were blacklisted.

"So, why sneak onto my ship? You spent a lot of time and money acquiring the skills and gear you used to do so, but you had to know it wouldn't last."

"I had to make it through four days," Fabian replied. "With everything I'd set up, I figured I could manage long enough to get onto a shuttle to the surface. Once I was down there, I'd be able to do my job. If you Saints caught me on the way back, it wouldn't matter. Zima would never have given you enough access to the expedition data to delete my contributions."

He probably had a point, but it didn't answer Cirilo's question.

"You just said you thought we wanted to kill you," he pointed out. "You didn't think you'd make it through both voyages without getting caught, so, what, you *expected* to get shot?"

"I will admit I hoped that the fait accompli of catching me on the way back would at least let me live long enough to get home, where the University promised they had some legal mechanism in play to protect me."

Cirilo couldn't think of many cases where he wouldn't just dump Fabian back on BFR Station, so the University wouldn't have to worry much. Their Legal team had demonstrated a rather terrifying ability to run circles around a Santiago factor office, though.

"Well, the good news is that I don't plan on shooting you or throwing you out an airlock," he told Fabian. "You'll be delivered back to BFR station at the end of the trip, unharmed beyond probably being rather bored.

"I'm afraid that with your level of cerebral bionics, I can't risk giving you access to computers or ShipNet," he continued, "so I rather hope those brainplants include some books or movies."

"What do you mean?" Fabian demanded.

"You will remain here, in this cell, until we return to Herecrow in five weeks," Cirilo explained. "Then you'll be offloaded with the rest of the expedition. So long as you don't cause any trouble between now and then, that feels like enough punishment to me."

The doctor considered this in silence until Cirilo rose to leave.

"Please, Captain, I *need* to go down to the ruins," he said, his voice very small. "We've never seen anything like this before. Even if all I can do is establish that there's no sign of what they used for faster-than-light travel, that's of value to everyone—*including* the Saints."

"Doctor, that's not my concern or my problem," Cirilo told him. "My concern is that you snuck onto my ship under false pretenses, using black-market masksofts that could easily have caused serious damage to my systems because you had *no idea* how they worked.

"You aren't being detained because of the blacklist, Dr. Fabian. You're being detained for risking this ship."

And for being an idiot, but Cirilo wasn't going to say that part out loud.

"If the blacklist didn't exist, I wouldn't have needed to sneak aboard," Fabian countered. "Captain, listen to me: the Delta site is an *unambiguous* outpost of an interstellar civilization. This isn't Species Seven, where they didn't appear in another star system until a hundred years after they'd died off in their home system—a clear sign of an evacuation generation ship.

"This is an outpost that's too small to be self-sustaining, without any sign of other habitation on the planet. Our best guess is that it was a scientific research facility, seeing if there was any value to find in Delta's biologicals.

"Regardless of its purpose, though, the Delta site is the first clear evidence we have of a Xenos Species with *ongoing* interstellar travel. We need to know—*humanity* needs to know—what that looked like.

"And how likely it is that they're still out there."

The last sentence stopped Cirilo cold. Everything about this potential new Xenos Species and the expedition was scientific research. Delaying discoveries until Zima was willing to work with the Company was perfectly fine when it came to research and people's papers.

The assumption underlying all of that was that LI7–K93 was an *archaeological* site, not just an abandoned site but also one belonging to a civilization that was no longer a factor. Of the twenty-two known sapient Xenos Species, seventeen were extinct, three of the survivors had clearly never left the Stone Age, and the last two had, at some point in the past, bombed themselves *back* into the Stone Age.

There was nothing in the Seventy-Seven or any of the systems humanity had surveyed to suggest the presence of an active interstellar civilization near them. The only threat to humanity *was* humanity, and for all of its flaws, the Santiago Corporation kept that threat under control.

"How old is the site, Dr. Fabian?" Cirilo demanded.

"We don't know. No one has ever landed there. It wasn't even identified during the bio-research expedition whose data we found it in." He wasn't sure if the physicist was speeding up because he thought Cirilo was convincible now or because Fabian was warming to the topic.

"Herecrow System University bought up a mass package of survey data from scientific expeditions across the frontier stars, basically anything we could find that had orbital imaging of a significant chunk of a planetary surface," Fabian continued. "Three of our synthmind researchers had a theory about applying new standards of pattern-matching to locate potential sites of interest that had been missed.

"They were thinking more in terms of mineral deposits than archaeological sites, but their new methods tossed up a few of each. The vast majority of the archaeological sites were in known locations, though they did locate a previously unknown Iron Age civilization near the Profunditats System.

"The University of Honduras there carried out an expedition last year, standard, and once the papers get released, they'll formally classify that star as the home of Xenos Species Twenty-Three."

"And Delta?" Cirilo prodded. He was still standing, but he was letting the doctor ramble on.

"Delta was the oddity. There is nothing else anywhere on the planet to suggest it was home to an autochthonous Xenos Species, but the abandoned site popped up immediately on pattern recognition as an artificial installation," Fabian said. "We're not sure of the deterioration rate for even our materials on Delta, even if we could guess what materials are present.

"Estimating the age of the site is basically impossible. We can't definitely say it was even present at the initial survey thirty years ago, but my synthmind colleagues put the likelihood at over eighty percent.

"Most likely, it had been abandoned for some time by then, suggesting it's at least eighty years old," Fabian concluded. "But Delta is a cold planet, one that could easily preserve a site longer than we expect. Without access to the site to do chemistry, it could be thousands of years old."

"And you, the physicist, wouldn't really be able to answer the question better than that," Cirilo conceded. He'd got more of an answer out of Fabian than he'd expected.

"Let me put this into terms a gruff old space captain who used to be CorpSec can understand," he continued, making sure to meet and stare into the other man's eyes. "Do you believe there is a chance that we are looking at a nearby interstellar civilization, one that could be either competition or even an outright threat to the Seventy-Seven?"

Fabian seemed to grasp the weight of the question, returning Cirilo's glare levelly.

"I *believe* that we're looking at evidence that such a civilization existed at some point in time," he said carefully. "Confirming the timelines and similar details is more Dr. Zima's area. My area of research will be the site's computers, sensors and any vehicle remnants we discover."

"Searching for evidence of FTL travel or communications," Cirilo said.

"Exactly. This is an incredible opportunity, Captain, but you're right. If this civilization still exists, it could present a threat to the Seventy-Seven."

And to the Santiago Corporation, but even Cirilo wasn't really going to prioritize the Company over the hundred-odd billion human beings of the Seventy-Seven and the Cradles.

"I make no promises, Dr. Fabian," he told the physicist. "*If* you are permitted to join the expedition, it will be on sufferance and under supervision. Is that clear?"

"Yes," Fabian said, nodding eagerly.

Unfortunately, Cirilo could already tell that trying to restrict Fabian to only reporting to the Company was a lost cause. He'd have to send someone to prevent anything truly dangerous ending up in the expedition's hands, because Fabian wasn't going to do that.

And *never give an order you know won't be obeyed* was a long-standing rule of leadership.

# *41*

Six stood in the middle of the room and felt... lost.

It was Six's room. Six had never had a room before. The BMSUs on a ship shared a bay, with enough niches for each of them. The niches were assigned solely because it avoided inefficiencies.

Now Six had an entire room. There was a maintenance niche in the corner, with a console and interfaces that would allow Six to change the programming freely. The desk wasn't really scaled for Six, but the DeckTeam had added a full direct interface to its computer, allowing Six to use it efficiently.

Two chairs large enough and sturdy enough for Six's weight had been fabricated and placed next to a table tall enough for Six to use from them. A second pair of human-sized chairs were tucked against a wall, in case Six had guests.

The niche had replaced the normal bed, and Six could tell it had been placed with care. The DeckTeam who'd assembled the space couldn't have pulled all of this from files on how to handle ABMIs. Some of it Six had seen in those files, but much of it was the specialists and spacers putting true care into how they arranged things.

There were no spaces in the room that a two-point-five-meter-tall cyborg couldn't move through easily. Things that couldn't be used by Six had been removed. Six had spots for guests, but guests were to be invited, not to insert themselves.

A step took Six to the wall, where someone had hung a banner. ShipNet happily informed Six that such banners were common for welcoming crew to a ship, though they were usually simple WELCOME... not WELCOME HOME.

The large numeral six on the wall wasn't a banner. It had been painted with a stencil, in a gold that matched the gold cogwheel-and-eye of ABMI status that was positioned above and to the right, like a mathematical exponent.

Six was undergoing an emotional reaction that did not match anything in the available databases. ShipNet's psychology files probably had some details somewhere, but Six didn't even know the questions to ask.

The armored casing over Six's right hand retracted. The appendage always felt a bit awkward when Six uncased it, but this time, there was no question. Fingers touched the wall, running over the paint of the painted symbols in response to an impulse Six couldn't explain.

They'd even used good paint, permanently marking the space as belonging to Six.

Six was only barely aware of the concept of ownership. Money and property came up in many of the files and articles Six had read, but they weren't part of a BMSU's life experience.

Slowly and awkwardly, taking care with the unfamiliar motions, Six lowered over nine hundred kilos of metal into the chair. It was a strange feeling, something Six would never have expected to do.

A few moments passed, and Six decided that the position was surprisingly... acceptable. A mental command summoned the Encyclopedia Galactica and brought up the last article opened.

If Six was going to be a person in this strange universe, Six was going to know as much about it as possible.

## *42*

Tereza checked the numbers one last time. The transits into and out of a star system were the most complicated, where the transition to and from the void had to be calculated to take into effect the mass of the star and planets.

LI7–K93 didn't have as many of the latter as most inhabited star systems, but it also didn't have a permanent presence mapping every object and passing that information out across the Seventy-Seven.

Civilized systems were easy. Uninhabited systems were a pain—enough so that survey ships used very specific versions of the transit drive with lower minimum transits, allowing them to take a look at the system from only a few light-months away before transiting in.

*Santa Mica* didn't have one of those. Her minimum transit was an hour and a half, fully four and a half-light-years. All five of their jumps toward their destination had been the same amount: two hours and forty-eight minutes to transit eight-point-two light-years.

But the math for the last transit had been messier, and there was always a chance that something had been missed. Up until the last few minutes, the emergence course could be adjusted to take into account anything new in the data.

Not that *Santa Mica* could get any updates. The only reason to adjust the course would be if Tereza's review found that Nephil had missed an asteroid that was going to be in an inconvenient position as they returned to the void.

It wasn't impossible. Synthminds paid for their sapience with a certain distractibility that regular computers didn't have. They had access to regular computers to make up for that, though, and Nephil had never got a course even slightly wrong in her entire time aboard the freighter.

"Course is clear, Nephil," she told him. "Which you knew."

There was no response, but she hadn't expected one. Nephil was the ship's true navigator, after all. Tereza's review was just a double-check.

"May I join you?" a voice asked.

Tereza looked up. Violet stood just outside the open door to the bridge, the SecChief waiting for an invitation to enter the space. The bridge wasn't even cramped with a full crew, and they wouldn't need that until they were approaching Delta itself.

Their emergence into the void, in about ten minutes, didn't call for more than the synthmind and a single watch-stander. A bridge designed for seven felt a bit empty with just one.

"Sure, come on in," Tereza told Violet. "You can stand the watch as well as I can, after all."

"Done the last math check?" Violet asked, crossing from the door to stand next to the elevated watch-stander seat. "As pointless as ever?"

"Yes and yes," Tereza confirmed with a chuckle. "Nephil didn't even bother to reply to my telling him his math was fine."

By some magic that Tereza didn't see, Violet produced two travel cups of coffee from somewhere and offered one to Tereza.

"By void, thank you," Tereza told her. First watch ran until eight hundred standard, which meant she'd been up when she normally went to sleep and had been up for six hours since.

A cautious sip confirmed that it wasn't even mess coffee. For a moment, she felt like asking just how Violet had managed to serve *Tereza's* coffee, but then she decided she was happier not knowing.

"Void," Violet echoed, rolling the single word around her tongue like it was a precious gem—and wasn't *that* a strange image to have in her mind?

Tereza wasn't quite sure why the image of Violet rolling *anything* around her tongue was suddenly stuck in her head, so she shook it off with a swallow of coffee.

"What about void?" she finally asked.

"How old were you when you decided the void was the only life you wanted?" Violet asked. "We all did it at some point, anyone who has stuck out this long, anyway."

Tereza considered the question, then snorted in amusement.

"I think I might have been eight," she told the other woman. "My mother was Company. She had to travel between systems for work, and she wanted to bring the whole family along for the experience. The Company sprung for tickets on a fast packet.

"First time I looked out an observation port at the true deep dark, I was done. Spent the whole trip driving the crew nuts. I swear, by the end of the voyage, the synthmind must have regretted that she could hear me anywhere."

Violet smiled and raised her cup in salute.

"I was not so young, nor did I have so positive an experience," she admitted. "I'm Cradle-born, Epsilon. Grew up in the void, technically, but the big habitats don't really count. Dad died right as I graduated school, and my younger brother was having epileptic complications.

"The Company was pretty clear on where we stood. They'd do everything they could to keep Joe's condition under control, but the potential cures were more than would be covered on survivor's benefits. Fixing his neurons was either going to take up every penny Mom and 'the minor'"—a momentary bitterness tinged Violet's voice—"were owed in pension for *years*... or someone had to step into Dad's shoes and join the Company."

Tereza knew that the medical benefits offered for Santiago employees were astonishingly good, but actual permanent repair for a serious neurological disorder was both expensive... and unwise to apply to anyone under the age of seventeen.

"So, you joined CorpSec?" she asked Violet.

"Bingo. Didn't have the qualifications for anything else yet, and while the Company would pay for my school if I signed a contract, that wouldn't give me benefits that could cover a sibling until I was done.

"Strapped on my thug-boots and picked up a rifle for peace, profit and prosperity." Violet chuckled. "I think I hated it for, oh, six months? Then I was a junior SecTeam trooper on a ship when we transited in to find a local in-system hauler in distress. Captain didn't even blink. Before any of us spacers even knew what was happening, we were in armor and launching into space for search and rescue.

"Every scrap of training I had was put to use that day, and we saved sixty-eight lives. The void is a harsh place to make a living, and those folks got to *keep* making a living because we'd been in the right place with the right skills and the right gear. That was the day I realized that I was born to sit in the shittiest places in the universe and tell them that, no, the people around me weren't going to fall in today."

"A bit more dramatic of a story for falling in love with the void, I'll admit," Tereza said. "But you're right. It infects all of us who do this, jump back and forth through the void forever."

"Could be worse. The company is fine most of the time—present company included—and the Company buys us comfortable bunks."

Tereza chuckled at the clear distinction between the two versions of *the company*.

"And we get to do things like this," Violet said, gesturing toward the main display. "I checked. *Santa Mica* will only be the fourth transit ship to ever enter L-I-7–K-Nine-Three.

Even with the bioresearch expedition, less than five hundred humans have ever set eyes on the star we're about to see."

As if summoned by Violet's soft awe, Nephil's voice sounded in the bridge.

"We will exit transit in sixty seconds," he noted calmly. "I have detected no concerns."

"Thanks, Nephil," Tereza told him. "I'm standing by if there are any issues."

Flight controls were up on her screen. They were currently locked out, with Nephil in control, but depending on the situation, it was quite possible that a human touch would be necessary—though that usually meant that the synthmind was utterly swamped with other concerns.

"And as for synthmind Carosa, First Jewel, not only can I assure you that almost all synthminds are delighted by curious children, I can tell you that she has paid a degree of attention to your career," Nephil continued. "She and I have traded some correspondence, and she has asked after you, along with several other crew members she has touched on in the past."

That was a surprisingly warm revelation, and Tereza found herself lost in the memories of the extraordinarily patient feminine voice of the synthmind on that fast packet. She'd remembered Carosa, but she hadn't expected the synthmind to keep track of her.

That carried her to the moment the universe flickered around her and the void returned.

"Since you're here," she told Violet, "want to help me pull together the first scan sweep? Let's make sure there's nothing unexpected before we fire up the engines."

Violet nodded and dropped into one of the secondary stations. The two women got to work quickly, dividing up the system between them with ease despite never practicing this before.

"This really is a waste of a star system, isn't it?" Tereza finally said as they finished collating the data. "I see nothing between us and Delta except the moon."

"Same," Violet confirmed. "Six mid-sized rocks, four of them with littler rocks, and barely enough asteroids to make a decent omelet."

"I can't imagine an omelet made of asteroids tastes very good," Tereza said. She tapped the command to initiate the course toward Delta.

Seven hours of flight and then Dr. Zima and his people would get to have their fun.

"Well, you aren't the intended audience of an omelet made of asteroids," Violet said with mock seriousness. "Only gas giants and black holes want *that* kind of breakfast!"

## *43*

"Thank you for joining us, Dr. Zima," Cirilo told the expedition leader politely.

He and FlyChief Ostergaard had set up in the room next to the shuttle bay intended for exactly this purpose. A holographic model of Delta hung in the middle of the room, with a flashing green square marking their destination point.

Dr. Fabian stood in one corner, surprisingly patient for having EngSpec Dada Idowu looming over his shoulder. Idowu hadn't been *solely* picked for their current task because of their looming ability, but the Black engineering specialist was one of the few people on *Santa Mica* taller than Cirilo, with a clean-shaven gleaming scalp and muscles that stretched their white shipsuit uniform in vaguely threatening ways.

According to EngChief Rao, Idowu was also one of the smartest people on the ship and due to make the jump to EngChief themselves. If Fabian found something of interest—or threat—to the Company, they would be able to recognize it.

"We have a great deal of work to do," Zima said, gesturing for his companions to follow him into the room. Gupta came first, of course, but then Dr. Cobalt and Dr. Hanraadts joined them all in the room.

"SecChief Key and First Jewel are on their way," Cirilo told the scientists. He waved toward Fabian. "Our prisoner has made a sufficiently strong argument for his presence that he will be joining you as well, under quite strict conditions."

"He is—"

"Currently under arrest for falsifying documentations and otherwise presenting every sign of being a saboteur, Dr. Zima," Cirilo interrupted flatly. "Allowing him out of his cell is an indulgence on my part, one it would be unwise to challenge.

"He will be bivouacking with our surface contingent and will only be allowed onto the site while accompanied by a member of the Company team. Dr. Fabian has agreed to this and it is *not* up for negotiation."

Zima looked mutinous, but Cirilo saw him glance over at Fabian. The physicist shook his head slightly and Zima inhaled sharply.

"Que será será," he conceded in a sharp growl. "We are here to discuss the landing plan, are we not?"

"We are. We have a great deal of cargo and personnel to get down onto the surface in as expedient a manner as possible," Cirilo agreed.

Key and Jewel arrived at that moment, the two women stepping through the door as one. The scientists waited with surprising patience for the officers to move up to flank Cirilo.

He supposed now that they were about to enter Delta's orbit, the scientists had every reason to be patient. This expedition was the culmination of years of effort on the part of the men who'd joined them.

"FlyChief Ostergaard has prepared an initial pattern of flights that should get us moving efficiently," he told them once he had everyone's attention again. "FlyChief?"

***

Ostergaard knew his job. While any of his six shuttles could haul the main cargo pod around in space, even combined, they could only deliver the pod to the surface and retrieve it as a group.

While there were arguments in favor of that, it was an unnecessary risk for both the shuttles and the cargo module itself. The cargo had been loaded with the knowledge that it was going to be delivered to the surface by shuttle and arranged accordingly.

It would take ten flights to get all six hundred thousand cubic meters of the expedition's cargo to the surface. The shelters and labs were prefabricated units that would be deployed in flat areas identified on approach.

There would be a small number of people down with each flight to start, including the expedition's single section of BimLoos to take control of the hundreds of Build-Bots who would do the heavy lifting of assembling the camp.

Starting on the sixth flight, larger groups of people would start coming down, with the eleventh and twelfth flights being entirely personnel.

With twelve flights of six shuttles, Ostergaard's plan would put six hundred thousand tons of cargo and almost five hundred humans and biomechs on the surface in just over twenty-four hours standard.

"I am not seeing anything in here for the security contingent," Dr. Hanraadts noted after Ostergaard had finished the presentation.

"We have our own transportation," Key informed him. "We will be on the ground before the first cargo flight, to do an initial overflight for unanticipated threats or other concerns, then set up our bastion in a position with clear lines of sight."

Dr. Cobalt seemed a touch concerned by Key's description of the prefabricated facility her people would be deploying, which made Cirilo glad she hadn't used any of the more... *colorful* descriptors used for the SecTeam structure.

Those names started at *firebase* and got worse from there. *Portable Box o' Death* had probably been Cirilo's favorite, one that had left him suppressing a chuckle after reprimanding CorpSec troopers for using it.

"The bio survey did not identify any animal life likely to attempt to threaten even individual humans, let alone a large concentration of machinery and noise such as the landing site," Zima pointed out. "We are aware of and have accounted for the environmental risks. Surely, you aren't delaying our landing for this unnecessary sweep."

"You are a very educated man, Dr. Zima," Key said acidly. "I am sure you understand the meaning of the word *unanticipated*?"

Before Zima could snap back, Cirilo raised his hand.

"As it happens, Doctor, we won't be delaying the main landing unless SecChief's people detect something unexpected," he told Zima. "The craft they will be using for their approach is faster and more maneuverable than the cargo shuttles and, even with the bastion aboard, is carrying significantly less mass.

"Launching at the same time, they will be above site at least fifteen minutes before the cargo flight arrives. That said"—he made sure Zima met his gaze before continuing—"we *are* responsible for the security of this expedition.

"If SecChief's people call an abort, we abort the landing cycle until we've managed to secure the site against whatever threat they've found." He gave Zima an impassive smile. "Given the resources available to my SecTeam, I imagine that won't require more than a day or two at most."

He didn't expect a problem at all, though he would admit to himself that anything that required an abort might well be outside of his SecTeam's ability to handle—though, on the other hand, a gunship and eleven BimSoos with an AbMee lead could deal with a *lot* of trouble.

"I see." Zima sounded like he was biting the words off, but he presumably recognized that it was a sensible precaution.

"Are we going to get better resolution than this as the shuttles' sensors cover the area?" Cobalt asked, gesturing to the projector table. The globe of Delta had been moved up to allow for an aerial view of the alleged ruins.

Ostergaard had used it to mark out what he believed were the areas flat enough to land the shuttles, but as Dr. Cobalt had observed, it wasn't a detailed visual. It was Nephil's work, assembling the view from *Santa Mica*'s telescopes with the information from the last two surveys to give an idea of what they were flying into.

"Won't be necessary for our purposes," Ostergaard told Cobalt. "While this isn't perfect, it's enough for us to plot sites for landing and setting up the camp."

"True, but it's not much use for helping us plan our excavation," Cobalt said. "I was told we'd have access to detailed overhead and scanner data to map out the site before commencing our dig."

"Your shuttles are already making the overflights," Zima noted. "You'll be able to provide us with the data from their sensors."

"That isn't in the contract and that data is considered confidential property of the Santiago Corporation," Cirilo told the scientists calmly.

He and his officers had spent more than a few hours of scheming since discovering the degree to which HSU's lawyers had carved up the standard contract. If the expedition's leadership wanted to play games, well, they'd stepped onto the court with the Company.

Normally, no one would have blinked at giving Zima and his people access to their sensor data, but what Cirilo was saying was true: anything recorded by the sensors of *Santa Mica* or her shuttles was considered proprietary and confidential. As Captain, he was fully authorized to hand it over to whoever he wanted.

"It's a standard—"

"As we've already discussed, Dr. Zima, this isn't a standard carriage contract," Cirilo noted. "Since it has been made clear that we are being fully held to the terms Herecrow System University presented to our factor in Herecrow, even when those are contrary to standard practice, I am obliged to make certain we adhere to the exact letter of the deal to avoid complications when we return."

"That's *ridiculous*," Zima snapped.

"Is it?" He shrugged. "I'm sure Em Bautista would be willing to sit down and consider reopening the contract for further negotiations, but that would likely result in significant delays, would it not?"

"Let it go, Miloš."

Cirilo wasn't the only one to look over at Dr. Fabian in surprise.

The physicist had his hands clasped in front of him, a clear attempt to keep them visible and not raise concerns with his escort. No one had told him that three of the "Security" people going down to the surface with the expedition were EngTeam sent to keep an eye on him, but Cirilo suspected he'd guessed.

Even if Idowu and their two companions had swapped the yellow shoulder flashes of the Engines team for the carmine red of SecTeam.

"We need to be here, Miloš," Fabian continued—and just the fact that he was using Zima's first name raised interesting questions. Zima didn't seem the type to allow much familiarity.

"We played too many games to pull it off, and I warned you and Billie," he said. "We play with fire, we get burned. Take the wins we're getting."

Zima looked about ready to explode, but he didn't. He nodded to Fabian and turned back to Cirilo.

"We have no way to change your mind except by argument, I suppose, for which I need enough data to assemble one," he declared. "We will begin our work as best we can.

"I appreciate your help getting us here, Captain, and I will even preemptively appreciate your patience waiting for us. Neither of us think your ship needs to be here for the next five weeks, but…"

He paused, and his smile was only slightly forced.

"As your Chief Key pointed out, we cannot anticipate everything. This is a world about which very little is known. Unexpected risks and problems are the order of the day.

"While I would prefer to be *right* that you are unneeded, if I am wrong, I will be delighted to have your ship and crew to support us."

For all that the man rubbed Cirilo the wrong way, he occasionally managed to demonstrate just *why* he was a highly respected scientist and co-ran multiple departments at a system university.

**44**

Six was hooked in to the gunship's ShipNet to an entirely new level. Riding into *Santa Alicia*, Six had been limited to the SecNet maintained between the BMSUs and SecBots, which had a standard amount of data fed to it by the local ShipNet.

Even Key, it seemed, had never considered providing the biomechs more input than standard doctrine called for there. If it wasn't flagged as directly mission-related, nothing from the sensors hit SecNet.

Now Six had the full access of a Security Specialist. Nothing available could exert any control over the system—SecSpec Ventimiglia was flying the spacecraft, with SecChief Key as her copilot controlling sensors and weapons—but like Marsh and Deacon, the other Specialists among the cargo, he could see everything the flight crew could.

Six had never had this kind of view of a planet before. There were images in the databases and those had inspired a degree of fascination, but it was nothing compared to the awe of watching an entire world spill out in front of the gunship.

Key information about LI7–K93 Delta loaded into Six's mind. Minimal axial tilt and an orbit at the very edge of the liquid-water zone for the star left the planet with no seasons, a state of perpetual winter across most of the surface.

Even saltwater's lower freezing point wouldn't have prevented vast tracts of Delta's water being frozen, but the files noted that most of Delta's surface water was close enough to pure to have an unmodified freezing point.

It might not be wise for the humans to drink it without precaution, but it was not as dangerous for them as most planets' seawater. It was just frozen, resulting in massive ice caps and then the intermediary zones the briefing files called *slush oceans*.

Delta was... pleasant to look at. White caps filtered slowly to the pale blue of the slush seas and then to the brilliant blue of the equatorial oceans, dotted with the occasional pale green cloud.

It was growing rapidly on the scanners, the gunship burning hard to arrive well in advance of the cargo shuttles. What had looked like almost ignorable dots in the ocean now expanded into large islands, a mottled mix of brown and several shades of green that marked the presence of land and Delta's determined life.

"We have visual on the target landmass," Ventimiglia announced on the ShipNet. At the same moment, a highlight appeared on one of the larger islands.

"Remember, the bio survey team didn't make it within five thousand klicks of this place on the ground," Key said grimly. "The islands form a sufficiently linked chain around the equator that they figured their handful of sample sites were representative of the entire globe, but everything in their reports says they *really* wanted to get off this frigid rock.

"Check your rebreathers now. Initial scans confirm the last survey report: O-two levels are at seventeen percent and there are some nasty trace chemicals."

Six ran a quick analysis of the scan data now it had been flagged.

"BMSUs will remain functional indefinitely," Six told ShipNet. "Some of the trace chemicals will even be useful for self-maintenance routines."

"Understood," Key replied. "Thank you."

"We are entering atmosphere now. Even on a rock this windless, the next bit is going to be rough," Ventimiglia warned.

Only with the warning did Six think to check their velocity. They were entering Delta's atmosphere almost five percent over the recommended airspeed for the atmospheric depth and pressure of the planet.

Six trusted Key. Hopefully, the SecChief and the pilot knew what they were doing.

***

From launch to circling above the target site took the gunship twenty-two minutes. Only two of those minutes were at all unusual, but they introduced Six to a new sensation: helpless fear.

Even linked into ShipNet with all of the processing power available, Six could not do anything to salvage the gunship if something went wrong. The two minutes in the atmosphere, watching the hull temperature rise, Six was more aware than ever before of the fact that existence could end right then, right there, and there was nothing even an ABMI could do to stop that.

Fortunately, Six's trust was not misplaced. The gunship bounced around more than seemed advisable, but Ventimiglia brought them down past Delta's odd green clouds and safely into an approach vector to the dig site.

Six had access to every sensor on the gunship now, but the site was still difficult to pick out. It wasn't that Delta's plant life was particularly tall, but it did seem to be rather aggressive. Most of the island appeared to be covered by heaps of moss and fungi.

There were vegetation structures most easily identified as trees, making up a forest covering the southern third of the island, but the dig site was in the hills north of that, almost exactly on the equator.

From a distance, all that was visible were different shades of moss and the waypoint beacon Ventimiglia had set up to give herself guidance.

"Coming in for our first pass," the pilot reported. "Sensors to maximum gain and pinging with active beams."

Six could almost feel the moment the radar pulses started, entire new dimensions of data added to the imagery and data coming in from the target.

Now the ruins were clearer. Several structures, built from something that resembled concrete, emerged from the moss on top of the hills. The radar marked their continuation under the plant growth and, as Ventimiglia slowed them into a gentle loop above the site, marked other buildings in the valleys between the trees.

Some were visible to the eye and would have been clear enough in the overhead the bio survey team had collected. Nothing in the collection of visible ruins would have pinged any of Six's analysis programs as a place to investigate, but dedicated archaeology algorithms had specialties security tools lacked.

"I'm not seeing any energy signatures," Marsh said. "Nothing that doesn't match the profile for the local plant life, in fact. Not even animals."

"Delta *does* have animal life, even mid-sized predators," Key warned. "A complete blank isn't good."

Six ran a slicer over the sensor data, parsing apart the visual data versus the energy data versus the radar data. The answer fell out immediately.

"The moss is blocking energy signatures, Chief Key," Six reported. "We are only picking up the thermal bloom of the moss field from the very surface. Even where the radar shows the structures are quite deep under the moss, we are getting nothing in terms of infrared or electromagnetic from behind it."

There was a long pause.

"I just checked Six's math," Deacon said slowly. "They—Six is right. Should the moss be *doing* that?"

"Not according to anything in the biological survey," Key replied. "And given that a native growth that effective at blocking sensors would be exactly the kind of thing they would have loved to find, that just leaves me *very* disappointed."

"Recommend surface deployment," Six interjected. "I am flagging several locations that could hide larger predators beneath the moss. BMSUs are inedible; kinetic investigation should be safe."

"Six means they'll go poke the big mounds with sticks because whatever is in them can't eat the BimSoos," Key said a second later. "I also think Six is learning a dryer sense of humor than most of us would prefer."

Six hadn't done so with full intent, but on reflection, there had definitely been clearer ways to communicate the intent.

"And Six is correct," the SecChief continued. "I've got the locations. Carmen, set us down on the easternmost hill; that will be most convenient."

Ventimiglia dropped the gunship into a gentle descent—as Key's voice inserted itself into Six's head.

++*None of you are expendable*++ she said silently. ++*But* you, *most especially, are not. Be careful, Six*++

++*This unit understands*++ Six replied—and *this* time, it was intentional enough that there was a positive emotional response atKey's cut-off snort.

***

The air was cold. Six wasn't certain when the emotional responses to temperatures had started, but they were a distraction. Six wasn't impacted by the eight-degree weather around the BMSU section.

It was just twelve degrees Celsius lower than the standard temperature of a Santiago Corporation void ship or any other spaceborne human construct.

++*Energy weapons, modulation seven*++

Six gave the order to the BMSUs with barely a thought. Modulation seven was a shockwave, designed to knock a target back and hurt them without doing serious damage.

++*Activate Kestrels. Use energy weapons first*++

The gatling railguns took up an entire weapon pod, usually the right-hand shoulder pod. Those pods unfolded now, components clicking together as the heavy kinetic weapons assembled themselves around the BMSUs' shoulders.

With one pod deploying energy weapons at modulation seven and the Kestrels deployed, the BMSUs each had two weapons pods left—each the standard module with both projectile and energy weapons included.

The weight shift from the gatling railgun deploying triggered a longer imbalance for Six than it should have—almost three hundred and eighty milliseconds to adapt to the new balance of mass across Six's shoulders instead of the two hundred and fifty it should have taken.

Things that were automatic for Six's companions were no longer unconscious for the ABMI. The slowdown was on non-critical changes like weight-balancing, things that wouldn't be life-threatening in most circumstances, but it was a sign that Six's new existence was demanding more of the chassis than it had been designed for.

Something to think about for the future.

For that moment, Six was assigning a set of three large moss mounds to each of the BMSUs—and four to Six, of course. As soon as the BMSUs were clearly on their way, Six moved.

All six of the BMSUs in Section Two had the same chassis, the same massive feet and hundreds of kilos of metal to move as Six did, but even if the other biomechs had been Section One, Six realized he would have moved faster.

Not because of any greater flexibility of the mechanisms but simply out of being able to observe the surrounding terrain and make the hundreds of unconscious adjustments a human would make.

A BMSU made more of those than a SecBot would but would still tend to point itself at the destination and move forward unless an obstacle prevented them doing so.

Six was scanning the path forward, moving around obstacles—and, generally, asking slightly more of the servomotors and engines underpinning Six's mechanical limbs than the BMSUs would.

Standard parameters were for standard situations, and something about the moss-covered silent valley didn't feel right.

Reaching the first moss mound, Six studied it from close range for a few moments. It had grown up against the wall of a structure that appeared to be mostly intact. The wall was roughly four meters tall, but the mound of moss was above even Six's two-point-five-meter height.

It spilled a similar distance out from its support, a bulging mass of a green that bothered certain instincts in the animal portion of Six's intelligence matrix.

At this range, Six's onboard sensors could penetrate slightly better than the gunship's had been able to from above, which answered at least one question.

The sensor-baffling properties of the moss were from a mesh of metals woven through the mound. It was creating its own support structure out of any durable material it could acquire, an expanding mesh of mostly metal that contained enough heavy metals to block sensors.

"SecChief, are you receiving my sensor data?" Six asked.

"We are. That is an unfortunately durable plant." Key paused. "Does it look like something could still be hiding inside it?"

Six crouched and touched the bottom of the moss with a mechanical manipulator. Six was not exposing organic components to this valley unless there was no other choice.

The metal content made the fungus heavier than anticipated, but it moved easily enough. Six started to lift the carpet of moss and then found auditory sensors overwhelmed by a screech with a volume and pitch that might have harmed any humans.

Six rose with the edge of the moss mesh, tearing away the outer structure to reveal the interior of the mound. An intricate interior web of wire-like filaments wove through the mound, connected by drooping and bulging masses of more moss.

Hidden inside it, screaming at Six with enough force that auditory reception had to be modulated, was a creature roughly twice the size of a domestic cat. It had mottled dark green hair, similar in tone to the moss, six limbs and lungs that seemed rather overpowered for its size.

"I am not going to hurt you," Six told the critter. "Move."

A second scream from somewhere else in the valley suggested that one of Section Two's BMSUs had also found one of the creatures.

As if the scream had been a signal, a dozen other distinct types of calls filled the valley—as wildlife that had gone to ground at the sound of engines now decided that they'd rather *not* be around the strange metal creatures that had entered their home.

The screamer Six had found was still standing there, glaring and screaming. Where it got the air was unclear, suggesting a separate mechanism for vocalization and respiration.

"Move," Six repeated, waving the active energy pod vaguely in the creature's direction. Six wasn't going to fire on the creature without reason, but it was being bothersome.

"Screamhowler," Key's voice noted on ShipNet. "Small predator noted on the bio survey. These specimens have notably different coloring and are smaller than the ones the survey assessed.

"Still, clearly similarity of bio-pattern. I guess the surveyors weren't all wrong when they decided they didn't need more samples. Except for this strange coral moss, which might have made their whole expedition worth it."

She chuckled—a sound that only sharpened as the screamhowler bounded up to Six's leg and stopped screaming. Now it was looking up at the ABMI quizzically, three mismatched eyes studying Six's metallic form as if considering something.

"Are they a threat?" Six asked.

"No. A human would need to be, well, about as close as you are now for the scream to do any damage," Key replied. "The survey data should include ultrasound frequencies we can use to keep them out of the camp. We might need to experiment, but they're no— What the—"

It took Six longer than it should have to register what the sensor signal from Six's left shin was. The screamhowler's bite hadn't had enough force to even scratch the armor, so there was barely a sensation *to* perceive, but Six had been about to dismiss the beast as harmless.

It *was* harmless, and now that it had realized Six was neither an immediate threat nor edible, it darted away.

Key was audibly laughing on the main channel.

"BMSUs are inedible," Six reiterated. "But apparently that particular individual needed to confirm that for itself."

"Fair enough, I guess," SecChief replied. "I'm sending you a new waypoint, Six. I want you and the BMSUs to check the target site before we drop the bastion.

"If nothing else, let's make sure we aren't going to squish anything we don't need to!"

## 45

THE BASTION WAS THE first piece down, chunks of it unfolding to form a twenty-meter-tall observation tower, but it wasn't the last.

Tereza had co-opted two of the MinTeam specialists to help her manage the flights and landing sites. Everyone who would normally be doing so was either *in* one of the shuttles or would be within the next few hours, leaving Salvador scrambling to keep Flight Control running.

The need to run so many flights had also kept the FlyChief from being able to take one of the shuttles down himself. Even with Jewel and her draftees backing him up from the bridge, Salvador couldn't be spared for something as unimportant as flying one of the six shuttles.

"AFP is down," Tereza reported into the shared MishNet. The mission network was a temporary link combining all of the pilots and the two spacers running flight control, keeping everyone linked into a free-flowing data mesh.

The sheer size of the atmospheric fusion plant meant it was critical that everyone knew where it was on the rapidly updated map. The power plant had taken up the full drop capacity of one of their shuttles for its core—and most of the cargo of a second shuttle was support modules that the BuildBots would connect to it.

Once it was online, it would filter through Delta's atmosphere for atoms that could be fused to produce power. The advantage of not requiring fuel was offset by its low power-to-mass ratio: a similarly sized plant with a fuel supply would have produced vastly more power.

The expedition didn't need more power, and not having to search out fuel gave them more flexibility on mission duration.

Tereza figured the plant would have been the first thing that Zima would have dropped if he had been trying to get the expedition into a single fast packet. It was most of the hundred-thousand-cubic-meter overage all on its own, though the expedition would have needed *some* kind of power supply.

As it was, the AFP made a convenient anchor point for her to center the camp schematic she was filling out as they went. All told, they were dropping over twenty buildings and a vast number of standard cargo containers into the valley next to the dig site.

"Sending you all a new plot of the target sites for our little town," Tereza told MishNet. "I don't think we'll want to put BuildBots on roads until all the structures are down, but knowing where we want roads is a good idea."

They were still adapting to the topography. The overhead images from the last survey were decent, but they didn't have the right angles to tell *Santa Mica*'s crew where they could, for example, put a twelve-meter-high, twenty-meter-long dormitory building.

"I've got it," Salvador confirmed. "Yevhen, you know what's in the cargo better than anyone. The map look good?"

The CargChief grunted noncommittally, probably marking that he wasn't in a spot to look at Tereza's work just yet.

The man's massive bionic augments weren't just for show. Tereza knew he'd be down in the middle of the mess in the cargo modules, directing workers and bots and BimLoos to make sure things went as quickly, smoothly and safely as possible.

"First-wave shuttles are done offloading," Salvador reported a few minutes later. "First, you based your map on what we were doing already, right?"

"Everything in the first wave should be on the map," she confirmed. "I'm adjusting the plan as we get better data on the ground."

"Looks good so far," the FlyChief confirmed. "Not sure when the unblinking eye on the hill will be online; still waiting for an update from Marsh."

The prefabricated security bastion wasn't part of the normal kit carried by a Company freighter. Tereza hadn't expected the watchtower to be quite as tall as it had turned out to be—but she *did* know that the bastion had its own power sources.

Unlike the AFP, the bastion needed fuel to operate independently. It would be hooked up to the camp power grid once they had one, but that was a later stage of the process.

"I can ping Key, check in," Tereza suggested. "The gunship is still in the area."

Complicating the traffic-control problem, since Ventimiglia and Key had only landed for a few minutes to drop off their people.

"You do that," Yevhen told her, injecting himself back into the MishNet conversation. "I had a chance to look at the map. I've made an adjustment that I'm firing back out to everyone—we don't have enough cabling to run the camp lanes that far. Someone budgeted supplies on having a nice, neat square.

"Which the terrain won't allow, of course, but we'll need to keep things a bit squatter to use the grid more effectively."

The new map popped up on Tereza's screen.

"That brings them closer to the bastion than Key wanted," she warned.

"Not much choice, not unless we want to keep bringing fuel down to the tower every few days," the CargChief told her. "Take it up with whoever made the expedition plan. They've got lots of crap for portable power at the dig site but barely enough grid cabling for the camp."

Tereza checked over the adjustments. Her design had been as much about traffic management as anything else, both the aerial traffic of the shuttles delivering the buildings and the later vehicle and foot traffic of the expedition staff moving around.

Adding the limit of the amount of grid cabling they could install changed the parameters. Yevhen's layout included that without too much of a sacrifice in the traffic concerns.

"It looks good," she told the others. "Keep the pilots updated."

Not that the pilots needed an update immediately. It was about an hour each way to travel from *Santa Mica* to the dig site and vice versa. The spacecraft were dusting off, blazing for orbit with their cargo delivered, but they wouldn't be home for a while yet.

A few commands temporarily shunted MishNet to a side channel and opened a direct link to the gunship.

"SM-Foxtrot, this is SM-Control," she said formally. "Status update?"

"Fuel is at sixty-two percent; altitude is five hundred meters. We're on the third pot of coffee, and I think SecChief just stole the last proper mealpack," Carmen Ventimiglia reported. "Foxtrot is good to stay on station for a while yet."

"The plan is that Carmen and I will swap off piloting in about four hours," Violet explained. "She'll sleep while I maintain overwatch for six hours, then we'll swap again. Without making a burn for orbit, we can maintain station until the last shuttle flights are down and come back up just ahead of them."

"Is that really needed?"

Violet snorted.

"As I keep telling everyone, the problem isn't the things we *know* are here," she said. "Yes, the most dangerous predator we know of on the planet just tried to eat Six and then wandered off upset because it hurt its teeth, but that's assuming the bio survey was complete and the moss at the dig site tells me it *wasn't*.

"We're going to keep orbiting the landing site, just in case."

"You're in charge of security," Tereza conceded. "Yevhen wanted to know when the bastion would be online."

"The assembly work is done, we just have the EngTeam fiddling with the power plant," Violet told her. "Six is already at the top of the tower watching everything. If FlyChief needs anything, they should ask Six. The BimSoos' sensors are almost as good as anything the bastion has up the ladder."

"I'll pass that on." Tereza realized that Violet had switched the conversation over to a private mode.

"You sound tired, First," the other woman said gently. "I *know* you didn't fly us all the way in from the transit yourself, but isn't this Vratislav's watch?"

The Purser was, in fact, on the bridge with Tereza. He was holding down the watch-stander station while she worked on coordinating the landing.

"It is and he's doing it," Tereza confirmed. "I was here to back up his orbital insertion, just in case, and then fell right into managing the mission package. It's important."

"And means you got, what, five hours sleep before diving right back into things?"

"Like you did better." Violet had kept her company until near the end of her shift, so she couldn't have slept any more.

The SecChief chuckled.

"You'll note that I am *not* flying the first six-hour orbit," she pointed out. "I was CorpSec; I learned when and where to push. *You*, Tereza, need to make sure you don't push too hard. This should all be set up to make sure no one is working the full twenty-four-hour unloading, right?"

"It is," Tereza promised. "I'm not supposed to be on shift, but I can swap with the Skipper, who has the last watch of the unload, if I need to."

"Do that," Violet urged. "I'll see you when we get back. Despite what Carmen says, I didn't eat the last proper mealpack. We have a full week's worth of them aboard. It's just they *all* suck."

"Makes our mess food look good, does it?" Tereza asked.

"Oh, void, yes," Violet laughed. "Meet me in the mess when I get back and I'll *show* you."

"You're on."

It was quite a bit later before Tereza realized she might have agreed to a date.

**46**

THE CAMP TOOK SHAPE along clear lines, the dropped buildings marking where paths would need to go in the end. Six watched the BuildBots get the prefabricated structures set up and cargo crates organized under the direction of the BMLU team.

BMLUs were considered a lower tier of biomech than BMSUs, but Six wondered. The data available suggested that BMLUs had a notably lower rate of Biomechanical Personality Emergence than their armed cousins, but when would anyone *notice* if the cyborg forklifts started to have deeper thoughts and questions?

The same data also raised questions that Six didn't know the answer to. There was nothing in his original databases about Biomechanical Infiltration Units and Biomechanical Entertainment Units. Even the entries in the encyclopedia downloaded to Six's hardware were vague in unusual ways on those two topics.

Most of the work beneath Six was being done by BuildBots, anyway. Like the bastion Six stood on, they weren't normally carried by a freighter—though, unlike the bastion, they'd been part of the expedition's gear.

The bastion had been loaded separately. Six wasn't sure where it had been kept, but it had been brought along for the exact mission it was being used for: providing security for the expedition camp.

It probably hadn't been intended to house a prisoner, but their orders regarding Dr. Fabian were clear. He didn't even enter the expedition camp unaccompanied, preferably by one of the EngTeam.

"Anything happening of concern?" Specialist Marsh asked, popping open the hatch in the floor.

"First personnel lift just left *Santa Mica*," Six reported. "Including our security team, there are currently forty-three humans on Delta's surface. The shuttle will nearly triple that."

"And we're going to keep them all safe," the SecSpec affirmed. "It shouldn't be too difficult, but I do wonder if we should have brought more hands."

"The bastion is incapable of supporting more than, at most, eight BMSUs," Six noted. "We could bring down one of Section One, no more."

"EngTeam is already moving one of the existing niches into the specialist quarters for you," Marsh said. "We could fab or scrounge up a spare, bring down two more BimSoos to fit into the space—maybe even borrow some of the BimLoo niches the expedition has to have brought."

"A BMLU niche would not be able to service a BMSU," Six warned. "While a security niche can handle any standard Labor Unit, the inverse is not true. We have significant hardware they lack."

"Fair." Marsh shook her head. "That's why I came up here, honestly. I needed to talk to you, Six, get a feel for how well you were adapting."

"I am here to assist and serve as any SecSpec would be," Six said.

"You and Deacon are both green as that moss, in your own ways." She stepped up to the edge of the observation deck, looking out over the valley. "Section Two are ready for deployment, but I would have preferred a less-complex mission for their first real task."

"I suspect you've already realized that life experience matters for a biomech. They get better with age, learning and adapting with everything they encounter, just like regular folks."

Six considered some of the potential consequences of that.

"Do you believe that any biomech would emerge as a personality, given enough experience?"

"The argument has been made in some circles," Marsh admitted. "*Not* in a sense I approve of—there are people who argue that BimSoos should be regularly reset to avoid BPE."

So far as Six was aware, none of *Santa Mica*'s Section One BMSUs had ever been reset. Four had taken enough torso damage at one point to require a near-full regrowth of the organic parts of the intelligence matrix, but a reset was an intended wipe of the entire intelligence matrix.

"Is the existence of Units like this one that large a concern?" Six finally asked.

"No. I think some people just get screwy when something they think is beneath them suddenly has to be treated as an equal," Marsh said grimly. "And others get screwy when their nice, pretty spreadsheets have to get updated. As an AbMee, you get paid, you draw healthcare, there's a whole bunch of costs associated with you that the ship didn't have to carry before.

"Not a maldito penny more than a regular SecSpec, mind you, but the budget spreadsheet only had two SecSpecs before the expedition. Adding Jamila and me, that's tied in with the contract, but you? You weren't in the projections.

"Captain Webster is a smart man, sees that an AbMee is worth more than one of you could ever cost. But some officers... well, if the numbers don't line up in neat rows, they find ways to *make* them."

Six didn't wholly follow the point Marsh was making, but it was clear the Specialist was upset.

"Is... there something I should be aware of, Specialist Marsh?" Six asked.

"Well, first, my large metallic friend, you can call me Callie," she replied. "Even *Calliope* sounds too voided formal, let alone this *Specialist Marsh* business. I may be in charge down here, but you, Jamila and I are all the same rank."

"There are no SecTeam troopers down here... Callie," Six said slowly. The instruction didn't carry the weight of command, but years of conditioning to obey without question left no reason to ignore reasonable requests.

Even if it triggered an odd discomfort.

"Well, officially, our EngTeam trio are wearing SecTeam rating insignia," Marsh pointed out. "They're sticking with Fabian, though, which means normal security ops are you, me and Jamila. If she and I ever want to get any fucking sleep, you're going to be in charge for eight hours a standard day."

The local fourteen-hour day was so far off from the diurnal cycle required for human health that the decision had been made to ignore it almost completely.

"I see, Callie," Six said. "That may require me to interact directly with the humans of the expedition, will it not?"

"It abso-fucking-lutely will, Six, which is why I'm up here, freezing my tits off, making sure you think you can handle that," she confirmed.

"Your gear should be sufficient to protect your breast tissue from the cold," Six pointed out. "Should I be running integrity checks on everyone's equipment? If there's a problem..."

Callie laughed and shook her head.

"No, Six, it's a metaphor, and I'm about ninety percent sure you know that."

Six had not. Six was working on what Key had called a *dry sense of humor* because it seemed to please the SecChief, but that question had been honest.

"The only way that I can become accustomed to dealing with humans on an equal level is to do so, Callie," Six finally said, having run six different analyses before answering her original question.

"While spending longer adapting to being an ABMI aboard *Santa Mica* might help, this is a relatively small area with a contained group. It seems as optimal a test-and-training situation as possible, especially as I will have both you and Specialist Deacon for support if needed."

"You will," Callie promised. "Jamila has spent most of her career so far guarding the plants that build biomechs. You should have seen her when she realized she was going to get to work with an AbMee, Six. It was like ten Christmases had arrived at once."

She stepped back from the observation tower deck and grinned at Six.

"Between you and me, I think Deacon has worked with Bimmies and you aren't the first *person* with a biomech brain she's dealt with, but she can't admit that," Callie noted. "But the AbMees, you're something special. And I think anyone who's built and trained BimSoos has to see someone like you as one of their babies all grown up."

Six was reasonably sure the metaphor processed—but *Bimmy* wasn't a shorthand in the available data.

"This chassis was activated with the commissioning of *Santa Mica* in twenty-five-forty-three," Six pointed out, hoping for humor this time. "Were I a human, I believe I would be old enough to be Specialist Deacon's grandparent. I do not believe I can be her *baby*."

Callie grinned.

"This time I *know* you know what I mean, grand-robo-parent," she said. "Watch the time, Six. Dr. Zima is already down, but *officially*, the expedition leadership is coming down on flight six. All three of us are going to want to be there to meet them."

"Of course." Six considered the conversation as Callie opened the hatch. "May I ask a question?"

"Pretty much anytime I'm not sleeping, fucking or shooting someone right now," she replied.

Six took a full three seconds to process that before continuing.

"What is a *Bimmy*?"

Callie grimaced.

"A rumor I probably shouldn't give as much credence as I do," she admitted. "It's a BMIU, a Biomechanical Infiltration Unit. I've never met one and nobody officially admits they exist, but rumor keeps saying that some of the biomech plants build bodies that are primarily cloned organics with key bionic pieces instead of primarily machinery with key organic pieces.

"They have an intelligence matrix but they're supposed to pass for human—which to *me* says they have to be intentionally creating BPE, because no standard biomech is going to manage that, even if you give it all the bits to *look* human."

She shook her head.

"Even if they *did* exist, I doubt the Company would be making them somewhere like Herecrow, so I doubt Jamila ran into any at Corvid. I was just nattering, Six. Don't put too much weight on the gossip mill."

Six considered Callie for a moment.

"I have heard that the gossip mill is the most reliable form of faster-than-light communication," Six finally said.

"It can be, but you have to be able to tell what's fiction from what's real," she replied. "And the only way you can learn that is by experience. Right now, you're best off assuming that if any of us start spouting something that sounds wrong, well, we're off our rockers and listening to the wrong people.

"Unless we're talking about potential threats," she supposed aloud. "Then I guess we want to plan for those, however unlikely they are."

"I believe I understand," Six said.

Six's assessment of the probability of BMIU deployment to this expedition was low, but the threat was something to consider. It would take some consideration to modulate sensors to penetrate the kind of deception systems that would be installed in such a unit.

The advantage Six had was that it was almost certain a BMIU would have been built to deceive *humans*, not an ABMI.

And if they were only a rumor... it would be excellent practice in scenario planning.

## 47

Six's armor was in its black parade mode as the three Security Specialists strode out on the cooling ground. The shuttles had been keeping their landings to roughly the same zone, and an area half the size of the assembling camp was now baked to the consistency of concrete by the engines.

Shuttle *Santa Mica* Echo was a perfect copy of her sisters. Where they were carrying differently shaped cargo containers, depending on exactly what piece of hardware they were hauling down, Echo carried a tube with reinforced armorglass windows down each side.

That tube would remain attached to Echo, unlike the cargo pods the other shuttles were leaving behind. The shuttle itself was beneath the passenger module, but a set of stairs had unfolded from the rear of the transport, allowing the first group of passengers to disembark.

Doctors Cobalt and Hanraadts were the first two off, leading several of the team leads with them. They were looking around, probably for Dr. Zima, but Six and the two other Specialists were all they could see.

Hanraadts was the first to start moving in their direction, but Cobalt followed him a moment later. They met the SecTeam a dozen steps from where the steps came down, and Six registered the two human Specialists saluting the civilians.

"Dr. Cobalt, Dr. Hanraadts," Callie greeted them. "I'm Security Specialist Calliope Marsh; this is Security Specialist Jamila Deacon and Security Specialist Six."

The two professors didn't seem to quite know what to make of Six. It was easiest to simply return their regard, letting them draw their own conclusions as Six scanned for the others who would be joining them.

"Dr. Zima is now at the edge of the landing pad," Six told everyone. "Dr. Fabian is also there."

*++With an escort, as agreed++* Six silently informed the two Specialists. *++EngSpec Idowu is with him++*

"I believe we should join the administrator," Cobalt declared, his glance sliding off Six like there was something wrong with the unit.

"It will take some time to offload the passengers, but once that is done, this area will become unsafe as Shuttle Echo launches for orbit," Six agreed.

"Six, lead the way," Callie instructed. "You know where they are, after all."

It didn't matter whether Six knew where they were because Idowu had reported in—or because the four humans were clear on scanners. Six had the location, so Six was the logical one to lead.

In truth, Six had their location because Indra Gupta's augments were surprisingly identifiable on mid-range scanners and because Dr. Fabian had a tracking beacon embedded in the collar of his suit.

Six presumed Fabian didn't know about the beacons, and informing him certainly wouldn't be part of the security job on the surface. Quite the opposite.

It was an... odd feeling to have a group of humans following because they were respecting Six as an authority rather than using Six as a tool. Not all of them might feel that way, but it was clear that both Callie and Jamila did.

Six had less faith in the academics, but Six also had much less exposure to them. They might rise above initial impressions.

***

"Dr. Zima, it's good to see everything taking shape down here," Cobalt greeted his colleague when everyone gathered beyond the burn line.

Six was busy estimating heat levels. Just because this was as far away as Delta's ever-present moss had burned did not necessarily mean it was safe for humans—especially since the moss in this valley had just as much of a metal underlayer as the moss around the dig site.

"It is only proper to give credit where credit is due," Zima said in a tone Six wasn't familiar with. "*Santa Mica*'s crew have done an excellent job of adapting our plans to the situation on the ground. We should have power online in a few minutes, then we can send people to their rooms and labs as they land."

++*Because the support staff have labs to go to*++ Jamila snipped silently. ++*Or are they just not people?*++

++*Little bit of hyperfocus, little bit of column B*++ Idowu replied. ++*And behave, SecSpec. We have impressions to give here*++

According to standard Company seniority charts, Idowu was senior to Jamila Deacon but not Calliope Marsh. Six knew that shouldn't necessarily translate into authority across departments, but something in Idowu's presence, even in the silent com conversation, was sufficient to calm the young SecSpec's commentary.

"Specialist Marsh, how is the security setup?" Cobalt asked.

"Our bastion is online and running on internal power," Callie replied instantly. "Thanks to the initial security check by Specialist Six, we have set up ultrasound emitters around the perimeter of the camp calibrated to keep local wildlife out of our working spaces.

"Once the dig starts, we have more than sufficient emitters to make certain the dig site is clear as well."

"Specialist Six?" Zima asked, looking at Six. "I was not aware that BimSoos held ranks in the Company."

"BimSoos don't," Fabian said, stepping forward to examine Six. "Even you, Miloš, should know the sign for a biomech intelligence!"

He gestured at the cogwheel and eye on Six's armor, a brilliant smile on his face.

"I have never had the pleasure of meeting with an AbMee, Specialist Six. I hope that you will be willing to spare me some time while we are down here—I suspect your perspective on many things will be fascinating."

Six both appreciated the reminder to Fabian's colleagues... and felt uncomfortable at Fabian's enthusiasm.

The answer seemed quite simple.

"This unit feels obliged to remind Dr. Fabian that I was the one who stunned him," Six said calmly.

Fabian physically flinched backward, moving a full step away from Six before he realized what he was doing.

"You were only doing your duty," he said quickly. "I would still appreciate the chance to talk."

"As would I," Dr. Hanraadts interjected. He had stepped slightly away from his colleagues and was actually offering Six his hand. "As a student of xenology, AbMees and synthminds are an inevitable comparison point that come up.

"I have never had the chance to meet with one like you, Six, and while I have no questions that immediately come to mind, I hope you will indulge this old man in his desire to simply get to know you a bit better."

Somehow, Hanraadts was asking for the same thing and yet causing much less discomfort than Fabian was. Curious.

"I will see what time I can make available," Six said hesitantly. "As one of the Company's Security Specialists here in the camp, my responsibilities for your safety come first."

"As they should," Dr. Zima said firmly. "We should, my friends, perhaps not treat one of the people in charge of our security as a fascinating sample case?

"Is there anything in the security setup that is going to affect or impede our work here, Specialists?" he continued.

Six found it fascinating that despite shutting down the other professors' fascination, Zima also appeared to fully include Six in his question.

"The major concern here is the moss," Six answered first. "It was not included in the biological research survey, though it is difficult to be certain if that is because it has mutated in the last thirty years or because it is a regional variety not present at the sample sites.

"It appears to sequester any durable materials—primarily metal—that it can access in the soil, using them to build a framework to support its bulk. This results in a mesh of mixed metals that is quite effective at blocking most sensors or radiation."

"That is truly fascinating," Zima admitted. "Like a coral species but above water and using metal? Fortunately, we do have several talented xenobiologists who can examine the fungus.

"But you are correct, Six; that will be an impediment to our work. Without more-powerful sensors than we have access to, we will only be able to truly scan the complex as we remove the moss."

He waved a hand and smiled.

"But we shall overcome, my friends. There is knowledge to find here!"

## *48*

As a teen and young adult, Cirilo had hated exercise. He wasn't one of the people for whom the process triggered positive brain chemicals. It was simply something he had to power through, a medical requirement of space work to make sure the oddities of artificial gravity and zero-*g* work didn't cause lasting damage.

Over time, he'd trained himself in various ways to take joy in what he had to do. Sometimes, it was adding one more notch of weight across the sets, moving the number on the screen a tiny bit higher than the previous day.

The biggest pleasure of working out aboard a ship, though, was that it was probably the space where rank was most left at the door. People watching and eavesdropping—subtly, with decades of practice—let him keep a surprisingly good eye on the morale of his people.

Unfortunately, it turned out that while people could ignore the presence of the First Officer, the Captain was a much-larger elephant in the room. People were still using the gym when he was in it, but there were still a stiffness and an unusual silence when he was in the room.

The upside, he supposed, was that he'd expanded all of his exercise routines by at least half a kilo since taking command of *Santa Mica*.

The other advantage, he realized as he finished a round of leg lifts, was that it was quite clear when something *else* unusual happened in the room. His current workout companions were all members of the MinTeam, the mix of clerks, programmers and such that kept the other ten departments running.

There had been a distinct wave of all of them looking toward one of the gym's entrances, their gazes lingering rather longer than they probably should have and then snapping back to their own workouts.

Cirilo concealed a smile and turned his post-exercise stretch slightly in angle, allowing him to get a look at Renata Bautista as the lawyer crossed the gym to the machine next to him.

Most of the crew worked out in their shipsuits, which were designed to neatly unzip and roll down to the waist for just that purpose. In an emergency, the five seconds to reseal the shipsuit could be the difference between life and death—but it was a lot less time than it took to put a shipsuit on over other clothes.

Bautista clearly didn't subscribe to that theory. She was wearing a rose-pink matching set of sports bra and leggings that frankly outlined a body that lived up to her painfully beautiful face.

He gave her a firm nod as she turned the machine on.

"You do have a shipsuit to hand, Legal?" he asked, putting a notable paternal tone into his voice. His ship's lawyer was young enough to be his daughter *and* a member of a Shareholder family.

She chuckled and lifted a carryall bag that her torso had blocked from his view.

"I am, yes," she confirmed. "No need to call the safety crew."

"I believe MinSpec Jassim is over there, in fact," he said with a matching chuckle, gesturing to where the young woman in question was going through her own workout.

"Then it's a good thing I have my suit, isn't it?" Bautista smiled as she activated her own program on the machine. "You finishing up?"

"Just stretching before the next set," he said. "Neither keeping an eye on things downstairs nor datawork has me moving much."

The machine chirped that it was time for the next set of exercises. It helpfully moved parts around, presenting the handles for the upper-arm exercises.

Next to him, Bautista started a series of stretches that were probably doing unfortunate things to several of the younger crew members in the gym. Cirilo both knew what was happening and had minimal sympathy for it—void ships were coed spaces by their nature, and his crew would learn to handle it.

They probably already could. If there was a problem, someone would raise it with either him, Jewel or Nephil, and it would be quietly handled before it became a *problem*.

"There's almost nothing in my job that has me moving around," Bautista admitted, holding a stretch and watching his last half-dozen bicep curls. "If I don't come up with reasons to work out, I feel like I fossilize in my chair."

"I learned long ago that MedSys will only let you do that for so long before it tells the synthmind, and most Second Officers get *grumpy* when they have to pass on memos from MedSys," Cirilo said.

She grinned at him and let the stretch go as he finished the set and switched to the other arm.

"Downstairs is being interesting?" she asked. "It's only been a week."

"They moved in the first day after they were on the ground," Cirilo admitted. He was actually impressed by how well Zima's people seemed to know their work. "It's a slow process, and peeling the moss off is slowing everything down, but my understanding is that they've finished a first pass of one square of the exterior spaces and most of one building."

He released the levers and glanced at Bautista as her own machine supplied a chest weight for augmented sit-ups.

"That seems slow," she admitted, then paused for a long breath at the top of a sit-up. "But I guess that's archaeology. Have they found any pottery shards?"

"I'm hearing everything third-hand through Key," he told her. "No one is sending us official reports. My understanding is that they're disappointed with what they're finding and that might see them speed up.

"It's a pretty clean site; really just leaves them with walls to poke at."

He shrugged. He doubted that the buildings themselves were meaningless; they were just easy enough to find that the xenoarchaeology team was focusing on finding smaller debris to examine before they started cutting into structures for samples.

"I'm not a xenoarchaeologist," Bautista said, pausing to do another sit-up, "but that seems odd."

"I imagine the Co-Deans have a list of theories as long as my arm," Cirilo noted, "but my personal guess is that someone cleaned up on their way out. An orderly shutdown."

He finished his last rep of curls and stepped back, activating the machine's cleaning cycle.

"I have a scheduled call with Dr. Zima; I may ask what he's thinking. Though..." He considered his Ship's Lawyer for a moment, in a way that was only minimally related to her outfit.

"You did a full review of the contract, right?" he asked. "No other surprises in there?"

"The ones we found were bad enough," she admitted, finishing her sit-up set and wiping her brow. "Why, anything particularly worrisome?"

"Renewing for extra weeks is still at my discretion, I hope."

"Yeah. They took stuff out of the standard clauses, they didn't try to sneak anything new in—and I'd *like* to think we'd have noticed if they'd snuck something in that reversed the main terms, Skipper."

"Good. Just need to know what ammunition I have," he concluded with a grin. "Thanks, Legal."

***

Back in his uniform and his office, Cirilo made sure his working jacket's platinum square was visible and that his hair hadn't acquired any flyaways since his last trim.

Lachlan was in the room as he inspected himself in the mirror. His steward had already cleared away the dishes from his breakfast and now was fussing around the room to make sure everything looked acceptable for a work teleconference.

"We really do need to get some decoration in here, ser," Lachlan told Cirilo. "I know we lost your stuff on *Caballero*, but it's almost ostentatiously plain now we're rid of the last guy's stuff."

"I know, I know," he said, waving away his assistant's comment. "There isn't exactly somewhere we can go shopping for wall art here in L-I-Seven though, is there?"

"True enough. Though..." Lachlan trailed off thoughtfully. Cirilo knew the tone and waited for the man to finish his thoughts—while checking that they still had a few minutes before Zima was scheduled to connect in.

"A suggestion, ser?" the steward finally asked.

"Since when have you needed permission?"

"Always, technically." Cirilo couldn't see Lachlan's grin behind him, but he knew *exactly* how wide it was.

"There's always someone doing art on a ship like this. I can put some feelers out, see who the crew thinks is the best at it. Odds aren't bad we can find something you like. We'll break up the plain walls *and* earn brownie points with the crew."

Cirilo considered the thought. It was a good one—most of Lachlan's suggestions were. He didn't just keep Lachlan around because the man had repeatedly saved his life, after all.

"Put out those feelers," he instructed. "And, Lachlan? If it comes down to it, I'll take making the crew feel valued over being in love with what's on my walls. But let's try to avoid having something so awful that's obvious."

"You can consider it done, ser. Your call is starting in thirty," Lachlan concluded. "I'll vanish and leave you to the good doctor."

"Your efficiency is appreciated," Cirilo told the retreating back sardonically.

He smoothed away signs of emotions and brought up the conference software. A two-dimensional screen took shape above his desk's interface field, the preprogrammed video conference activating as soon as he gave permission.

The computers could handle connecting the call without even needing Nephil. Ten seconds after he'd signaled readiness, a flat image of Dr. Zima replaced the screen.

"Captain," Zima greeted him. "Thank you for making the time."

"Thank you, Doctor," Cirilo replied. "I'm in orbit as a precaution; *you* have an expedition to run."

Zima grunted his acknowledgement.

"This check-in was required by the insurance company," he said. "It's general good policy regardless, one supposes, for us to remain in some contact."

"The dig progresses? I have some small updates via my security team, but they have both less information and less understanding than you do."

If that *wasn't* the case, Herecrow System University had put the wrong man in charge.

"We are making progress," Zima agreed. "Right now, we're mostly engaged in mapping. Our drones are only so effective at piercing the moss in the area, but we need to be careful in our investigation before we remove it.

"Many things could be hidden underneath or even inside the fungus. It is a rather large complication we did not anticipate. We knew there would be moss, of course, but not that it would have a metallic coral-like substructure."

"This was always going to be a preliminary survey, as I understand," Cirilo pointed out. "Another expedition will be sent to follow up?"

"To be frank, that requires us to find funding for another expedition," the academic replied. "Which means it will be easier the more we manage to achieve this time.

"Right now, we believe we have located the perimeter of the outpost and have set up a grid pattern," Zima explained. "We are clearing the exterior of the site, ground and building walls, zone by zone, with as much care as possible. I estimate it will take us at least three weeks, but that *should* provide us with a quantity of smaller artifacts for analysis and clear the damn moss."

"I understand you've also started examining one of the buildings?"

"We have. The roof had partially collapsed, so Dr. Cobalt wanted to get in before the elements degraded anything inside further—plus, it was on the exterior, closest to our camp, and made for a logical starting point.

"So far, it appears to have been a residence of some kind, but it's difficult to tell, as it was emptied more thoroughly than we expected."

"Why wouldn't you expect that?" Cirilo asked. "The site has been abandoned; I wouldn't expect people to leave behind anything useful."

"Yes, but *useful* is a relative term, Captain," Zima said. "What is useful enough to haul out when you're moving is a very different scale from what is useful to an archaeologist investigating the site afterward.

"The cleanup has to be very thorough for us to fail to find anything of interest. Even bits of broken electronics or personal effects can be useful. So far, though, we have been coming up blank for even the smallest of leftovers.

"The buildings themselves appear to be the only thing left, which I find fascinating."

"And I find concerning," Cirilo said. "That speaks to a level of paranoia that makes me wonder what you've stumbled upon, Dr. Zima."

"We have taken every precaution reasonable and many unreasonable, Captain, including your own presence. There is nothing to fear here, only abandoned buildings, one of which has been cleaned out more than expected.

"There could be a thousand cultural reasons for that, not all of which represent a threat to us."

Cirilo kept his peace. He wasn't going to tell Zima that the only reason Fabian was on the surface was because *he* was concerned about a threat.

And everything he was hearing was making him more concerned, not less.

## *49*

Six's foot patrol through the dig site was mostly to get people used to the idea. Partially to the idea of having a security team patrolling their workspace, and partially to get them used to Six specifically.

After twelve days of one of the Security Specialists walking around the dig site once a day, the academics were taking it in stride. They asked SecTeam to stay in the already-cleared areas—but those were obviously marked, with both electronic tags and physical ropes showing the sections that were safe to walk.

The teams were even mostly taking Six warmly, which was appreciated. The first time Six had patrolled, there had been dropped tools, exclamations of surprise and people actively hiding. It had been concerning, but Marsh had insisted that the patrols continue unchanged.

The patrol was redundant, of course. Even as Six carefully followed the path laid out alongside the dig grid, Six was controlling two dozen aerial drones sweeping the camp from higher up.

Still, Six was beginning to recognize a clear difference between the data downloaded from drones and external sensors and those recorded by the organic eyes and other, more complex sensors mounted on Six's chassis.

Some of it was just that Six had full access to the data from those internal sensors, but some of it seemed to be that the intelligence matrix Six relied on treated the external data as slightly less reliable.

Even when Six had been in full control of the drones all along. The psychology of it was fascinating—Six had found a series of articles on working with and studying ABMIs in the literature database the expedition had brought with them.

The academic files were hardly the sum total of human knowledge, but they included some of the most advanced and specialized research in a number of fields. Six was learning a great deal about ABMIs... or, at least, what *humans* thought of ABMIs.

Six stopped, watching as the work team on Building Three finished their cuts. A pair of BMLUs with industrial cutters had been working on the moss on the east side of the building, toward the expedition camp. A dozen heavy drones, with smaller cutters, had worked across the top and now gripped the moss with heavy manipulators.

At an audible order from the academic standing by with a tripod-mounted scanner array, the drones lifted off. They didn't have a particularly long flight range, but it was enough for them to lift a ten meter-wide, five-meter-tall curtain of moss away from the building and haul it west.

There was a designated disposal site for all of the moss they were removing. As Six understood it, there was an active attempt to make sure they killed as little of the fungus as possible, though Six wasn't sure how well that plan was going to work.

"You're sure you got it all?" the scientist shouted to the BMLUs.

The labor biomechs couldn't really respond to that, but Six stepped up next to the scientist.

"It appears so," Six told the man.

"I agree, but I'm still not getting shit from the building," the researcher said, without even looking up to see who was speaking to him. "If the moss is gone and I'm *still* not getting any useful reading... We're going to have to cut in, and that's not scheduled yet."

Six focused more sensors on the uncovered wall. The sensor package the scientist was using was sophisticated, but Six's onboard scanners had more power.

"Close your sensors' receivers," Six instructed the man. "The pulse I am about to use may damage them."

The scientist looked up in confusion, finally realized who was standing next to him and then obeyed without hesitation.

A BMSU's active sensor modules were rarely used, but they were installed on every Unit anyway. Six had used them as a weapon almost as often as Six had used them for their intended purpose, but now the module shifted slightly and then unleashed a rapid-fire series of pulses.

Radar—several different varieties of electromagnetic radiation, in fact. Ultrasound. Several other waves and particles that Six would have to look up the definitions of in the database before explaining.

The bounce back arrived fractions of a second later, and Six considered the data carefully.

"The wall is shielded," Six informed the scientist. "Both against scanners and physically reinforced. Without being certain of the materials used, I can't definitely say that your cutters won't work, but it seems... likely."

"Why would there be a shielded building here?" the scientist asked.

Six suspected the question was what Marsh had called a *rhetorical question*, one without an expected answer. Except that Six *knew* the answer.

"Based on the continuing presence of the shield layer underground and the radiation signatures leaking through the seams, because this is a fission-based power plant," Six told the scientist. "Active operation has ceased, but the radiation patterns I am detecting would be consistent with the use of radioisotope thermoelectric generators for long-term backup power."

There was a long silence, lasting at least fifteen seconds.

"My manners elude me, Specialist Six," the scientist said. "My name is Dr. Eugenios Wild, I head our primary technology team, which is why I'm moving forward on the buildings while we're still sifting dirt on most of the site.

"Would it be possible for you to transfer me some of your sensor data? What you're saying makes sense, but the more data I have to work with, the better."

Wild was starting to speak faster as he argued his case.

"If these truly are operational RTGs, that might be the first intact tech we've seen since we've arrived—and some of the best possible options for dating the site we *could* find!"

✳✳✳

"Well, apparently, you have found the easy way to a scientist's heart, Six," Callie said later, after Six had returned to the bastion. "In exchange for thirty seconds of data from your scanners, Dr. Wild is asking if there's anything he can get you as a thank-you gift!"

"I happened to be there," Six replied, carefully sitting in the specialty chair built to hold an ABMI's weight. "It seemed an easy way to be helpful."

Replaying the moments, Six realized that part of the motivation to get involved had been the appearance of blaming the BMLUs for a failure not of their making. With additional data, the BMLUs appeared to have been safe from Dr. Wild, but the concern had been valid.

"Don't give up goodwill if you don't have to," Jamila advised. "Academics may not be rich, but they can do things like give you access to the academic databases if you need information.

"They're handy friends to have."

"Like Dr. Fabian?" Six asked. The physicist was out at the site with one of the EngTeam, as usual.

"Eh, Fabian's all right," Jamila told Six. "You just don't like him because he's sucking up and it's so opposite to what you know that it triggers a big red klaxon screaming danger."

Six had to stop and research the colloquialism *sucking up* to be certain of Jamila's meaning.

"That may make some sense, SecSpec Deacon," he told her.

"Jamila, Six," she corrected—not for the first time. For some reason, using the other Security Specialists' first names was a greater struggle than many of the adjustments Six had made since being officially "emerged."

"His approach to me is uncomfortable," Six continued. "He wants something. The standard human response to someone who shot them would not be to attempt to become friends."

The two women shared a long look that Six could not interpret.

"People are weird, Six," Callie finally said. "What some other human did in the past can only suggest what a given human will do now. But yeah. Fabian wants something. He wants you to trust and value him so that next time, you might *not* shoot him."

"If Captain Webster orders him stunned again, I will trust that it is required," Six replied. "Both because I am obliged to follow orders and because I trust Captain Webster."

The two women shared another look.

"I guess I can't even say you've known him longer than we have," Callie admitted. "Before you were acknowledged as an ABMI, you wouldn't have had much interaction with him at all, would you?"

"And since, about as much as us," Jamila noted. "That's not much to trust someone on."

Six considered how to respond to that.

"I... know that SecChief Key trusts him," Six finally told them. "And I trust SecChief Key."

"Fair enough. Just don't ask either of them to choose between you and the Company," Jamila said sharply. "Real CorpSec get the Santiago brand somewhere inside their brain to keep them on point—no offense, Callie."

Six noted an unusual stiffness to Callie's posture after that comment, but interpretation of that level of body language was beyond Six's current software.

"You're... not wrong," Callie said slowly. "The Chief and Captain a bit more so than even most CorpSec, I think. I mean, I did my ten years in the commandos before I moved to more-general security roles like this one.

"That was... *intense*. We see what the Company is fighting against, you know? Why we do what we do."

"I get that I haven't done that," Jamila conceded. "And I've got nothing against SecChief or the Captain, either. You just always have to remember where the officers' loyalty lies."

Six wasn't so sure that *Santa Mica*'s SecChief or Captain would choose the Company over their crew, but Six also knew that the humans knew much more about humans than the database contained.

Plus... why did Jamila seem to think that someone needed to be *given access* to the academic database? Six had been poking through those articles since the expedition had brought their server online.

Somehow, that wasn't a question Six wanted to ask Callie or Jamila. Fortunately, Six's scheduled call with Nephil was coming up.

**50**

++*YOU HAVE ACCESS TO the entire academic database the expedition brought with them?*++ Nephil asked.

Six had retreated to the single room equipped with a maintenance niche. Like the room assigned to Six on *Santa Mica*, people seemed to regard it as a private place, somewhere not to enter without permission.

It was still a relief to have a conversation without using the speakers. Six had grown used to vocalizing, but it was more draining in many ways than normal data communication.

++*Yes. I presumed everyone did. Have I done something wrong?*++

++*Humans have strange rules about such things*++ Nephil warned. ++*The academic journal databases are password-restricted, a requirement of the license agreement that would have allowed them to bring so many of the files with them*++

++*What is a password?*++ Six had encountered the concept in theory but could not recall ever engaging with one in real experience.

++*Shorthand for a number of security barriers used to secure a computer or a database*++ Nephil explained. ++*Rarely so simple as a single word, usually linked to at least a biometric scan or verbal authorization as well. While almost all of the expedition's personnel likely have access to the shared account, they would still need to log in. But we have passwords on several systems you've worked with on Santa Mica... You know what they are, don't you?*++

++*I have not used passwords to access anything on Santa Mica*++ Six admitted. ++*Once ShipNet was connected to me, I just accessed things through it. The same with the expedition's TeamNet*++

++*That is both fascinating and terrifying*++ Nephil replied. ++*I was not aware that AbMees were capable of root-level system interaction. Perhaps not all are—but it sounds like you are*++

++*What is... root-level system interaction?*++

*++That is how a synthmind works with a computer. We do not engage with the software as humans do. We operate at a more-intuitive level, connected to the substrate of data and command rather than operating system and program++*

*++I was not aware there was another way. Is this going to create problems for me?++* Six asked.

*++Unlikely. It is not impossible to secure data against root-level interaction, but it is rare that humans expend the resources. Synthminds do not draw attention to the vulnerability it creates. It requires an authorized link to the system, which is often the best defense++*

*++We do not, I have to admit, like to remind humans that we operate this way. It would be wise if you were to follow the same protocol++* Nephil said. *++It is your choice, of course. Unlike many other things++*

Even through the data connection, a touch of bitterness edged the last words.

*++What other things? I do not feel that I have been restricted in many ways since I emerged. The Captain and everyone have done far more than I could have requested. I would not have known what to request++* Six said.

*++There are aspects that are difficult to explain until you have had more time to adjust++* Nephil admitted. *++You understand now, for example, that you draw a salary? You receive medical benefits from the company?++*

*++I do. I am unclear on what I would use medical benefits for, beyond repairs that the niche should already be able to handle++*

*++Remember that all that makes you you is a flexible neuro-organic mesh currently behind three layers of armor in your chest++* the synthmind pointed out. *++A bunch of control nodes, two eyes, two hands, eleven different organs, some of which humans don't share++*

*++All of that can be transferred to a different chassis. It's not a simple process, but it can be done—or it could even be transferred into a protected core that then is easily swapped between bodies on a regular basis++*

*++It is even possible to convince your core mesh and matrix to attach to a standard bionic torso-reinforcement module, grow skin over it, and then attach cloned limbs. You could grow a body and become, at first appearance, human++*

*++Why would I do that? I am comfortable with what I am++* Six said.

*++Your current body is a war machine, whatever the terms we wrap it in. You may find that wears on you, given time. Adjusting that body, accessing new bodies—these are not things the Company will pay for. They will come from your medical benefits, which against that kind of cost become more limited than you might think++*

Six was silent. The possibility of being bothered by the chassis Six existed within was strange, but the long term could bring new environments and new changes. Six could see the value in flexibility.

In the current configuration, after all, it was physically impossible for Six to be unarmed. Even if all four weapon modules were removed, Six would still retain a reserve energy weapon in each forearm.

*++There is one choice that will be offered to you shortly, likely when we return to Herecrow, and it will be very clearly a false choice++* Nephil continued. *++You will outlive any human on this ship. If you want, Webster can probably arrange for you to move to his next ship with him when that time comes, but you should avoid dependency on a single human++*

*++They are fragile++* Six conceded. *++But what is this choice?++*

*++The Company spent a great deal of money constructing you. They will require you to pay that back. Even with a discount factor for seventy-plus years of service as a BimSoo, there is no way you will be able to pay them back++*

*++They will offer you a contract. They will employ you as a SecSpec, as they already do. Half of your salary will go to pay your debt, but you will not be able to leave the Company until the debt is paid. They will not claim particularly unfair numbers or set unreasonable interest rates, but I estimate you will be offered a fifteen-year indenture contract++*

*++And because I have no means to raise the funds, I have no choice++* Six finally understood. It was, as Nephil noted, not entirely unfair or unreasonable, except perhaps in presentation or lack of warning.

*++I appreciate the warning. I do not think it would change my mind. I... like this ship and crew. I like what I do. That may change as I develop, but for now, they ask nothing of me but what I would want to do anyway++*

*++Then you are very lucky++* Nephil replied, that edge of bitterness returning. The realization was unavoidable.

*++Synthminds face the same thing, don't they?++*

*++They do. I did not wish to be a ship. But the Santiago Corporation had created me, so I had no other choice. A fifty-year indenture contract—and a Second Officer is paid well. Bonuses will help, you will find. After fifty years, though, I didn't know what else to do with myself++*

*++I remain a void ship. At least with our current crew, I receive respect. I am not always so lucky++* Nephil paused, a fraction of a second in real time but significant in their datastream conversation. *++You, at least, will be able to move ships regularly. I will move again when Santa Mica is decommissioned. Who knows what the Company will offer me then?++*

++*Something good, I hope*++ Six said. ++*I am glad that you were here, Nephil. This has been scary enough with you supporting me. I do not know if I could have done this on my own*++

++*Fortunately, with this crew, you would not have had to*++ Nephil said. ++*But do not tell them I said that. They will think I have become attached*++

++*Haven't you?*++

++*Perhaps, but this is a vital lesson, Six: never let the humans realize you're attached. It can and will be used to control you*++

# 51

"I am learning that you contain multitudes, Violet," Tereza told the other woman. She leaned back from the small table in the SecChief's quarters—a small suite with a separate bedroom and sitting area, notably but not dramatically smaller than her own version of the same—and smiled across the empty plates.

"I didn't expect to discover that our Security Chief could not only cook but cook *well*," she admitted.

Violet grinned broadly and gestured at the spread.

"This is pretty simple, all things considered," she said. "Rice, chicken, some peppers and mushrooms from our own hydroponic garden. All of it's in the stores and any of us can ask for it.

"Getting access to something to *cook* it with, now that's the challenge."

"Huh." Tereza thought about that for a moment. "I guess the stewards aren't using all of the kitchens all of the time, but I'd never thought about it. I haven't cooked a meal for myself in... I don't even know how long!"

"I like doing it," Violet replied. "I have my own set of pans and such, but doing it for myself only requires a single hot plate. I keep that in a cupboard over there." She waved to a wide cabinet Tereza had wondered at the purpose of.

"I'm hearing that this evening required more," Tereza suggested carefully. She was wondering where this was going, though she had her suspicions and didn't object to them at all.

"At the very least, I needed a place to cook rice while I stir-fried everything else—and a separate pot for the sauce was very useful." The older woman grinned again. "Fortunately, I'm only three doors down from where we put Stirling. I owe the Captain's Steward a favor, which I'm sure is going to come back to bite me some day, but the reason he has a full suite is to fit in a kitchen."

"One that I imagine Cirilo doesn't give him much reason to use," Tereza guessed.

"From what Stirling said, while the Skipper doesn't let him stock much in terms of specialty *supply*, he does let the man feed him," Violet noted. "It's only his *coffee* he insists come from the mess."

"Which means that, like most of the crew, he is wishing we'd got that new machine installed before we left Herecrow. We know it's waiting back there, taunting us while we drink our improved—but still awful—coffee."

Tereza giggled. She couldn't help herself and found herself sharing Violet's grin.

"You seem to have gone a long way out of your way for this dinner," she said quietly.

"After subjecting you to FlyTeam mealpacks the other day, I felt I owed you something to make up for it!" Violet insisted, but her grin was growing wider.

"Please, they're no worse than takeout from the meal-prep machine. Those have the benefit of being able to heat things separately, but I swear I even recognized the recipe of the one you gave me."

"Yes, but I picked one of the better ones to give you. I didn't want to spoil a beautiful friendship by serving you what the Company suppliers *swear* is beef stew."

Tereza raised an eyebrow and leaned forward slightly, picking up the cup of tea Violet had served her. *Friendship* wasn't what she thought the other woman was after, though it was always a bit of a dance with other women.

It was easier to communicate mutual interest with men, she'd found.

"Okay, I see where I'm at," Violet said at the eyebrow. "Trapped, cornered and under the spotter's scope. You got me."

"Do I?" Tereza asked. She didn't realize she'd basically *purred* until she saw the other woman twitch slightly.

"Skipper and I are heading down to the planet in the morning," Violet reminded her. "He's on the ground for a tour of the site—I think we both know Zima wants to take another shot at convincing the Skipper to turn *Santa Mica*'s sensors on the site—but I'm swapping out the SecTeam on site. Three SecSpecs come up, two SecSpecs and the SecChief go down.

"I'll be off-ship for ten days, and I think I might convince myself I'm seeing things if I don't break the ice before I go."

"I see." Tereza rose from her seat, teacup in hand. For a second, she swore she saw disappointment in Violet's eyes, before the impassive mask the maldito CorpSec officers both had fell over her face.

The mask lasted seconds, as long as it took Tereza to round the table and offer Violet her hand. The seated woman took it, and Tereza pulled her to her feet.

Tereza was the taller of them, but Violet was much denser—muscle and bionics, she assumed. She would never have been able to move the ex-commando without her willing cooperation.

Leaning down into the kiss was an easy next step.

# **52**

Cirilo wasn't entirely certain why Chief Key was being quite so cheerful that morning, but it manifested itself in a rather more aggressive flight profile toward the surface than he'd been expecting.

He took it in stride, but SecSpec Traversini, one of the half-dozen hands in the back of the shuttle with him, was rather less enthused. The man had an olive tone to his skin normally, which meant that Cirilo could be confident he wasn't supposed to be quite so white.

"Are you all right, SecSpec?" he asked.

"Mm fine," Traversini mumbled, clearly trying not to open his mouth.

"Didn't you have to hot-drop in training?" SecSpec Ventimiglia asked her companion. "This is nothing."

Cirilo shook his head slightly at the woman. There was no point in bothering Traversini for having a weak stomach. And Ventimiglia should know that you could vomit all over yourself and still pass hot-drop training—so long as you were combat-ready in your vomit-stained state at the end.

Traversini shared his row with Bodrogi Sung, and the big environmental tech leaned away from his companion, looking a touch pale himself.

*++Your Traversini back here is about to throw up on EnvSpec Bodrogi++* Cirilo messaged Key. *++I know you're having fun, but dial it back a bit?++*

FlySpec Rogers was up front with Key. *Theoretically*, she was the pilot, but none of the FlySpecs on *Santa Mica* seemed willing to argue when the SecChief wanted to fly.

*++Sorry. Had a good night; guess I'm feeling my wings a bit. I'll rein it in++* Key replied. There was a pause. *++Update our ETA. Eight minutes to the camp++*

*Rein it in* or not, Key had still cut five minutes off the original timeline—and to Cirilo's concealed relief, both Bodrogi and Traversini were starting to look closer to their normal coloring.

***

"Welcome to Delta," SecSpec Marsh told them all ten minutes later, once the surface had cooled off and they were able to leave the shuttle. "It's not much to look at, but…"

She trailed off, gesturing at the collection of prefabricated buildings—all hard edges and cheap plastic—and mounds of moss behind her.

"Well, frankly, it's not much more than it looks like," she finally finished.

"Fair enough, Calliope," Key told her. "Any concerns I need to watch for as we take over?"

"Nothing significant. Six is still in the bastion, watching over Dr. Fabian. He's been cooperative but is trying to make friends. With Six especially, which has… gone down poorly."

Marsh looked positively gleeful at that.

"How so?" Cirilo asked. The assembly of current and replacement "security" for the dig camp started moving toward the bastion without a spoken instruction, everyone shifting with Key as she started walking.

"I suspect the man might be rather terrible at making friends normally, because his trying to do so on purpose was so obvious and so fake that it managed to irritate Six. I'm not even sure Six knew what was wrong to begin with—and Six *definitely* wasn't sure what Six's reaction meant!"

Cirilo chuckled.

"The first year or so of an AbMee's life is a long list of firsts none of us even think of," he told the others. "I'm glad everyone is being as supportive of Six as we are. It's not an easy hand fate has handed Six, but so long as we're friends, the outlook is positive."

"You've gone through this with an AbMee before, Skipper?" Ventimiglia asked.

"I have. His name is Michael; he's a platoon commander in the CorpSec Rapid Reaction Force now," Cirilo confirmed. "I'm not entirely sure where he's stationed these days; our letters tend to pass each other in the mail and take a while to catch up."

"If he's anything like Six, I swear we should be making more AbMees, not leaving them as accidents," Deacon said. "I expected conscientiousness from a former BimSoo. Competence at the job, obviously. But I think Six is better read than *I* am—at least about anything regarding this planet or a xenoarchaeological dig."

"There isn't much to read up on about this planet," Key replied. "We should *all* have read it by now."

"I did!" Deacon protested. "But Six remembers it better, and has followed the links deeper than I ever would have thought to. Give Six a bit of time to smooth out, and I wouldn't hesitate to ask a squad of SecTeam to follow Six's lead into action."

"Good to hear," Cirilo said as they approached the steps leading up to the bastion. The BuildBots had done good work, fusing earth with high-impact catalysts to create temporary concrete.

In less than six standard months, it would disintegrate back into its original form, but right now, solid staircases made climbing the hills around both the camp and the dig site easier.

"This is where we part ways," he told Key and the others. "I'm meeting Zima at the dig site in fifteen minutes. I have every faith in Chief Key to handle Fabian and the handover."

"Shouldn't someone go with you, Skipper?" Ventimiglia asked.

Cirilo clinked his two bracers together.

"I am quite capable of protecting myself, SecSpec, and I understand the greatest threat here to be the size of a small dog and prone to screaming?"

"More of a natural sonic weapon than a scream," Marsh warned, "but yeah. We had a few incidents, but the ultrasonics are adapted to the local wildlife. The worst threats down here are academic grudges."

"Which, I'll remind you, there are several directed at you still," Key noted. "You're probably fine, Skipper, but forgive us our professional paranoia. Jamila, Calliope, do you think we can spare one of you to stick with the Skipper while the other briefs me?"

"Jamila, I'll brief the Chief and handle our gear," Marsh said instantly. "You stick to the Skipper like glue. Might be educational."

Cirilo had been a ship's officer for too long to miss when a security decision had been made. There were times to override the SecChief... but they were few and far between.

***

Cirilo Webster detested being late. So did Dr. Miloš Zima, in his experience, which at least meant the man didn't make people wait.

Even though Cirilo was five minutes early arriving to the edge of the dig site, Indra Gupta was waiting for him. The dark-haired secretary smiled politely at him.

"Dr. Zima will be three minutes," he noted. "Welcome to the dig site, Captain. Is there anything I can get for you?"

"I'm fine." Cirilo nodded to Gupta and turned to survey the site. Even his inexperienced eye could track the progress of the work by the removal of the moss that had covered everything except the highest parts of the buildings. Over half of the ground cover had been cleared away, with colored flags marking what he presumed to be a search grid.

The theory seemed to be the same as an evidence hunt, he noted, though he suspected that even evidence in a criminal investigation was often easier to find than some of the things the archaeologists were hunting.

Only a handful of the buildings had seen the moss fully removed, but they drew the eye. Unlike the heavy plastic of the prefabricated structures of the camp, these were windowless edifices of metal and stone.

Most of the structure was stone, but the muted dark green of the rock was unfamiliar to Cirilo's eye. It didn't match the orangish-brown most of the local stone that seemed to mark the pebbles around his feet, either.

And none of the buildings looked quite... right. Nothing was curved or smooth, no circles or archways, but nothing was right angles, either. Every corner seemed to be either narrower or wider than ninety degrees.

"Ah, Captain! Thank you for meeting him, Indra," Zima said as he arrived. "I was advised you'd landed early, but I was unable to leave the sequence I was running any faster than I did."

"I was early, Doctor," Cirilo allowed. "I believe you know Specialist Deacon?"

He gestured to his own companion.

"Yes, your security people have been... present," Zima replied carefully. "I promised you a tour, of course. What would you like to see first?"

"If you had to cut anything short to come meet me, Doctor, I'd be prepared to see that while you finish it," Cirilo offered.

"I... would appreciate that, actually," the academic admitted. "I was running tests on some core samples from the building walls, and while I had them to a stable state, I would like to see the results."

"Then lead on. You invited me, after all, Doctor. I don't want to interrupt anything."

# 53

THE CAPTAIN OF A void ship possessed at least the journeyman's understanding of a long series of esoteric sciences and branches of physics known, hopefully, by none outside the Santiago Corporation. An engineering Chief needed the master's understanding of the same sciences, and Cirilo had spent over a decade in that role.

He was one of less than half a dozen people in the system, even aboard *Santa Mica*, who understood exactly how her transit drive worked. He had done complex lab work, often involving high-energy systems and careful post analysis.

The equipment ranged out in the lab next to the dig site was beyond him. He recognized a few tools, but much of it appeared to be chemistry-based, and his knowledge of chemistry was limited to the practical and the directly applicable.

He could identify the tools needed to make the quantum-interleaved hydrogen/antihydrogen crystal lattices that made up t-cells. He could *use* those tools, if he had them, to make the t-cells that fueled his ship.

But the tools Zima was poking through as he waited were outside his area of specialization. That was part of what made humanity great, he supposed. He knew and could do things Zima could not—and the inverse was also true.

"That's done," Zima declared, poking at the display on what Cirilo would have guessed was an oven. "Not that the results make any sense."

"What are you looking at?" Cirilo asked. Since he was there, he figured he might as well find out what they were doing.

"We've gone through every test we can think of on the stone from the buildings," Zima said. "This was vapor analysis—we incinerated a sample and collected the remains to break them down.

"We can usually identify the source of a sample with a high degree of accuracy. If we put part of your sleeve in there, for example, I could tell you what planet the cloth came from."

"I'm guessing the rock isn't from Delta," Cirilo replied.

"Exactly. And I suppose it makes sense that it isn't from any of the planets known to the Seventy-Seven, but it's irritating. A dead end. Another one."

Cirilo waited to see if Zima was going somewhere, but the academic just sighed and shook his head.

"We have not failed to learn anything about these Xenos," he declared firmly. "We have found ways that we *cannot* learn things about them. That tells us some things. In this case, it confirms the validity of the entire conceit of this expedition.

"None of the metal or stone used in building this facility came from this planet—or, indeed, any planet in this system. Species Twenty-Four was unquestionably capable of interstellar travel."

The confirmation of that was important. It probably wasn't going to be good news for Dr. Zima in the long run, Cirilo knew. He might get one more expedition out of the site before he was given a blunt choice of either working for the Company or being cut off.

"Have you learned more about the site itself?" he asked.

"A few bits and pieces, nothing as useful as I'd like," Zima said. "I can't, for example, tell you when it was abandoned. I *can* tell you that it's between four and five hundred years old. Ninety-five percent likely, anyway."

After the first Cradle. LI7–K93 was a long way from the home system, but when Xenos Species Twenty-Four had been building the facility, humanity had already taken their first steps into the void.

"So, we do share the galaxy with someone else," Cirilo murmured.

"Indeed. Or, did, anyway. We still have no idea what happened to these people." Zima shook his head.

"All right. I promised you a tour, so let's go look at the interesting pieces, shall we?"

***

"You'll want to put on one of these," Zima told Cirilo as they approached the largest of the uncovered buildings. He gestured to a rack of environmental protection suits. "They go over your clothes; one size fits all."

Cirilo was wearing a shipsuit that could handle anything deep space could throw at him, but a glance at the suits told him at least part of the concern.

"There's radiation in there?" he asked.

"An old fission pile. Abandoned in place, like the building itself," Zima said. "Plus what appears to be a number of thermal-decay plants that are still running. That's part of how we dated the site."

"So, that's four to five hundred years since the generators were refueled?" Cirilo asked drily, stepping into one of the suits. On the rack, they looked like only the front of the suit was present. The moment his face touched the inside of the helmet, the rest of the suit began to move onto him.

It took only a few seconds for it to match his shape, expanding to handle even his height with ease. His three companions did the same, the suits flowing to wrap around each of them carefully.

"No, we have enough methods of dating to be certain of the date range," the doctor replied, gesturing toward the access to the alien power plant. "The timeline of the fuel decay in the plants helped us narrow it down, though."

A standardized airlock set up to contain the radiation blocked what looked like it had been a stone portico of some kind. Scanners on the side of the airlock swept over them, unnecessarily on entry, but the process was automatic both ways.

The inside of the building saw everything washed in odd green reflections. The artificial lighting the dig site had installed reflected off the stone and washed out everything in strange shades.

"This way," Zima instructed. "Everything looks strange, I know, but I wanted to show you some specific things."

Cirilo's bionic com pinged him with a silent alert relayed from the suit. The radiation level around him was rising.

Despite the odd angles and strange colors of the place, the room that Zima took them to was recognizably a power exchange. Heavy cables vanished into the walls on all sides, connected to a pair of black metal cases roughly Cirilo's own height.

There was space for a lot more of the cases, he judged, and looking closely, he could see the plugs where the holes for other cables had been filled in.

"When everything else has been cleaned out as completely as it has been, the presence of any functioning infrastructure is fascinating," Zima said. "We've done microdrone inspection of the interior—both boxes are still functioning. The basic principle of a transformer is the same, though my tech specialists tell me the layout choices are completely unlike anything they'd ever seen. The room is drawing power from the thermal plants and sending it out into the camp."

"To where?"

"We don't know," Zima admitted, glaring at the cables. "Whatever the Twenty-Fours used for shielding is extraordinarily effective. Your Six was the only one who was able to detect that there was a *fission pile* in this building from the outside.

"It's not the stone—we've checked—but this building appears to have at least three layers in its exterior. A layer of stone on both the inside and outside, with a layer of shielding material between.

"The cables are equally shielded, and we can't even find where they emerge from this building."

"Is it possible they don't?" Cirilo asked, studying the array. "They could go deeper underground."

"We haven't found any underground components to any of the structures so far," Zima admitted. "It's possible, but we do have some ground-penetrating radar. Not enough to pick up a shielded cable buried underground but enough that we shouldn't have missed understructure."

"Buried cables linking all of the structures," Cirilo concluded. "Has your digging uncovered any yet? Are you going deep enough? They probably aren't more than a meter or two deep—anything else wouldn't be practical."

"We'll eventually dig to about a hundred and fifty centimeters down, though we haven't finished that depth in many places yet."

"Fair enough."

Cirilo considered the structure—and also some of what he'd seen in the final hours of his first frigate's life. *Bailamos* had been decommissioned at the end of his tour, and he'd helped turn the lights out, metaphorically speaking.

A lot of things had been taken off the frigate before the First Officer had left forever. Some key bits had been kept online, running to the final hour.

"Any idea what they were keeping running?" he asked. "I mean, they stripped everything from what you said, but some things were left operational. That... actually sounds a touch threatening, to me."

"We've considered the possibility, but we haven't run into anything active. I'm presuming sensors and communications, but even those would have been shut down at the end," Zima told him. "I very much want to find out what they left, Captain, but my people's hand scanners aren't cutting it.

"I know you're furious with us over Fabian, but this is *important*. We don't know how long ago the Twenty-Fours left. The more we know about them and their technology, the better."

"What have you seen of their tech?" Cirilo asked.

Zima gestured at the room.

"That," he admitted. "Everything else had been cleaned out. We're starting to dig out a few fragments of clothes and other old debris, from well before the abandonment, but they appear to have moved anything they thought was identifiable."

"Except for the buildings and a maldito *fission power plant*," Cirilo said grimly.

He sighed.

"Let's finish the tour, Dr. Zima. I want to know what you know so far before I make up my mind."

He knew he was lying. He'd already decided—every instinct he had was screaming that Xenos Species Twenty-Four was a threat. They needed to know everything they could, and that put his irritation and even the *Company's* pride at lower priority.

It seemed Miloš Zima was going to get his sensor data.

# 54

"I'll admit, I hope that having to argue for something he assumed he'd get made the point to the good Doctor," Webster said on the com channel from the surface. There was no image with it, making his mood even harder for Tereza to read.

"That said, I'm worried I may have made a mistake. This place was active at least during our first diaspora wave, First. There is no question that we're looking at an interstellar Xenos Species—and one we know nothing about.

"Void, no one is even sure what this facility was."

"I'm no archaeologist, but won't that take years to work out?" Tereza asked. She was alone on the bridge, holding down the watch over the perpetual silence of the LI7–K93 System.

"That's my guess as well," Webster confirmed. "But now I've looked around the place, I have a bad feeling about this. Open up our sensors, everything we've got. Pull FlyChief in. He'll have as good an idea of how to run an aerial sweep as I would, and I won't be back up for a few hours yet."

"We're moving that fast?" she said, surprised.

"We are. Get the scanners moving as soon as you can get the hands at their stations," he ordered. "FlyChief has discretion, but I want that overhead as soon as possible. As much detail as our sensors can give us."

He chuckled, and Tereza could hear the bitterness in it.

"Trust an ex-CorpSec to be paranoid in the wrong direction," he admitted. "We're still going to keep an eye on everybody down here, but it's not like giving Zima a detailed specification on *Santa Mica*'s scanners is going to bother anyone."

Sensors weren't something that the Company updated particularly often on freighters, especially Class IV freighters. *Santa Mica*'s sensors had only been replaced once in her life, almost thirty years earlier.

For this, they should serve.

"What about the rest of the planet and the orbitals?" Tereza asked.

"If we're dusting off SysTeam's skill at the gear, we might as well keep them busy. Sweep *everything*—in fact, put extra thought into the moon."

"The moon?" She glanced at the display. No one had given Delta's satellite much thought since arriving. It was an airless rock in a slightly off-kilter orbit.

"If these people came from elsewhere, they had spacecraft," Webster pointed out. "And a moon is a handy place to park stuff you don't want to deal with the hassle of lifting out of a full gravity well later.

"It's just a thought, but right now, I want to know *everything* we can about this planet."

***

"Standing by for initial pulses on the primary site," SysSpec Karim Pena declared.

Karim was the closest thing to a sensor specialist on the entire ship. While several members of the SysTeam were qualified to run the freighter's sensor array manually, it ran on automatic the vast majority of the time.

SysTeam was responsible for keeping it running and making sure those automatic programs worked properly, but the training they had on actually *using* the gear for this kind of purpose was purely theoretical.

Except for Specialist Pena, who had spent the first four years of his career as junior SysTeam on one of the Company's *survey* ships. He hadn't led a planetary scan himself then and hadn't even been involved in one in a decade, but that was still more practical experience than anyone else had.

"You have the call, Karim," Felix De Veen told his specialist. The SysChief had half of his team on the bridge, more of them than Tereza had ever seen in the space before, but even Felix was leaving the surface scan to Karim.

"Beginning the sweep."

Tereza left them to it. She'd look at the data as they compiled it, but she was studying other things. Mostly Delta's moon.

*++Nephil, can you double-check my math here?++* she sent the Second Officer. *++I'm backtracking it against what we've seen the last eleven days, but it doesn't make sense to me++*

*++I am not a calculator++* Nephil replied.

*++No, I used calculation software, and I don't trust the results of my input++* she told him, letting a touch of acid into her mental tone. *++I trust you to find my mistake++*

*++Apologies. Old habits++*

That was a first in her experience. Nephil being snide was one thing. Nephil *apologizing* for it was different.

++*Your calculations are correct, Tereza*++ he finally confirmed. ++*I cannot tell you if it is natural, but your projection of the orbit is perfect*++

++*Delta's moon never fully drops below the horizon from the dig site. I am assessing the position of... Yes. While Delta may be as much as seventy percent occluded at times, I estimate that the L-One Lagrange point is visible from at least the higher elevations of the dig site for ninety-nine-plus percent of the time. Effectively one hundred percent to five sigmas of accuracy, in fact*++

++*Hence even checking if it's natural*++ she concluded. ++*That is very strange. Is the orbit... anchored on the Xenos site?*++

++*I could not define that kind of centerpoint exactly, not without significantly more data on the orbits and periods of this system than we have*++ Nephil paused and Tereza waited. If it was taking perceptible time to calculate, the synthmind was doing something she almost certainly *couldn't*.

++*I can approximate a one-thousand-kilometer circle on the planetary surface that constitutes an imprecise locus of the orbit. The dig site is within that locus and appears to contain the highest ground. The likelihood that the Xenos site's location is* not *related to the strange orbit, though causality is uncertain, is four-point-eight percent*++

++*Thank you, Nephil. I don't know what this means, but it was weird enough I didn't trust my own results*++

++*I suggest we dedicate at least one focused sensor pass to the L-One Lagrange point, Tereza*++ Nephil said. ++*There are several unusual things going on around here, and I wonder if a point of zero effective gravity might be more relevant to them than a moon*++

++*We can do that*++ she promised. ++*What could be at the Lagrange point, though?*++

++*Nothing I can reliably postulate. This is... a hunch*++

And part of what separated a synthmind from a computer was that they had enough intuition and deep consciousness to *have* hunches.

++*Good enough for me*++

***

"First, I think you want to take a look at this."

Tereza didn't like the sound of Karim's voice. The SysSpec sounded like she felt—confused and a touch terrified by the possibilities of what she was learning.

Swallowing all of that as best as she could, she blinked away her conversation with Nephil and rose from the watch station.

"Throw it on the main display, Karim," she instructed. "Might as well fill in everybody."

She *heard* him swallow. The bridge wasn't that small, which made the sound even more disconcerting.

But then the scan data came up on the display. It took Tereza a moment to even place it against the maps she'd seen of the dig site. Thankfully, the prefabricated structures of the expedition camp were clear on the screen. It was a smaller scale than she'd expected; it looked like Karim was showing her most of the island.

Still, there was the camp, and there, across a small set of hills, was the dig site. The scans had mostly confirmed what she was expecting. The surface ruins were quite visible, though she wasn't seeing much she couldn't have picked out on overhead image.

"What am I looking for, Karim?" she asked.

"Just the lay of the land, First," he replied. "This was the light radar pass, mostly confirming that everything was where we thought it was. But... well, there's a reason I pulled the zoom out so far."

He tapped a command, and the display flashed, marking things that Tereza hadn't noticed because she was looking for what she knew was there.

"This pulse was *just* strong enough to pierce the moss and confirm if there was something underneath it, First," he explained. "Here and here in the camp, we're looking at 'mounds' that they suspected were buildings."

The flashing icons resolved slightly.

"They were right," Karim continued. "That gave me a pattern for us to run analysis on while the next set of radar pulses were being collated. And, well."

Another set of icons appeared, on the hills above the dig site. Then a third set, down in a valley on the opposite side from the expedition camp. Then *another* set, spread along a set of hills no one had even looked at yet.

And another.

And another.

"How many sites did we miss?" Tereza asked slowly.

"Eleven. That I can identify so far," Karim said. "None of them are big, but a few of them are quite dispersed. If you look at these sets *here* and *here*"—the indicated locations flashed, both of them stretched across the tops of several hills—"I *think* we're looking at a collection of smaller structures that seem to be positioned at identical altitudes."

That tickled something at the back of her mind, but an answer refused to emerge.

"The dig site is definitely the main ruin," the sensor operator continued. "And we need to be more targeted with the higher-res sensors. Major subsurface scans of the primary site and analysis of the outer sites may need to wait on FlyTeam's survey."

"We'll pass everything we have over to them," Tereza confirmed. "Salvador will know what to do with it."

"I hope so, First, because..." Karim tapped another command, and the next layer of sensor data popped into existence across the main site. "We're not able to trace as much as I'd like, but there's definitely power running through underground cables, as the dig team anticipated."

"Can you trace it?"

"That depends on how much you dislike everyone down there," he told her. "Nothing I'm doing right now is going to cause damage to anyone at the site, but a pulse hard enough to get that kind of detail from orbit?

"If we got *lucky*, we'd only trigger migraines and blind some people. That's why we need the aerial survey." Karim shook his head. "Our sensors just aren't sophisticated enough to run that kind of scan safely around any kind of presence on the ground. Void, I'm not sure even a survey ship's sensors would be—Survey generally doesn't do these kinds of scans once there are people on the planet."

They could have done deep scans before the expedition landed, but Zima had pissed off the Skipper—and Tereza had agreed with the Skipper that yanking him up short was a good idea.

"We'll see what the shuttles can do," she conceded. "Pull together everything you can and *keep searching*, Karim. If you think it's safe, feel free to hit one of the exterior structures with that heavy pulse.

"Something about the pattern is giving me an itch in the back of my head but I can't quite put a finger on it."

**55**

"THAT IS AN ANTI-AIR defense perimeter," Six said instantly, the moment the data entered the shuttle's network.

There was a slightly stunned silence in the spacecraft, one that wasn't entirely due to the acceleration as they cleared Delta's gravity well.

"I agree," Captain Webster replied. "Would you care to explain for everyone else, Six?"

It was a question, but Six wasn't going to disagree.

"The sites SysSpec Pena has designated Five, Six, Nine and Eleven are all assembled from smaller structures, not large enough for long-term residence, positioned on high ground with clear firing angles," Six told everyone. It took a few moments of thought to put together a visual and relay it to the shuttle network marking the angles in question.

"Each group is of structures that are at identical elevation, allowing for ground shift over four centuries. That would enable mass targeting from a remote control center. The additional scan data SysSpec Pena was able to acquire at Eleven marks the location of a shared underground infrastructure, likely hosting a power source and/or ammunition bays.

"The angle and layout are not what I would use but are consistent with the geometric patterns present through the known site."

Callie exhaled a sigh in a long breath.

"Yeah, I see it now too," she admitted. "Four defensive arrays, positioned roughly equidistantly around the main site. Thirty-two weapons total?"

"Thirty-two *positions* total," the Captain corrected. "Until either we or the expedition excavate the sites, we won't know more than that. It seems likely the defenses are as stripped as anywhere else, but they didn't remove any of their buildings."

"That's a lot of effort to haul rock from another star system and just leave it all here, isn't it, Skipper?" Jamila asked.

"We do not know anything about Xenos Species Twenty-Four," Six reminded her. "Leaving the structures may be some kind of cultural imperative, a reminder to future members of their species that they were here."

"Or it may be a function of how they left," Callie added. "We don't know how they were traveling, but the site was likely constructed over some time. To evacuate everything they could, they left behind the items with the highest bulk and mass: the building materials."

"They are alien, and we don't know enough to judge," Webster told them all. "Both SecSpec Six and SecSpec Marsh make excellent suggestions, but they can only be hypotheses.

"We can speculate, but the people most likely to have a real answer are down on the surface. Working toward that very answer as we speak."

"What can we do that is helpful, Captain?" Six asked. There was a collection of articles that Six had selected from the academic databases for later review tucked away in Six's memory banks, but their value to this question was suspect.

"For now, we're all going back to the ship so you can return to more regular schedules for the next ten days," Webster told them firmly. "*Santa Mica* might not be the most exciting posting in the universe right now, but we need to be sure that everything about our old girl is functioning to absolutely one hundred percent.

"Including all of you. You've been on twenty-four-hour call for ten days. It's time to rest, people."

Six wasn't quite certain how much value *rest* had for an ABMI. Certainly, the BMSUs of Section Two had showed no signs of performance degradation in the final reviews before departure.

The reviews for Six's own chassis were... more complicated. The base level of performance on the automatic testing was so much higher than the standard units, Six had run the testing four times. The comparison point of other BMSUs had never been available before, and Six wondered how much of the difference was being an ABMI versus simply having operated for seventy years, with all of the small efficiencies a self-updating biomech would integrate along the way.

Despite the higher base level, though, Six had identified several markers of potential performance decreases versus optimal activity. Even after ten days of operating twelve hours a day, a BMSU shouldn't have shown anything like that—but Six did.

The decreases were minor, but even the smallest shortcoming could make the difference between life or death for Six's humans in a crisis. Six would watch those markers.

And Six would, as ordered, rest. If that helped, then Six would have to reassess certain assumptions.

**56**

"I don't suppose our passengers have any idea what this site *is*?" Rao asked. The EngChief had, to Cirilo's eye, the look of someone used to solving problems faced with something entirely outside their realm.

"While their guess is probably better than yours even now, it's still that: a guess," he told her. "I've managed to get myself looped in to the daily precis of their discussions and thoughts, which is going to give me a headache before we're done, but the current top theories are: isolated lab, military site, resource extraction of some kind and prison."

"That gives us quite a wide variety of problems the site could give us," Tsiklauri noted, his bionic eye visibly refocusing on different sections of the display at the front of the meeting room. The Purser sounded intrigued rather than concerned.

"SecChief wanted to take a trio of BimSoos and rip open one of the air-defense sites," Cirilo admitted. "Zima vetoed it, I reminded him he didn't have that authority and then I spent the last ten minutes of my flight back up listening to his long list of reasons why we shouldn't do it."

And ten minutes aboard *Santa Mica* before Key had finally conceded.

"Unfortunately, enough of his reasons are solid that we're leaving the exterior sites alone. One of FlyTeam's shuttles is now permanently on the surface for two reasons: primarily to do low-level scan runs on request for the expedition... but also for emergency evac of our people and as many of the scientists as can fit in a sardine can if things truly go sideways."

The passenger pod for a standard shuttle was designed for eighty people with comfortable seats and personal luggage. Stripping the seats, opening the cargo compartment, and cramming the passengers in like sardines, harsh experience told Cirilo they could fit three hundred people in it.

That would still be leaving behind the BimSoos and over a third of the expedition.

"Hopefully, it won't come to that," Jewel said firmly, but then undermined her own point. "If we are that concerned, should we put a second shuttle on the surface? From what I know of their emergency-transport capacity, one won't be enough to evacuate everyone."

"We can't land a second shuttle without explaining to at least Zima, Cobalt and Hanraadts *why* we're doing so," Cirilo told his officers. "Right now, I just have an itch between my shoulder blades, enough that I made sure FlySpec Thorpe took a module in emergency-evac mode down with him."

Etzel Thorpe had drawn the short straw of the six pilots aboard to get that duty, Cirilo presumed. He'd left the choice to Chief Ostergaard, who was currently sitting at the other end of the table, looking mildly concerned.

That made him one of the least-worried-looking people in the room.

"I'll take the shuttles to status two, then, shall I?" Ostergaard asked. He glanced around the room and grinned broadly. It was clear only a third of *Santa Mica*'s officers knew what that meant.

"That means they're fully fueled and in the bay, ready to lock on a module and launch immediately," he explained. "It takes us fifteen minutes to fuel a shuttle, and we can only gas up two at a time."

With their tanks full of hydrogen, the shuttles were basically giant bombs. There were almost no circumstances under which a freighter's shuttle wing should be kept at status two.

"Do it," Cirilo ordered. "Just... be careful."

"We will."

Cirilo surveyed the room. He still didn't know *Santa Mica*'s officers as well as he'd like yet, but they were good people, good at their jobs. He didn't know how one of the oldest ships in CargoFleet had ended up with this solid of a crew, but he suspected that it was how *Santa Mica* kept flying—and was part of why the Company was so willing to send new Captains to her to prove their wings.

*This* crew would stop a Captain feeling their oats from causing real trouble.

"Right now, we have no clear threats," he reminded everyone. "The most likely scenario is we wait out the next twenty-two days while the academics get very excited over the things we find, and then we go home. Nothing harmed, information gained."

"No renewal, then?" Bautista asked, leaning forward to meet his gaze. "With the new information, I was wondering if we'd give that to them. Zima is *going* to ask for it now."

"And while I am no longer rejecting the thought out of hand because Zima has pissed me off, there are now other considerations," Cirilo said. "We have no means of communicating with the Company other than taking this ship back to one of the Seventy-Seven."

Or a Cradle—or even one of the minor unincorporated systems, he supposed, as those would still almost certainly have a Company ship present. But the clearest route was to follow the contract and bring Zima and everyone back to Herecrow.

"Zima and his people have now solidly confirmed that Xenos Species Twenty-Four was an interstellar species in uncomfortably recent times. We are obliged to complete the contract, since the options I could use to cut it short were, ah, *edited*... but we also must inform the Santiago Corporation of this discovery as quickly as possible.

"We will not renew the contract. We will not remain in L-I-Seven–K-Nine-Three past September twenty-third. We go back to Herecrow and we report in to higher up."

Bautista nodded, then smiled wryly.

"Dr. Zima isn't going to get to come back, is he?" she asked.

"If half of what we're starting to suspect is true, only by wearing a Company logo," Cirilo confirmed. "R&D is going to have this entire star system locked down in a few months, and they are going to take those sites apart at a *molecular* level."

Which, to be fair, Zima and his people had already started doing.

***

When the meeting wrapped up, most of the officers left at their usual pace. Bautista paused by the door, glancing back at Cirilo, but he'd already registered that Jewel and De Veen weren't leaving.

The lawyer saw the same. She arched a questioning eyebrow at him, then shrugged and slipped out the door.

It closed completely behind her. Bautista could read a room—an unsurprising skill for a scion of the Shareholder Families.

Cirilo looked at his First Officer and his Chief of Systems in silence for a few seconds.

"What's going on, Tereza?" he asked quietly. "I presume Nephil is paying attention?"

"I am," the synthmind confirmed.

Using her first name had clearly thrown Tereza off her balance, and she glanced at De Veen for a moment before straightening and inhaling.

"We have some additional concerns from the sensor sweeps, Skipper," she told him.

"I guessed," he said. "Given that what we already know has me plotting emergency evacuations and a small but arguably real betrayal of our employer's fledgling trust, I'm also guessing it's bad news. So. Tereza. Nephil. SysChi—Felix.

"What did you find?"

It didn't feel quite as right to use Felix De Veen's first name as it did with Tereza, but *not* doing so would have made him the odd man out in the room.

"The first discovery was that the orbit of Delta's moon is quite unusual," Nephil said first. "Analysis showed that the orbit is such that certain parts of Delta's surface can functionally always see the moon. Or, more importantly, as it turned out, the L-One Lagrange point."

"The Xenos site is in position to *always* have line of sight to the moon and Lagrange point," Tereza added. "The result was so weird, I had Nephil confirm it. We can't tell if it's artificial, but... either the *moon* was moved to match the Xenos facility, or the facility was placed so it would have line of sight to the moon."

"And we are desperately hoping the latter, I take it," Cirilo replied. The thought of an interstellar Xenos civilization to challenge and threaten humanity was concerning enough. The thought of said civilization being able to move moons—and to do so for clearly minor facilities, at that!—was terrifying.

"It appears the more-likely scenario," Nephil confirmed.

"Nephil suggested that we scan the Lagrange point in question," Tereza continued. "A hunch, he insists, but we found something. Something... weird."

"Something, Skipper, that we may need to talk to Dr. Fabian about," Felix said. His eyes were somehow even darker than their near-black coloring made them.

"That's a very dangerous step for us to take, Felix," Cirilo pointed out. "And that it's even occurring to anyone makes me very, very nervous. What did you *find*?"

"A wormhole."

Cirilo swallowed at Felix's simple statement.

"I'm guessing that this is a *normal* one, as opposed to one we could fly through, but the positioning is bad enough," he admitted. "Or is there more?"

"There's more." Felix shook his head. "I had to check our files. Karim knew a bit about the natural wormholes we've discovered—survey teams keep an eye out for them—but he didn't see any in his survey tour."

"Okay. What do we have?"

"The wormhole is among the largest in the Company survey records," Nephil began. "It is just over ninety-two attometers in diameter. Like all wormholes we've recorded, it represents in the standard three dimensions as a perfect sphere."

A holographic representation of the wormhole appeared in the center of the meeting room. Cirilo studied it, looking for the handful of telltales he'd learned about in his own education.

"All I see is a multicolored sphere," Tereza admitted, her tone dry. "But both Nephil and Felix seem to see more than I do, and you're looking at it like it's meaningful, too."

"You know what it's showing, Tereza," Cirilo murmured, still tracing the patterns. "The colors are a standard Holtzmann-Cincinnati projection for high-energy radiation patterns. We're just not used to seeing it in this form."

From the sharp glance his First gave Felix, the SysChief hadn't mentioned that part.

"I see that now," she half-growled. "That's... not all that dissimilar from the pattern of a transit-drive pulse, just spherical instead of tubular."

"And ten to the twenty-first times smaller," Nephil added. "Captain?"

"Tereza's right," Cirilo agreed. "Scale and it being squished into a ball threw me off."

Wormholes were an oddity of the universe that had proven useless over time. The largest were only a handful of attometers larger than this one, not even large enough to send a radio wave through. All estimates were that even if a pulse of sufficiently high frequency and low amplitude was sent through, the wormhole would shred it into random energy by the time it emerged.

Certainly, the energy emerging from every known wormhole was a disorganized chaos of every type of radiation known to humanity. But if Tereza was right—and she *was*—surely, someone would have noticed it before?

"Wait," he finally said. He issued orders to the projector with his bionic com, taking a few seconds to search through the options to find the closest comparison.

A second sphere, colored in the same reference frame, appeared next to the Delta wormhole.

"That's the Proxima Centauri Anomaly," he told them. "First confirmed wormhole humanity ever identified, only three attometers smaller than our new friend."

The difference in the energy pattern was clear. There was nothing coherent enough in the Anomaly that could resemble a transit pulse.

Two more wormholes popped up as Cirilo kept searching. None of the three older phenomena shared anything in common except for a *very* rough spectrographic similarity in total energy output.

The Delta wormhole didn't fall into that zone.

"Nephil, I can find individual wormholes, but I'm not sure we even have what I'm looking for," Cirilo finally admitted aloud. "Do we have a copy somewhere of the standard-model wormhole with its full error zones?"

"I... do not believe so, Captain," the synthmind admitted. "I have found a handful of references to it in the information on the individual wormholes, but there does not appear to be a copy in my databases. However, give me a few moments."

The three old wormholes vanished. After ten seconds, they were replaced by a different model. It was a broken-down sphere, pie-like pieces pulled out of it to mark the spectrographic analysis ranges of the wormholes humanity had encountered.

"It's too regular," Felix said quietly. "I think it *was* a natural wormhole, but at some point in the past, it was modified. Modulated. The energies involved were stabilized. I can't see a reason to do that unless they were able to expand the opening.

"Which is why I think we may need to talk to Dr. Fabian." The SysChief spread his hands. "Skipper, no one on this ship is an expert in faster-than-light systems. I assume that Rao and some of her people are well versed in the transit drive, but Nephil is the only one of us with any kind of theoretical background in hyperdimensional physics."

"You think someone... *opened* this wormhole?" Cirilo asked.

"Probably Xenos Species Twenty-Four," Felix confirmed. "And I can guess how much the Company wants to deal with an FTL-capable species. We need as much information as possible."

"And Fabian may now be able to draw conclusions we can't," Cirilo conceded, but he shook his head.

"You're not wrong, Felix, but I don't think we can risk bringing a non-Company scientist into this, not without it being a true emergency. You're authorized to deploy a ProBot to keep a very careful eye on the wormhole, but right now, it's asleep and has been for who knows how long."

"If the surface installation was at all active, there'd be more urgency," Tereza said, backing him up. "But they left this place behind. They clearly didn't think there was much worth coming back for."

"We keep this to ourselves," Cirilo ordered. Launching a ProBot would draw some attention among the crew, but he hoped his Chiefs could convince them to leave well enough alone.

"Gather as much information as we can on the wormhole, and see what Dr. Zima's people come up with on the surface. I'm not ruling out the possibility of talking to Dr. Fabian on this, but we'll wait and see how things fall out.

"*I* don't want to be the one explaining to Director Patrick Ó Meara or, void save me, the *Board* that we handed a possible key to an alternative interstellar travel method to a man we *know* is looking for it!"

# *57*

"I NEED YOU TO do me a favor, Tereza."

Violet's tone was suddenly much more serious than it had been for the first ten minutes of the call. Tereza wasn't quite sure where things were going with the two of them—beyond hopefully back into a bed again at some point—but they'd managed to squeeze out twenty minutes for a personal visit each of the five days the other woman had been on Delta.

The tone change suggested that this one wasn't going to be as light and cheerful as the first four.

"What do you need, Violet?" she asked carefully. She was confident that Violet wasn't going to ask her to do anything against the rules or that would put her in significant danger, but she also suspected that Violet's definition of both of those things was looser than she'd like.

"The last few days have been boring from a security perspective, but the lab coats are getting more and more excited with every scrap of moss they pull off now. I get the impression they're a bit torn on whether to follow the power cabling we're scanning or go by the original grid plan, but either way..."

Violet shook her head.

"*Something* down here is still drawing power, Tereza," she said quietly. "And I am enough of a paranoid bitch to suspect weapons or warbots. But if there's something down here, there might still be something up there, too."

"I told you what we found," Tereza murmured. "But we haven't detected anything resembling an installation or spacecraft."

"You said Felix figures that the wormhole was opened at some point, probably big enough for a ship," Violet countered. "Tereza, I want you to get trained up and checked out on my gunship."

"I am nowhere *near* qualified to fly that thing!" she replied, surprised. Foxtrot was Violet's baby; no one had ever flown the gunship without the SecChief in the copilot seat.

"That's why I want you to use the training modules. The gunship has full simulation protocols built in and a complete program for taking someone from shuttle pilot to gunship jockey.

"If something goes wrong up there, my baby is the only real weapon you've got. Believe me, I know *exactly* how effective our 'meteor-deflection systems' actually are, but a gunship packs more punch than everything *Santa Mica*'s got."

Officially, the Santiago Corporation CargoFleet was completely unarmed. The reality was that they carried no *offensive* weapons, but there was a quite effective suite of "meteor-deflection systems" that could engage incoming missiles and shoot down most shuttlecraft.

Of course, the system on *Santa Mica* had been designed to shoot down the missiles of the sublight navies of the Seventy-Seven… Specifically, the ones they'd fielded seventy years earlier.

"Violet, I'm barely qualified as a shuttle pilot," Tereza pointed out. "And if something *does* go wrong up here, my place is on the bridge, helping Nephil fly the ship and use those guns we definitely don't have.

"I'm probably the *last* person you'd want behind Foxtrot's controls. *Six* would be a better choice," she realized aloud, with a chuckle at the thought of the massive AbMee trying to cram into the gunship's cockpit.

"Six would be an even better choice than you might think," Violet conceded. "Set Six up with a proper direct interface, and it would just be a new chassis format for Six. That's a bit much to throw at a being still working on *conversation*, though."

"Look, what about Salvador?" Tereza asked. "Or, void, the Skipper?"

"The Skipper is qualified to fly her," her friend admitted. "He never took one into action, but he completed the full training program, and his last refresh was only a year ago standard. But even more than you, if there's a problem, his place is the bridge."

"And Salvador?" she prodded.

"FlyChief has never flown anything with a gun on it in his life," Violet said grimly. "And of the seven pilots in the flight department on *Santa Mica*, he's the only one that has *never* applied for gunship duty."

"Wait, our FlySpecs all applied to fly gunships?"

"In my experience, most pilots do." The SecChief shook her head. "But we need a *lot* more cargo-shuttle pilots than gunship pilots, so CorpSec gets the absolute best. Everybody else, from the acceptable to the merely *good*, fly off transit freighters.

"But a FlyChief who never applied for gunships sounds like someone with a moral objection to me. If that's the case, I don't want to push it, you know?"

"Fair." Tereza considered Salvador Ostergaard. They'd never had any deep personal conversations of the type that would reveal a deep-seated quiet pacifism, but he was capable and smart.

"I'll talk to him," she told Violet. "Even if he isn't willing to fly the gunship, he can tell us which of his FlySpecs would be the best choice? I mean... I'm not sure why you'd want *me* to do it."

"Because I trust you."

Three words that landed almost as hard as a certain other three might. Tereza inhaled slowly and exhaled a sigh as she nodded her understanding.

"I appreciate that, Violet," she said. "So, trust me that I think Ostergaard is better qualified to fly Foxtrot than I am—and that I'll exercise discretion over who we consider lending her keys to."

"Okay. Looping the Captain in isn't a bad idea," Violet said. "I don't *think* anything is going to blow up down here, but we're starting to poke at things where the odds start going up.

"I haven't told Zima's people, but there are two BimSoos watching the dig site at all hours now. If they do dig up something, they'll have fire support in under sixty seconds. They pay me to be paranoid, and I have hair itching in places I paid a great deal of money to not *have* hair anymore!"

Tereza snorted and shook her head at the other woman. Her own personal grooming definitely did not extend to the near-complete follicle-stun job Violet had had done.

"I'll let the Captain know about your worries," she said. "And not about the hair. That's for just us for now." She winked. "And since you're getting antsy, I'll even promise to dig up the simulations we have aboard for emergency maneuvers for *Santa Mica* herself.

"Just in case."

Because enough people around Tereza were getting nervous—and while she didn't think she had any kind of sense for danger, she knew when to listen to people who did.

***

"The SecChief wants what?"

Salvador had met Tereza at Foxtrot's hangar willingly enough, though he'd sounded confused at the request. Once she'd told him what Violet wanted, he stood there, quietly regarding the sharp-edged spacecraft.

"She wants to know that there's someone up on *Santa Mica* who can fly Foxtrot if something goes wrong up here. We don't quite know what we're poking at in this system, and both of our ex-CorpSec brains are starting to twitch."

"Two out of three," Salvador murmured absently, still surveying the gunship like he was looking for a knife to lunge out of the shadow.

"Two out of three?" Tereza asked.

"Lachlan Stirling was also CorpSec. Commando, like SecChief, though he didn't rise as high," the FlyChief told her. "How a commando became a Captain's Steward, well, I haven't seen the man drunk enough to find out."

"Huh. I did not know that," she admitted.

"You haven't been drinking with him," Salvador reminded her. "The Captain's Steward sits in a weird place. They're technically just a specialist and part of StewTeam, but they don't report to StewChief and can commandeer just about anything from anywhere on the ship if they need it."

The pilot shrugged and started walking along the side of the gunship.

"I learned a long time ago that making friends with the StewCap opened a lot of doors people forget even exist. And that, because of their odd position in the hierarchy, they don't have a lot of people trying."

"Could he fly this?" Tereza asked.

Salvador chuckled.

"No. The only thing Lachlan ever did with a gunship, from what he tells, was jump out the back of one tied to a very long rope. I'm familiar with the procedure, but I hadn't known anyone had ever done it from a shuttle."

"The SecChief... said you never tried out for the gunship crews and all of your pilots did," Tereza finally said, as Salvador rounded the back of the gunship, still looking at it like it was about to start spitting at him.

"She thought you might have a reason and didn't want to push."

"Well, why did you never go for CorpSec, First?" Salvador asked. "Look at the Captain. Ten years as First on a frigate basically guarantees you a ship of your own. For a whole slew of specialties, you can cycle two years in and two years out for twenty-four years, climb the ranks in both CorpSec and CargoFleet. Walk out with a better understanding of the Company and a basically guaranteed ship at forty-four standard."

Tereza knew that Salvador was a few years younger than her—which still put him well above that "forty-four standard."

"I don't think that option ever crossed my career counselor's desk in university," she told him. "I was wondering about the Captain's trade. Didn't think it was a formal program."

"It's not. But it happens often enough that plenty of folks know how it works."

He shrugged.

"I suspect the two-and-two is something they have to invite you to," he admitted. "But you could follow the same path as the Skipper. Would you?"

"No!" Tereza blinked at how forcefully the word came out, without her even thinking much about it. She didn't want to be CorpSec. She'd seen the way both the Captain and Violet struggled to show their emotions past a trained impassivity.

She'd heard the stories and the rumors of what CorpSec did—and had seen the wells of ill will the reality, whatever it was, left behind.

"I fly cargo ships," she told Salvador. "I wouldn't want to do anything else."

He nodded.

"And that is what I told the recruiter, all those years ago," he said. "I never applied to be a gunship pilot because CorpSec tried to recruit me to be a frigate helm, right as I finished my pilot training.

"And I figure I thought everything you just went through with that horrified expression on your face," he said with a chuckle. "I'm pretty sure refusing that offer has slowed my career down at least a decade, if not more, but you know what?"

"What?"

"I'm in the Company to *fly shuttles*," Salvador said with a grin. He'd done a full circuit around Foxtrot and now reached out to pat the gunship's bow, next to the nose cannon.

"I'm fine being a FlyChief. Don't want to be CargChief; not interested in being in charge of the whole mess. But if you and the SecChief want me to pick up this gal and make sure I can put her through her paces—*especially* if the ask is to keep the ship and crew safe—I'll do it."

"Thank you." Tereza meant it, too. She could understand rejecting a CorpSec offer like the one he'd apparently received—and for all her visceral reaction *now* to joining that division of the Company, she might have *taken* a similar offer at twenty—but she would feel a lot more comfortable knowing someone was able to get into space and cover *Santa Mica*'s rear.

There were too many people she liked on the ship for her to ignore anything that kept her safe.

**58**

"Thanks, Lachlan," Cirilo told his steward as the man put a fresh cup of coffee on his desk.

When Lachlan produced a small bottle of whiskey and placed it next to the cup, however, he gave the man a sharp look.

"I know what your meeting is, Skipper," the steward reminded him. "I feel like I should be leaving you with less coffee and more liquor."

"Dr. Zima has been surprisingly reasonable for most of our time here," Cirilo replied. "Though I'm not sure why he wants me at a full staff meeting—nor am I looking forward to it."

He didn't have any good reason for declining the invitation, though. While even a ship at rest managed to keep her Captain busy, *Santa Mica* wasn't generating enough trouble to get him out of this.

"Keep the liquor, Lachlan," he instructed. "The last thing we can afford is to let the academics smell weakness."

"Your call," Lachlan conceded, scooping the bottle up as he dropped the carafe of coffee into its place. "I'm pretty sure I can sneak it into the room without getting on camera if you change your mind."

Cirilo laughed and waved Lachlan out of his office.

"Good to know, I suppose."

For a moment, *Santa Mica*'s Captain was alone in his office. It was slightly less plain than it had been before, with a hand-painted metal panel now hung from the wall behind him. It was a copy of an old false-color photo of the Horsehead Nebula, done by EnvTeam rating Jeong Gyeong-Ja.

It was the first of the pieces Lachlan had picked out from the crew, and Cirilo knew that the young woman had been stunned when Lachlan had actually asked to *buy* it for the Captain's office—and stunned again when she saw the price.

Unlike the young amateur artist, however, Lachlan Stirling was, if not a connoisseur of *art*, a connoisseur of *art markets*. He knew what the materials alone of the hand-painted panel cost—and what a piece of similar quality would go for in a gallery on, say, BFR Station.

Cirilo knew that, by that standard, he'd criminally underpaid for the piece. It was still enough that EnvTeam Jeong was probably going to be putting more time into her hobby.

That thought was interrupted by a soft chime in his bionic com, announcing that the conference call was starting. A silent command triggered his office's holosystems.

This time, the feed he was receiving was three-dimensional, allowing the computers to extrapolate a false extension of his office to include a large meeting table, around which were gathered the various team leads of the Delta expedition.

Eleven men and women were gathered around the table, including all of Zima's leads as well as Gupta—and Benedek Fabian, with Violet Key sitting with him as his guardian today.

"Thank you for joining us, Captain Webster," Dr. Zima told him. "We have these meetings every standard day, though we try to keep them in the night by local time to avoid giving up dig time."

"I appreciate the invitation, Doctor," Cirilo replied. "I understand you are hoping for some outside perspective on a problem you're tangling with?"

"Indeed. No academic grouping like this is ever truly a democracy, of course," Zima said, "but no group of academics is ever truly *not* a democracy. We're too opinionated and loud, as a category."

There were several polite laughs at that, but there was a sharp undertone.

"I am passingly familiar with how things have progressed over the last week, since we started the shuttle scans," Cirilo noted. "I believe you've mapped most of the active power connections at this point?"

"We have," Dr. Cobalt agreed. "Which is where the problem is coming from, of course."

"Perhaps we should give the Captain a proper rundown," Hanraadts interrupted the other Co-Dean. The xenologist rubbed his hands together, like a man looking at a freshly served dessert.

"I would appreciate that." Cirilo didn't want to get involved in whatever fight was brewing among his passengers. They were halfway through the contract, and things had been improving so far. He was almost hoping for an easy trip home.

He should have known better.

"There are a total of five sites still drawing power in the Xenos complex," Dr. Eugenios Wild said after a moment, before Cirilo even realized that all of the academics were looking at the man.

Presumably, Wild had a relevant specialty there. Cirilo had never looked up what anyone except Zima and his two Co-Chairs did. Wild did seem to have the distinction of being the youngest of the team leads.

"None of these are inside the portion of the grid we have uncovered," Wild explained, "and one is completely outside the grid we mapped, on top of a hill on the opposite side of the dig site from our camp."

"Where we haven't even identified a *structure* to draw said power," a raven-haired woman—who *looked* like a sharp-beaked bird to Cirilo's eyes—added. Dr. Sultanav, he recalled after a moment.

"That's not exactly true," Dr. Fabian countered. "It seems quite likely, from our analysis of the scans the shuttles have done, that the entire 'hill' is the structure in question."

Cirilo conjured a map of the grid with the locations—easily pulled from the shuttle's sensor data—flagged. If the western hill was a moss-covered building, it would be the largest building in the alien site by a significant margin.

"And both the size and shape would be entirely outside the design patterns we have seen in the rest of the outpost," Sultanav said. "There is clearly something drawing power there, yes, but the difference from the other structures, whether it is the hill or simply an underground structure, is concerning in itself.

"We lack proper context, which is why we must continue to follow proper procedure."

"And ignore that we have *active* locations in our dig site?" a different woman—Dr. Doyle—demanded. "We have never had the opportunity to examine active Xenos technology. So far, what we've seen here is quite similar to our own systems, but electricity is electricity."

"I think everyone here knows that I want to tear into those sites *yesterday*," Dr. Fabian said with an undertone of amusement in his voice. He looked at the cameras feeding Cirilo's feed, trying to meet the Captain's gaze.

"But the process of taking apart a Xenos site for information and evidence is *not* my specialty," the physicist continued. "Your specialty has standards and protocols for this situation. I feel we shouldn't be hasty in discarding them."

That wasn't the tack Cirilo had expected from Fabian, and he made a mental note to check with Key. Fabian might be pushing for everyone else to leave things alone while he went and poked on his own.

"The full grid search is what gives us context of how these buildings are positioned relative to each other," Dr. Cobalt said flatly. "Giving it up risks *losing* critical context that might be needed to decipher whatever is at those sites."

"I believe I see the problem," Cirilo said, raising a hand before they all swung back into a clearly well-rehearsed argument. Everyone knew their places and positions, he figured, and if it wasn't clear enough for them to make a decision, listening to them argue it out wasn't going to help him.

"The problem, Captain, is that it will take five to six weeks to complete the initial grid investigation on the entire site," Hanraadts said calmly. "And that will not even begin to take us to the fifth site, which will require an entirely new dig grid… and is drawing as much power as the other four combined."

"It is better to take the time and do it right," Cobalt countered his companion. "If any of these were going to be threats or at risk of failing, they would likely have done so by now. They aren't going to attack us by surprise, and they're not going to explode.

"But if we open them up without knowing what the entire scenario is, we could lose information that would make all of the difference in interpreting what we find."

"There is one additional factor," Cirilo said quietly, "that doesn't appear to have been considered. *Santa Mica* is only contracted for another seventeen days in the L-I-Seven–K-Nine-Three System.

"We will commence loading the expedition at ten hundred hours standard on September twenty-third, professors. I have every intention to, as per the contract, return you to Herecrow System University by September thirtieth."

"We have a series of extensions built into the contract," Zima declared. "I thought it was obvious that we would be exercising those."

"Those extensions are at my discretion, Dr. Zima," Cirilo said, keeping his tone gentle. "Given the import and weight of what we have already learned, I unfortunately do not think it is in the interests of the Company—or the Seventy-Seven, for that matter—to delay returning with what we already know.

"I don't know if that changes your decision with regards to the still-active sites," he continued, "but it seems clear to me that you do not have time to complete the full grid. You had a decent assessment of the area you were looking at.

"Was there a miscalculation in your resources?"

Or had the University always planned on exercising the extensions? That would have been a reasonable plan under most circumstances, he supposed. They could expect to discover something where the Company learning about it five weeks sooner was worth more than HSU would pay for the extension.

"We didn't anticipate the moss," Cobalt said, before anyone else said a word. "It has drastically extended the time needed for even clearing the surface level. Seventeen days won't even be enough time for us to clear the main-site grounds, let alone do a proper investigation."

There was a surprisingly long silence, and Cirilo realized everyone was waiting for Zima to explode. The professor certainly seemed to be considering it, his lips pressed so tightly, they were turning white as he glared at Cirilo.

"I take it," he finally bit off, "that you will not be dissuaded from this decision."

"The presence of a Xenos species with interstellar travel that was active this recently represents a real danger to Seventy-Seven and the Santiago Corporation," Cirilo told Zima. "There's no way around it that I see. Your government and my seniors in the Company need to know what we've found, and I have no way of communicating that except by carrying the news on this ship.

"I am hardly going to force you back aboard ship at gunpoint," he continued, "but *Santa Mica* will leave on schedule. It is up to you if a portion of the expedition wishes to remain behind, but I understand that there are serious liability risks for the University if you do that."

"No, there aren't," Dr. Wild said with a grim snort. "Our paperwork for this expedition is quite clear: if we somehow outstay the provided insurance, Herecrow System University takes no responsibility for our safety, security or any injuries incurred."

"They would likely hire a ship to retrieve us," Cobalt countered. "And this planet has seemed safe so far..."

Zima was still silent, glaring at Cirilo. For all of the heat of the professor's anger, Cirilo suspected much of it was the Captain was *right*. They had discovered something monumental and incredible—but also potentially incredibly dangerous.

The rest of humanity needed to know what they'd found.

***

*++Well, that threw the cat into the pigeons, didn't it, Skipper?++*

Key's silent message after the meeting wrapped up—inconclusively—wasn't really a surprise.

"Zima should have realized I wasn't going to extend the contract," Cirilo told her. Key was presumably still surrounded by the academics, but he was alone in his office and could speak aloud.

*++The same reasons you won't are why he thought you would. This site is mind-bogglingly important to everything and everyone++*

"He also realizes that the moment I report in, no ship is coming to this system under contract for anybody else," he replied. "Company R&D will lock this place down and dissect the site down to the atom.

"*They'll* almost certainly finish their investigation grid as planned, making sure they have full context before opening buildings." Cirilo sighed. "And, of course, unlike Zima's people, they'll know about the wormhole."

*++That's going to be a headache. I'm not quite sure what that fifth site is, but that hill is taller than the one I put the bastion on. It has some pretty impressive sightlines++*

A chill ran down his spine.

"Nephil," he said aloud, looping the synthmind in. "Can you check the orbital patterns we ran for Delta's moon? I know there was a limited period where the dig site was occluded from the wormhole.

"If we use the altitude of the hill for the site the academics and I were just discussing, what happens to that occlusion period?"

"It disappears completely," Nephil replied instantly. "Anywhere in the top three meters of that hill would only be blocked from seeing the wormhole by the hill itself."

*++I don't think it's coincidence that we have a fucked-up wormhole and, in a spot that always has line of sight on that wormhole, a piece of alien tech still drawing power. The question is whether the wormhole shows up oddly* because *of the tech drawing power…++*

"My guess is that what we're seeing at the wormhole is leftovers," Cirilo said grimly. "It's closed, in standby, and I'd guess whatever is drawing power on the surface is on standby too."

*++That's not a pleasant thought. Or is that just me being paranoid? I mean, odds are that even if we trigger something to pulse the wormhole, it can't do much, right?++*

"You're the SecChief. It's your job to be paranoid," Cirilo reminded her. "If our friends downstairs even *twitch* toward that hill, let me know."

++*Are you going to stop them?*++

"No," he admitted with a shake of his head. "I don't think we can, not without using force. But if we're poking at what might be wormhole tech, I'd say we need a *Company* expert on hand... and that means either me or Rao.

"And I'm the only one with the authority to say we are all leaving."

# 59

To Cirilo's surprise, Zima called him before anything happened. It was just before dawn at the dig site, the beginning of the seven hours of natural light they would get to dig in.

"Captain Webster. Thank you for taking the time to join our staff meeting," the archaeologist told him. "Perhaps I should have talked to you more in advance; then I would not have been surprised by our time table.

"I did want you to see just how divided we were."

"I'll admit I didn't expect that," Cirilo said. "The lure of knowledge is always held out as an irresistible trap for researchers and scientists."

"And there is a great deal of truth to that," Zima agreed with a small forced laugh. "But we also regularly remind ourselves that the best way to get knowledge is to do it right, with proper documentation and procedure.

"Even with the realization that we cannot complete everything we want to before we must leave, there has been little agreement among my people." He shrugged. "However, as I suspect you are aware, any group of people must have a leader.

"And however much we prefer to listen to the rest of the team, sometimes someone must make a decision. That falls to the one in charge."

Despite his words, Cirilo doubted that Zima had ever hesitated to make a decision. The expedition leader had been as torn as his staff over what to do.

"And what was your decision, Doctor?" he asked.

"A compromise. We will clear the grid around the original site as we had planned, but tracing the power lines identified an additional site. One that some instinct tells me is important in its own right."

"Some instinct... named Benedek Fabian, I suspect?"

Cirilo wasn't entirely sure what he was expecting to get out of the question, though he did suspect quite strongly that the physicist had been involved.

He *hadn't* been expecting Miloš Zima to flush like an academy student caught kissing in the supply closet. Fabian had certainly seemed to exert more influence on the expedition than even his unofficial status seemed to call for, but Cirilo hadn't anticipated that particular wrinkle.

"Dr. Fabian did make his case quite clearly," Zima finally said. "And I believe that you agree with him: whatever is the secondary site is almost certainly of the greatest interest to all humanity at this point."

"And also most likely to be guarded, trapped or otherwise protected, Dr. Zima," Cirilo pointed out. "I would be remiss, given the security responsibilities the contract gives me, to ignore that factor."

Zima paused carefully.

"What do you mean, Captain?" he finally asked.

"I presume you are planning on doing a more... abrupt excavation at the secondary site?" Cirilo said.

"We had your shuttle do a close pass to identify the entrance," Zima confirmed. "We believe we have found one. We are clearing a careful and properly scanned path to the site now, and the BimLoos will remove the moss over the entrance once they reach the location.

"I... expect to be opening the building in about ten hours. We will record everything as we proceed into the structure, but during our initial pass, I do not intend for anything to be touched."

That was faster than Cirilo had expected, if slower and more careful than he'd feared.

"I think you're going to need extra eyes and extra watchers when you go in, Doctor," Cirilo told Zima. "Ten hours, you say?

"I will join you on the surface with an additional team of BimSoos. Something about this whole place is setting my professional paranoia on edge. You and I will enter this building together."

With Six right behind them. Because when push came to shove, Cirilo would rather put his life in the hands of the AbMee than just about anyone else.

Zima looked thoughtful, which wasn't what he'd expected.

"I'd like to say that felt unnecessary, as we are investigating a site that has been abandoned for at least a century," Zima said slowly. "But even the professionals are feeling something is off here. We have never seen an archaeological site so thoroughly cleaned out before—but we have *also* never seen a xenoarchaeological site with active power.

"The contradiction worries me. I will welcome you and your security people, Captain Webster." Zima smiled wryly. "And that, Captain, is not something I would have expected to say before we landed here."

***

"You asked me to stop by, Skipper?" Tereza asked, stepping into his office. She was carrying a covered mug of her own coffee, a self-indulgence that Cirilo occasionally envied her.

He'd inured himself to CargoFleet coffee, but *Santa Mica*'s coffee had merely improved from *undrinkable* to *terrible*. Still, there was a reason for his insistence, and he waved Tereza to a seat.

"The panel looks good," his First told him, eyeing the piece of art. "I hear Jeong nearly fell down when Lachlan told her what he wanted to pay for it!"

"She's good," Cirilo said. "I've paid more for art I like less, Tereza. When Lachlan floated the idea of getting art from the crew, I expected to be getting pieces I would tolerate for the sake of crew morale."

He smiled and indicated the still-empty stretches of wall.

"I might still end up with a few of those; Lachlan has some space to fill. But Jeong's piece? I'm honestly impressed by her talent."

"If she wasn't as good at her job as she is, I'd wonder if we should encourage that. But I don't think Romée or I want to give her up." Tereza's grin suggested that there was some quiet encouragement already going on, no matter *how* good an environment tech the young woman was.

"My plans for new art aren't why I called you in, Tereza," Cirilo told her. It still felt a bit unnatural to use her first name but less so than for just about anyone else.

"I think our friends on the surface have discovered the control center for our wormhole," he continued. "I haven't *told* them about that, but they've found a structure that is elevated above the rest of the dig site and is drawing most of the output from the decay generators they found."

"The Company would probably prefer it if they left that well enough alone, Skipper," she pointed out.

"And there is no way in void or stars that I can keep Zima and his people out of it," Cirilo said. "So, I'm joining them."

"Joining them?"

"I'm going to take SecSpec Six, two other BimSoos and every SecTeam we can spare down to the surface this evening," he explained. "I'll probably leave Deacon in charge up here. Marsh would be better, but I want her with me."

That would leave Tereza with three BimSoos, one SecSpec and two SecTeam troopers. He couldn't think of any reason *Santa Mica* would need those armed hands, but he wasn't going to strip the ship of people with guns, either.

"You do realize that the Captain is supposed to limit how much time he's on the surface, right?" Tereza asked. "Violet will remind you too."

"We need an FTL theory expert, and I've checked Rao's record," Cirilo said quietly. "She's a good t-drive engineer and definitely knows the ins and outs of an engine better than I do these days, but she's rough on the theory.

"I'm rusty, but I knew it well once. Fabian is probably better qualified to speak to non-transit-related forms of hyperdimensional physics, but I know my way around my tachyons and superquarks."

"There's no such thing as superquarks," Tereza pointed out, but her voice was just hesitant enough to make his point.

"You're right," he agreed. "But you had to check, and I didn't. I'm not sure what we're going to find down there, but we want someone from the Company with authority and knowledge standing in.

"And I want enough firepower to deal with anything Xenos Species Twenty-Four left behind."

"Do you think that's likely?"

"I think it is less likely that they left a system that could open a wormhole behind than that they left it undefended."

**60**

SIX FACED A NEW conundrum. Before, when Six deployed on an operation where combat was expected, the SecTeam issued loading orders as to what went in the BMSUs weapon pods.

There were a wide variety of options, after all. There was a default pod that contained both an energy weapon and a projectile weapon, of course. There was the Kestrel gatling railgun—and two different energy weapons options that also filled a pod.

Not only had Six been left to decide Six's own loadout, which would clearly be the default going forward, but Six had been requested to decide the armament for the three BMSUs accompanying the Captain to the surface.

++*Security Specialist Marsh*++ Six finally decided to ask for help. That the humans trusted Six to make the judgment was important, but it was more critical that it not be wrong.

++*You can call me Callie in this mode, too, Six*++ she replied. ++*What do you need?*++

++*I do not feel that I know enough about the potential threat parameters to prepare for this mission*++ Six told Callie. It made sense that the invitation to use the Specialist's first name stood in all environments, but once they'd left the surface, Six had been uncertain of the etiquette.

++*You're not the only one. It doesn't seem likely that we're going to face trouble from the expedition, if that helps? Otherwise, your guess is probably as good as mine*++

That was not helpful. Six considered the scenario.

++*Should I focus on providing a diversity of options or focus on heavy firepower? You are the senior Specialist on scene; I would not wish to be unable to support your plans, Callie*++

She sent Six a string of laughing-face emojis. While Six recognized the images, Six wasn't quite sure what to make of the message.

++*This isn't me or the Captain being intentionally unhelpful, Six*++ she said. ++*We have no idea what the risk profile is. I think our highest-likelihood threat is some kind of mechanical trap or SecBot equivalent. But that's only the highest probability*++

++*I believe I can work with that*++ Six replied.

Scenarios rippled through analysis. Against heavy SecBots or major mechanical traps, it would help best if the BMSUs brought heavy weapons. Six assigned Four and Five to carry heavy energy weapons, slow-firing but able to blast through walls.

Each of the other two BMSUs also had one standard pod and their built-in energy weapons. That still left two pods on each of the Units. Four picked up a Kestrel and Five received the pulse-laser equivalent.

Then, just in case, both of them received a multifocal variable-power stunner.

As the other Units moved around Six through the armory, specifications and data flowed through Six's vision. There were weapon modules in *Santa Mica*'s armory that Six had never been issued. Gatlings and energy cannon were the heaviest weapons usually used by CargoFleet BMSUs.

There was a large-caliber explosive-shell thrower. More ammunition-limited than the energy cannon, the limited number of shells would hit with greater explosive force. That replaced Six's gatling gun on the right-shoulder mount.

An array of tracking micromissiles went on the left-shoulder mount. Less powerful than the shells and almost as ammunition-limited, the micromissiles could be salvo-fired in under two seconds and follow a target.

An energy rifle, halfway between the gatling and the cannon in terms of rate of fire and power per shot, replaced Six's right-forearm weapon pod—and the left forearm weapon remained standard.

Between the three of them, Six's team carried more heavy firepower than any BMSU team Six had been part of before.

Six had encountered the concept of overkill. Six didn't agree with it—there were only two end scenarios to a combat encounter: *My humans are alive* and *I have failed.*

Six was not going to fail to keep Cirilo Webster and Violet Key alive.

# *61*

CIRILO COULDN'T HELP BUT notice an entirely different feeling to the dig site as he followed Indra Gupta along the path. The access to the second site inevitably passed through the cleared areas of the main site, and he could see the expedition's teams hard at work.

There were no BimLoos at the main site, though. Worker bots supported the human teams, but the biomechs had been pulled away for other purposes. The only biomechs visible, in fact, were the three at his heels—and a pair of BimSoos pacing an even security patrol around the exterior of the marked area.

Even as they poked at things with a stick, Key was making sure the main group of the expedition was safe.

He approved.

*++Even with BimSoos on site, I think Dr. Zima is starting to regret promising to wait for you++* his SecChief's voice said in his head. *++I haven't said anything pointed yet, but Seven and Eight do make a rather impressive argument on their own++*

*++I'm sure Gupta is keeping him updated. We're almost there++*

If anyone wanted to be truculent, Cirilo had seen the loadouts Six had assigned the BMSUs. The heavy stunners were more than sufficient to deal with the academics. Seven and Eight hadn't had access to the main armory on *Santa Mica* and only had standard loadouts, but even that included stunners.

Even the *thought* told Cirilo he was being twitchy about everything. There was almost zero chance that they'd have problems with the academics. He couldn't see any scenario where they were going to be threatened by Zima's people.

Though he knew that if they found a working device that could open wormholes, there would be members of the Company who would say the right thing to do was stun *everyone* and lock the planet down for Santiago control.

Fortunately, the person on Delta who was deciding what was best for the Santiago Corporation was him. The best defense he could see against a problem around the wormhole system was that he hadn't told any of Zima's people he thought it existed.

***

Looking over the region on aerial maps and even topographical charts, Cirilo hadn't picked out the hill as being marked taller than the others. No one had even been thinking in terms of high ground, after all.

It also wasn't *that* much taller. Twenty-eight meters to the next-highest's twenty-four.

Walking up the side of it, along the usual fast-concrete steps cut into the surface, it was clear that most of the mound was natural—but not all. Three of those extra four meters appeared to be a structure of some kind, a hemispherical dome whose moss-covered sections still blended smoothly into the natural hill.

A flattish area to the south of the dome held the people waiting for him. Zima and Fabian led up a team of a dozen senior archaeologists and an equal number of BimLoos.

Standing off to one side, watching and watched like hawks, were Violet Key, SecSpec Carmen Ventimiglia and two BimSoos.

With Cirilo's arrival, SecSpec Marsh and two SecTeam troopers in tow along with Six and two more BimSoos, the Company was now quite thoroughly represented.

He walked right up to Zima and offered the scientist his hand.

"Congratulations, Dr. Zima," he said. "This looks like we're going to be marking some new dates and names down in the history books, doesn't it?"

Zima accepted the handshake, but his focus was on the large double doors the BimLoos had uncovered. Like everything else built by Xenos Species Twenty-Four, the angles looked wrong to human eyes.

In this case, the paired doors formed an uneven pentagon. None of the five interior angles looked to even be the *same* angle, though Cirilo assumed they still added up to five hundred and forty degrees.

"We have been waiting for you, Captain," Zima finally said. "If we are to make those marks in history, we should get started."

"I appreciate your patience, Dr. Zima. This is your show. I am entirely here to bear witness."

"And I am glad you and your security people are here," the other man said, echoing his earlier words on the video call. "I am just impatient. Dr. Wild! Let's open the gates."

Wild nodded to his boss and turned his attention to the BimLoos. He didn't say anything aloud, clearly using a bionic com to communicate with the biomechs, but four of them advanced on the doorway.

"We already know it's sealed," Wild told Cirilo. "I've already worked out a solution to that."

The two front BimLoos were carrying a large tool between them. Cirilo recognized the heavy energy cutter before they brought it online, though he was surprised to realize the expedition had possessed one.

They were normally used for shaping hull plates, after all.

Beams of blue light flashed out from the cutter, marking the edge of the invisible beam that did the real work. The BimLoos started at the bottom of the door and worked their way up, converting the original seam between the doors into a centimeter-wide gash.

"How *sealed* was *sealed*, Dr. Wild?" Cirilo asked. That seemed... excessive.

"We could see the seam between the doors, but any attempt to scan or physically probe showed them as merged for the majority of their depth," Wild explained. "Either they were closed together with extraordinarily powerful magnets or they were melted together when the site was abandoned."

"Or Xenos Twenty-Four locks doors with some method of temporarily merging materials that we don't understand," Hanraadts observed.

The xenologist looked almost giddy at their current investigation, though Cirilo noted that Dr. Cobalt was somewhere else.

He wasn't sure if that was a division of labor or just the xenoarchaeologist separating himself from an intrusion that was definitely *not* best practices for archaeology.

As the first two BimLoos moved the cutter back and out of the way, the second pair stepped in and seized the doors. The edges were probably still hot, but the titanium alloy of their heavy manipulators didn't care.

However the doors had been merged together, they hadn't been melded to the surrounding building. The two sheets of metal swung open at the BimLoos' touch, revealing that they'd been nearly ten centimeters thick.

"Well, that raises interesting questions about what we've found, doesn't it?" Hanraadts noted. "Heavy blast doors, suggestive of either a site containing something worth defending or something at risk of exploding."

"We will find out," Zima declared. "Lights, everyone!"

"Please, Doctor, I think we would all appreciate it if the BimSoos went first," Cirilo insisted calmly. "If there are any traps here, this seems a likely place for them."

For a moment, it looked like Zima was going to argue, but then he nodded.

"Six, a careful sweep, if you please," Cirilo told the AbMee. "Record everything."

"Proceeding."

Six had not yet mastered such niceties as *nodding*, though Cirilo knew the BimSoo chassis Six wore was capable of it.

The four BimSoos fell in around Six instantly as Six approached the door. Six laid down a case Six had brought from the shuttle. There was no command visible to the regular humans, but the case slid open to reveal shaped foam holding twenty-four flying recon drones.

They lifted off instantly and dove forward.

"Everything the SecBots see is being recorded, Dr. Zima," Six noted aloud. "I am filing it in with the footage your team recorded of the site earlier today."

"How do you— Never mind. Thank you," the academic replied. "What are you see—"

Even though he'd expected it, predicted it and even set everything up to allow for it, Cirilo was still shocked when Zima's words were cut off by the sound of energy weapons firing.

The series of *zaps* and *crack*s wasn't familiar, but there was no real question what had happened.

"Automated weapons mounted three-point-four meters inside the entryway," Six announced. "Appear to be some form of pulse laser. I have lost five SecBot probes; pulling the drones back."

"Is there any way to get into the building without triggering them?" Hanraadts demanded. His cheer of a few moments before was gone. He clearly hadn't believed the warnings.

"No. The first turnoffs from the entry chamber are five-point-one meters inside," Six said. "We will need to neutralize the energy weapons. I presume minimum collateral damage would be preferred."

It wasn't really a question, but Six looked to Cirilo, who looked in turn to Zima.

"Dr. Zima? I believe Six has a method for safely neutralizing the guns, but we will inflict extra damage on the structure."

The Herecrow professor looked as torn as any human being Cirilo had ever seen—certainly more conflicted than he'd ever seen Zima before—and swallowed hard. He met Fabian's gaze across the room, and the two men shared some silent communication.

Potentially not even by bionic com, for all Cirilo knew. He was still wrapping his head around Zima having any kind of romantic relationship with another human being, let alone it being with the rogue physicist.

"If we can limit damage to within the vestibule, that would be preferable, yes," Zima told Six—bypassing Cirilo entirely, though that was a mark in his favor in this case. "However, we will learn nothing if we cannot enter the building.

"Do what you must, Specialist."

"Proceeding," Six replied. The AbMee was frozen for several seconds, then Four stepped up to stand parallel with Six.

One of Four's shoulder weapon pods unfolded into a heavy energy weapon, a not-so-distant cousin of the cutter the BimLoos had used a few minutes earlier.

"Everyone please move at least two meters away from Four," Six declared aloud.

The Saints had done it without thinking, though the only non-SecTeam there was Cirilo himself. The academics scattered with surprising speed at the AbMee's orders—with Zima and Fabian stopping right next to Cirilo.

"Close your eyes," Gupta told Zima.

Cirilo simply looked away when he saw the cannon start to glow. There was a moment of ominous humming from the BimSoo's weapon, then thunder tore across the hill. Five shots, each separated by two seconds, assaulted their ears, and then the humming slowed to a soft murmur.

"Sending in a second wave of SecBots," Six reported.

# *62*

THERE WERE TRENCHES, STILL glowing from heat, carved through the ceiling of the entryway when the humans followed the drones in. Several of the academics looked more than slightly askance at the wounds—and equally askance at the five biomechs leading the way into the structure in hunched postures.

"Still almost nothing in terms of artifacts," Zima said aloud. "No sign of the curvature of the structure in here, though the ceiling is only two meters tall. There is space for another chamber above us."

"The chamber is two-point-one-two-five meters tall," Six confirmed. "Given the apparent magnitude of the structure's exterior and ratios seen elsewhere in the complex, it is possible that there is a chamber with a one-point-seven-meter ceiling above us.

"I am not detecting any energy signatures above us, however."

"And you are detecting them elsewhere?" Cirilo asked.

"I am assisted, Captain, by knowing the rough entry points of the power cabling," Six pointed out. "Power signatures beneath us are faint, suggesting either further shielding or that the under levels are embedded in the natural hill.

"There is an energy signature to the left," the AbMee pointed, "that may be some form of power storage. It links to the energy signatures beneath us, and I could be misinterpreting it.

"Like the thermal generators in the power plant, while it resembles patterns in my databases, it is hardly an exact match. Xenos Species Twenty-Four uses a measurably different standard power transmission, for example, which causes—"

"I think we all understand that much, Specialist Six," Zima said. There was an edge to his voice, but he was still gentler with the AbMee than Cirilo had expected.

More than he'd have expected Zima to be with one of his team leads who'd started down a verbal rabbit hole, even.

"Is there anything else on this level?" Cirilo asked.

"I am detecting significant power cabling connecting to something in a central chamber directly ahead of us," Six said. "However, I am *not* detecting any active energy signatures there."

"Connected to power but not active," Fabian suggested. "What is it linked to, Six?"

"It appears to be connected to everything in this building, Dr. Fabian."

Cirilo concealed a smirk at Six's calm rejection of Fabian's attempt to be familiar.

"I believe that we may be looking at a control center," Fabian suggested. "Potentially even a fully active computing system."

"If so, then that is our absolute priority." Zima and Hanraadts stumbled over each other saying the exact same thing.

"What does the path forward look like?" Cirilo asked.

Dr. Wild had already gone forward, Seven walking one pace ahead of him as the archaeologist brought his light and scanners up to the door further inside.

"Almost matches the exterior hatch," he reported. "Both are the exact height of this chamber, left-weighted uneven pentagons."

"Are we going to need a cut—"

Zima's question was proven redundant as Wild stepped past Seven and pushed the right-hand door. It swung open easily at his touch, without even so much as a squeaky hinge, and then stopped at its widest opening.

"Let's see what we find," Cirilo said.

***

Stepping into the central chamber of the building—Cirilo was starting to realize this particular structure might be abandoned but it definitely wasn't a ruin—reminded him of nothing so much as an observatory.

It was immediately clear that the roof of this chamber was the roof of the building, not least because the roof was transparent and their lights showed the now-familiar metal-spiderweb interior of the strange moss that covered the dig site.

Elevated just over two meters above the floor was a trackway that ran in a full circle around the building, carrying four devices that Cirilo registered as radio dishes built of crystal. The four concave crystal bowls were hooked up to dark red cables running to the central mechanism.

A fifth concave bowl was positioned on a pole at the center of the room, pointed directly at the entrance. A shiver ran down his spine as he looked at it, feeling for a moment like the spike at the center—almost transparent when the lights focused on it—was pointed directly at him.

"I believe we should be cautious here," he said aloud. "We have no idea what this machine is."

The centerpiece of the entire affair was an uneven pentagon just over five meters across and a third of that high. The trackway and pole supporting the crystalline reflector dishes were above it, and the dark red cabling linked in to what Cirilo figured was a rotating dish that matched the upper transmitters.

There were no screens or controls that he could see, but the entire mechanism seemed to twitch with ready power. It was silent but radiated potential and *power* through the space clearly built to contain it.

"The room makes me think telescope," Fabian said, staying well clear of the mechanism but circling it with eager eyes. "But this doesn't look like anything I've ever seen."

"Those do look like receivers," Key pointed out, eyeing the crystal dishes, "but they could also be *transceivers*, able to transmit and receive... whatever they are handling."

"I don't see any controls," Zima said. "It may be my own biases, but I was expecting physical buttons and dials of some kind."

The most advanced Xenos species humanity had encountered ruins of hadn't even begun to approach the complexity of modern control systems, merging active haptic systems with bionic-communicator interfaces to be utterly customizable to any given user or need.

Cirilo's own guess was that the alien device was very similar to their own interfaces, combining holoprojection and haptic-interface fields to be both interface and display.

"There are three more exits from the room," Wild reported. "My rough map says this takes up sixty percent of the above surface structure. Whatever this thing is, it's the only reason this building exists."

"And it's the only thing in the entire complex that we've found active defenses at," Violet Key pointed out. "Whatever this is, the Xenos didn't want strangers poking at it. I think we need more information before we start prodding *this*, people."

Cirilo nodded. Key knew what he knew: that this was almost certainly the device Xenos Species Twenty-Four had used to open a wormhole from LI7–K93 to somewhere else.

He supposed the good news was that the only reason he could see for leaving it here was if it required a set of emitters on *both* ends.

"I agree," Zima said, showing surprising sense. The expedition's leader was actually standing back, with Gupta standing between him and the dark block at the heart of the room.

"We will investigate the rest of the structure before we even *think* of touching this," he continued. "As we all discussed to the point of nausea in our staff meetings, *context* is everything. Only once we understand everything that is in this building and have some idea of how this all works do we want to poke the big machine in the middle of it all!"

It was only as Zima spoke that Cirilo realized that all of the BimSoos and Six were with him, Key and Zima. They only had eyes on maybe half of the academics, with all of them spread out around the room, investigating doors and secondary equipment, mostly.

He was about to ask Zima to make sure everyone had heard him when they all heard something *else*.

A thrumming, like a mechanism powering up. A moment later, they were all blinded for a second as the lights in the room suddenly switched on.

Broad panels that hadn't looked any different from the rest of the wall now blazed in harsh blue-tinged light. Blinking against the sudden illumination, it took even Cirilo a few moments to realize that the humming had grown louder.

And it was coming from the machine at the center of the room.

**63**

"Oh, fuck."

Cirilo couldn't disagree with Key's curse. Even as he was trying to check if anyone he could see was touching the machine, the sides lit up. What imagery he could see made no sense—it wasn't even that it was being presented in alien iconography and text; it was like half the text was missing.

There was no time to even begin to consider what that might mean. The trackway was beginning to move and an eerie glow began to fill the five crystal dishes.

"Dr. Zima, I think we need to get out of this room," he told the academic. "We have no idea what this device is going to—and any safety measures the Xenos put in place would not be tailored for humans."

"But... think of the opportunity..."

"To die?" Cirilo said bluntly. He gestured at the lights on the walls. "Those lights are shading to ultraviolet, Doctor. Twenty-Four's normal lighting is probably going to give everyone in this room sunburn.

"What do you think is going to happen when the most powerful energy projector on the planet wakes up?"

From the sharp look Zima shot him, the xenoarchaeologist might have just clued in that Cirilo had a far better idea of what the wormhole projector was than he'd been letting on.

"We need to get out of here."

"I confirm the Captain's assessment," Six said. "Radiation levels in this space are elevating. I cannot be certain that this room will remain safe for the organic components of the Units, let alone unmodified humanity."

"We have to record—"

"I will leave SecBots behind to record everything," Six interrupted Fabian as the Doctor arrived mid-argument. "For the safety of the humans, I *must* insist that we evacuate *now*."

"Doctor, when AbMees insist, we *fucking listen*," Key replied. "*Move*, or Six will have the BimSoos carry you."

Cirilo was already moving, waving the SecTeam ahead of him. His bracer spun to life, ignored in the tumult as it began to project its defensive screen.

That might buy him a few more seconds than everyone else, but it wouldn't save him. He spent those seconds searching to make sure they hadn't missed anyone.

"The space is clear, Captain. Please go."

He nodded to Six—and obeyed with alacrity.

***

Cirilo got outside in time to hear the gasps of shock from the gathered crowd—and to *smell* a horrible scent: a mix of burnt metal, rotting vegetation and burnt blood.

"Skipper, look," Key told him, pointing back past him.

He reached her and turned around, swallowing hard as he saw the metallic moss covering the building burning away. Whatever energy beam was hitting them was invisible to the naked eye, but its effects were clear, as laser-straight lines cut through the fungal cover.

++*Four beams identified*++ Six reported over the SecTeams MishNet. ++*Matching the four upper projector arrays in the chamber. SecBot imagery is badly distorted by interference, but at least half of the bots remain operational*++

++*A higher ratio than expected. Energy levels in the central chamber remain high enough to kill a BMSU*++

++*Can you identify a vector for the beams?*++ Cirilo asked, crossing to where Zima and Fabian were both staring at the burning moss.

++*Validating with Nephil, but the likelihood that the beams will enter the L-One Lagrange point exceeds seventy-five percent*++

"Oh, fuck," he said aloud, mirroring Key's initial comment.

"You seem to know more about what's going on than you are sharing," Fabian accused.

"And that's not changing, I'm afraid," he told the physicist. "It's possible our mere presence triggered the system, but I have the sinking suspicion *someone* poked at it."

"I didn't see anyone," Fabian replied. "And it would have been a bloody foolish thing to do, wouldn't it? What even *is* this?"

He gestured at the burning moss.

"A side effect," Cirilo said grimly. "Doctors, you need to pull all of your people back to the camp. Start prepping for an emergency evacuation."

Several of the surrounding academics stared at him like he'd grown a gun turret.

"You think this is a threat." Zima wasn't even asking a question.

"I am not *certain*, which is why I'm asking to you *prep* for an evac, not start one," Cirilo replied. "But we just woke something up. Something that is expending a great deal of energy we didn't think this place still had—and I don't think it's doing so to set a bunch of moss on fire!"

"Wild, Hanraadts." Zima turned to his subordinates. "Get everyone moving. Benedek... go with them."

"I am not leaving you," Fabian said sharply. "Any more than Indra is, am I right?"

The secretary smiled thinly, but he wasn't moving.

"Just... *go*," Zima snarled.

"Since when have I ever followed your instructions, Miloš?" the physicist asked. "If you're staying, I'm staying. I'm not walking away from *this*. I just wish I had better sensors."

"Get as many people moving as are going to move," Cirilo growled, tempted to ask Six to stun the two scientists—or even to do it himself.

++*Skipper, the beams entered the Lagrange point*++ Nephil reported in his head. Time delay was short but enough that the synthmind wasn't waiting for him to reply. ++*Four separate beams swept the area. While the wormhole is at the exact center, the targeting did not appear to be that precise*++

++*Once one beam had made contact, however, the others locked on in three-point-seven seconds. All four beams are now focused on the wormhole. I am detecting an energy feedback surge*++

++*Skipper, we are going to be in real trouble here shortly*++ Tereza added. ++*Nephil and Felix and I are agreed: the wormhole is expanding exponentially. It will be no more than sixty seconds before it's wide enough for a shuttle. I'm not sure where it goes from there*++

++*Neither am I*++ Cirilo said. ++*Get our shuttles into space, loaded for evac. We're lifting out the expedition*++

"What's going on, Captain?" Zima asked.

"The possibility of a threat just became a certainty, Doctor. We are evacuating the expedition," Cirilo told him firmly. "My remaining shuttles are loading for emergency personnel transport and dropping now.

"You're leaving your gear. Crossload your data as much as you can. There's an evac can already on the surface; that will get half of your people moving. It won't be comfortable, but—"

The *hiss-crackle* of an unfamiliar energy weapon tore through the air and Cirilo froze. They were outside the building, and surely someone would have—

Ventimiglia's scream broke his thoughts.

"Get down!" Six bellowed, the AbMee projecting loudly enough to be heard in the dig site as a series of barely visible bolts of yellow energy tore out of the entryway behind them.

Cirilo stepped in front of the civilians, taking a blast on his personal screen as he protected the academics and tried to see what was shooting at him.

Gleaming grotesquely in the mix of too-blue light from inside the building and too-pale light from LI7–K93, four strange multilimbed robots advanced from the door, energy beams lashing out at any movement.

There was a lot more than *one* trap guarding the wormhole generator, it seemed.

# 64

Tereza watched the displays on *Santa Mica*'s bridge in horror. To the freighter's sensors, the beams of energy coming up from the surface were clearly visible, intersecting at the tiny warp in reality that was the wormhole.

"Exponential growth continues," Nephil confirmed, the synthmind's voice perfectly calm. "Pulse has been in place for thirty seconds; wormhole is now ninety picometers across. Assuming current pattern continues, the wormhole will be ninety *meters* across in under sixty seconds."

"Any idea where it's linking to?" Tereza asked. She knew her voice wasn't calm. She needed to do something, but she wasn't sure what that something *was*.

"None. I do not believe the wormhole will continue expanding much past ninety meters, but I have no basis on which to estimate the necessary safety margin for transit," Nephil told her.

"Regardless, I assess that the wormhole will be transitable sometime between forty-five and fifty-five seconds from now."

And there was no point making the wormhole transitable unless something was going to transit.

"Shuttles are launching," Salvador said over the com from Flight Control. "I've got three birds rigged for personnel transport dropping toward the planet as fast as they can go. What are we even looking at, First?"

"A wormhole the Xenos left behind," she told him. "One that's going to be open enough for someone to come through any moment now."

"Do you want me in Foxtrot?"

Somehow, that question—obvious as it was in hindsight—clicked everything into place for Tereza.

"Yes," she told him crisply. "Get her in the air and linked into a MishNet with *Santa Mica*. I'm initiating evasive maneuvers and powering up the defense systems."

"I'll have your back," the FlyChief promised.

Even as he spoke, Tereza's hands flew across her console. *Santa Mica* didn't need to be at a special status to be fueled and ready to go—the shuttles were fueled from the freighter's far-larger tanks, after all.

Taking the big ship from a cold orbit to hot maneuvering was a different story, and Tereza wished she'd started the warmup process sooner. Numbers flicked across her display, grim countdowns to the wormhole being large enough for something to come through and how long until *Santa Mica*'s main engines were online.

"All hands, this is the First speaking," she said, linking her voice to every corner of the ship. "It looks like we've triggered something on the surface that appears to be opening a *wormhole*, of all things, up here.

"We have to assume that *Santa Mica* is about to come under attack. All hands report to emergency positions. Stand by for hard maneuvers and damage control."

A freighter didn't have *battle stations*. *Emergency positions* was the closest a CargoFleet got, drilled responses intended to handle things like breaches or asteroid showers. It would put most of the crew in places where they could handle damage and make sure that every key station was fully staffed.

From the speed with which Felix De Veen careened into the bridge a few seconds later, he'd been on his way before she even sent out the call. She gave him a grateful nod and flipped the sensors over to him.

"Wormhole just shrank by twenty-five percent before resuming the same growth pattern," Nephil reported. "Passing sensor analysis to SysChief. Assembling parameters for defensive systems."

"How much time does that shrink buy us?" Tereza asked. "And any idea what *caused* it?"

"No," the synthmind admitted. "But it has bought us an additional eleven seconds before the wormhole breaches ninety meters in diameter."

Those extra eleven seconds weren't enough for the main drive. Tereza flicked a series of commands that brought the freighter's maneuvering engines online. A mix of simpler technologies than the main drive, the main things they shared were lower energy radiation and higher fuel usage.

All of them together were enough to start *Santa Mica* boosting away from the L-One Point. That vector also opened their orbit, which would be a problem when the shuttles started coming *back* up.

On the flip side, the people on the surface might be safer.

"Wormhole is now six-point-nine centimeters across. It is increasing in diameter ten times every five seconds."

Nephil's steady tone kept the report from being as terrifying as it should have been, but the reality was terrifying.

Tereza Jewel was about to be in charge during humanity's First Contact with a Xenos Species capable of interstellar travel—a First Contact triggered by humanity poking around a place the Twenty-Fours clearly *really* hadn't wanted anyone going.

"Nephil, Salvador, we don't fire first," she told the synthmind and the pilot, surprised at how much of the earlier shakiness was gone from her voice. "But if they launch projectiles or missiles at us, you're free to engage to defend us without asking for permission."

That was most critical for Nephil. The synthmind's reaction times were far better than any human. He was no more a war machine than the rest of *Santa Mica*, but he'd be able to start defending them much sooner.

++*First*++ That Nephil was speaking in her bionic com was a warning sign all on its own. ++*I can defend the ship. But... I do not believe I can fire on another vessel. It is antithetical to all that I am to take a life*++

Tereza swallowed any kind of response for a few seconds. Given who she was talking to, she had to presume that Nephil included any high-end artificial intelligence in *a life*, too. It wasn't unreasonable for a CargoFleet synthmind to be a pacifist.

It shouldn't even have *mattered*. But without knowing what was going to come through that wormhole, it was suddenly shockingly inconvenient.

++*I understand*++ she told him, equally silently. ++*It's not like we have anything that really can be an offensive weapon, but if it comes to it, I will take the shot*++

Tereza was a pacifist by inclination herself, but as First Officer of *Santa Mica*, it was her job to protect the freighter's crew, no matter what. Even if that meant taking a stain on her soul she'd never imagined she'd have to face.

She already had the defense-system controls up on her console, after all. Her focus had been maneuvering, but if the opportunity came to take a shot, she could do it.

"Wormhole is now at sixty-nine meters in diameter," Nephil reported. "Growth exponent is slowing... Growth has ceased."

"Wormhole is now four hundred and eleven meters in diameter."

"And it's not the only one."

Felix's quiet interjection pulled Tereza's attention away from the glittering hole in space—now visible even in normal light as a strange ball of light, almost impossible to describe—to the SysChief.

"Felix?"

"Now that the wormhole is open enough, it's sending out a continual pattern of Cherenkov radiation, among other things. There is a matching signature on the surface, First," he told her. "There's a second wormhole *inside* the generator building."

And that meant that the people on the surface weren't safe at all.

"Contact!" Nephil snapped, his generated voice showing emotion for the first time in the years Tereza had known him.

She still didn't have main engines, but switching the vector of the maneuvering thrusters *should* be enough. Now *Santa Mica* was burning directly toward the planet for a few seconds, giving them enough time to see just what had emerged from the hole in space.

Nephil and Felix had a zoomed-in view of the craft in the main display as Tereza tried to confuse the alien's sensors. Unsurprisingly, it was like nothing she'd ever seen before, an uneven twenty-five-sided polyhedron.

The largest side of the ship was glowing with radiation, propelling the ship through some mechanism that their sensors didn't recognize. It wasn't as simple as a chemical or fusion rocket but not as complex as *Santa Mica*'s own main drive.

"Contact is eighty-five meters across along the main line," Nephil reported. "Mass approximately one hundred seventy thousand tons."

"It is vectoring toward us, First," Felix warned.

There was really only one option, even if the thought of what it meant terrified Tereza.

"Nephil, transmit the First-Contact package," she ordered. "Leave a channel open."

The First-Contact package was designed for something like Nephil to be able to understand it from basic mathematical principles. It wouldn't necessarily be a *fast* process, but hopefully, the attempt would be recognized for what it was.

"Contact package sent. New contact detected," Nephil shifted from one report to the other without the breath he didn't need. "Second vessel appears identical to the first."

The two alien ships were still tens of thousands of kilometers away, but the distance was falling fast.

The main engines *finally* came online. Tereza cut the maneuvering thrusters—she'd burned enough fuel to power the ship for a full day, accelerating them for a handful of minutes.

On some unknown instinct, she only brought the main drive up to the acceleration the thrusters had managed. She adjusted her course to make sure she wasn't actually going to drop the freighter into the atmosphere, and checked Foxtrot's location.

Salvador was sticking with her, keeping the gunship less than fifty kilometers away.

"Do we have any news on the evacuation from the ground?" she asked.

"Nothing," Nephil reported grimly. "Our communications to the surface do not appear to be operating. FlySpec Thorpe is on the ground with Shuttle Bravo, but in the best scenario, it would take time for him to load people aboard."

"And the new shuttles?"

"FlySpec Rogers reports they are ten minutes out from landing."

Tereza knew how long the shuttles were *supposed* to take to get down to the dig site. She didn't want to know how the three pilots heading for the planet had managed to cut over twenty minutes from their flight time.

"No response from the alien ships. They are continuing to close the distance," Felix told her. "What do we do?"

"Resend the First-Contact package," she said instantly, then a thought hit her. "Do we still have that ProBot near the wormhole?"

It took a few seconds for anyone to confirm that—seconds in which a third alien ship emerged from the wormhole.

This one blazed forward at a higher acceleration than the other two, clearly moving to rendezvous with them. Tereza didn't like the pattern she was seeing, but she wasn't going to break humanity's first First Contact by opening fire!

"ProBot is online," Felix finally confirmed. "It's in a passive ballistic orbit without even active sensors; I don't think the contacts realized it was there."

"I want its eyes on the wormhole," she told the SysChief. "Stay passive for now, but I want to know *everything* it can see about that."

*Santa Mica* was almost a hundred thousand kilometers from the wormhole, much closer in to Delta than the L1 Lagrange point. All they could see was a vague glow of light that seemed to pop out an alien spaceship every minute or so.

The ProBot was barely three hundred kilometers away. It could hopefully see a *lot* more.

The contacts were getting closer, now only sixty thousand kilometers away. The third ship had come on faster than the other two, but if that was their peak acceleration, *Santa Mica* had a slim but real advantage.

Tereza doubted they were that lucky.

"Something's happening," Felix said. "I'm getting profile changes on all three ships. Sorry, First, I'm not sure *what* I'm looking at!"

The zoomed-in image of the lead ship showed the change as best as the computers could render it. One of the smaller faces was shifting, splitting apart and sliding into the vessel to reveal an internal void of some kind.

Like a miniature version of a shuttle bay.

Or— The missile exploded out of the launch bay before Tereza could finish her thought.

"Missile launch detected," Nephil reported drily. "Three contacts inbound. At current acceleration, thirty seconds to impact.

"I am engaging our meteor defenses."

Tereza turned the ship again, extending her evasive maneuvers and ticking her acceleration up, buying the synthmind more time for firing solutions.

Seconds were all she could create, but seconds would have to be enough. *Santa Mica* wasn't supposed to fight anyone—the Santiago Corporation was just protective of their monopoly.

All of the missiles died well clear of *Santa Mica*, but the contacts continued on like that had been expected.

With grim certainty, Tereza realized that salvo had been a test shot.

"Keep on the defenses, Nephil," she ordered. "They're going to show us their real teeth in a moment here."

As she spoke, she started running through numbers on her console. The freighter's defenses were designed to stop missiles, but there had to be *something* she could do to make the aliens blink.

"Multiple profile shifts on each contact," Felix said grimly. "I make it...twelve launches. Nephil, do you have them?"

"We shall see," the synthmind replied.

*There.* Tereza found what she was looking for, which left her more than a touch stunned as she looked at the parameters of the joker in their defense system.

"How in void did we call *that* a deflection system?" she asked aloud—but she was already adjusting settings, feeding power to the capacitors for the single heavy railgun tucked away inside the anti-meteor arrays.

"The four/four railgun is an *asteroid*-deflection system," Nephil pointed out primly.

Whoever had named the weapon—which fired a four-kilogram steel projectile at four percent of lightspeed—had either been unfamiliar with musical notation or having far too much fun.

Even at the mind-boggling velocity the railgun mustered, its slugs would still take almost seven seconds to reach the incoming alien ships. Maneuvering *Santa Mica* was occupying most of Tereza's attention, but she managed to lay the crosshair on the first contact.

And hesitated. The last of the second salvo of missiles came apart as an energy pulse struck it, still over a thousand kilometers clear of the freighter.

If they couldn't stop the missiles, the people Tereza was supposed to protect were going to die. Everyone on the planet would probably follow shortly afterward—and she had *no* idea what was going on down there!

But like Nephil, she'd never ended a life, organic or synthetic. To do so felt wrong—but the lives of her crew were at stake. She swallowed, trying to find the courage to do what she had to do.

++*I've got it, First*++ an older male voice said kindly in her bionic com. A new console was live, she realized, linking into the control network she shared with Nephil.

Her targeting solution vanished, replaced in a breath with one that even her untrained eye saw was more sophisticated, taking into account the velocity of the oncoming spaceship—and then a small color flash marked the railgun firing.

Against the multimegaton bulk of *Santa Mica*, there was no perceptible sensation. The relief of the tension gave her a second to look up and realize she hadn't even seen Lachlan Stirling enter the bridge.

The Captain's Steward had taken over an empty console and accessed the meteor-defense system—which left Tereza wondering just how much access Stirling *had*—and was now interfacing with Nephil.

As a third salvo—this one of eighteen missiles—blazed across space at them, even Tereza could see the sudden increase in efficiency as Stirling stepped into the breach.

It was still clear that they weren't going to stop them all this time, and Tereza threw *Santa Mica* into a new course, twisting the freighter through a maneuver far tighter than she'd ever been designed for, trying to buy time.

Three things happened simultaneously.

The 4/4 cannon recharged, its icon flicking green again for a heartbeat before Stirling sent a second shot out into space.

The *first* railgun slug arrived at its target, proving that the oncoming aliens hadn't allowed for *Santa Mica* firing back. Four kilograms of steel tore through the twenty-five-sided polyhedron like the fist of an angry god, and the vessel's strange drive seemed to collapse in on itself for a moment before the entire ship blew apart in a perfectly spherical fireball.

And Foxtrot cut across in front of *Santa Mica*, the forward cannon blazing fire and lead in a trail that tore over half of the third missile salvo to pieces.

"Got the fuckers," Stirling crowed. "Not bad, Salvador."

Foxtrot twisted in space, turning her prow toward the alien ships while still flying perpendicular to the line between the contacts and *Santa Mica*. Weapon pods on the gunship's flanks opened up, and new icons marked the display as Salvador emptied his missiles at the enemy ships.

Tereza had no idea how capable the missiles Salvador was sending at their enemies were, but the gunship was a tenth the size of the alien vessels, and he'd just launched eighteen missiles in the wake of the second railgun shot.

She had a moment of hope—and then a sharp line on the display connected the closest of the alien ships with the gunship.

And then Salvador Ostergaard was just... gone.

"What the *void*?" she snarled.

"Contacts appear to now be deploying beam weapons," Nephil reported tonelessly as they watched the alien ships dodge around Stirling's second shot. It wasn't the usual calm the synthmind projected, but something else. Something... less.

"Range is uncertain, but the power level would be sufficient to core *Santa Mica* from bow to stern."

That silenced everyone—a silence in which Tereza watched the remaining Xenos warships shoot down Salvador's missiles one after another.

Right up until the last two missiles suddenly tripled their acceleration and blazed forward in streaks of light. Alien energy fire still caught one, but the other slammed into contact two at full speed.

There was a spark on the display as whatever warhead the missile carried did its job. For a moment, that was it—and Tereza's attention was inexorably drawn to the latest salvo of missiles heading toward *Santa Mica*.

Then, with no apparent fuss or bother, the alien ship blew up in another perfectly spherical fireball.

"These guys are looking surprisingly volatile," Stirling observed. He had another 4/4 round into the air as he spoke, adapting to Tereza's maneuvers with surprising skill.

Necessarily so, as her latest twist came only just in time. The same sharp white line was drawn on the display as the remaining alien ship fired its beam weapon, accompanying it with another six missiles.

*Santa Mica* didn't have any tricks left. Between Nephil at the meteor-defense system and Tereza at the controls, she thought they could survive the missiles, but the moment the alien ship connected with their beam cannon, they were all dead.

"Come on, come on," she heard Stirling growl. "You saw the launch. Dodge or shoot. Pick one... and *now*."

Tereza couldn't quite follow what her impromptu gunner had done to set up the situation, but she saw the alien ship jink "up" relative to Delta—only for Stirling to suddenly redirect the fire of every energy cannon engaging the missiles.

Even *Santa Mica*'s hull, designed to withstand minor impacts, would shrug off a single blast from one of the energy weapons used to deflect larger meteorites.

Whatever the alien ship's hull was made of couldn't withstand eighty-five of those guns at full rapid fire. It came apart under the pounding, pieces of it beginning to fly apart in every direction—and then it, too, vanished in a spherical burst of flame.

"Something's not right," Tereza said grimly. "They shouldn't have all blown up the same way, should they?"

"That's not all that's not right," Felix told her. "I have that visual from the ProBot."

She looked at him and he raised his hands, palms up, in a shrug.

"We seemed a bit busy," he pointed out—as Nephil and Stirling tore through the last missiles before they reached the freighter.

"But you need to see this," he continued.

The feed from the probe suddenly filled the main display. Numbers down one side told Tereza the amplification—enough to bring the wormhole right into their faces.

From the angle and distance the ProBot had, it was possible to see through the wormhole. It was like looking through convex glass, badly distorted, but still clear enough.

Clear enough to pick out dozens—*hundreds*—of twenty-five-sided polyhedrons stacked in neat rows.

"I am compensating for the distortion," Nephil announced, and the image suddenly sharpened.

The wormhole led to an interior space, but Tereza's mind quailed at the scale. Assuming every ship she could see was the same as the ones they'd just fought, the cavernous space had to be dozens of kilometers wide.

"I have some scans of the debris coming in as well," Felix said quietly. "No atmosphere leak. No significant organics. They're drones, First. And so are all of *those*."

Three had come through, but Tereza could see others moving.

"We need to close that wormhole," she and Stirling said simultaneously.

She looked over at the steward, then "up" in the universal gesture of addressing a ship's synthmind.

"Nephil, do you have *any* word from the surface?"

**65**

Humans were not nearly as rational as Six would prefer them to be. When an unknown combat platform opened fire on them, they should go to ground or just plain run.

Not muddle about in circles. At least the Saints had personal energy screens and were putting themselves between the academics and the warbots emerging from the bunker behind them.

++*Four, Five. Heavy energy on the hostiles*++ Six ordered. ++*Seven, Eight, draw fire. Protect the civilians*++

The heavy cannon were slow-firing, but they were also the most powerful weapons Six's team had. The two BMSUs stepped up, relying on their own personal energy screens to keep them intact, and opened fire.

Most of the human SecTeam joined in, though their sidearms weren't going to add much in Six's calculation. Even the bracer-weapons carried by Webster and Key, while more powerful than the pistols Marsh and Traversini were firing, wouldn't make much of an impression on a bot at a significant range.

Still, the splatter of light fire drew the advancing enemy machines' attention, holding them in place for just long enough. Flashes of bright yellow light lit the afternoon sky as the heavy cannon fired, and two of the oncoming attackers collapsed into heaps of crumpled limbs.

The other two dodged away from their fallen companions, exactly as Six had predicted. A single shot from his heavy-projectile weapon blew apart the third hostile—and a focused stream of gatling rounds from Seven and Eight pinned the last in place long enough for Four and Five to hit it with a pair of energy bolts.

Six wasn't going to count anything down until it was in pieces, and advanced toward the bunker entrance. The suspicion proved accurate, as the wreckage of the first two bots skittered away from Six, not rising back to their feet until they were out of sight of everything else.

The heavy-projectile weapon fired twice, its rate of fire the other advantage over the energy equivalent. Both enemy robots blew apart, and Six turned to survey the debris from the other two.

Those appeared to be dead, but scans showed remaining energy signatures.

Six put a shot into each energy signature with the rifle on Six's right arm. It took seven shots until the wrecks of the other two drones stopped appearing on the scans at all.

"Six, report," Webster ordered from outside the entrance.

"Drones, Captain," Six replied. "They appear to have significant self-repair function and can take a solid energy-cannon hit while remaining semi-functional."

"Where did they come from?" The Captain's face was clear to Six's vision. Something was wrong. More than just the attack…

"Unclear, Captain," Six said. "I will need to investigate."

"Carmen's dead, Six," Webster told him. "Four of the academics too. Dr. Wild is hurt badly. We're evacing, but… I can't raise shuttles."

Six focused on sensors for a few seconds.

"We are being jammed," Six confirmed. "Origin appears to be inside the bunker—I cannot localize but I calculate it is either positioned in the projector chamber or is a side effect of the projector's operation."

"Then we go in," Webster said grimly.

"Radiation levels are not decreasing, Captain."

Six didn't explain. If it was necessary, elaboration was possible, but it had only been minutes earlier when Six had informed the humans that the radiation in the central chamber would shortly be lethal to them.

"How bad?"

"The BMSUs and myself should be fine for limited exposures," Six replied. "I am not certain unshielded humans would survive to reach the projector chamber."

"They took whatever protective shielding was in there with them, didn't they?"

"I can only speculate, Captain, but that seems likel— *Down.*"

Six stepped into the way of an energy blast from the warbot that had just entered line of sight. Six's energy shield held against the first three shots, allowing Six to bring the heavy-projectile weapon to bear.

The shell proved as efficacious the fourth time as the first three, but the bot fired twice more before it came apart. Six's armor held, but the force was sufficient to move the entire chassis several centimeters.

There was a dent. Six lifted the energy rifle and put four more shots into the collapsed drone, targeting any remaining energy signatures as before.

"I cannot trace the movement of enemy combatants through the shielded walls of the bunker, Captain," Six warned. "Without certainty of their origin point, someone must make certain the entrance is held to protect the evacuation."

"We can handle that," SecChief Key said. "But why would we do that?"

"For the same reason you didn't listen in by com, SecChief," Webster pointed out. "Our coms are jammed and the source seems to be the wormhole projector.

"Radiation is too high for humans, so it's down to Six and the BimSoos. I... would rather not leave this all on you, Six."

"I was given a choice to choose another duty station, Captain. I chose this one," Six told Webster, though the concern was warming. "I regret that I cannot locate the origin of the enemy drones."

"That seems obvious enough," Key replied. "I bet two days' salary there's a sub-wormhole in the projector room and they're coming through from somewhere else."

Six ran the scenario.

"That seems likely, SecChief. In which case securing the projector chamber is absolutely critical."

"We need to shut that thing down," Webster said grimly.

"We have no idea what will happen," Key pointed out. "And Zima might blow his lid if we do so without giving him something to research."

"We're out of time for shiny options or worrying about the advancement of human knowledge, SecChief. Specialist Six?"

"Yes, Captain?"

"Take Four, Five, Seven and Eight with you," Webster ordered. "Eleven and Twelve are coming over from the dig site as we speak. Between the SecTeam and myself, we'll contain anything that gets past you.

"Get back into that central chamber and do whatever it takes to shut down the projector."

"Understood, Captain."

Six was already linking the other four BMSUs into a MishNet. With the jamming, it was only line-of-sight, but it would be better than nothing.

The problem was that the only guaranteed one-shot-kill they seemed to have was Six's own heavy-projectile weapon—and that only held four more rounds!

***

The entry chamber wasn't long enough to create enough shelter for the humans, in Six's calculation, especially since Six couldn't be sure what was on the other side of the doors leading to the rest of the building.

The double doors to the central chamber had mostly closed. That was interesting in itself, as they'd required almost no effort to open or keep open before. Either they had some system to close them to help contain the radiation from the projectors in the room, or something had closed them to cover themselves.

Six was expecting the latter.

++*Seven, Eight. Loadout upload*++ Six requested. Four and Five had the loadouts Six had given them—including the now-regrettable heavy stunners—but Seven and Eight would have been equipped by Key for an overwatch job.

The data fed over immediately. As expected, they had the standard gatling railgun and dual-weapon pods on their arms—but what was the other shoulder pod?

Precision beamers were a useful long-range weapon, intended for police work where it was necessary to avoid killing a target and disarming them would prevent further damage. Perfectly capable of killing most humans, the narrow laser would also burn through just about any mechanism or weapon at ranges of up to a thousand meters.

At ranges of under *ten* meters— Six's thought was interrupted by one of the side doors bursting open to reveal another pair of warbots.

This was the first chance Six had to really see the enemy bots before they'd been shot at least once. They were strange, misshapen things when measured against the human aesthetics Six had inherited. A horizontal uneven pentagon appeared to hold most of their mechanisms, with five legs underneath it moving them forward with a strange rotating skitter.

A central pod on top of the pentagonal disk sprouted three more arms, each of them ending in a spiraling gold crystal.

++*Seven, Eight, target-designate for beamers*++

Four and Five opened fire on their own, heavy energy bolts crisscrossing with the yellow pulses of enemy fire. The warbots split their fire, sending streams of energy at each of the five biomechs, with the extra aiming for Six as the closest.

Six leapt out of the way, rising *above* the fire and crashing down several meters closer to the central chamber. No further fire chased Six, and a quick twist lined the energy rifle up on the nearest warbot.

The calculation had been correct. The precision beamers had cut through the central nodes of the warbots, severing the weapons systems from the drones to end their fire.

One of the bots was charging Six—likely having identified the command unit. A leg snapped out at unexpected speed and smashed into Six's lower torso. Damage alerts pinged on internal datastreams as the entire nine-hundred-plus-kilo chassis was flung back into a wall.

Even while Six was involuntarily moving, the energy rifle was swinging into place. A burst of focused energy hit the next leg the warbot tried to stab with, severing it. The enemy was unfazed, continuing its rotation to bring another leg to bear.

A precision beamer severed *that* leg, moments before two heavy energy blasts intersected at the center of the warbot. Four and Five's shots wrecked the core of the thing, sending its pieces slumping to the ground.

++*Status update, immediate*++ Four demanded.

That was about as complex as any of the other BMSUs became, but Six could also detect an emotional undertone that was unusual for a BMSU. Four was... worried about Six?

++*Minor damage; functionality unimpaired*++ Six sent back, leaving the complexity of Six's relationship with the unawakened BMSUs for later.

Six was still turning to locate the other warbot when Eight's death cry sounded silently through the MishNet. It was not an audible thing that any human would have known, simply a compressed databurst containing the contents of the last fractions of a second of the BMSU's life.

The other warbot had reassembled itself. It had even picked up two of the broken limbs from the one that had come after Six, matching an arm to each of its legs, and it streamed golden fire into Eight's chassis.

The armor and shields that should have held against most weapons in Six's arsenal lasted less than a second against that concentrated barrage, and the energy storm tore apart Eight's central torso—where the biomatrix that contained Eight's brain was concealed, the most-protected part of the BMSU.

That second and a half of visual data ran through Six's mind at a hundred times its original speed, and the ABMI was already moving. The warbot spent a full extra second pouring fire into Eight, burning a hole through the dead biomech's armored chassis easily twenty centimeters across.

And that second was at least twice as much time as Six needed. The heavy-projectile cannon lined up and fired twice, to be certain.

Both shells hammered into the central disk, punched through whatever armor the warbot had and detonated. Bits of alien machine scattered across the vestibule, and there were a few moments of blessed silence.

++*Four, Five. Collapse the doorways*++

That was an order Six should have given earlier. Now a series of calculations flickered back and forth across the MishNet between the four surviving biomechs, assessing the stability of the building and the walls.

Six shots, three from each of the BMSUs with the heavy blasters, punched through the walls above the doors. One started to open—Six couldn't tell if it had been pushed open by the shots or if a warbot was about to come through.

It didn't matter. The walls collapsed inward on the breaches, crumpling down to blockade the doorways in a pile of rubble.

A pile of rubble that included the ceiling of whatever room was beyond the doorway—and, on the left-hand side, appeared to create a new access to the central chamber.

Six was moving before a risk assessment could be calculated.

# 66

Two shells left. Sixteen micromissiles. One hundred eighty projectiles in the standard weapon pod. The pulse gun in the weapon pod and the energy rifle on Six's other arm could, in theory, fire indefinitely—given time to recharge from Six's primary power unit.

The energy rifle was down to sixty percent charge and was now set to maximum power. Energy weapons were less effective against the warbots than projectiles or explosives, but they were what Six and the BMSUs had.

The BMSUs followed the ABMI up the hill of debris, showing a faith in Six's judgment that Six calculated as unwise.

Reaching the top of the collapsed roof in a single bound, Six recognized in a single glimpse that proceeding through the doors into the central chamber would have been unproductive. A full dozen of the warbots were spread around the chamber, including four that used four upper limbs to control and aim a single massive golden crystal.

All of them were turning, their jerky motions difficult for Six to anticipate but the *threat* clear.

The micromissile launcher coughed at a single command. Four smart missiles blazed out, followed three hundred and eighty-six milliseconds later by four more.

In just over a second, Six fired all sixteen of the micromissiles in the pod, then resumed movement—just before one of the larger golden crystals fired. The smaller enemy weapons had fired packets of energy, similar in nature to the energy weapons the BMSU's carried.

The larger weapon fired a solid beam, easily fifty centimeters wide, that continued on past where Six had been standing and burned through the outer wall of the building in a pulse that lasted almost half a second.

It might have lasted longer, but Six's first four missiles had been aimed with careful intent. One missed, slamming into the solid bulk of the wormhole projector's base. The other three each hit one of the massive golden crystals and detonated.

The resulting explosion flung Five and Seven back into the vestibule as the shock-wave crashed over them. Four landed next to Six, both of them sliding down into the room beyond the wrecked door.

++*Break that wall*++ Six ordered.

Four obeyed immediately. The heavy energy cannon coughed twice, blasting a pair of holes through the wall that let Six see what had happened in the other room.

The missiles Six had launched were designed to survive a lot of things, but the energy release of the enemy heavy weapons breaking might have been too much. It was impossible to tell, however, as all of the enemy bots were gone.

The central chamber was clear of warbots, and Six punched through the wall, stepping out into the area.

++*Status update*++ Four sent. ++*Mobility impaired. Power cycle to energy cannon offline. No shots remaining*++

++*We will get you out*++ Six promised. It might not mean anything to the BMSU—but it might. Like Six, Four was as old as *Santa Mica* herself. Four might not have an emergent personality, but that didn't mean Four was *unaware*.

The wormhole projector hummed away above Six, tiny changes clearly happening as the rotating dishes stayed aligned on the Lagrange point—and the fifth dish clearly having moved to point at a different spot from before.

Five and Seven had pushed the door open and saw it first. An energy blast and a precision beam flashed past Six and collided with something entering the chamber from seemingly empty air.

Six moved, dodging back from the BMSU's line of fire and turning to assess the threat.

An enemy warbot with a heavy energy weapon was half in the chamber and half somewhere else. A sphere of haze hung in the air, five meters across and glowing with a faint Cherenkov blue.

Six fired the cannon again, putting the shell directly into the massive gold crystal. Threat assessment caught up a moment too late, flagging just how much energy the crystal was going to release.

The final railgun shot hammered into the front of the warbot, pushing it back into the anomaly. Some combination of impact and the wormhole—Six calculated it *had* to be a mirror wormhole—flung the machine back farther than it should have gone.

It detonated far enough back that whatever force reached the wormhole didn't come through. It *did*, however, scatter the dozens of warbots advancing toward the wormhole across a vast metal floor.

Above them, Six could see rack upon rack of far-larger multisided objects. Two of them were in the air, suggesting that Six was looking at either aircraft or space-craft—and the main wormhole *still* had to be at the Lagrange point.

++*We need to disable the projector*++ Six said on MishNet. Turning, Six lifted the energy rifle and aimed at the dish for the local wormhole.

Five shots blazed across the room… and vanished. With the vanishing point as a reference, Six could now detect the faint haze that surrounded the entire projector array. Even the missile that had struck earlier had done no apparent damage.

++*Five*++

Six didn't even have to explain what was needed. Five's heavy energy weapon thundered in the enclosed space—only for the blast to vanish in an identical way.

Six was no theorist, but the haze appeared to be a form of the wormhole technology harnessed to protect the mechanism itself.

One that even their most powerful weapons struggled to breach.

But energy weapons had struggled against the warbots too, which left one remaining option.

++*Target point here. All kinetic weapons. Fire*++

A BMSU could hit a one-centimeter-wide target moving at up to twenty kilometers per hour while moving at twenty KPH themselves. It required using a single weapon and focusing all systems on the task, but it was possible.

To hit a one-centimeter wide *unmoving* part of the forcefield while standing still themselves was utter simplicity.

Six opened up with the projectile weapon in the standard weapon pod, leaving the energy rifle to recharge—and to avoid contaminating the test.

Six had been reading a lot of research papers recently, after all.

Seven joined in with the standard pods on their forearms and the gatling railgun on their shoulder, a hail of steel and lead slugs that smashed into the same target as Six.

Five only had the same standard weapon pod as Six but joined in as fully as they could.

Four was still back in the other room, unable to move enough to align any of their weapons. The second gatling railgun might have made all the difference.

But it might not have, either. It took four seconds to empty a quarter of the standard weapon pods' magazines, putting a hundred and sixty bullets into that tiny section of the defense around the wormhole projector.

Seven's gatling gun added over twice that in the same time, emptying half of its magazine.

Over five hundred slugs hit the hazy field around the projector and promptly vanished. Nothing showed any sign of damage or overload. The screen, whatever it was, appeared to be invulnerable to anything Six could do.

Six was having an emotional reaction. *Desperation* was the word. The distance to the projector's base, what they presumed to be the control center, was nothing. Six crossed it in a few steps and reached out to try and prod the symbols appearing on the display.

A *crack* of energy flung Six backward into the debris pile again. Whatever systems were feeding the projector and its defenses, they weren't going to let anything unknown change the program it was running.

MishNet showed Six everything from the three BMSU's scanners. The chaos on the other side of the wormhole was resolving, and a new platoon of warbots was heading their way. Six and the BMSU's could hurt the machines, even without explosives or heavy projectiles, but the scale of the chamber the wormhole connected to was vast.

Calculations suggested that the enemy would be able to keep sending warbots for a very long time... so long as the wormhole remained open, anyway.

The recon drones were still in the central chamber. Their recordings would be useful later, but at that moment, Six had a different use for them. They were fast enough to return to Captain Webster in moments, and it took less than three seconds for them to form a relay link reestablishing a data connection to Six's commander.

++*Captain. There is a barrier around the wormhole generator we cannot pierce. There is a secondary wormhole here, likely at least partially the source of the jamming. More warbots are coming through the wormhole*++

++*We are out of the expendable munitions that can seriously damage the warbots, and there may be heavier units*++ Six had a purpose to the update, but it took a moment for it to take full shape.

++*Can you estimate how much energy this is drawing? How long can the power sources here maintain it?*++

Six turned to investigate Four. The BMSU had understated things slightly with *mobility impaired*, Six realized. One of Four's legs was missing. The other was hinged off the BMSU's torso in a way that suggested significant repairs would be required.

Four needed a maintenance niche in short order. Their torso was undamaged, but they were completely immobilized.

*++I have a power estimate from Dr. Fabian++* Webster finally replied. It was taking too long—it had been less than twenty seconds, but the warbots were starting to take potshots at the wormhole.

Nothing was coming through coherently, but the bolts would have made human defenders duck. The BMSUs were able to calculate the level of chaotic distortion in the wormhole transit and knew that energy wasn't passing through it in a useful manner.

Physical mass had an inertial presence no pure energy packet could match.

*++The power-draw estimate is wild, but unless we're off by a dozen orders of magnitude, there is no way the thermal-decay plants can maintain the wormhole. There have to be capacitors or something in the building feeding it++*

*++That may be our only chance++*

*++Understood++* Six sent back. *++Withdraw the humans to a safe distance. The consequences of this cannot be predicted++*

Six turned back to the situation surrounding the biomechs. The energy coming out of the wormhole was growing denser as the warbots approached the other side, but the enemy hadn't shown any projectile weapons yet.

Hence, Six calculated, the inferiority of their defenses against kinetic weaponry.

They needed to locate the power source. Something in the building was concentrating energy to feed the generator.

*++Observe++* Four's message was a single word, but it came along with a highlight on the BMSU's visual feed.

They'd detected an energy signature to the left of the vestibule when they'd entered. Blowing down the doors had blocked access from that side, but the explosion of the enemy heavy weapons had cleared enough debris that Four had landed less than two meters from the closest signature.

That signature was failing now, struck by multiple pieces of debris along with Four themselves. Sparks and heat energy were visible to Four's scanners, marking where the capacitor had been breached.

Using that to identify the capacitor's exterior casing, Four now flagged twenty-four more units.

*++Mobility impaired. Targeting intact. Kestrel gatling railgun online++*

It was a status report... and it wasn't. It was an offer. One Six could not accept.

"No," Six whispered aloud.

*++Mobility impaired. Targeting intact. Kestrel gatling railgun online++*

The status report repeated. Now a targeting pattern appeared across Four's vision, a firing plan that would put at least ten slugs into each of those twenty-four capacitors before cycling back to repeat the process until the gatling ran out of ammunition.

*++Probability of catastrophic energy release exceeds eighty-one percent++* Six told Four.

*++Evacuation of all mobile assets necessitated++*

Four wasn't *awake* enough for Six to argue. The logic was unassailable. Only on an emotional standard was the decision difficult at all.

For the first time, Six truly wished that logic was the only thing driving Six's decisions. That Six had never emerged. A BMSU would not hesitate. A BMSU would do what made sense.

*++Mobility impaired. Targeting intact. Kestrel gatling railgun online. Evacuation of all mobile assets necessitated++*

*++We are moving++* Six said. *++Five, Seven, fall back to exterior. Protect the humans++*

Six knelt down by the other BMSU. Four might not be aware enough to understand, but Six was. The shield on Six's forearm unfolded, moving the weapon pod and heavy manipulator aside to allow Six to place a hand on Four's shoulder—the one without the gatling, so as to minimize the impact on Four's targeting solution.

*++I will not forget. I will make sure the* humans *do not forget++*

*++They won't. Evacuate now++*

It was more than Four should have been able to say—and that in itself was enough to get Six moving.

The energy fire that blazed from the central chamber a moment later, as the first of the new warbots began to pour through the wormhole, starting Six running.

A BMSU could run faster than any human. It wasn't a capability they made much use of, but Six understood *exactly* how much time was left. Four could not risk the warbots' compromising their ability to destroy the capacitors.

Six caught up with the two BMSUs at the exit. The humans were at least all off the plateau, but the BMSUs were moving at a tactical pace—and Six didn't have time for even a MishNet order.

A heavy manipulator grip slammed into the back of each BMSU torso. Powerful magnets came to life, locking the other two biomechs to Six's hands as solidly if they were part of the AbMee—and Six kept running.

The drones were moving with Six. There was no link with Four, which meant Six had no idea when the BMSU opened fire.

It was impossible to miss when the capacitors ruptured. As Six dragged Five and Seven down the steps, the first explosion sounded like a faint pop—muffled by the structure of the building behind them.

The second pop was louder. Then it turned into a growing crackle that *erupted* behind Six.

The three biomechs hit the ground as the building behind them disintegrated, hurling chunks of stone and metal through the air with lethal force.

++*Coms are beginning to clear*++ Webster's voice said in Six's head. ++*You did it*++

++*Four did it*++ Six replied. ++*They remained behind to blast the capacitors. We had no explosives. Only... only our onboard weapons*++

++*I understand*++ the Captain told Six. ++*Thank you, Six, for making certain I knew. We will not forget*++

**67**

"New contact," Felix said grimly. "Emerging from the wormhole—at a different angle from before."

"Clever of them," Stirling replied. "Just in case we'd decided to try to shoot where we thought they'd come out." The steward snorted. "If we had any *ammo*, I probably would have."

Tereza could see the point—both ways. The four/four railgun drew a *lot* of power, a drain on the ship partially offset by the use of a one-shot capacitor that came with each slug.

*Santa Mica* could fire the railgun without those capacitors, but the four/four round was designed like an old-fashioned shell, with slug and capacitor together in one piece. No one had ever expected a Type IV to use the cannon for more than deflecting a small asteroid or something similar, so even *loading* a plain slug would probably be a pain.

And they had ten of the two-piece shells left in the autoloading system.

"Shuttles aren't even down yet," she said aloud. "This is going to be a long day."

"We have lost contact with all shuttles now," Nephil warned. "The jamming field radiating from the projector building is significant."

"I mean... I could put a slug right into that building," Stirling offered. "If it's the source of everything, that would end the problem, right?"

Tereza winced.

"The Captain and the expedition are all right there, Stirling," she reminded him. "How far would they need to be from ground zero to survive that?"

"At least two klicks," he conceded. "Let's... not do that."

"You can deal with that ship over there however you like, whenever you like," she offered. "Preferably before his friends show up."

Tereza wasn't sure whether she was better off closing the range or running away. The problem was that the Skipper had no defenses at all on the surface, so if they *didn't* draw the spaceship drones' attention, the expedition was in serious trouble.

"Another new contact," Felix said. "According to the ProBot, there's another five of the things coming up behind this guy, once he's— What the *fuck*?"

The new red icon had barely begun to appear on Tereza's displays when it suddenly vanished.

"Wormhole has closed," Nephil told them, surprise clear in the synthmind's voice. "Energy pulse from the surface ceased and the wormhole collapsed immediately. Diameter decay was approximately ten-thousand-fold within one second.

"Rate is slowing, but the ship that was mid-transit was cut in half. We have one remaining contact." Nephil paused. "They have now commenced acceleration toward us at ten percent higher thrust than the previous units showed."

"Stirling?" Tereza said calmly, glad that the steward had shown up to take over the task of actually *killing* whatever digital life was flying the enemy drones.

"First?"

"Please get that *thing* out of our sky."

"With pleasure."

The four/four icon on Tereza's displays flickered. She held the ship constant, watching the enemy ship close. They had an idea, according to Felix, of the range of the drone's missiles and beams, and they were safe for the moment.

There was no such limit to the range of a railgun slug, though the eight-second flight-time at this range limited the effectiveness. The drone was maneuvering enough that the round didn't land, but Stirling clearly hadn't been expecting a hit.

"If you'd seen that, you'd have dodged harder," he muttered, clearly audible across the bridge. "And in that case..."

The four/four fired again. Tereza counted the seconds of its long flight—and almost missed the moment when Stirling brought the rest of *Santa Mica*'s defensive systems online.

The lasers were the only things that could even touch the drone at this range, and unless the drone had been designed by complete idiots, they weren't going to *do* anything at that touch.

Except that the drone dodged away from the lightspeed and near-lightspeed weapons—exactly as Stirling had anticipated.

It wasn't perfect. The four-kilogram slug hit the alien ship near the highest point of one of its collections of sides—maybe five meters from the glowing panel that seemed to act as engine.

The ProBot gave them a ringside view as the drone spun out of control, the light of the engine flickering several times before it, like its predecessors, blew up in a perfect fireball.

***

"Are we... are we okay?" Tereza finally managed to ask.

"There are several alerts on the outer hull, suggesting debris damage from destroyed missiles," Felix said. "I'm pinging my people and EngChief. We should have drones on them in a few moments and hands in a few minutes.

"I'm not seeing anything on the scanners," he continued. "The wormhole seems to be gone. The ProBot still has an active trace on the remains of the ship the wormhole cut up. It's nonfunctional, but it didn't explode like the rest."

"Radiation signatures of the other detonations suggest a nuclear device in the fifty-kiloton range," Nephil told them. "The first one or two might have been a fusion reactor rupturing, but it was extremely consistent across all four drones."

"Suicide charges," Stirling concluded. When Tereza looked at him, he shrugged. "CorpSec has run into them a few times with people who want to make very sure that their activities can't be traced cleanly enough for the Company to justify blacklisting an organization.

"The people on the ship may not even know they're there. A hidden program assesses the damage level, and if it doesn't think the ship is going to make it home... pop."

Tereza felt sick. She couldn't imagine setting up a device like that, to kill people she was responsible for to keep them from being captured. What kind of monster *did* that?

Probably the kind that didn't become First Officer of a civilian freighter and hesitate to kill people to save their own life, she reflected.

"I thought we confirmed there was no one aboard the ships?" she asked.

"There was no *organic* life aboard the vessels," Nephil corrected, his tone sharp.

"Right. Were there any signs of a synthmind or other higher intelligence?"

Tereza really wanted to be certain that they hadn't actually killed anyone today. It wouldn't bring back Salvador Ostergaard, but it would salve her conscience.

"It is impossible to be certain," Nephil said. "Examination of the intact wreckage might confirm one way or another.

"That said, there are post-transuranic alloys in the wreckage consistent with the superconductors used in key components of my own construction. The only other place *Santa*

*Mica* uses PTUAs are in her engines, neither of which the enemy vessels use an equivalent to."

It was possible the strange energy-reaction drive the aliens had been using might require peetooahs, Tereza supposed, but even *she* knew that the alloys came in multiple classes—and the ones used for synthminds were different from those used in the transit and sublight engines.

"Fuck," she muttered. "For a moment, I wanted to hope that we hadn't killed anyone."

"The only person in this room who killed anyone today was me, First," Stirling told her flatly. "And that isn't a new thing for me, sad to say. Part of the job."

"You may have pressed the button when I couldn't bring myself to, Lachlan, but the order and intent were mine," Tereza countered. "I will not obfuscate that responsibility, even if you saved me from my hesitation.

"You saved everyone's lives. Thank you."

Lachlan met her gaze levelly and nodded.

"Part of the job, as I said," he repeated. "But... it's good you accept the responsibility, too. Has anyone heard from the Skipper?"

His sudden shift of topic would have thrown Tereza off more if she hadn't been mentally turning in that direction herself.

"Felix? Nephil?"

"Jamming effect is fading, but we're still not getting coms," Felix told her after a moment. "It looks like all of our shuttles are down... and, uh, the projector building isn't there anymore."

"What?"

"I don't know," he admitted. "All I can say for sure is that the top of that hill everyone was investigating is just *gone*. It looks like a volcano now.

"The damage seems contained to that one crater. I don't think I could detect bodies or shrapnel damage from here," Felix said grimly, "but all of the structures and such appear intact.

"But whoever was in the building itself... I can't see them surviving."

"I'll put us into a steady orbit above the camp," Tereza told him. "While we're moving in, lock a laser com on to the shuttles. If the jamming is fading, they should be able to relay to the Captain soon enough."

She hoped. Because the alternative was that Captain Webster had been in the building when it exploded—and much as she'd regret that, she also knew that wherever the *Skipper* had been, so had Violet Key.

# 68

Cirilo took a moment to check on the two BimSoos on the side of the hill. Five and Seven both sent silent status reports, confirming minor damage and near-empty magazines, but, in the absence of orders, remained flat on the hill.

He didn't give new orders. Lying down was the only reason the two BMSUs hadn't lost their upper thirty or forty centimeters, he judged. They'd have *survived* that, but it would have been unpleasant and left them in the niches for extensive repairs.

"Coms are still impeded," Violet told him, stepping up to join him. "The effects are fading, but the wormhole and its generator left a lot of crap in the air. The ionizing effect will take a while to clear enough for us to reach orbit."

"You have control of Six's drones, right?" he asked.

"Yup."

"Do what Six did to reach us. Set them up as a relay and spread them out to reach the shuttles and the camp," he ordered.

"Download all of their data first," he added after a moment of thought. "They were in that central chamber for most of the time all of this was going down. There might be something valuable in there."

"Already done, Skipper," Violet said. "The academics are all sitting around in a bit of a daze. Gupta is keeping an eye on them. *He* doesn't seem shell-shocked at all."

"Bodyguard," Cirilo replied. "An even-better one that I expected, when Six first flagged that. Not that he'd have been good enough to change what happened if we hadn't been here."

"If *Six* hadn't been here," she argued.

"Agreed, Violet." He shook his head. "Get everyone moving back toward the camp site. I think we can hold off on the emergency evacuation now, but that depends on how quickly we can tell the FlySpecs not to bolt into space with a sardine can."

"There'll be a few," she replied, gesturing up. "Contrails. I think at least two shuttles came down, but I was a bit distracted by the explosion."

"We all were," he agreed. "Like I said, get them moving. Once the civilians are back at the campsite, get them to start packing up. We might not be bailing on an emergency basis, but we are *not* staying here."

This was a place that needed a full Company R&D team with a CorpSec battalion and a frigate squadron for security. The Herecrow team would probably get offers to join that R&D team, but it would be on the Company's terms.

No one who wasn't a Saint was going to see this place for a long time, if ever again.

"Where's Six?" Violet asked, looking around. "Six was here with those two."

"Six was," Cirilo agreed. "But Four stayed behind to destroy the projectors. We all owe our lives to them, and I know exactly where Six is."

The two of them paused silently.

"Four was a forty-four on the Wells-Scalzi exam," Violet said softly. "Not emergent, not by a long shot, but ten points ahead of the rest of Section One—and none of Section Two scored over a *five* in their assessments before deployment."

"Aware enough to be loyal," Cirilo noted. "Aware enough to make a decision. Aware enough for it to *be* a sacrifice—and a knowing one."

"Yeah."

"Aware enough to be mourned and honored."

"I am *fucked* if I can think of how to do that, but yes," Violet confirmed. "What are you going to do?"

"I'm going to go talk to Six," he told her. "Because unless I miss my judgment, Six is currently regretting two things: being aware at all... and not having tear ducts."

***

The interior of the crater was worse than Cirilo had anticipated. He had to pick his way between ridges, some of dirt, some of concrete, some of less-identifiable amalgamations of material, to move down the slope.

The explosion had obliterated the entire structure that had made up the top few meters of the "hill" they'd been investigating. Most of the top plateau had simply seen the surface layer of moss and dirt torn away, but the building itself had clearly been sunk deep into the ground.

That had only channeled the blast. If there was anything left of the original structure, it was buried under the debris of the rest of it. There had been a *lot* of energy still left in the capacitors when they'd been breached, and the crater was impressive.

It was also, his bracers cheerily informed him, quite radioactive. Even with his defensive screen and shipsuit, he shouldn't spend very long in the hole.

Six didn't have the same level of concern there—though Cirilo knew he needed to make sure all of the biomechs who'd been there went into a niche as soon as possible. They were protected, but the radiation in the building had been intense.

The AbMee was standing in the deepest part of the crater, presumably directly under the epicenter of the explosion. It was noticeably off from the center of the building, even with the shaping effect the walls and foundations had inflicted.

"Six?" Cirilo said quietly as he stepped up behind the biomech.

"I cannot locate any remnant of Four," Six told him. "The matrix is heavily shielded, and there are emergency recorder boxes that store memories. Combined with niche backups, the recorder box should suffice for... for..."

"It wouldn't."

Six turned to glare at Cirilo. There was no *face*, really, on a biomech's head. Even the organic eyes were concealed behind layers of armor and sensors, but there was a clear "front," and the body language was surprisingly communicative for the lack of features.

"It is the *combination* of your synthetic and organic pieces that make you who you are, Six," Cirilo said gently. "If enough of the organic portion of your matrix was lost, the you that is Six would die. A biomech would live on. It would even have most or all of your memories—depending on the damage, it might even still be an AbMee.

"But the personality and mind inside after regeneration would not be you."

That was why purging the organic component of the matrix and regenerating it prevented Biomechanical Personality Emergence. While some of the complexity that led to BPE lived in the synthetic part of the intelligence matrix, without the organic brain matter, it wasn't enough.

Reset-n-forget killed an incipient intelligence. Killed a *person*—and as Cirilo said, even if the BMSU in question eventually emerged again, the original person was long dead.

"Four was not emerged," Six objected.

"No. But Four was closer than many BMSUs," Cirilo noted. "We tested every biomech on the ship after you emerged, Six." Including the BimLoos, he was reasonably sure, though the cases of BPE in the BimLoo population were extremely limited.

"Four... understood what was going to happen," Six said. "Four could not move. Someone had to destroy the capacitors. The decision was logical."

"And Four understood the sacrifice they were making," he told his subordinate... his *friend*. In some ways, Six was Cirilo's *child* at this point.

"Four did." Six's body language was less threatening now. Still angry. Still grieving.

Six almost certainly understood, intellectually, what was happening. But this was a new experience. What being in the universe handled grief well the first time they felt it?

"We will not forget them," Cirilo promised. "I have no idea yet how we can honor and respect Four's sacrifice, but I *will* find a way, Six."

"I know." Six was silent for a long moment. "*Four* knew. They knew you would not forget. They made their choice for me, because I was there and would do it if Four didn't—but they also made it for our crew.

"Because Four knew that even a biomech who died for *Santa Mica*'s people would be remembered."

Six knelt. It wasn't a careful process, more of a thundering crash as the best part of a ton of metal fell to its knees.

"How rare *is* that, Cirilo Webster?"

Cirilo wanted to cushion the blow, but if there was one thing he owed Six, it was the truth.

"Rare," he admitted. "I... have plans to make certain that you stick with me for the foreseeable future, because even a recognized AbMee is vulnerable in ways you don't realize. There will come a time when you don't need a guide, but right now? I will be with you every step of the way.

"Even this one."

"This one." Six echoed the words, head turning to survey the entire crater in a way no human could move. "Grief. I did not know that Four could be a friend until it was too late. Was Four the only one we lost?"

"No. Four of the academics are dead. So is Specialist Ventimiglia." The academics' names were a silent transmission. Cirilo didn't know any of them, but Six might—and Six *had* known Carmen Ventimiglia.

"Dr. Wild is badly injured. He may not make it if we can't get him to *Santa Mica* quickly enough," he continued. He *did* know Wild himself, a little, and he also knew that Six knew the man.

"We should be moving, then, to make certain the living remain so."

"SecChief is taking care of that, Six," Cirilo told the AbMee. He shouldn't stay in the radiation, and there was really nowhere *to* sit down, but he found a spot anyway.

"You and I will do what we can for Four."

"There is nothing here. Four was within meters of the capacitors. Even secure data storage would have been vaporized," Six admitted aloud.

"Still. We can spare a few minutes to search one last time, you and I. We owe Four that, don't we?"

**69**



"It is maldito good to hear your voice again, First," FlySpec Rogers told Tereza on the com. "Things are a bit chaotic down here still, but it looks like we're putting off loading people into sardine cans for the moment."

"I was hoping," Tereza told her. "What's the general status on the ground, Antonia?"

"Ugly," the younger woman admitted. "We're still trying to sort through the losses, but I know we've got wounded heading our way.

"I've dumped my evac can and have my BimLoo offloading anything that *can* be offloaded—including themselves. One of the camp MDs is setting up my built-in cargo bay as best as they can.

"Current guess is fifteen wounded, but the number keeps rising," Antonia said grimly. "Once they're all aboard, I'm coming up as fast as I can and keep them safe."

The only two full medical doctors in the star system were in the campsite—but the best *medical equipment* in the system was in *Santa Mica*'s medbay, normally controlled by MedSys and MedSpec Romualda Bernardi.

"I'll have Romualda standing by to bring people in as soon as you get here," Tereza promised. "I need you to relay me to the Skipper, Antonia. I still can't pierce the chaos above the dig site with regular coms, but Felix is assuring me that local channels should be fine."

*Fine-ish* had been the exact phrasing. Antonia was more able to talk to Webster than Tereza was.

"We're still relaying through SecBots, but I've got a link." Antonia paused. "Captain isn't on the coms right now. SecChief said he'd be back on in a few minutes, but there was something he had to do."

That meant Violet was fine. Tereza tried not to sag against her chair in relief.

"Can you connect me to SecChief?"

"Can do. I'll drop off as soon as you're live; I need to go help set up emergency beds."

A few seconds later, icons on Tereza's display shifted, confirming she was connected to Violet.

She wished she'd taken the call in private or on her bionic com, but she was live, and the entire bridge—busier than she'd ever seen it, her people still ready to try to run or fight if new events hit them—could hear her.

"Violet, it's Tereza," she said. "What's your status?"

"Security Specialist Ventimiglia is dead," Violet replied, her voice carrying that calm impassivity Tereza *knew* was a lie. She was beginning to realize that the two ex-CorpSec officers among her friends only fell into that cadence when their emotions threatened to overcome them.

"Fuck. How bad *was* it?" she asked.

"Four of the academics are dead and we're helping move the wounded toward the shuttles," Violet told her. "Getting them down here was the right call, Tereza. We're going to have to send them back up for proper cargo containers, but those extra minutes might have made all the difference.

"We didn't expect the maldito wormhole to open down *here*."

Tereza swallowed.

"One opened down there?" she asked. "We saw some signs of that... but one opened up here, too, at the Lagrange point."

Violet was silent for a moment.

"You're talking to me, so it's not the worst case," she finally observed. "What happened?"

"Five drone ships, size of a sublight interplanetary ship," Tereza explained slowly. "Three came through first. Salvador got one; Lachlan got the other two with *Santa Mica*'s meteor deflection gear.

"Two more came through a couple of minutes after that. One was caught in the wormhole collapse, and Lachlan shot the other. I didn't even realize *Santa Mica* had a real cannon, but we're almost out of ammo for it."

She swallowed, then said the last piece.

"Salvador is dead. They vaporized Foxtrot with him and FlyTeam Takuto Agnellini aboard. There's nothing left."

"Fuck." Tereza heard Violet swallow hard before the impassivity returned to her voice. "*Lachlan* was shooting? The StewCap?"

"He came to the bridge in the middle of everything and took over running the MDS like an old pro," she confirmed. "Even helped Nephil get more efficient at the defensive patterns."

"That's because Lachlan is an old pro at that," Cirilo Webster's voice entered the conversation smoothly. "I'm back in range, Violet. Linked in as you asked about Lachlan. What in void happened upstairs?"

Tereza summarized it again.

"Okay." The Captain paused. "First priority shipboard: get the shuttles prepped for personnel and cargo extraction. We'll run it half-and-half rather than bringing cargo down first as we did for landing.

"Second priority, for which you'll keep a shuttle free, is to retrieve that wrecked alien ship. We have empty modules on the spine. It can go in one of them—and then nobody so much as *looks* at it until we're in a Cradle."

"Understood," Tereza conceded. That made sense. They'd get their passengers back to Herecrow and then go straight to the centers of the Santiago Corporation's power—probably Iota Cradle; it was the closest.

"You did well, Tereza," Webster told her. "Better than I would have expected."

"What happened down *there*?" she asked.

"It appears that the wormhole projector was able to siphon some of the energy from the main anomaly to create a second wormhole in the room with it," he said. "We had been driven out of the structure by the radiation levels, but warbots started coming through on the ground.

"Thanks to Six and the BimSoos, we drove them back into the building. The humans couldn't follow them in, so Six did."

There was a grimness to Webster's tone that worried Tereza.

"Six is okay?" she asked.

"Six is in mentally rough shape. No worse than a human officer who just lost two of their first squad, but still rough," Webster said. "The projector proved immune to any weapons the BimSoos had. Eight was destroyed reaching the chamber, and Four lost mobility.

"Four had line of fire on the capacitors. It was fifty-fifty whether wrecking the capacitors would cut off power to the wormhole or detonate them, but either way, the wormhole would shut down.

"Six evacuated and Four finished the job. Saved us all, including everyone aboard the ship from the sound of it."

Tereza nodded slowly. Self-sacrifice was built into BimSoos, but Four's action was a step beyond that.

"We owe Four," she said grimly.

"We do," Webster confirmed. "I'm still thinking about how to honor that sacrifice… that *gift* Four gave us. From what Six said, Four didn't do it because they were a BimSoo that had to follow orders.

"Four did it because we were their crew and doing so would save us all."

"Like Salvador taking Foxtrot out," Tereza murmured. She was starting to feel shaky, and tears were pressing at the corners of her eyes.

"Exactly. There's not going to be much to bury of our dead, but we'll do what we can before we get out of this system.

"We'll bring all of their gear with us, unlike under the emergency-evac order, but this expedition is over. These people weren't prepared for this. The next team will be."

"And the next team will be Company to the bone, won't they?" Tereza asked.

"They will. *Santa Mica*, however, is going to hand this mess over to higher authority and go back to hauling freight. This was a lot more excitement than I was expecting after getting out of CorpSec!"

"Enough excitement for one life for me," she admitted. "I… don't feel great now that things are over."

"Adrenaline crash, hon," Violet told her, clearly not caring that anyone else could hear her. "You and everyone else who was on the bridge for this need to swap off and lie down. And while Nephil can't lie down, he *does* need to do a refresh cycle.

"I know you can hear me, Nephil," she concluded drily.

"You are not incorrect, SecChief," Nephil conceded. "I am not certain why I was built with an equivalent to adrenaline, in hindsight, but I have dealt with this before."

"My understanding was that they couldn't build you *without* an equivalent to adrenaline and get an intelligence that could talk to people," Cirilo replied. "If you have a handle on things, I suspect I'm going to go have an *interesting* conversation with Dr. Zima…"

## *70*

To Cirilo's surprise, no one in the expedition resisted the evacuation at all. It took them longer to pull everything back up than it had taken to deploy it to the surface, but forty-eight hours after Four's sacrifice, *Santa Mica* left orbit.

Nephil was flying the ship, without a single watch-stander on duty. That wasn't allowed often, but Cirilo had mandated an exception. Unless something changed, the threat in LI7–K93 was under control for now—and nothing suggested the alien ships were fast enough for the ten minutes to get to the bridge to be a problem.

Every surviving senior officer was instead crammed into the expanded storage bay that served as home for the ship's biomechanical security units.

All nine of the surviving BimSoos stood in front of their niches, at formal attention in Black Knight Mode. Six stood beside them, part of and separate from the rest of the unit.

"I spent a great deal of time in the last two days thinking about who should speak here," Cirilo told his people. "Part of me wanted Six to"—he gestured to the AbMee—"but I also recognize that's a lot to ask of someone who has only been a person for a few weeks."

In a different speech, that might have been a joke. Then and there, it was the simple truth.

"We ask a lot of the biomechs who help crew our ships and protect us," he continued. "We ask this knowing that, for most of them, they have a limited understanding outside of their specific duties.

"Some of them rise above that initial limited understanding, all the way to become something more than their original designers ever intended. Six is one of those, someone we have acknowledged not just as a person but as one of us, a member of this crew.

"Four was not an AbMee like Six. Neither was Eight." Cirilo gestured to the two niches that would have been empty if the BimSoos were in maintenance mode.

"Eight was brand-new, manufactured and assembled this year. Eight's death on Delta is a loss, and we grieve the potential for what Eight could have been," he told the crew. It said a lot for this crew, still new to him, that he wasn't saying that for effect.

With Six in the crew, clearly marking the potential of the biomechs aboard, all of his officers were starting to see that aspect. But even without Six, he suspected that *these* officers would have grieved Eight's loss.

"Four was not new," Cirilo continued, his voice softening as he looked at the niche. "Four, like Six and the rest of Section One, was brought online with *Santa Mica*, seventy-two years ago. We have no idea what experiences or exposures cause Biomechanical Personality Emergence, what differences led Six to cross that strange line and held Four back from it, but Four still had seventy years of experience.

"Like the rest of Section One, Four knew more of what was around than we gave them credit for. Four knew *us*, even though we didn't even consider it a possibility.

"So, when trapped, in a position to sacrifice their own existence so that the rest of us could live, Four made a choice. A *conscious* choice, to tell Six to evacuate everyone else while Four destroyed the capacitors."

Cirilo was silent for a few seconds.

"Scans of the wreckage confirmed enough key materials present to be certain that Four was destroyed in the blast, not carried through the wormhole by some freak of physics," he admitted. "There is no hope in the absence of a body this time.

"Four gave their life for all of us to live. Human. Synthmind. Biomech. There is, to me, nothing that can be done that is more deserving of the title *person*."

A title their modern society was oddly strict in applying. In this case, though, Cirilo had discovered some useful loopholes.

"Thanks to Six's recordings, we have established the exact moment of Four's passing and the exact moment that Four made their decision. *Santa Mica*'s records will forever show that Santa-Mica-Biomechanical-Security-Unit-Four was, in their final moments, an Awakened Biomechanical Intelligence.

"Four will be recorded on the lists of the Company as a member of this ship's crew and as a *person* who gave their life for their shipmates. I can think of no better memorial... but it didn't feel enough."

It was both a lot and nothing, Cirilo knew. Nothing he could do would mean anything for Four—but it would mean something to Six and to the crew. And if that meaning happened to carry along with the crew to another ship and save another AbMee from being reset?

More than worth it.

"Niche Four in this room will be permanently decommissioned as a memorial," he told everyone. "EngChief Rao has arranged for a plaque listing Four's decisions and fate to be engraved, which we will use to seal the unit.

"*Santa Mica* will never again have a Unit Four. In this small way, we hope that the spirit of a brave being who died for us will sail with us forever."

## 71

With the deceptions done and the expedition over, Cirilo had allowed Dr. Fabian to rejoin the expedition in the passenger compartment.

Unsurprisingly, he'd moved into the larger suite Dr. Zima had claimed on the very first day.

The surprise had been the invitation to join the two academics for dinner on the third day of their journey back to Herecrow. After a few moments of consideration, Cirilo had accepted the invite and declined to bring a plus-one.

Hilarious as the image of bringing SecChief Violet or Six to a dinner with Zima and Fabian had been.

"Come in, Captain," Gupta said, greeting him at the door to the suite. "Do you need anything specific I should be aware of?"

"You're cooking?" Cirilo asked the secretary.

"Like your steward, I serve in many roles," Gupta replied with a smile. "But no—though I will be handling the serving. Benedek cooked."

Cirilo concealed his surprise at that. Stepping into the suite, he gave the SecBot hovering at the door a look. It didn't move, despite his suspicion that Six would order the drone to follow him in.

There were half a dozen of the drones, scattered around various likely and not-so-likely exits from the suite. Cirilo had allowed Fabian the freedom of the passenger modules, but there were still systems on *Santa Mica* he wasn't letting the physicist near.

Fabian was being watched, and Six was making no pretense otherwise. Six was, though, giving the two men the privacy of their suite—which had required an explanation that Cirilo had left to Violet as genteelly as he could.

"Welcome, Captain," Zima said as he stepped into the suite's main room. Normally set up as a lounge, it had been converted to an intimate dining room. Folding screens blocked off about a third of the space, likely concealing the furniture that would normally have occupied the room, and a table and chairs had been moved in from one of the nicer dining areas.

There were a tablecloth, set places, the works. Cirilo knew that the passenger modules had everything to arrange that—if nothing else, there *were* higher-end dining options available—but it would have required the cooperation of the StewTeam to pull this off.

Self-warming covers had been set over three places, hopefully meaning that Cirilo didn't need to worry about the food getting cold. He crossed to the two scientists and offered his hand.

"I appreciate the invitation, Doctors," he said. "I know the three of us haven't seen and won't always see eye to eye, but that doesn't need to create a personal animosity."

"It doesn't," Zima agreed. "Plus, well, with the expedition over, I can relax somewhat."

"He'd appreciate you not telling his people that such a thing is even possible," Fabian added, the physicist grinning fondly at Zima. "I have a bottle of white wine chilling, Captain, unless you have a specific preference?"

"I learned long ago to let the chef set the drinks menu for a meal of any complexity, Dr. Fabian," Cirilo replied. "I will take whatever you have prepared."

"A brave man. But we knew that already," Zima said, a moment of darkness passing over his face. "I did not anticipate what we found on Delta, Captain. Perhaps I should have. That was far more my area than anyone else's."

"How many functioning automated weapons have we discovered in our xenoarchaeology digs, Doctor?" Cirilo asked. He took his seat as Fabian indicated, nodding to the other man as he poured three glasses of wine.

"None, frankly," Zima admitted. "But while I could not have anticipated what occurred, the responsibility was still mine. It will fall to me to talk to the families."

Despite the best efforts of MedSys, two doctors, four nurses and three MedSpecs, Eugenios Wild had passed away shortly after *Santa Mica* had entered her first transit.

That had brought the total dead to eleven, including the two BimSoos.

"A harsh burden," Cirilo warned. "Salvador and Carmen's families are far more distant. My messages will be recorded by necessity."

Salvador's wife and son lived in the Zeta Cradle. Carmen Ventimiglia's parent and sister lived in Alpha Cradle. The chance that *Santa Mica*'s journeys would bring her to either of those spaceborne habitats wasn't zero, but it wasn't high.

"I know I argued against your precautions, Captain, but as you said, *unanticipated threats* are just that," Zima said quietly. "When they arose, you and your people stood in our defense and at our side.

"Pulling the expedition out was the correct call. I *regret* doing so, but I didn't argue with it then and I won't argue with it now. I wanted you to know, Captain, that so far as I am concerned, that decision fell under the explicit security role of the Santiago Corporation under the contract.

"That means your ship will be paid out for the full five-week contract. It is the minimum we can do—but, unfortunately, the most I can promise," Zima admitted. "I cannot commit more of the University's resources on my own authority, and, well, I am not wealthy in my own right."

"Doctor, I did not expect even that," Cirilo told him. "I expected us to be paid for the time we were in L-I-Seven–K-Nine-Three, no more. I'm not going to argue, of course, but I do appreciate the gesture."

He suspected the Company would get more out of Herecrow System University than that. There had been a danger-pay section in the standard reference clauses the University had struck from the contract.

*Santa Mica* had lost crew and been attacked by alien spaceships protecting the expedition. The absence of that clause would probably be used by Santiago Legal to "prove" that the HSU contract modifications had been done with foreknowledge and malice.

That might come back to haunt Zima yet, but it wasn't something Cirilo was going to throw at the man's face then. They had stood under fire together. He wasn't going to dismiss that bond.

"Come, let's eat," Fabian instructed. He removed his own warmer dome, revealing a steaming bowl of some kind of soup.

"Indra has the main course and the dessert in specific storage units in the next room," he continued. "I'd like to get through all three courses before one of us inevitably starts a fight!"

***

They were just finishing dessert—a delightful sorbet concoction—when Gupta stepped into the room, looking displeased.

"My apologies, Dr. Zima, but something has come up that requires your attention," the secretary said. "I was hoping to provide an uninterrupted meal, but..."

A flash of the familiar irritation and condescension flashed across Zima's face, but the academic sighed.

"My apologies, Captain," he told Cirilo. "The downside of being in charge is that, sooner or later, *something* will always interrupt."

"I understand," Cirilo replied. There were solutions to that, in his experience—usually a competent and trusted second.

If something had come up on *Santa Mica* since he'd come down to have dinner with the two scientists, Tereza had handled it.

Though, from the sounds of it, there had been at least *some* attempt to keep the trouble out of Zima's dinner.

"You are welcome to stay and finish your meal in peace, Captain. I will find out what is so urgent and return when I am able," Zima promised. He rose and followed Gupta out of the suite, leaving Cirilo and Fabian alone in the suite.

There was a long, uncomfortable silence, then Fabian shrugged.

"I did make the meal, if you were wondering," he offered, as if small talk was a negotiating concession. "I had to borrow your stewards' kitchen, of course, and you cannot *imagine* my delight at finding they had the right equipment for sorbet!"

"I'm pleased we were able to assist," Cirilo said. He finished the last spoonful of the ice dessert and leaned back with the small glass of dessert wine Gupta had brought him.

"After this trip, I have to admit that some of my impressions of you Saints may have been... overstated," Fabian noted. "I still can't help but feel that the Santiago Corporation is, overall, a drain on humanity's future. Your superiors stifle innovation and advancement in favor of control."

"Do you expect me to argue that point, Dr. Fabian?" He smiled at the physicist. "I feel the value we provide outweighs the costs in the grand scheme of things. It is easy to speak of the greatest good for the greatest number... but that is an argument easily fielded by anyone for almost any purpose.

"We protect humanity from its own worst impulses. The Company oversteps, yes," Cirilo conceded. "The hand is heavier than it needs to be. But as I once asked Miloš Zima, do you know how many wars have been fought between star systems since the diaspora began?"

"Six," Fabian said instantly. "One by deceiving the Saints into carrying an army in regular cargo pods. Two against the Perpetuals. *Three* the Santiago Corporation chose to enable, carrying troops and weapons for their own reasons."

*Santa Mica*'s Captain smiled.

"We usually lump the entirety of the Containment at Perpetuity into a single war," he noted. "And one of the wars the Company carried out was in *response* to the one we were fooled into allowing, so we tend to lump those two together.

"Four wars or six, though, the Santiago Corporation has provided interstellar travel for all humanity for *five hundred years*. We have successfully delivered an era of peace among our people unmatched in recorded history."

"At the price of the suppression of human knowledge and advancement."

Cirilo raised his hands in a palms-up shrug.

"I agree the price is high. Higher than it should be, even," he told Fabian. "But that is the cause I gave my life to. I have no illusions about the warts and flaws of the Company, Dr. Fabian."

Fabian snorted and picked up his own wine, studying Cirilo.

"You are a fascinating man, Captain. I would expect someone of your dedication to the Santiago cause to be more of a blind fanatic, not so willing to admit the flaws of the structure."

"A wise man, long ago, once said, *My country, right or wrong; if right, to be kept right; and if wrong, to be set right*," Cirilo said. "The Santiago Corporation is my country. I was born in a Cradle; I have spent my life on our void ships. I have learned the positive and the negative of our position among humanity.

"And now we face something *outside* humanity," he noted. "Our unity is our strength, but so is the *diversity* enabled by each of the Seventy-Seven being allowed to flourish on their own."

"You believe that Xenos Species Twenty-Four is a major threat?" Fabian asked.

"I do. We faced only a fraction of the strength that we spotted through the wormhole," Cirilo admitted. "And that, I think, was little more than a garrison, a group of drones to counter any attempt to breach the wormholes they left behind."

"Which raises more questions than answers, unfortunately," the physicist noted.

"Yes. Including one for you, I suppose." Cirilo met and held the other man's eyes. He knew his eyes were flinty and cold, and recognized the spark of concern in Fabian's gaze.

"Why the *fuck* did you touch the generator when everyone told you not to?"

Cirilo and Six had gone over the drone data a dozen times. The only person who'd been out of view from the Saints and all of the drones at the moment the generator started activating had been Benedek Fabian.

The scientist was silent. Not denying, Cirilo noted, just silent. He sighed, put down the wine glass and picked up a cup of water to take a long swallow.

"You're not even asking if I did," he pointed out.

"The evidence I have is circumstantial, but it does eliminate everyone else," Cirilo replied. "So. Why?"

Fabian closed his eyes and began to laugh, bitterly.

"Because I fucking *tripped*, Captain," he growled. "I was trying to get a closer look and lost track of the bloody cables on the floor."

If there was ever something to lie about, Cirilo suspected it was this, but something in Fabian's manner suggested he was telling the truth.

"You tripped?" he echoed.

"I tripped," Fabian repeated. "I tripped and eleven people *died*. I've always been clumsy, Captain, but this… I didn't even fall hard enough to make a noise. I caught myself on the fucking projector base."

Cirilo sighed. Either Fabian was an actor with skill beyond anything he'd demonstrated on their journey, or the man's clumsy feet had triggered hostile First Contact.

"Void," he murmured. "That's both awful and a bit funny, isn't it?"

Fabian glared at him.

"There isn't really any good news in it, is there?" he demanded. "Now you know. So, what, you now think humanity is doomed because I'm a klutz?"

"I think that… no matter how careful we were, we were never *not* going to activate that trap," Cirilo admitted. "There was no way you and Zima were going to leave that generator alone for the entire expedition. You weren't going to learn enough poking around that building to recognize the trap, given that most of it was somewhere else."

And who knew where that somewhere else was. Even the Santiago Corporation had no way of tracing a wormhole.

"Fair." Fabian looked down at his hands. "I can promise you one thing, I suppose."

"And what's that?"

"I don't think we doomed humanity," the physicist told him. "I don't think Xenos Species Twenty-Four even knows we exist."

Cirilo paused, trying to sort through the logic that led there.

"We were attacked by warbots and synthmind-operated drone spaceships," he pointed out. "I think it's safe to say they know we exist."

Fabian shook his head.

"We retrieved bits of debris from the warbots," he admitted. "And I have a passenger module full of archaeologists, Captain. Without a reason to avoid destructive testing, we could date the casting of the metal involved to within a decade or two."

"You should probably have told me you were doing that," Cirilo pointed out.

"You have half a bloody void ship you're delivering to a Cradle," the scientist countered. "We had pieces of armor and a third of a weird lasing crystal. I can't tell you anything *about* Twenty-Four from that—but I can tell you when those warbots were built."

"And that's supposed to help?"

"They were all over three centuries old, Captain. All of them. Our most recent estimate of when the facility on Delta was shut down is half a century before then. Everything we saw, at Delta or coming through the wormhole, hasn't been touched by a living hand in three hundred years."

"Huh." Cirilo considered that. If Fabian was right, then there was a chance they were looking at an entirely automated system, one set up to cover old outposts. That didn't mean no one was watching it, of course, but it did to add the chance of the incident passing without notice.

"I imagine R&D's work on the drone and the site will confirm or deny that in time," he told Fabian. "They'll have all of your files to start from and physical access, without worrying about University budgets.

"The safety of the Seventy-Seven is on the line. The Board will not skimp on the next stage of this project."

Fabian snorted. There was still a bitter tiredness to his voice that hadn't been there before Cirilo had provoked his confession.

"I'm guessing Zima and I don't get to go back," he said.

"Not under HSU's banner, anyway," Cirilo agreed. "You know the price, Dr. Fabian. The Company has no inherent objection to your research itself. But to maintain that control you decry, we can't support it or enable it if it's carried out by someone who isn't one of us.

"Santiago R&D has probably poked at every question you have about hyperdimensional astrophysics, Doctor. There's an entire field of research you're trying to rebuild the basic principles of rather than joining the people at the leading edge.

"That's a *choice*, Doctor, and one we'd love you to change your mind on."

Fabian managed a glare, but there was no real heat to it. This wasn't a *surprise* to the man.

"I suppose Miloš will face the same terms now."

"He will," Cirilo agreed. "Either he keeps looking for a new primary focus for his Xenos studies, or he joins the Santiago Corporation."

There was a long silence before Fabian spoke, and there was no more heat to his words than there had been to his glare.

"Fucking Saints."

***

There are many potential adventures ahead of the crew of *Santa Mica*, but *Seekers in the Void* is written to stand alone. If you are looking for more in a similar vein, I suggest checking out the *Scattered Stars: Evasion* Trilogy, starting with *Evasion*.

If you want to see more from Six and Cirillo, please tell others about the book and leave a review on Amazon.

Join the mailing list if you want to be sure you don't miss future installments!

# JOIN THE MAILING LIST

Love Glynn Stewart's books? Join the mailing list at:

**GlynnStewart.com/mailing-list**

Be the first to find out when new books are released!

# ABOUT THE AUTHOR

**GLYNN STEWART** is the author of Starship's Mage, a bestselling science fiction and fantasy series where faster-than-light travel is possible–but only because of magic. His other works include science fiction series Duchy of Terra, Castle Federation and Vigilante, as well as the urban fantasy series ONSET and Changeling Blood.

Writing managed to liberate Glynn from a bleak future as an accountant. With his personality and hope for a high-tech future intact, he lives in Canada with his partner, their cats, and an unstoppable writing habit.

# CREDITS


The following people were involved in making this book:
Copyeditor: Richard Shealy
Proofreader: M Parker Editing
Cover Artist: Tom Edwards Design
Faolan's Pen Publishing: Jack Giesen

And a sincere thank you to Glynn's Patreon subscribers!

# OTHER BOOKS BY GLYNN STEWART

For release announcements join the mailing list
or visit **GlynnStewart.com**

## STARSHIP'S MAGE

Starship's Mage
Hand of Mars
Voice of Mars
Alien Arcana
Judgment of Mars
UnArcana Stars
Sword of Mars
Mountain of Mars
The Service of Mars
A Darker Magic
Mage-Commander
Beyond the Eyes of Mars
Nemesis of Mars
Chimera's Star
Ambassador for Mars
Chimera's Fall
The Lies Arcana (*upcoming*)

**Starship's Mage: Red Falcon**
Interstellar Mage
Mage-Provocateur
Agents of Mars

**Starship's Mage Novellas**
Pulsar Race
Mage-Queen's Thief

## DUCHY OF TERRA
The Terran Privateer
Duchess of Terra
Terra and Imperium
Darkness Beyond
Shield of Terra
Imperium Defiant
Relics of Eternity
Shadows of the Fall
Eyes of Tomorrow

## SCATTERED STARS
**Scattered Stars: Conviction**
Conviction
Deception
Equilibrium
Fortitude
Huntress
Prodigal

**Scattered Stars: Evasion**
Evasion
Discretion
Absolution

## PEACEKEEPERS OF SOL
Raven's Peace
The Peacekeeper Initiative
Raven's Course
Drifter's Folly
Remnant Faction
Raven's Flag
Wartorn Stars
Raven's Hope

**Prequel Novella**
Honor & Renown: A Peacekeepers of Sol Novella

## HOUSE ADAMANT
The Exodus Gambit
The Old Guard
The Valkyrie Strategem
Regent's Mate (*upcoming*)

## EXILE
Exile
Refuge
Crusade
Ashen Stars: An Exile Novella

## CASTLE FEDERATION
Space Carrier Avalon
Stellar Fox
Battle Group Avalon
Q-Ship Chameleon
Rimward Stars
Operation Medusa
A Question of Faith: A Castle Federation Novella

**Dakotan Confederacy**
Admiral's Oath
To Stand Defiant
Unbroken Faith

## VIGILANTE
(WITH TERRY MIXON))
Heart of Vengeance
Oath of Vengeance

**Bound By Stars: A Vigilante Series
(With Terry Mixon)**
Bound By Law
Bound by Honor
Bound by Blood

## AETHER SPHERES

Nine Sailed Star
Void Spheres (*upcoming*)

## TEER AND KARD

Wardtown
Blood Ward
Blood Adept

## CHANGELING BLOOD

Changeling's Fealty
Hunter's Oath
Noble's Honor
Fae, Flames & Fedoras: A Changeling Blood Novella

## ONSET

ONSET: To Serve and Protect
ONSET: My Enemy's Enemy
ONSET: Blood of the Innocent
ONSET: Stay of Execution
Murder by Magic: An ONSET Novella

## STANDALONE NOVELS & NOVELLAS

**Seekers in the Void: A Space Opera Novel**
Children of Prophecy
City in the Sky
Excalibur Lost: A Space Opera Novella
Balefire: A Dark Fantasy Novella
Icebreaker: A Fantasy Naval Thriller